Perpetuity Blues
AND OTHER STORIES

Neal Barrett, Jr.

GOLDEN GRYPHON PRESS ★ 2000

Foreword, copyright © 2000, by Terry Bisson.
"Perpetuity Blues," copyright © 1987, by Davis Publications, Inc. First published in *Isaac Asimov's Science Fiction Magazine*, May, 1987. Reprinted by permission of the author.
"Diner," copyright © 1987, by Omni Publications, Ltd. First published in *OMNI*, November, 1987. Reprinted by permission of the author.
"A Day at the Fair," copyright © 1981 by Mercury Press, Inc. First published in *The Magazine of Fantasy & Science Fiction*, March, 1981. Reprinted by permission of the author.
"Sallie C." copyright © 1986 by Western Writers of America. First published in *Best of the West* (Doubleday). Reprinted by permission of the author.
1: "High Fashion," an excerpt from "The Hereafter Gang," copyright © 1991 by Neal Barrett, Jr. Firt published by Mark V. Ziesing. Reprinted by permission of the author.
"Cush," copyright © 1993 by Bantam Doubleday Dell Magazines. First published in *Asimov's Science Fiction*, November, 1993. Reprinted by permission of the author.
"Class of '61," copyright © 1987 by Davis Publications, Inc. First published in *Isaac Asimov's Science Fiction Magazine*, October, 1987. Reprinted by permission of the author.
"Trading Post," copyright © 1986 by Davis Publications, Inc. First published in *Isaac Asimov's Science Fiction Magazine*, October, 1986. Reprinted by permission of the author.
"Winter on the Belle Fourche," copyright © 1989 by The Western Writers of America, first published in *The New Frontier* (Doubleday). Reprinted by permission of the author.
"Stairs," copyright © 1988 by Davis Publications, Inc. First published in © Isaac Asimov's Science Fiction Magazine, September, 1988. Reprinted by permission of the author.
2: "Mummies," an excerpt from "The Hereafter Gang," copyright © 1991 by Neal Barrett, Jr. First published by Mark V. Ziesing. Reprinted by permission of the author.
"Under Old New York," copyright © 1991 by Davis Publications, Inc. First published in *Isaac Asimov's Science Fiction Magazine*, February, 1991. Reprinted by permission of the author.
"Highbrow," copyright © 1987 by Davis Publications, Inc. First published in *Isaac Asimov's Science Fiction Magazine*, July, 1987. Reprinted by permission of the author.
"Ginny Sweethips' Flying Circus," copyright © Davis Publications, Inc. First published in *Isaac Asimov's Science Fiction Magazine*, February, 1988. Reprinted by permission of the author.
3: "The Model Shop," an excerpt from "The Hereafter Gang," copyright © 1991 by Neal Barrett, Jr. First published by Mark V. Ziesing. Reprinted by permission of the author.

Copyright © 2000 by Neal Barrett, Jr.

LIBRARY OF CONGRESS CATALOG CARD NUMBER: 99-76110
Barrett, Jr., Neal.
    Perpetuity blues and other stories / Neal Barrett, Jr. — 1st ed.
        ISBN 0-9655901-4-3 (hardcover : alk. paper)

All rights reserved, which includes the right to reproduce this book, or portions thereof, in any form whatsoever except as provided by the U.S. Copyright Law. For information address Golden Gryphon Press, 3002 Perkins Road, Urbana, IL 61802.
Printed in the United States of America.
First Edition.

Contents

Foreword, Terry Bisson	ix
Perpetuity Blues	3
Diner	32
"A Day at the Fair"	47
Sallie C.	60
From the Novel: The Hereafter Gang 1. High Fashion	82
Cush	84
Class of '61	119
Trading Post	136
Winter on the Belle Fourche	157

Stairs	174
From the Novel: The Hereafter Gang 2. Mummies	186
Under Old New York	189
Highbrow	212
Ginny Sweethips' Flying Circus	224
From the Novel: The Hereafter Gang 3. The Model Shop	243

*FOR JIM TURNER,
IN LOVING MEMORY*

*YOU CONCEIVED THIS
COLLECTION, JIM,
AND MADE IT HAPPEN.
I WILL ALWAYS
CHERISH YOUR FRIENDSHIP.
THAT'S SOMETHING THAT
DOESN'T GO AWAY.*

—NEAL

Forward

HEMINGWAY ONCE SAID THAT ALL AMERICAN LITERAture begins with a book called Huckleberry Finn. What he meant by this (and you can take my word for it; I was an English major) is that the richest, the most original, the cleverest and quite often the best American writing is both regional and vernacular —rooted in the talk of the South.

The South, like Science Fiction, has very flexible boundaries. It's been called a state of mind, but it's actually an intonation, an angle of approach, an accent if you will. It includes scraps of Maryland, most of Kentucky, the bootheel of Missouri (and thanks to the river, the tube socks all the way up to Hannibal), and grandest and most aggravating of all, Texas, which has the peculiar distinction of being the only state that is at the same time a Deep South and a Border state.

Which brings us back to literature, for the American novel's South (Faulkner, like Billie Holiday, is an influence without imitators) is a Border South; an edgy, an Upper or a Western South: poor in spirit, polyester in texture, trashy and talky, sexy and steeped in Sin; a weedy garden easier to rob than tend. (Forget the myth that stories hover ready-made in the Southern air like mosquitoes or traffic copters; in fact, they were used up long ago, reducing writers to making up new ones.)

Which brings us back to Science Fiction, the most influential and at the same time most despised genre in modern American literature; a close-to-the-ground field that has always welcomed experimentation but has only recently (let's admit it) made room for the kind of complex literary writing that distinguishes the best American prose from Twain through Flannery O'Connor to Charles Portis to today.

Which brings us to Neal Barrett, Jr.

I came late to Barrett's work, and not via his gleaming (and fast) V-8 tail-finned masterpiece, "The Hereafter Gang." It was the short fiction. Prowling through the pulps one afternoon, I read an incandescently loopy Cinderella tale called "Perpetuity Blues" and I thought I had discovered another writer as hooked as I was on happy endings. (I was wrong but that's another story.)

I read it again, then called my friends and got, "where have you been?" (I just discovered Utah Phillips last year.) But the fact that I had like Columbus stumbled onto an already discovered strand didn't diminish my own pleasure. My next Barrett thrill was the dark and menacing "Diner" which hangs in the air like an unanswered call for help. Then came the spectacular "Cush," a funereal encounter with the blind hogs of fate that out-o-connors O'Connor herself.

It kept getting better. Much as I admired the ideas, the humor, the rumor and the roar, I had to keep reminding myself: "It's the writing, stupid." Read the opening lines of "Belle Fourche" if you ever admired Hemingway's weather reports. Careful writing sets a tone, and Barrett's stories all sing. He's particularly good with margins, edges—dawn ("before the earth changed hands and the sun beat the desert flat") and dusk ("the sky settling into a shade inducing temporary wisdom."). This kind of work might not get you a seat on the inaugural platform, two butts down from the President, but it will win you immortality, which is almost as good.

I finally got to hear Neal Barrett, Jr., read—in Texas of course. Even there, amid the Bradley Dentons, Bruce Sterlings and Howard Waldrops, he shone like a star. (What's with these Texans anyway? How come they always tell the best jokes, write the best stories, and get all the credit? It has always kind of pissed me off. Which is why I wrote two books in which there is NO TEXAS AT ALL, only a long, windswept Oklahoma/Mexico border. But that's another story.)

Barrett is both a faux primitive and a high modernist. Like Portis, he has mastered the low cadences of mule, of car, of common speech. Like Lafferty (another south/westerner) he has turned high rhetoric on its head. He can write from top down and bottom up at once, and break most (if not all) of the rules. How many writers are willing to switch POVs in the middle of a short story (as Chekhov and Carver twirl in their graves)? Or undress Emily Dickinson? Or put Wilbur Wright to work sweeping out a cantina?

And so I commend to you this book which contains at least two of the stories that will make 20th Century's short fiction final cut. Not with the tired dictum that Barrett is a serious writer in SF drag—surely after Dick, LeGuin, Russ, Wolfe, we no longer have to suffer that sorry disclaimer. Rather, I would remind you that just because these stories sing with that Alfred Kazin called the "exalted naturalness" of authentic American literature, don't think that they somehow aren't really SF.

"There's a scientist and a girl in every one, almost.

— TERRY BISSON

Perpetuity Blues

AND
OTHER
STORIES

Perpetuity Blues

On Maggie's seventh birthday, she found the courage to ask Mother what had happened to her father.
"Your father disappeared under strange circumstances," said Mother.
"Sorghumdances?" said Maggie.
"Circumstances," said Mother, who had taught remedial English before marriage and was taking a stab at it again. "Circumstances: a condition or fact attending an event or having some bearing upon it."
"I see," said Maggie. She didn't, but knew it wasn't safe to ask twice. What happened was Daddy got up after supper one night and put on his cardigan with the patches on the sleeves and walked to the 7-Eleven for catfood and bread. Eight months later, he hadn't shown up or called or written a card. Strange circumstances didn't seem like a satisfactory answer.
Mother died Thursday afternoon. Maggie found her watching reruns of *Rawhide* and *Bonanza*. Maggie left South Houston and went to live with Aunt Grace and Uncle Ned in Marble Creek.
"There's no telling who he might of met at that store," said Aunt Grace. "Your father wasn't right after the service. I expect he got turned in Berlin. Sent him back and planted him deep in

Montgomery Ward's as a mole. That's how they do it. You wait and lead an ordinary life. You might be anyone at all. Your control phones up one day and says 'the water runs deep in Lake Ladoga' and that's it. Whatever you're doing, you just get right up and do their bidding. Either that or he run off with that slut in appliance. I got a look at her when your uncle went down to buy the Lawnboy at the End-of-Summer Sale. Your mother married beneath her. I don't say I didn't do the same. The women in our family got no sense at all when it comes to men. We come from good stock, but that doesn't put money in the bank. Your grandfather Jack worked directly with the man who invented the volleyball net they use all over the world in tournament play. Of course he never got the credit he deserved. This family's rubbed elbows with greatness more than once, but you wouldn't know it. Don't listen to your Uncle Ned's stories. And for Christ's sake, don't ever sit on his lap."

Maggie found life entirely different in a small town. There were new customs to learn. Jimmy Gerder and two other fourth graders took her down to the river after school and tried to make her take off her pants. Maggie didn't want to and ran home. After that, she ran home every day.

Uncle Ned told her stories. Maggie learned why it wasn't a good idea to sit on his lap. "There was this paleontologist," said Uncle Ned; "he went out hunting dinosaur eggs and he found some. There was this student come along with him. It was this girl with nice tits is who it was. So this paleontologist says, 'Be careful now, don't drop 'em, these old eggs are real friable.' And the girl says, 'Hey, that's great, let's fry the little fuckers.' " Uncle Ned nearly fell out of his chair.

Maggie didn't understand her uncle's stories. They all sounded alike and they were all about scientists and girls. Ned ran the hardware store on Main. He played dominoes on Saturdays with Dr. Harlow Pierce, who also ran Pierce's Drugs. On Sundays he watched girls' gymnastics on TV. When someone named Tanya did a flip, he got a funny look in his eyes. Aunt Grace would get Maggie and take her out in the car for a drive.

Maggie found a stack of magazines in the garage behind a can of kerosene. There were pictures of naked girls doing things she couldn't imagine. There were men in some of the pictures, and she guessed they were scientists, too.

Aunt Grace and Uncle Ned were dirt-poor, but they gave a party for Maggie's eighth birthday. Maggie was supposed to pass out invitations at school, but she threw them all away. Everyone knew Jimmy Gerder chased her home and knew why. She was afraid Aunt Grace would find out. Uncle Ned gave her a Phillips screwdriver in a simulated leather case you could clip in your pocket like a pen. Aunt Grace gave her a paperback history of the KGB.

Maggie loved the freedom children enjoy in small towns. She knew everyone on Main who ran the stores, the people on the streets, and the people who came in from the country Saturday nights. She knew Dr. Pierce kept a bottle in his office and another behind the tire in his trunk. She knew Mrs. Betty Keen Littler, the coach's wife, drove to Austin every Wednesday to take ceramics, and came back whonkered with her shoes on the wrong feet. She knew about Oral Blue, who drank wine and acted funny and thought he came from outer space. Oral was her favorite person to watch. He drove a falling-down pickup and lived in a trailer by the river. He came into town twice a week to fix toasters and wire lamps. No one knew his last name. Flip Gator, who ran Flip Gator's Exxon, tagged him Oral Blue. Which fit because Oral's old '68 pickup was three shades of Sear's exterior paint for fine homes. Sky Blue for the body. Royal blue for fenders. An indeterminate blue for the hood. Oral wore blue shirts and trousers. Blue Nikes with the toes cut out and blue socks.

"Don't get near him," said Aunt Grace. "He might of been turned. And for Christ's sake, don't ever sit in his lap."

Maggie kept an eye on Oral when she could. On Tuesdays and Thursdays she'd run home fast with Jimmy Gerder on her heels and duck up the alley to the square. Then she'd sit and watch Oral stagger around trying to pinpoint his truck. Oral was something to see. He was skinny as a rail and had a head too big for his body. Like a tennis ball stabbed with a pencil. Hair white as down and chalk skin and pink eyes. A mouth like a wide open zipper. He wore a frayed straw hat painted pickup-fender blue to protect him from the harsh Texas sun. Uncle Ned said Oral was a pure-bred genetic albino greaser freak and an aberration of nature. Maggie looked it up. She didn't believe anything Uncle Ned told her.

Ten days after Maggie was eleven, Dr. Pierce didn't show up for dominoes and Ned went and found him in his store. He took one look and ran out in the street and threw up. The medical examiner from San Antone said Pierce had sat on the floor and opened forty-two-hundred pharmaceutical-type products, mixed them in a five-gallon jug, and drunk most of it down. Which accounted for the internal explosions and extreme discoloration of the skin.

Maggie had never heard about suicide before. She imagined you just caught something and died or got old. Uncle Ned began to drink a lot more after Dr. Pierce was gone. "Death is one of your alternate lifestyles worth considering," he told Maggie. "Give it some thought."

Uncle Ned became unpleasant to be around. He mostly watched girls' field hockey or Eastern Bloc track-and-field events. Maggie was filling out in certain spots. Ned noticed her during commercials and grabbed out at what he could. Aunt Grace gave him hell when she caught him. Sometimes he didn't know who he was. He'd grab and get Grace, and she'd pick up something and knock him senseless.

Maggie stayed out of the house whenever she could. School was out, and she liked to pack a lunch and walk down through the trees at the edge of town to the Colorado. She liked to wander over limestone hills where every rock you picked up was the shell of something tiny that had lived. The sun fierce-bright and the heat so heavy you could see it. She took a jar of ice water and a peanut butter sandwich and climbed up past the heady smell of green salt-cedar to the deep shade of big live oaks and native pecans. The trees here were awesome, tall and heavy-leafed, trunks thick as columns in a bad Bible movie. She would come upon the ridge above the river through a tangle of ropy vine, sneak quietly to the edge, and look over and catch half a hundred turtles like green clots of moss on a sunken log. Moccasins crossed the river, flat heads just above the water, leaving shallow wakes behind. She would eat in the shade and think how it would be if Daddy were there. How much he liked the dry rattle of locusts in the summer, the sounds that things made in the wild. He could tell her what bird was across the river. She knew a crow when she heard it, that a cardinal was red. Where was he? she wondered. She didn't believe he'd been a mole at Montgomery Ward's. Aunt Grace was wrong about that. Why didn't he come back? He might leave Mother, and she wouldn't much blame him if he did. But he wouldn't go off and leave *her*.

"I don't want to be dead," she said aloud. "I can think of a lot of people who it's okay if they're dead, but not you."

She dropped pieces of sandwich into the olive-colored water. Fish came up and sucked them down. When the sun cut the river half in shadow, she started back. There was a road through the woods, no more than ruts for tires but faster than over the hills. Walking along thinking, watching grasshoppers bounce on ahead and show the way. The sound came up behind her, and she turned and saw the pickup teeter over the rise in odd dispersions of blue, the paint so flat it ate the sun in one bite. Oral blinked through bug spatters, strained over the wheel so his nose pressed flat against the glass. The pickup a primary disaster, and Oral mooning clown-faced, pink-eyed, smiling like a zipper, and maybe right behind some cut-rate circus with a pickled snake in a jar. He spotted Maggie and pumped the truck dead; caliche dust caught up and passed them both by.

"Well now, what have we got here?" said Oral. "It looks like a picnic and I flat missed it good. Not the first time, I'll tell you. I smell peanut butter I'm not mistaken. You want to get in here and ride?"

"What for?" said Maggie.

"Then don't. Good afternoon. Nice talking to you."

"All right, I will." Maggie opened the door and got in. She couldn't say why, it just seemed like the right thing to do.

"I've seen you in town," said Oral.

"I've seen you, too."

"There's a lot more to life than you dream of stuck on this out-of-the-way planet, I'll tell you that. There's plenty of things to see. I doubt you've got the head for it all. Far places and distant climes. Exotic modes of travel and different ways of doing brownies."

"I've been over to Waco and Fort Worth."

"That's a start."

"You just say you're a space person, don't you," said Maggie, wondering where she'd gotten the courage to say that. "You're not really, are you?"

"Not anymore I'm not," said Oral. "My ship disintegrated completely over the Great Salt Lake. I was attacked by Mormon terrorists almost at once. Spent some time in Denver door-to-door. Realized I wasn't cut out for sales. Sometime later hooked up with a tent preacher in Bloomington, Indiana. Toured the tristate area, where I did a little healing with a simple device concealed upon my person. Couldn't get new batteries and that was that. I was taken in by nuns outside of Reading, Pennsylvania, and treated well, though I was forced to mow lawns for some time. Later I was robbed and beaten severely by high-school girls in Chattanooga, where I offered to change a tire. I have always relied on the kindness of strangers. Learned you can rely on 'em to kick you in the ass." Oral picked up a paper sack shaped like a bottle and took a drink. "What's your daddy do? If I'm not mistaken, he sells nails."

"That's not my daddy, that's my uncle. My father disappeared under strange circumstances."

"That happens. More often than you might imagine. There are documented cases. Things I could tell you you wouldn't believe. Look it up. Planes of existence we can't see, or not a lot. People lost and floating about in interdimensional yogurt."

"You think my father's somewhere like that?"

"I don't know. I could ask."

"Thank you very much."

"I got this shirt from a fellow selling stuff off a truck. Pierre Cardin irregular is what it is. Dirt cheap and nothing irregular about it I can see. Whole stack of 'em there by your feet."

"They're all blue."

"Well, I know that."

"Where are we going now?"

"My place. Show you my interstellar vehicle and break open some cookies. You scared to be with me?"

"Not a lot."

"You might well ask why I make no effort to deny my strange origin or odd affiliation. I find it's easier to hide out in the open. You say you're from outer space, people tend to leave you alone. I've lived in cities and I like the country better. Not so many bad rays from people's heads. To say nothing of the dogshit in the streets. What do *you* think? You have any opinion on that? People in small towns are more tolerant of the rare and slightly defective. They all got a cousin counting his toes. I can fix nearly anything there is. Toasters. TVs. Microwave ovens. Everything except that goddamn ship. If Radio Shack had decent parts at all, I'd be out of here and gone."

Oral parked the truck under the low-hanging branches of a big native pecan. The roots ground deep in the rigid earth, squeezed rocks to the surface like broken dishes. The tree offered shade to the small aluminum trailer, which was round as a bullet. Oral had backed it off the road some time before. The tires were gone, tossed off in the brush. The trailer sat on rocks. Oral ushered Maggie in. Found Oreos in a Folger's coffee can, Sprite in a minifridge. A generator hacked out back. The trailer smelled of wine and bananas and 3-In-One oil. There was a hot plate and a cot. Blue shirts and trousers and socks.

"It's not much," said Oral. "I don't plan to stay here any longer than I have to."

"It's very cozy," said Maggie, who'd been taught to always say something nice. The trailer curved in from the door to a baked plastic window up front. The floor and the walls and the roof were explosions of colored wire and gutted home computers. Blue lights stuttered here and there.

"What's all this supposed to be?" said Maggie.

"Funky, huh?" Oral showed rapid eye movement. "No wonder they think I'm crazy. The conquest of space isn't as easy as the layman might imagine. I figure on bringing in a seat from out of the truck. Bolt it right there. Need something to seal up the door. Inner tubes and prudent vulcanizing ought to do it. You know about the alarming lack of air out in space?"

"I think we had it in school."

"Well, it's true. You doing all right at that place?"

The question took Maggie by surprise. "At school you mean? Sort of. Okay, I guess."

"Uh-huh." Oral hummed and puttered about. Stepped on a blue light and popped it like a bug. Found a tangle of wire from a purple Princess phone and cut it free. Got needle-nose pliers and twisted a little agate in to fit. "Wear this," he told Maggie. "Hang it round your waist and let the black doohickey kind of dangle over your personal private things."

"Well, I never!" Maggie didn't care for such talk.

"All right, don't. Run home all your life."

"You've been spying on me."

"You want a banana? Some ice cream? I like to crumble Oreos over the top."

"I think I better start on home."

"Go right up the draw and down the hill. Shortcut. Stick to the path. Tonight's a good night to view the summer constellations. Mickey's in the Sombrero. The Guppy's on the rise."

"I'll be sure and look."

When Maggie was twelve, Aunt Grace went to Galveston on a trip. The occasion was a distant cousin's demise. Uncle Ned went along. Which seemed peculiar to Maggie, since they wouldn't *eat* together, and seldom spoke.

"We can't afford it, God knows," said Aunt Grace. "But Albert was a dear. Fought the Red menace in West Texas all his life. Fell off a shrimper and drowned, but how do we know for sure? *They'd* make it look accidental."

She left Maggie a list of things to eat. Peanut butter and Campbell's soup. Which was mostly what she got when they were home. Aunt Grace said meat and green vegetables tended to give young girls diarrhea and get their periods out of whack.

"Stay out of the ham and don't thaw anything in the fridge. Here's two dollars, that's for emergencies and not to spend. Call Mrs. Ketcher, you get sick. Lock the doors. Come straight home from school and don't look at the cable."

"I'm scared to stay alone," said Maggie.

"Don't be a 'fraidy cat. God'll look after you if you're good."

"Don't tell anyone we're gone," said Uncle Ned. "Some greaser'll break in and steal us blind."

"For God's sake, Ned, don't tell her *that*."

Uncle Ned tried to slip a paper box in the backseat. Maggie saw him do it. When they both went in to check the house, she stole a look. The carton was full of potato chips and Fritos, Cheetos and chocolate chip cookies. There was a cooler she hadn't seen iced down with Dr Peppers and frozen Snickers and Baby Ruths. There were never any chips or candy bars around the house. Aunt Grace said they couldn't afford trash. But all this stuff was in the car. Maggie didn't figure they'd be bringing any back. When the car was out of sight, she went straight to the garage and punched an ice pick hole in the kerosene can that hid Uncle Ned's stash of magazines. She did it on a rust spot so Ned'd never notice. Then she went out back and turned over flat rocks and gathered half a pickle jar of fat brown Texas roaches that had moved up from Houston for their health. Upstairs she emptied the jar where Aunt Grace kept her underwear and hose. Downstairs again she got the ice pick and opened the freezer door and poked a hole in one of the coils. In case the roasts and chickens and Uncle Ned's venison sausage had trouble thawing out she left the door open wide to summer heat.

"There," said Maggie, "y'all go fuck yourselves good." She didn't know what it meant, but it seemed to work fine for everyone else.

When Maggie was thirteen, Jimmy Gerder nearly caught her. By now she knew exactly what he wanted and ran faster. But Jimmy had been going out for track. He had the proper shoes, and it was only a matter of time. Purely by chance she came across Oral's gimmick in the closet. The little black stone he'd twisted on seemed to dance like the Sony when a station was off the air. Why not, she thought, it can't hurt. Next morning she slipped it on under her dress. It felt funny and kinda nice, bouncing on her personal private things. Jimmy Gerder caught her in an alley. Six good buddies had come to watch. Jimmy wore his track outfit with a seven on the back. A Marble Creek Sidewinder rattler on the front. He was a tall and knobby boy with runny white-trash eyes and bad teeth. Maggie backed against a wall papered with county commissioner flyers. Jimmy came at her in a fifty-meter stance. His mouth moved funny; a peculiar glaze appeared. A strange invisible force picked him up and slammed him flat against the far alley wall. Maggie hadn't touched him. But something certainly had. Onlookers got away fast and spread the word. Maggie wasn't much of an easy lay. Jimmy Gerder suffered a semimild concussion, damage to several vertebrae and ribs.

She hadn't seen Oral in over a year. On the streets sometime, but not at the extraterrestrial aluminum trailer by the river.

"I wanted to thank you," she said. "I don't get chased anymore. How in the world did you do that?"

"What took you so long to try it out? Don't tell me. I got feelings, too."

Nothing seemed to have changed. There were more gutted personal home computers and blue lights, or maybe the same ones in different order.

"You wouldn't believe what happened to me," said Oral. He brought out Oreos and Sprites. "Got the ship clear out of the atmosphere and hit this time warp or something. Nearly got eat by Vikings. Worse than the Mormons. Fixed up the ship and flipped it out again. Ended up in medieval Europe. Medicis and monks, all kinds of shit. Joined someone's army in Naples. Got caught and picked olives for a duke. Look at my face. They got diseases you never heard of there."

"Oh my," said Maggie. His face didn't look too good. The bad albino skin had holes like a Baby Swiss.

"I taught 'em a thing or two," said Oral, blinking one pink eye and then the other. "Simple magic tricks. Mr. Wizard stuff. Those babies'll believe anything. Ended up owning half of Southern Italy. Olive oil and real estate. Not a bad life if you can tolerate the smell. Man could make a mint selling Soft 'n Pretty and Sure."

"I'm glad you're back safe," said Maggie. She liked Oral a lot, and didn't much care what he made up or didn't. "What are you going to do now?"

"What can I do? Try to get this mother off the ground. I'm thinking of bringing Radio Shack to task in federal court. I feel I have a case."

Maggie listened to the wind in the trees. "Do you really think you can do it, Oral? You think you can make it work again?"

"Sure I can. Or maybe not. You know what gets to me most on this world? Blue. We got reds and yellows and greens up the ass. But no blue. You got blues all over." Oral put aside his Sprite and found a bottle in a sack. "You hear from your daddy yet?"

"Not a thing. I'm afraid he's gone."

"Don't count him out. Stuck in interstellar tofu, most likely. Many documented cases."

"Daddy hates tofu. Says it looks like someone threw up and tried again."

"He's got a point."

"What's it like where you come from, Oral? I mean where you lived before."

"You said you been to Fort Worth."

"Once when I was little."

"It doesn't look like that at all. Except out past Eighth Avenue by the tracks. Looks a little like that on a good day."

Maggie did fine in school after Jimmy Gerder left her alone. He cocked his head funny and walked with a limp. His folks finally sent him to Spokane to study forest conservation. By the time she reached sixteen, Maggie began to make friends. She was surprised to be chosen for the Sidewinderettes, the third finest pep squad in the state. She joined the Drama Club and started writing plays of her own. She was filling out nicely and gave Uncle Ned a wide berth.

They were still dirt-poor, but Uncle Ned and Aunt Grace attended several funerals a year. Two cousins died in Orlando not far from Disneyland, a car mishap in which both were killed outright. A nephew was mutilated beyond recognition in San Francisco, victim of a tuna-canning machine gone berserk. A new family tragedy could be expected around April, and again in late October when the weather got nice. Maggie was no longer taken in. She knew people died year round. They died in places like Cincinnati and Topeka where no one wanted to go. What Aunt Grace and Uncle Ned were doing was having fun. There wasn't much question about that. Maggie didn't like it, but there was nothing she could do about it, either.

When Maggie was eighteen, her play *Blue Sun Rising* was chosen for the senior drama presentation. It was a rousing success. Drama critic Harcourt Playce from San Angelo, Texas, told

Maggie she showed promise as a writer. He gave her his personal card and the name of a Broadway theatrical producer in New York. The play was about a man who was searching for the true meaning of life on a world "very much like our own," as the program put it. There was no night at all on this world. A blue sun was always in the sky. Maggie wanted to ask Oral but was sure the principal wouldn't let him in.

Aunt Grace died a week after graduation. Maggie found her watching reruns of M*A*S*H. She secretly wrote a specialist in Dallas. Told him what had happened to her mother and Aunt Grace. The specialist answered in time and said there might be genetic dysfunction. They were making great strides in the field. He advised her to avoid any shows in syndication.

Life with Uncle Ned wasn't easy. With Aunt Grace gone, he no longer practiced restraint of any kind. Liquor came out of the nail bin at the store, and found its way to the kitchen. Girl and scientist magazines were displayed quite openly with *National Geographic*. Maggie began to jump when she heard a sound. There was a good chance Uncle Ned was there. Standing still too long was a mistake.

"You're going to have to stop that," said Maggie. "I mean it, Uncle Ned. I won't put up with it at all."

"You ought to get into gymnastics," said Uncle Ned. "I could work with you. Fix up bars and stuff out back. I know a lot more about it than you might think."

Maggie looked at Uncle Ned as if she were seeing him for the first time. His gaze was focused somewhere south of Houston. There seemed to be an electrical short in his face. His skin was the color of chuck roast hit with a hammer.

"I'm going to go," said Maggie. "I'm getting out of here."

"On what?" said Uncle Ned.

"I don't care on what, I'm just going. You try to stop me, you'll wish you hadn't."

"You haven't got busfare to the bathroom."

"Then I'll walk."

"You do and you'll get raped and thrown in a ditch."

"I can get that first part here. I'll worry about the ditch when I come to it."

"Don't expect any help from me. I haven't got two dimes to rub together."

"You will," said Maggie. "Some cousin'll get himself hacked up in a sawmill in Las Vegas."

"Now that's plain ignorant," said Uncle Ned. "Especially for a high-school graduate. There isn't a lot of timber in Nevada. That's something you ought to know."

"Good-bye, Uncle Ned."

It took maybe nine minutes to pack. She took *Blue Sun Rising* and a number two pencil. Left her Sidewinderette pep jacket and took a sensible cloth coat. It was the tail end of summer in Texas, but New York looked cold on *NYPD Blue*. She searched for something to steal. There were pawnshops all over New York. People stole for a living and sold the loot to buy scag and pot and ludes and whatever they could find to shoot up. There was no reason you couldn't buy food just as well. In the back of her aunt's closet she found a plastic beaded purse with eight dollars and thirty cents. Two sticks of Dentyne gum. Downstairs, Uncle Ned was watching the French National Girls' Field Hockey Finals. Maggie stopped at the front door.

"It was me poured kerosene on your magazines," she said. "I thawed all the meat out, too."

"I know it," said Uncle Ned. He didn't turn around. A girl named Nicole blocked a goal.

Hitchhiking was a frightening experience. She felt alone and vulnerable on the interstate. Oral's protective device was fastened securely about her waist. But what if it didn't work? What if she'd used it up with Jimmy Gerder? A man who sold prosthetic devices picked her up almost at once. His name was Sebert Lewis, and he offered to send her to modeling school in Lubbock. He had helped several girls begin promising careers. Many were now in national magazines.

When Sebert stopped for gas, Maggie got out and ran. There were trucks everywhere. A chrome black eighteen-wheeler city. They towered over Maggie on every side. In a moment she was lost. Some of the trucks were silent. Others rumbled deep and blinked red and yellow lights. There was no one about. She spotted a café through the dark. The drivers were likely all inside. It seemed like the middle of the night. French fries reached her on a light diesel breeze.

"I don't know what to do next!" she said aloud, determined not to cry. A big red truck stood by itself. A nice chrome bulldog on the front. It wouldn't hurt to rest and maybe hide from Sebert Lewis. She wrapped her coat around her and used her suitcase for a pillow. In a moment she was asleep. Only a short time later, a face looked directly into hers.

"Oh, Lord," said Maggie, "don't you dare do whatever it is you're thinking."

"Little lady, I'm not thinking on anything at all," the man said.

"Well, all right, then. If you mean it."

He was big, about as big a man as Maggie had ever seen. Dark brown eyes nearly lost in a face like a kindly pie. "You better be glad I'm a bug on maintenance," he said. "If I'd of took off you lyin' there under the tire, I'd a squashed you flatter'n a dog on the road to Amarillo. You got a name, have you?"

"I'm Maggie McKenna from Marble Creek."

"You running away?"

"I'm going to New York City to write plays."

"You got folks back home?"

"My mother's dead and my father disappeared under strange circumstances. I'm a high-school graduate and a member of the Sidewinderettes. They don't take just everybody wants to get in. If you're thinking about calling Uncle Ned, you just forget it."

"Not my place to say what you ought to do. I'm Billy C. Mace. How'd you get to here?"

"A man named Sebert Lewis picked me up. Said he'd put me through modeling school in Lubbock."

"Lord Jesus!" said Billy Mace. "Come on, get in. Nothing's going to happen to you now."

Riding in the cab of an eighteen-wheeler wasn't anything at all like a '72 Ford. You towered over the road and could see everything for miles. Cars got out of the way. Billy talked to other truckers on the road. His CB handle was Boomer Billy. He let Maggie talk to Black Buddy and Queen Louise and Stoker Fish. The truck seemed invulnerable. Nothing could possibly reach her. The road hummed miles below. There was even a place to sleep behind the driver. Billy guessed she was hungry, and before they left the stop he got cheeseburgers and onion rings to go. Billy kept plenty of Fritos and Hershey bars with almonds in the truck, and had Dr Peppers iced in a cooler. Maggie went to sleep listening to Waylon Jennings tapes. When she woke it was morning. Billy said they'd be in Tulsa in a minute.

"I've never even been out of the state," said Maggie. "And here I am already in Oklahoma."

Billy pulled into a truck stop for breakfast. And then to another for lunch. He measured the distance in meals. "Two hundred miles to lunch," he'd tell Maggie, or "a hundred seventy to supper."

Maggie read him *Blue Sun Rising* while he drove.

"I don't know a lot about plays," said Billy when she was through, "but I don't see how that sucker can miss. That third act's a doozie."

"It needs a little work."

"Not as I see it, it don't. You might want to rein in the Earth Mother symbolism a little, but that's just a layman's suggestion."

"You may be right," said Maggie.

She already knew Billy was well read. There was a shelf of books over the bunk. All the writers' names were John. John Gunther. John Milton. John D. MacDonald.

"John's my daddy's name, God rest him," said Billy. "A man named John tells you something, you can take it for a fact."

She told him about Uncle Ned and Aunt Grace. She didn't mention Oral Blue, as they had not discussed the possibilities of extraterrestrial life. Billy was livid about her experience with Sebert Lewis.

"Lord Jesus himself was looking after you," he said. "No offense meant, but a girl pretty as you is just road bait, Maggie. That modeling studio thing is likely a front. I expect this Sebert's a retired Red agent and into hard astrology on the side. Probably under deep cover for some time. I imagine there's a network of such places spread right across the country. Sebert and his cohorts cruise the roads for candidates, like yourself. Couple of days in a little room, and you're hopeless on drugs, ready to do unspeakable acts of every kind. There's a possibility of dogs. You wake up in bed with some greaser with a beard that gets military aid from this godless administration. That's where your tax dollar goes. I don't want to scare you, but you come real close to a bad end."

"I guess I don't know much, do I?" said Maggie. "I feel awful dumb."

"You learn quick enough when you drive the big rigs. There's things go on you wouldn't believe. The Russians got the news media eatin' out of their hands. I could give you names you'd recognize at once if I was to say 'em. There are biological agents in everything you eat. Those lines and numbers they got on the back of everything you buy? What that is is a code. If you're not in the KGB or the Catholic Church, you can't read it. Don't eat anything that's got three sixes. That's the sign of the beast. I wish to God I had control of my appetite. I can feel things jabbing away inside. White bread and tomatoes are pretty safe. And food isn't the only way they got you. TV's likely the worst. I can't *tell* you the danger of watching the tube."

"I already know about that," said Maggie.

Billy Mace had it all arranged. As good as any travel agent could do. He left her with a Choctaw driver named Henry Black Bear in St. Louis. Henry took her to Muncie, Indiana. Gave her over to a skeletal black man named Quincy Pride. Quincy's CB handle was "Ghost." He taught her the names of every blues singer who had lived in New Orleans at any time. He played their tapes in order of appearance. At Pittsburgh she transferred to Tony D. Velotta, a handsome Italian with curly hair. Maggie thought he was the image of John Travolta.

And then very early in the morning, she woke to the bright sun in her eyes and crawled down from the bunk and Tony pointed and said, "Hey, there it is, kid. We're here."

Maggie could scarcely believe her eyes. The skyline exploded like needles in the sun. A lonely saxophone wailed offstage. She could see the trees blossom in Central Park. Smell the hot dogs cooking at the zoo. They were still in New Jersey, but they were close.

"Lordy," said Maggie, "it looks near as real as a movie."

As they sliced through upper Manhattan, Tony pointed out the sights. Not that there was an awful lot to see. He tried to explain the Bronx and Brooklyn and Queens, drawing a map with his finger on the dash. Maggie was thoroughly confused, and too excited to really care.

"So what are you going to do now? Where you going to stay?"

"I don't know," said Maggie. "I guess I'll find a hotel or something."

"How much money you got, you don't mind me asking?"

"Eight dollars and thirty cents. Now I know that's not a lot. I may have to look for work. It could take some time before I get my play produced."

"Holy Mother," said Tony. "You'd better stay with us."

"Now I couldn't do that. I'll be just fine."

"Right. For six, maybe eight minutes, tops."

The Velottas lived in Brooklyn. It might as well have been Mars as far as Maggie was concerned. There were eight people in the family. Tony and his wife Carla and little Tony, who was two. Tony's father and mother, two younger brothers and a sister. They took in Maggie at once. They said she talked funny. They loved her. Carla gave her dresses. There was always plenty to eat. The Velottas had never heard of peanut butter. Maggie ate things called manicotti and veal piccata. Carla made spaghetti that didn't come out of a can. Nothing was like it was at Aunt Grace's and Uncle Ned's. The family was constantly in motion. Talking and running from one end of the house to the other. Everyone yelled at each other and laughed. Maggie tasted wine for the first time. She'd never seen a wine bottle out of a paper sack. Everyone worked in the Velotta family bakery. Maggie helped out, carrying trays of pastry to the oven.

Tony stayed a week and went back on the road. Maggie talked to Carla one evening after little Tony was in bed.

"I've got to go see my producer," she said. "You all have been wonderful to me but I can't live off you forever. The sooner I get *Blue Sun Rising* on Broadway, the better."

"Yeah, right," said Carla. She looked patient and resigned. The whole family conferred on directions. An intricate map was drawn. Likely locations of muggers and addicts were marked with an X.

"Don't talk to *anyone*," said Tony's mother. She crossed herself and gave Maggie a medal. "Especially don't talk to blacks and Puerto Ricans. Or Jews or people with slanty eyes or turbans. No turbans! Avoid men with Nazi haircuts and blue eyes. *Anyone* with blue eyes."

"Watch out for men in business suits and ties," said Papa Velotta. "They carry little black cases. Like women's purses only flat. There's supposed to be business inside but there's not. It's dope, is what it is. Everybody knows what's going on."

"Don't talk to anyone on skates with orange hair," said Carla.

"A Baptist with funny eyes will give you a pamphlet," said Papa. "Don't take it. Watch out for white socks."

"I'll try to remember everything," said Maggie.

"I'll light a candle," said Mama Velotta.

Maggie called Marty Wilde, the Broadway producer. Wilde said she had a nice voice and he liked to encourage regional talent. He would see her at three that afternoon.

"What's the name of this play?" he wanted to know.

"*Blue Sun Rising*," said Maggie.

"Jesus, I like it. You don't have an agent or anything do you?"

"I just got in town," said Maggie.

"Good. I like to work with people direct."

Her first impression was right. Manhattan was as real as any cop show she'd ever seen. It was all there. The sounds, the smells, the people of many lands. There was a picture show on nearly every block. Everything was the same, everything was different. The city changed before her eyes. A man lying in the street. A kid tying celery to a cat. A woman dressed like a magazine cover, getting out of a cab. She watched the woman a long time. Maybe she'll come to see my play, Maggie thought. She looks like a woman who'd see a play.

Marty Wilde had a small office in a tall building. The building was nice outside. Inside, the halls were narrow. There was bathroom tile on the floors. A girl with carrot hair said Mr. Wilde would see her, and knocked on the wall. Marty came out at once.

"Maggie McKenna from Marble Creek, Texas," he said. "That's who you are. Maggie McKenna who wrote *Blue Sun Rising*. Hey, get in here right now."

Marty ushered her in and offered a chair. The office was bigger than a closet and had faded brown pictures on the wall. Maggie realized these were Broadway greats, people she would likely meet later. There was very little light. The window looked out on a window. Black men in *Kung Fu* suits kicked at the air. There were piles of plays in the room. Plays spilling over tables and chairs and onto the floor. This sight left Maggie depressed. If there were that many plays in New York, they might never get around to *Blue Sun Rising*.

Marty Wilde took her play and set it aside. He perched on the edge of his desk. "So tell me about Maggie McKenna. I can read an author like a page. I can see your play right on your face. A character sits down stage right. The phone rings. I can see that."

"That's amazing," said Maggie. Marty Wilde seemed worn to a nub. A turkey neck stuck out of his shirt. His eyes slept in little hammocks. "There's not much to tell about me. I think my play's good, Mr. Wilde. If it needs any changes I'm willing to do the work."

"Every play needs work. You take your Neil Simon or your Chekhov. A hit doesn't jump out of the typewriter and hop up on the stage."

"No, I guess not."

"You better believe it. Who's this guy give you my name?"

"Harcourt Playce, he works on the San Angelo paper."

"Short little man with a clubfoot. Wears a Mexican peso on a chain. Sure, I remember."

This didn't sound like Mr. Playce, but Maggie didn't want to interrupt.

"You say you haven't got an agent."

"No, sir, I sure don't."

"Let's cut the sir stuff, Maggie. I'm older than you in years, but there's a spirit of youth pervades the stage. You're a very pretty girl. How you fixed for cash?"

"Not real good right now."

"My point exactly. Here's what I suggest. It's just an idea I'm throwing out. I take in a few writers on this scholarship thing which is, hey, my way of paying Lady Broadway back in a small way. You stay at my place, we work together. I got a friend can give you good photo work. He's affiliated with a national modeling chain. All semi-tasteful stuff. You'd know his name the minute I said it."

"You want to take my picture?"

"Just an idea. Let's get you settled in."

"This sounds a lot like girls and scientists, Mr. Wilde. I don't see what it has to do with my play."

Marty came off the desk. "I want you to be comfortable with this."

"I'm not very comfortable right now."

"So let's talk. Tell me what you're feeling."

"You just talk from over there."

"You remind me a lot of Debra Winger. In a very classical sense."

"You remind me of someone, too."

"Jesus, what a sweet kid you are. We won't try to push it. Just let it happen." He took a step closer. A strange invisible force picked him up and hurled him against the wall. Pictures of near-greats shattered. Some crucial fault gave way in the stacks of plays. Acts and scenes spilled over Marty on the floor.

"I think you broke something," said Marty. "Where'd you learn that hold? You're awful quick."

The girl with carrot hair came in.

"Call somebody," said Marty. "Get me on the couch."

"I don't think we can work together," said Maggie. "I'm real displeased with your behavior."

"I can see you don't know shit about the theater," said Marty. "You can't just waltz in here and expect to see your name in lights."

"You ought to be in jail. If you try to get in touch with me, I'll press charges."

*   *   *

Carla said she could stay as long as she wanted. There wasn't any reason to go look for another place.

"I've got to try it on my own," said Maggie. "I believe in my play. I don't believe everyone on Broadway's like Marty Wilde."

Carla could see that she was determined. "It's not easy to get work. Tony thinks a lot of you, Maggie. We all do. You're family."

"Oh, Carla," Maggie threw her arms around her. "You're the very best family I ever had."

Carla persuaded her to wait for the Sunday *Times*. Mama Velotta filled her up with food. "Eat now. You won't get a chance to later."

The room was on East Twenty-first over an all-night Chinese restaurant. Maggie shared it with three girls named Jeannie, Eva, and Sherry. They all three worked for an insurance company. Maggie got a waitress job nights at the restaurant downstairs. There was just enough money to eat and pay the rent. She slept a few hours after work and took the play around days. No one wanted to see her. They asked her to mail copies and get an agent. Maggie cut down her meals to one a day, which allowed her to make a new copy of *Blue Sun Rising* every week. She even started a new play, using Sherry's old Mac computer and the backs of paper placemats from the job. The play was *Diesel and Roses*, a psychological drama set in a truck-stop café. Billy Mace was in it, and so was Henry Black Bear and Quincy Pride and Tony Velotta. Carla called. There was a postal money order from Marble Creek for $175 and a note.

"It's not good news," said Carla.

"Read it," said Maggie.

" 'Dying. Come home. Uncle Ned.' "

"Oh Lord."

"I'm real sorry, honey."

"It's okay. We weren't close."

The thing to do was take the money and eat and make some copies of *Blue Sun Rising*. And forget about Uncle Ned. Maggie couldn't do it. Even Uncle Ned deserved to have family put him in the ground. "I'll be back," she told New York, and made arrangements to meet Carla and get the money.

The first thing she noticed was things had changed in the year she'd been away. Instead of the '72 Ford, there was a late model Buick with a boat hitch on the back. Poking out of the garage was a Ranger fishing boat, an eighteen-footer with a big Merc outboard on the stern.

"You better be dead or dying," said Maggie.

The living room looked like Sears and Western Auto had exploded. There was a brand new Sony and a VCR, and hit tapes like *Gymnasts in Chains*. The kitchen was a wildlife preserve. Maggie stood at the door but wouldn't go in. Things moved around under plates. There were cartons of Hershey bars and chips. Canned Danish hams and foreign mustards. All over the house there were things still in boxes. Uncle Ned had dug tunnels through empty bottles and dirty books. There were new Hawaiian shirts. Hush Puppies in several different styles. A man appeared in one of the tunnels.

"I'm Dr. Kraft, I guess you're Maggie."

"Is he really dying? What's wrong with him?"

"Take your pick. The man's got everything. A person can't live like that and expect their organs to behave."

Maggie went upstairs. Uncle Ned looked dead already. There were green oxygen tanks and plastic tubes.

"I'm real glad you came. This is nice."

"Uncle Ned, where'd you get all this *stuff*?"

"That all you got to say? You don't want to hear how I am?"

"I can see how you are."

"You're entitled to bad feelings. I deserve whatever you want to dish out. I want to settle things up before I go to damnation and meet your aunt. Your father had an employee stock plan at Montgomery Ward's. Left your mother well off, and that woman was too cheap to spend it. We got the money when she died and you came to us. We sort of took these little vacations. Nothing big."

"Oh Lord."

"I guess we wronged you some."

"I guess I grew up on peanut butter and Campbell's soup is what happened."

"I've got a lot to answer for. There are certain character flaws."

"That's no big news to me."

"I can see a lot clearer from the unique position I got at the moment. Poised between one plane of being and the next. When your aunt died, weakness began to thrive. I didn't mean to buy so much stuff."

"I don't suppose there's anything left."

"Not to speak of, I wouldn't think. All that junk out there's on

credit. It'll have to go back. The bank's got the house. There's forty-nine dollars in a Maxwell House can in the closet. I want you to have it."
"I'll take it."
"I wish you and me'd been closer. I hope you'll give me a kiss."
"I'd rather eat a toad," said Maggie.

Maggie saw Jimmy Gerder at the funeral. He still had a limp and kept his distance. She walked along the river to see Oral. It was fall, or as close as fall gets in that end of Texas. Dry leaves rattled and the Colorado was low. The log where she used to watch turtles was aground, trailing tangles of fishing line. The water was the color of chocolate milk and the turtles were gone. Oral was gone, too. Brush had sprung up under the big native pecan. The place looked empty without the multiblue pickup and the extraterrestrial trailer. Maggie wondered if he'd gotten things to work or just left. She asked around town, and no one seemed to remember seeing him go. After a Coke and a bacon and tomato at the café, she figured she had enough to get back to New York if she sold a couple of things before Sears learned Uncle Ned was dead. Put that with her forty-nine-dollar inheritance and she could do it. There was fifteen dollars left from the ticket. Even dying, Uncle Ned had remembered to pay for only one way.

Winter in New York was bad. The Chinese restaurant became an outlet for video tapes. Sherry and Jeannie and Eva helped all they could. They carried Maggie on the rent and ran copies of *Blue Sun Rising* down at the insurance company. The Velottas tried to help, but Maggie wouldn't have it. She got part-time work at a pizza place on East Fifty-second. After work, she walked bone-tired to the theater district and looked at the lights. She read the names on the posters and watched people get out of cabs. There was a cold wet drizzle every night, but Maggie didn't mind. The streets reflected the magic and made it better. When the first snow fell, she sewed a blanket in her coat. The coat smelled like anchovies, and Sherry said she looked like a Chinese pilot. "For God's sake, baby, let me loan you a coat."
"I can manage," said Maggie, "you've done enough."
She could no longer afford subways or buses, so she walked every day from her room. She lost weight and coughed most of the time. The owner asked her to leave. He said customer's didn't like people coughing on their pizza. She didn't tell the girls she'd

lost her job. They'd want to give her money. She looked, but there weren't any jobs to be had. Especially for girls who looked like bag ladies and sounded like Camille. She kept going out every day and coming back at night. Hunger wasn't a problem. She felt too sick to eat. One night she simply didn't go home. "What's the point? What's the use pretending? No one wants to look at *Blue Sun Rising*. I can't get a job. I can't do anything at all."

The snow began to fall in slow motion, flakes the size of lemons. Broadway looked like a big Christmas tree someone had tossed out and forgot to take the lights.

"Look at the blues," said Maggie. "Oral liked the blues so much."

A man selling food gave her a pretzel and some mustard. The pretzel came up at once. A coughing fit hit her. She couldn't stop. First-nighters hurried quickly by. Maggie pulled her coat up close and looked in the steamy windows of Times Square. Radios and German bayonets were half off. There was a pre-Christmas sale on marital aids. She could still taste the mustard and the pretzel. A black man in sunglasses approached.

"You hurtin' bad, mama. You need something, I can maybe get it."

"No, thank you," said Maggie.

I can't just stand here, she thought. I've got to do something. She couldn't feel her feet. Lights were jumping about. There was a paper box in the alley. The thing to do was to sit down and try to figure things out. She thought of a good line for *Diesel and Roses* and then forgot it. A cat looked in and sniffed; there were anchovies somewhere about. Maggie dreamed of Daddy when he took her to the zoo. She dreamed of Oral under a tree and riding high with Billy Mace. The cab was toasty warm and Billy had burgers from McDonald's. She dreamed she heard applause. The cat started chewing on her coat. Oh Lord, I love New York, thought Maggie. If I can make it here, I can make it anywhere . . .

Carla looked ethereal, computer-enhanced.

"I guess I'm dying," said Maggie. "I'm sorry to get you out in this weather."

"Oh, baby," said Carla, "hang on. Just hang on, Maggie."

Everything was fuzzy. The tubes hurt her nose. The walls were dark and needed painting. Sherry and Eva and Jeannie were there and all the Velottas. They bobbed about like balloons. Everyone had rings around their eyes.

"I want you to have *Blue Sun Rising*," said Maggie. "All of you. Equal shares. I've been thinking about off-Broadway lately. That might not be so hard. Don't see a man named Marty Wilde."

"All right, Maggie."

"She's going," someone said.

"Good-bye, Daddy. Good-bye, Oral," said Maggie.

The room looked nice. There was a big window with sun coming in. The doctor leaned down close. He smelled like good cologne. He smiled at Maggie and wrote something and left. A nice-looking man got up from a chair and stood by the bed.

"Hello. You feeling like something to drink? You want anything, just ask."

"I'd like a Dr Pepper if you have one."

"You got it."

The man left and Maggie tried to stay awake. When she opened her eyes again, it was late afternoon. The man was still there. A nurse came in and propped her up. The man brought her a fresh Dr Pepper.

"You look a lot like Tony," said Maggie. He did. The same crispy hair and dark eyes. A nice black suit and a gray tie. Maybe a couple of years older. "You know Tony and Carla?"

"They ask about you every day. You can see them real soon. Everybody's been pretty worried about you."

"I guess I 'bout died."

"Yeah, I guess you did."

"This place looks awful expensive. I don't want the Velottas or anyone spending a bundle on me."

"They won't. No problem."

"Hey, I know a swell place like this isn't *free*."

"We'll talk about it. Don't worry." The man smiled at Maggie and went away.

Maggie slept and got her appetite back and wondered where she was. The next afternoon the man was back. He helped her in a wheelchair and rolled her down the hall to a glassed-in room full of plants. There were cars outside in a circular drive. A fountain turned off for the winter. A snow-covered lawn and a dark line of trees. Far in the distance, pale blue hills against a cold and leaden sky. Men in sunglasses and overcoats walked around in the snow.

"I guess you're going to tell me where I am sometime," said Maggie. "I guess you're going to tell me who you are and what I'm doing in this place I can't afford."

"I'm Johnny Lucata," the man said. "Call me Johnny, Maggie. And this house belongs to a friend."

"He must be a friend of yours, then. I don't remember any friends with a house like this."

"You don't know him. But he's a friend of yours, too." He seemed to hesitate. He straightened his tie. "Look, I got things to tell you. Things you need to know. You want, we can talk when you feel a little better."

"I feel okay right now."

"Maybe. Only this is kinda nutsy stuff, you know? I don't want to put you back in bed or nothing."

"Mr. Lucata, whatever it is, I think I'll feel a lot better when I know what's going on."

"Right. Why not? So what do you know about olives?"

"What?"

"Olives. They got olives over in Italy. There's a place where the toe's kicking Sicily in the face. Calabria. Something like a state, only different. The man lives here, he's got a lot of the olive oil business in Calabria. Been in his family maybe four, five hundred years. You sure you want to do this now?"

"I'm sure, Mr. Lucata."

"Okay. There's this city called Reggio di Calabria right on the water. You can look and see Sicily real good. A couple of miles out of town is this castle. Been there forever, only now it's a place for monks. So what happens is a couple of months back this monk's digging around and finds this parchment in a box. It's real old and the monk reads it. What he sees shakes him up real bad. He's not going to go to the head monk because Catholics got this thing about stuff that even *starts* to get weird. But he's a monk, right? He can't just toss this thing away. He's got a sister knows a guy who's family to the man who lives here. So the box gets to Reggio and then it gets to him." Johnny Lucata looked at Maggie. "Here's the part I said gets spooky. What this parchment says, Maggie, is that the old duke who started up the family left all the olive business to *you*."

Maggie looked blank. "Now that doesn't make sense at all, Mr. Lucata."

"Yeah, tell me. It's the straight stuff. The experts been over it. I got a copy I can show you. It's all in Latin, but you can read the part that says Maggie McKenna of Marble Creek, Texas. We got the word out, and we been looking all over trying to find you. But your uncle died and you came back to New York. We didn't know where to take it after that. Then someone in Tony's family mentions your name and it gets to us. The thing is now, the man lives here, he doesn't know what to make of all this, and he don't want to think about it a lot. He sure don't want to ask some cardinal or the Pope. What he *wants* to do is make it right for *you*, Maggie. This duke is his ancestor and he figures it's a matter of honor. I mean, he doesn't see you ought to get it *all*, but you ought to be in for a couple of points. He wants me to tell you he'd like to work it where you get maybe three, four mill a year out of this. He thinks that's fair and he knows you're pressed for cash."

Maggie sat up straight. "Are you by any chance talking about dollars? Three or four million *dollars?*"

"Five. I think we ought to say five. He kind of left that up to me. Don't worry about the taxes. We'll work a little off-tackle Panama reverse through a Liechtenstein bank. You'll get the bread through a Daffy Duck Christmas Club account."

"I just can't hardly believe this, Mr. Lucata. It's like a dream or something. No one even knew I was going to *be* back then. Why, there wasn't even a *Texas!*"

"You got it."

"This castle. There's just these monks living there now?"

"Palazzo Azzuro. Means blue palace. I been there, it's nice. Painted blue all over. Inside and out. Every kind of blue you ever saw."

"*Blue?* Oh, my goodness!"

"You okay?"

"Oral," said Maggie, "Oh, Oral, you're the finest and dearest friend I ever had!"

When she was feeling like getting up and around, Johnny Lucata helped her find a relatively modest apartment off Fifth Avenue. Five mill or not, Maggie had been poor too long to start tossing money around. She did make sure there were always Dr Peppers and Baby Ruths in the fridge. And steaks and fresh fruit and nearly everything but Chinese food and pizza. Carla helped her find Bloomingdale's and Saks. Maggie picked out a new cloth coat. She sent nice perfume to Jeannie and Sherry and Eva, and paid them back triple what they'd spent to help her out. She gave presents to the Velottas and had everyone over for dinner. Johnny Lucata dropped by a lot. Just to see how she was doing. Sometimes he came in a cab. Sometimes he came in a black car with tinted windows and men wearing black suits and shades. He took her out to dinner and walks in the park. Sometimes Maggie made coffee, and they talked into the night. She read him *Blue Sun Rising* and he liked it.

"You don't have to say that, just because it's me."

"I mean it. I go to plays all the time. It's *real*, Maggie. You don't have to wonder what everybody's thinking, they just say it. I want you to talk to Whitney Hess."

"Whitney Hess the producer? Do you know him?"

"Yeah, sure I know him."

"I don't want to do that, Johnny. I don't want to get help from somebody just because he's a friend of yours. That's not right. I want *Blue Sun Rising* to stand on its own."

"Are you kidding?" said Johnny. "Whitney Hess wouldn't buy a bad play from his dying mother. Besides, I want five points of this up front. You're not going to cut *me* out of a winner."

Tony and Carla and Tony's brothers and his sister and Mama and Papa Velotta dressed up for opening night. Johnny Lucata sent a limo to pick them up, and another to get Jeannie and Sherry and Eva. Tony got out the word, and the truckers found Billy Mace and Henry Black Bear and Quincy Pride. They all had seventh-row center seats.

Maggie thought sure she was dreaming. Her name up in lights at the Shubert Theatre. Ladies in furs and jewels dressed up for opening night. Spotlights and TV cameras and people she'd only seen in the movies. She stayed outside a long time. Standing in the very same spot where she'd thrown up pretzels in the street. Not far from the alley where she'd curled up in a box and nearly died. You just never know, she told herself. You just don't.

There was no need to wait for the reviews. After the first act, Whitney Hess said they had a smash on their hands. After the third-act curtain, even Maggie believed it was true. The audience came to its feet and shouted, "Author! Author!" and someone told Maggie they meant *her*.

Johnny hurried her out of the Shubert by the side door. He wouldn't say where they were going. A black car was by the curb around the corner. There were men in overcoats and shades.

"I want you to meet somebody," said Johnny, and opened the rear door. "This is Maggie McKenna," he said. "Maggie, I'd like you to meet my father."

Maggie caught the proper respect in his voice. She looked inside and saw an old man sitting in the corner. He was lost in a black suit, a man no more substantial than a cut-rate chicken in a sack.

"That was a nice play," he said. "I like it a lot. I like plays with a story you can't guess what's going to happen all the time. There's nothing on the television but dirt. The Reds got people in the business. They built this place in Chelyabinsk looks just like Twentieth Century Fox. Writers, directors, the works. They teach 'em how to do stuff rots out your head, then they send them over here. This is a great country. You keep writing nice plays."

"Thank you," said Maggie, "I'm very glad you liked it."

"Here. A little present from me. Your big night. You remember where you got it."

"I'm very grateful," said Maggie. "For everything." She leaned in and kissed him on the cheek.

"That's very nice. You're a nice girl. She's a nice girl, Johnny."

Johnny took her back inside, and on the way home after the big party Whitney Hess gave at the Plaza, Maggie opened her present. It was a pendant shaped like an olive. Pale emeralds formed the olive, and a ruby sat on top for the pimiento.

"It's just lovely," said Maggie.

"The old man's got a lot of class."

"Why didn't you tell me that was your father's house, Johnny? I kinda guessed later, but I didn't know for sure."

"Wasn't the right time."

"And it's the right time now?"

"Yeah, I guess it is."

"Whitney Hess wants to go into rehearsal on *Diesel and Roses* next month. I'm going to ask Billy Mace and Henry Black Bear and Quincy Pride to come on as technical advisers. There's not a thing for them to do, but I'd like to have them around."

"That's nice. It's a good idea."

"Whitney says everyone wants the movie rights to *Blue Sun Rising*. Which means we'll get a picture deal up front for *Diesel and Roses*. Oh Lordy, I can't believe all this is really happening. Everything in my life's been either awful or as good as it can be."

"It's going to stay good now, Maggie." He leaned over and kissed her quickly. Maggie stared at the tinted glass.

"You've never done *that* before."

"Well, I have now."

Maggie wondered what was happening inside. She felt funny all over. She was dizzy from the kiss. She liked Johnny a lot, but she'd never liked him quite like this. She wanted him to kiss her again and again, but not *now*. Not wearing Oral's protective device, which she'd worn since her very first day in New York. It was something she'd never thought about before. What if you really *wanted* someone to do something to you? Would the wire and the black stone know that it wasn't Jimmy Gerder or Marty Wilde? She certainly couldn't take the chance of finding out.

The phone was ringing when they got to her apartment.

"You're famous," said Johnny. "That'll go on all night."

"No, it won't," said Maggie, "just take it off the hook. I can be famous tomorrow. Tonight I just want to be me."

Johnny had a funny look in his eyes. She was sure he was going to kiss her right then. "Just wait right there," she said. "Don't go away. Get me a Dr Pepper and open yourself a beer." She hurried into the bedroom and shut the door. Raised up her skirt and slipped the little wire off her waist. Her heart was beating fast. "I hope you know what you're doing, Maggie McKenna."

Johnny gave a decidedly angry shout from the other room. Another man yelled. Something fell to the floor.

"Good heavens, what's that?" said Maggie. She rushed into the room. Johnny had a young man backed against the wall, threatening him with a fist. The man wore a patched cardigan sweater and khaki pants. He was trying to hit Johnny with a sack.

"Who the hell are *you*," said Johnny, "what are you doing in here!"

"Oh, my God," said Maggie. She stopped in her tracks, then ran past Johnny and threw her arms around the other man's neck. "Oh, Daddy, I *knew* you wouldn't leave me! I knew you'd come back!"

"Maggie? Is that you? Why, you're all grown up! Say, what a looker you are. Where am I? How's your mother?"

"We'll talk about that. Just sit down and rest." She could hardly see through her tears. "I'll explain," she told Johnny. "At least I'll give it a try. Oh, Oral, I hope you're wherever it is you want to be. Johnny, get Daddy a Dr Pepper." She gave him the sack. "Put this in the kitchen and you come right back."

"It's just catfood and bread," said Daddy. "I think that fella there took me wrong."

"Everything's all right now."

"Maggie, I feel like I've been floating around in yogurt. Forever or maybe an hour and a half. It's hard to say. I don't know. I'm greatly confused for the moment. I *ought* to be more than five years older'n you."

"It happens. There are documented cases. Just sit down and rest. There's plenty of time to talk." Johnny came back with a Dr Pepper. She gave it to her father and led Johnny to the kitchen.

"I don't get it," said Johnny.

"You got all that business with the monks, you can learn to handle this. Just hold me a minute, all right? And do what you did in the car."

Johnny kissed her a very long time. Maggie was sure she was going to faint.

"I'm a real serious guy," said Johnny. "I'm not just playing around. I got very strong emotions."

"I like you a lot," said Maggie. "I'm not sure I could love a man in your line of work."

"I'm in olives. I got a nice family business."

"You've got a family in overcoats and shades, Johnny Lucata."

"Okay, so we'll work something out."

"I guess maybe we will. I keep forgetting I'm in olive oil, too. Maybe you better kiss me again. Johnny, there's *so* much I want us to do. I want to show you Marble Creek. I want to show you green turtles on a log and the Sidewinderettes doing a halftime double-snake whip. I want to see every single shade of blue in that castle, and I've got a simply *great* idea for a play. Oh, Johnny, Daddy's back and you're here and I've got about everything there *is*. New York is such a knocked-out crazy wonderful town!"

Diner

HE WOKE SOMETIME BEFORE DAWN AND BROUGHT THE dream back with him out of sleep. The four little girls attended Catholic junior high in Corpus Christi. Their hand-painted guitars depicted tropical Cuban nights. They played the same chord again and again, a dull repetition like small wads of paper hitting a drum. The light was still smoky, the furniture unrevealed. He made his way carefully across the room. The screened-in porch enclosed the front side of the house facing the Gulf, allowing the breeze to flow in three directions. He could hear rolling surf, smell the sharp tang of iodine in the air. Yet something was clearly wrong. The water, the sand, the sky, had disappeared, lost behind dark coagulation. With sudden understanding he saw the screen was clotted with bugs. Grasshoppers blotted out the morning. They were bouncing off the screen, swarming in drunken legions. He ran outside and down the stairs, knowing what he'd find. The garden was gone. A month before, he'd covered the small plot of ground with old window screens and bricks. The hoppers had collapsed the whole device. His pitiful stands of lettuce were cropped clean, razored on the ground as if he'd clipped them with a mower. Radishes, carrots, the whole bit. Eaten to the stalk. Then it occurred to him he was naked and under attack. Grasshopper socks knitted their way up to his knees. Something considered his crotch. He yelled and struck out blindly, intent on knocking hoppers silly. The fight was next to useless, and he retreated up the stairs.

Jenny woke while he was dressing.
"Something wrong? Did you yell just a minute ago?"
"Hoppers. They're all over the place."
"Oh, Mack."
"Little fuckers ate my salad bar."
"I'm sorry. It was doing so good."
"It isn't doing good now." He started looking for his hat.
"You want something to eat?"
"I'll grab something at Henry's."
She came to him, still unsteady from sleep, awkward and fetching at once. Minnie Mouse T-shirt ragged as a kite. A certain yielding coming against him.
"I got to go to work."
"Your loss, man."
"I dreamed of little Mexican girls."
"Good for you." She stepped back to gather her hair, her eyes somewhere else.
"Nothing happened. They played real bad guitar."
"So you say."

He made his way past the dunes and the ragged stands of sea grass, following the path over soft, dry sand to solid beach, the dark rows of houses on stilts off to his right, the Gulf rolling in, brown as mud, giving schools of mullet a ride. The hoppers had moved on, leaving dead and wounded behind. The sun came up behind dull anemic clouds. Two skinny boys searched the ocean's morning debris. He found a pack of Agricultural Hero cigarettes in his pocket and cupped his hands against the wind. George Panagopoulos said there wasn't any tobacco in them at all. Said they made them out of half-dried shit and half kelp and that the shit wasn't bad, but he couldn't abide the kelp. Where the sandy road angled into the beach, he cut back and crossed Highway 87, the asphalt cracked and covered with sand, the tough coastal grass crowding in. The highway trailed southwest for two miles, dropping off abruptly where the red-white-and-blue Galveston ferries used to run, the other end stretching northeast up the narrow strip of Bolivar Peninsula past Crystal Beach and Gilchrist, then off the peninsula to High Island and Sabine Pass.

Mack began to find Henry's posters north of the road. They were tacked on telephone poles and fences, on the door of the derelict Texaco station, wherever Henry had wandered in this merchandising adventure. He gathered them in as he walked, snapping them off like paper towels. The sun began to bake, hot wind stinging up sand in tiny storms. The posters said: FOURTH OF JULY PICNIC AT HENRY ORTEGA'S DINER. ALL THE BARBECUE PORK YOU CAN EAT. EL DIOS BLESS AMERICA

Henry had drawn the posters on the backs of green accounting forms salvaged from the Sand Palace Motor Home Inn. Even if he'd gotten Rose to help, it was a formidable undertaking.

No easy task to do individually rendered, slightly crazed, and plainly cockeyed fathers of our country. Every George Washington wore a natty clip-on Second Inaugural tie and, for some reason, a sporty little Matamoros pimp mustache. Now and then along the borders, an extra reader bonus, snappy American flags or red cherry bombs going *kapow*.

Mack walked on picking posters. Squinting back east, he saw water flat as slate, vanishing farther out with tricks of the eye. Something jumped out there or something didn't.

Jase and Morgan were in the diner, and George Panagopoulos and Fleece. They wore a collection of gimmie caps and patched-up tennis shoes, jeans stiff and sequined with the residue of fish. Mack took the third stool down. Fleece said it might get hotter. Mack agreed it could. Jase leaned down the counter.

"Hoppers get your garden, too?"

"Right down to bedrock is all," Mack said.

"I had this tomato," Panagopoulos said, "this one little asshole tomato 'bout half as big as a plum; I'm taking a piss and hear these hoppers coming and I'm down and out of the house like that. I'm down there in what, maybe ten, twenty seconds flat, and this tomato's a little bugger and a seed. You know? A little bugger hanging down, and that's all." He made a swipe at his nose, held up a finger, and looked startled and goggle-eyed.

Mack pretended to study the menu and ordered KC steak and fries and coffee and three eggs over easy; and all this time Henry's standing over the charcoal stove behind the counter, poking something flat across the grill, concentrating intently on this because he's already seen the posters rolled up and stuffed in Mack's pocket and he knows he'll have to look right at Mack sooner or later.

"Galveston's got trouble," Jase said. "Dutch rowed back from seeing that woman in Clute looks like a frog. Said nobody's seen Mendez for 'bout a week."

"Eddie's a good man for a Mex," Morgan said from down the counter. "He'll stand up for you, he thinks you're in the right."

Mack felt the others waiting. He wondered if he really wanted to get into this or let it go.

Fleece jumped in. "Saw Doc this morning, sneaking up the dunes 'bout daylight. Gotta know if those hoppers eat his dope."

Everyone laughed except Morgan. Mack was silently grateful.

"I seen that dope," Jase said. "What it is there's maybe three tomato plants 'bout high as a baby's dick."

"I don't want to hear nothin' about tomatoes," said Panagopoulos.

"Don't make any difference what it is," Fleece said. "Man determined to get high, he going to do it."

Panagopoulos told Mack that Dutch's woman up in Clute heard someone had seen a flock of chickens. Right near Umbrella Point. Rhode Island Reds running loose out on the beach.

Mack said fine. There was always a good chicken rumor going around somewhere. That or someone saw a horse or a pack of dogs. Miss Aubrey Gain of Alvin swore on Jesus there was a pride of Siamese cats in Liberty County.

Mack wolfed down his food. He didn't look at his plate. If you didn't look close, you maybe couldn't figure what the hot peppers were covering up.

When he got up to go, he said, "Real tasty, Henry," and then, as if the thought had suddenly occurred, "All right if you and me talk for a minute?"

Henry followed him out. Mack saw the misery in his face. He tried on roles like hats. Humble peon. An extra in *Viva Zapata!* Wily tourist guide with gold teeth and connections. Nothing fit. He looked like Cesar Romero, and this was his cross. Nothing could rob him of dignity. No one would pity a man with such bearing.

Mack took out the roll of posters and gave them back. "You know better than that, Henry. It wasn't a real good idea."

"There is no harm in this, Mack. You cannot say that there is."

"Not me I can't, no."

"Well, then."

"Come on. I got Huang Hua coming first thing tomorrow."

"Ah. Of course."

"Jesus, Henry."

"I am afraid that I forgot."

"Fine. Sure. Look, I appreciate the thought, and so does everyone else. This Chink, now, he hasn't got a real sense of humor."

"I was thinking about a flag."

"What?"

"A flag. You could ask, you know? See what he says. It would not hurt to ask. A very small and insignificant flag in the window of the diner. Just for the one day, you understand?"

Mack looked down the road. "You didn't even listen. You didn't hear anything I said."

"Just for the one day. The Fourth and nothing more."

"Get all the posters down, Henry. Do it before tonight."

"How did you like the George Washington?" Henry asked. "I did all of those myself. Rose did the lettering, but I am totally responsible for the pictures."

"The Washington was great."

"You think so?"

"The eyes kinda follow you around."

"Yes." Henry showed his delight. "I tried for inner vision of the eyes."

"Well, you flat out got it."

Jase and Morgan came out, Jase picking up the rubber fishing boots he'd left at the door. Morgan looked moody and deranged. Mack considered knocking him senseless.

"Look," Mack told him, "I don't want you on my boat. Go with Panagopoulos. Tell him Fleece'll be going with me and Jase."

"Just fine with me," Morgan said.

"Good. It's fine with me, too."

Morgan wasn't through. "You take a nigger fishing on a day with a *r* in it, you goin' to draw sharks certain. I seen it happen."

"You tell that to Fleece," Mack said. "I'll stand out here and watch."

Morgan went in and talked to Panagopoulos. Jase waited for Fleece, leaning against the diner, asleep or maybe not. Mack lit an Agricultural Hero and considered the aftertaste of breakfast. Thought of likely antics with Jenny's parts. Wondered how a univalve mollusk with the mental reserve of grass could dream up a wentletrap shell and then wear it. This and other things.

Life has compensations, but there's no way of knowing what they are.

* * *

Coming in was the time he liked the best. The water was dark and flat, getting ready for the night. The bow cut green, and no sound at all but a jazzy little counterbeat, the crosswind snapping two fingers in the sails. The sun was down an hour, the sky settling into a shade inducing temporary wisdom. He missed beer and music. Resented the effort of sinking into a shitty evening mood without help.

Swinging in through the channel, Pelican Island off to port, he saw the clutter of Port Bolivar, the rusted-out buildings and the stumps of rotted docks, the shrimpers he used to run heeling drunkenly in the flats. South of that was the chain-link fence and the two-story corrugated building. The bright red letters on its side read SHINING WEALTH OF THE SEA JOYOUS COOPERATIVE 37 WELCOME HOME INDUSTRIOUS CATCHERS OF THE FISH.

This Chinese loony-tune message was clear a good nautical mile away; a catcher of the fish with a double cataract couldn't pretend it wasn't there.

Panagopoulos's big Irwin ketch was in, the other boats as well, the nets up and drying. Fleece brought the sloop in neatly, dropping the sails at precisely the right moment, a skill Mack appreciated all the more because Morgan was scarcely ever able to do it, either rushing in to shore full sail like a Viking bent on pillage or dropping off early and leaving them bobbing in the bay.

The Chinks greatly enjoyed this spectacle, the round-eyes paddling the forty-three-foot Hinckley in to shore.

Mack and Jase secured the lines, and then Jase went forward to help Fleece while the Chinks came aboard to look at the catch. The guards stayed on the dock looking sullen and important, rifles slung carelessly over their shoulders. Fishing Supervisor Lu Ping peered into the big metal hold, clearly disappointed.

"Not much fish," he told Mack.

"Not much," Mack said.

"It's June," Fleece explained. "You got the bad easterlies in June. Yucatán Current kinda edges up north, hits the Amarillo Clap flat on. That goin' to fuck up your fishing real good."

"Oh, yes." Lu Ping made a note. Jase nodded solemn agreement.

Mack told Jase and Fleece to come to the house for supper. He walked past the chain-link fence and the big generator that kept the fish in the corrugated building cooler than anyone in Texas.

The routine was, the boats would come in and tack close to the long rock dike stretching out from the southeast side of the peninsula, out of sight of the Chinks, and the women and kids would wave and make a fuss and the men would toss them fish in canvas bags, flounder or pompano or redfish if they were running or maybe a rare sack of shrimp, keeping enough good fish onboard to keep the Chinese happy, but mostly leaving catfish and shark and plenty of mullet in the hold, that and whatever other odd species came up in the nets. It didn't matter at all, since everything they caught was ground up, steamed, pressed, processed, and frozen into brick-size bundles before they shipped it out.

Mack thought about cutting through the old part of the port, then remembered about Henry and went back. There were still plenty of posters on fence posts and abandoned bait stands and old houses, and he pulled down all he could find before dark.

They ate in front of the house near the dunes, a good breeze coming in from the Gulf strong enough to keep mosquitoes and gnats at bay, the wind drawing the driftwood fire nearly white. Henry brought a large pot of something dark and heady, announcing it was Acadia Parish shrimp creole Chihuahua style, and nobody said it wasn't. Mack broiled flounder over a grill. Jase attacked guitar. Arnie Mace, Mack's uncle from Sandy Point, brought illegal rice wine. Not enough to count but potent. Fleece drank half a mason jar and started to cry. He said he was thinking about birds. He began to call them off. Herons and plovers and egrets. Gulls squawking cloud-white thick behind the shrimpers. Jase said he remembered pink flamingos in the tidal flats down by the dike.

"There was an old bastard in Sweeny, you know him, Mack," George Panagopoulos said. "Swears he had the last cardinal bird in Texas. Kept it in a hamster cage long as he could stand it. Started dreaming about it and couldn't sleep, got up in the middle of the night and stir-fried it in a wok. Had a frazzle of red feathers on his hat for some time, but I can't say that's how he got 'em."

"That was Emmett Dodge," Mack said. "I always heard it was a jay."

"Now, I'm near certain it was a cardinal." Panagopoulos looked thoughtfully into his wine. "A jay, now, if Emmett had had a jay, I doubt he could've kept the thing quiet. They make a awful lot of noise."

Mack helped Fleece throw up.

"Georgia won't talk to me," Fleece said miserably. "You the only friend I got."

"I expect you're right."

"You watch out for Morgan. He bad-talkin' you ever chance he get."
"He wants to be pissant mayor, he can run. I sure don't care for the honor."
"He says your eyes beginnin' to slant."
"He said that?"
"Uh-huh."
"Well, fuck him." Fleece was unsteady but intact. Mack looked around for Henry and found him with Rose and Jenny. He liked to stand off somewhere and watch her. A good-looking woman was fine as gold, you caught her sitting by a fire.
He took Henry aside.
"I know what you are going to say," Henry said. "You are angry with me. I can sense these things."
"I'm not angry at all. Just get that stuff taken down before morning."
"I only do what I think is right, *mi compadre*. What is just. What is true." Henry tried for balance. "What I deeply feel in my heart. A voice cries out. It has to speak. This is the tragedy of my race. I feel a great sorrow for my people."
"Okay."
"I shall bow to your wishes, of course."
"Good. Just bow before Huang gets here in the morning."
"I will take them down. I will go and do it now."
"You don't have to do it now."
"I feel I am an intrusion."
"I feel like you've had enough to drink."
"Do you know what I am thinking? What I am thinking at this moment?"
"No, what?"
"I am thinking that I cannot remember tequila."
"Fleece has already done this," Mack said. "I don't want you doing it, too. One crying drunk is enough."
"Forgive me. I cannot help myself. Mack, I don't remember how it tastes. I remember the lime and the salt. I recall a certain warmth. *Nada*. Nothing more."
Tears touched the Cesar Romero eyes, trailed down the Gilbert Roland cheeks. *If Jase plays "La Paloma," I'll flat kill him,* thought Mack. He left to look for Rose.

Jenny told him to come out on the porch and look at the beach. Crickets crawled out of the dunes and made for the water. The sand was black, a bug tide going out to sea. The crickets marched into the water and floated back. In the dark they looked like the ropy strands of a spill.

"The ocean scares me at night," Jenny said.

"Not always. You like it sometimes." He wanted to stop this but didn't know how to do it. She was working up to it a notch at a time.

"It's not you," she said.

"Fine, I'll write that down." He worked his hand up the T-shirt and touched the small of her back. She leaned in comfortably against him.

"Things are still bad, you get too far away from the coast. I don't want you just wandering around somewhere."

"I haven't really decided, Mack. I mean, it's not tomorrow or anything."

"I don't think you're going to find anyone, Jenny." He said it as gently as he could. "Folks are scattered all about."

She didn't answer. They stood a long time on the porch. The house already felt empty.

The chopper came in low out of the south, tilted slightly into the offshore breeze, rotors churning flat, snappy farts as it settled to 87, stirring sand. Soldiers hit the ground. They looked efficient. Counterrevolutionary acts would be dealt with swiftly. Fleece and Panagopoulos leaned against the diner trading butts. Henry came out for a look and ducked inside. The morning was oyster gray with a feeble ribbing of clouds. Major Huang waved at Mack. Then Chen came out of the chopper and started barking at the troops. Mack wasn't pleased. Huang was purely political—fat and happy and not looking for any trouble. Chen was maybe nineteen tops, a cocky little shit with new bars. Mack was glad he didn't speak English, which meant Jase wouldn't try to sell him a shark dick pickled in a jar or something worse.

The Chinese uniforms were gallbladder green to match the chopper. Chen and three troopers stayed behind. The troopers started tossing crates and boxes to the ground. One followed discreetly behind the major.

"Personal hellos," Huang Hua greeted Mack. "It is a precious day we are seeing."

Mack looked at the chopper. "Not many supplies this time."

"Not many fishes," Huang said.

It's going to be like this, is it? Mack followed him past the diner down the road to Shining Wealth Cooperative 37. He noticed little things. A real haircut. Starched khakis with creases. He wondered what Huang had eaten for breakfast.

Sergeant Fishing Supervisor Lu Ping greeted the major effusively. He had reports. Huang stuffed them in a folder. The airconditioning was staggering. Mack forgot what it was like between visits.

"I have reportage of events," Huang began. He sat behind the plain wooden table and folded his hands. "It is a happening of unpleasant nature. Eddie Mendez will not mayor himself in Galveston after today."

"And why's that?"

"Offending abuse. Blameful performance. Defecation of authority." Huang looked meaningfully at Mack. "Retaining back of fishes."

"What'll happen to Eddie?"

"The work you do here is of gravity, Mayor Mack. A task of large importance. Your people in noncoastal places are greatly reliant of fish."

"We're doing the best we can."

"I am hopeful this is true."

Mack looked right at him.

"Major, we're taking all the fish we can net. We got sails and no gas and nothing with an engine to put it into if we did. You're not going to help any shorting us on supplies. I've got forty-one families on this peninsula eating nothing but fish and rice. There's kids here never saw a carrot. We try to grow something, the bugs eat it first 'cause there's no birds left to eat the bugs. The food chain's fucked."

"You are better off than most."

"I'm sure glad to hear it."

"Please to climb down from my back. The Russians did the germing, not us."

"I know who did it."

Huang tried Oriental restraint. "We are engaging to help. You have no grateful at all. The Chinese people have come to fill this empty air."

"Vacuum."

"Yes. Vacuum." Huang considered. "In three, maybe four years, wheat and corn will be achieved in the ground again. Animal and fowl will be brought. This is very restricted stuff. I tell you, Mayor Mack, because I wish your nonopposing. I have ever shown you friendness. You cannot say I haven't."

"I appreciate the effort."

"You will find sweets in this shipment. For the children. Also decorative candles. Toothpaste. Simple magic tricks."

"Jesus Christ."

"I knew this would bring you pleasure."

Huang looked up. Lieutenant Chen entered politely. He handed Huang papers. Gave Mack a sour look. Mack recognized Henry's posters, the menu from the diner. Chen turned and left.

"What is this?" Huang appeared disturbed. "Flags? Counterproductive celebration? Barbecue pork?"

"Doesn't mean a thing," Mack explained. "It's just Henry."

Huang looked quizzically at George Washington, turning the poster in several directions. He glanced at the cardboard menu, at the KC Sirloin Scrambled Eggs Chicken-Fried Steak French Fries Omelet with Cheddar Cheese or Swiss Coffee Refills Free. He looked gravely at Mack.

"I did not think this was a good thing. You said there would be no trouble. One thing leads to a something other. Now it is picnics and flags."

"The poster business, all right," Mack said. "He shouldn't of done that. I figure it's my fault. The diner, now, there's nothing wrong with the diner."

Huang shook his head. "It is fanciment. The path to discontent." He appeared deeply hurt. The poster was an affront. The betrayal of a friend. He walked to the window, hands behind his back. "There is much to have renouncement here, Mayor Mack. Many fences to bend. I have been lenient and foolish. No more Henry Ortega Diner. No picnic. And better fishes, I think."

Mack didn't answer. Whatever he said would be wrong.

Huang recalled something of importance. He looked at Mack again.

"You have a black person living here?"

"Two. A man and a woman."

"There is no racing discrimination? They are treated fairly?"

"Long as they keep picking that cotton."

"No textiles. Only fishes."

"I'll see to it."

Mack walked back north, past a rusted Chevy van waiting patiently for tires, past a pickup with windows still intact. Rose hadn't seen Henry. She didn't know where he was. "He didn't mean to cause trouble," she told Mack.

"I know that, Rose."

"He walks. He wanders off. He needs the time to himself. He is a very sensitive man."

"He's all of that," Mack said. He heard children. Smelled rice and fish, strongly seasoned with peppers.

"He respects you greatly. He says you are *muy simpático*. A man of heart. A leader of understanding."

A woman with fine bones and sorrowful eyes. Katy Jurado, *One-Eyed Jacks*. He couldn't remember the year.

"I just want to talk to him, Rose. I have to see him."

"I will tell him. He will come to you. Here, take some chilies to Jenny. It is the only thing I can grow the bugs won't eat. Try it on the fish. Just this much, no more."

"Jenny'll appreciate that." A hesitation in her eyes. As if she might say something more. Mack wouldn't ask. He wasn't mad at Henry. His anger had abated, diluted after a day with Major Hua. He left and walked to the beach. Jase and Fleece were there. Jase had a mason jar of wine he'd maybe conned from Arnie Mace.

"Tell Panagopoulos and some of the others if you see 'em," Mack said, "I want to talk to Henry. He's off roaming around somewhere; I don't want him doing that."

"Your minorities'll do this," Jace reflected. "I'm glad I ain't a ethnic."

"It's a burden," Fleece said. "There going to be any trouble with the Chinks?"

"Not if I can help it."

"Fleece thought of two more birds," Jase said. "A cormorant and a what?"

"Tern."

"Yeah, right."

"Good," Mack said. "Keep your eyes peeled for Henry. He gets into that moon-over-Monterey shit, it'll take Rose a month to get him straight."

"I think I'm going to go," Jenny told him. "I think I got to do that, Mack. It just keeps eatin' away. Papa's likely gone, but Luanne and Mama could be okay."

He put out his cigarette and watched her across the room, watched her as she sat at the kitchen table bringing long wings of hair atop her head, going about this simple task with a quick unconscious grace. The mirror stood against a white piece of driftwood she'd collected. She collected everything. Sand dollars and angel wings, twisted tritons and bright coquinas that faded in a day. Candle by the mirror in a sand-frosted Dr Pepper bottle, light from this touching the bony hillbilly points of her hips. When she left she would take too much of him with her, and maybe he should figure some way to tell her that.

"I might not be able to get you a pass. I don't know. They don't much like us moving around without a reason."

"Oh, Mack. People do it all the time." Peering at him now past the candle. "Hey, now, I'm going to come on back. I just got to get this done."

He thought about the trip. Saw her walking old highways in his head. Maybe sixty-five miles up to Beaumont, cutting off north before that into the Thicket. He didn't tell her everything he heard. The way people were, things that happened. He knew it wouldn't make a difference if he did.

Jenny settled in beside him. "I said I'm coming back."

"Yeah, well, you'd better."

He decided, maybe at that moment, he wouldn't let her go. He'd figure out a way to stop her. She'd leave him in a minute. Maybe come back and maybe not. He had to know she was all right, and so he'd do it. He listened to the surf. On the porch, luna moths big as English sparrows flung themselves crazily against the screen.

The noise of the chopper brought him out of bed fast, on the floor and poking into jeans before Jase and Panagopoulos made the stairs.

"It's okay," he told Jenny, "just stay inside and I'll see."

She nodded and looked scared, and he opened the screen door and went out. Dawn washed the sky the color of moss. Jase and Panagopoulos started talking both at once.

Then Mack saw the fire, the reflection past the house. "Oh, Jesus H. Christ!"

"Mack, he's got pigs," Panagopoulos said. "I seen 'em. Henry's got pigs."

"He's got what?"

"This is bad shit," Jase moaned, "this is really bad shit."

Mack was down the stairs and past the house. He could see other people. He started running, Jase and Panagopoulos at his heels. The chopper was on the ground, and then Fleece came out of the crowd across the road.

"Henry ain't hurt bad, I don't think," he told Mack.

DINER

"Henry's hurt?" Mack was unnerved. "Who hurt him, Fleece? Is someone going to tell me something soon?"

"I figure that Chen likely done a house-to-house," Fleece said, "some asshole trick like that. Come in north and worked down rousting people out for kicks. Stumbled on Henry; shit, I don't know. Just get him out of there, Mack."

Mack wanted to cry or throw up. He pushed through the crowd and saw Chen, maybe half a dozen soldiers, then Henry. Henry looked foolish, contrite, and slightly cockeyed. His hands were tied behind. Someone had hit him in the face. The rotors stirred waves of hot air. The diner went up like a box. Mack tried to look friendly. Chen lurched about yelling and waving his pistol, looking wild-eyed as a dog.

"Let's work this out," Mack said. "We ought to get this settled and go home."

Chen shook his pistol at Mack, danced this way and that in an unfamiliar step. Mack decided he was high on the situation. He'd gotten hold of this and didn't know where to take it, didn't have the sense to know how to stop.

"We can call this off and you don't have to worry about a thing," Mack said, knowing Chen didn't have the slightest notion what he was saying. "That okay with you? We just call it a night right now?"

Chen looked at him or somewhere else entirely. Mack wished he had shoes and a shirt. Dress seemed proper if you were talking to some clown with a gun. He was close enough to see the pigs. The crate was by the chopper. Two pigs, pink and fat, mottled like an old man's hand. They were squealing and going crazy with the rotors and the fire and not helping Chen's nerves or Mack's, either. Mack could just see Henry thinking this out, how he'd do it, fattening up the porkers somehow and thinking what everybody'd say when they saw it wasn't a joke, not soyburger KC steak or chicken-fried fish-liver rice and chili peppers. Not seaweed coffee or maybe grasshopper creole crunch. None of that play-food shit they all pretended was something else, not this time, *amigos*, this time honest-to-God pig. Maybe the only pigs this side of Hunan, and only Henry Ortega and Jesus knew where he found them. Mack turned to Chen and gave his best mayoral smile.

"Why don't we just forget the whole thing? Just pack up the pigs there and let Henry be. I'll talk to Major Huang. I'll square all this with the major. That'd be fine with you, now, wouldn't it?"

Chen stopped waving the gun. He looked at Mack. Mack could see wires in his eyes. Chen spoke quickly over his shoulder. Two of the troopers lifted the pigs into the chopper.

"Now, that's good," Mack said. "That's the thing you want to do."

Chen walked off past Henry, his face hot as wax from the fire, moving toward the chopper in this jerky little two-step hop, eyes darting every way at once, granting Mack a lopsided half-wit grin that missed him by a good quarter mile. Mack let out a breath. He'd catch hell from Huang, but it was over. Over and done. He turned away, saw Rose in the crowd and then Fleece. Mack waved. Someone gave a quick and sudden cheer. Chen jerked up straight, just reacting to the sound, not thinking any at all, simply bringing the pistol up like the doctor hit a nerve, the gun making hardly any noise, the whole thing over in a blink and no time to stop it or bring it back. Henry blew over like a leaf, taking his time, collapsing with no skill or imagination, nothing like Anthony Quinn would play the scene.

"Oh, shit, now don't do that." Mack said, knowing this was clearly all a mistake. "Christ, you don't want to do that!"

Someone threw a rock, maybe Jase. Troopers raised their rifles and backed off. A soldier near Chen pushed him roughly toward the chopper. Chen looked deflated. The rotors whined up and blew sand. Mack shut it out, turned it back. It was catching up faster than he liked. He wished Chen had forgotten to take the pigs. The thought seemed less than noble. He considered some gesture of defiance. Burn rice in Galveston harbor. They could all wear Washington masks. He knew what they'd do was nothing at all, and that was fine because Henry would get up in just a minute and they'd all go in the diner and have a laugh. Maybe Jase had another jar of wine. Mack was certain he could put this back together and make it right. He could do it. If he didn't turn around and look at Henry, he could do it. . . .

"A Day at the Fair"

WE WEREN'T EVEN PAST HUMMER'S HILL AND I COULD smell it already. Beanspice and weed-cake and a hundred other yum things to eat. The smells were floating up from all the little stands and cookpits and coming right out to meet us.

"I can smell it, Grandpa. I can smell the Fair!"

Grandpa just laughed. "We're getting mighty close, Toony, but I didn't figure we was *smellin'* close."

"Toony's always doing things 'fore she's supposed to," said Lizbeth Jean. I glared back at the wagon, but Lizbeth Jean just nudged up to Mother and looked the other way.

I *do* kind of catch stuff sometimes, and Lizbeth Jean knows it. Just little things, like smells, or maybe who's coming over. Not even Grandpa knows about that, and he knows near everything.

Folks never can get over me and Lizbeth Jean. If you were looking for kids that didn't have any business being sisters, you'd come straight to us. She's about the prettiest girl on Far, and I'm near the plainest. Lizbeth Jean's got skin like brand new milk, and gold-silky hair down to here. *My* hair looks like it come out of a armpit somewhere, and I'm fat as a bubble.

All you got to do is set Lizbeth Jean and Mother up side by side to see where she got her good looks — including my share.

Grandpa says Mother was more'n just pretty, before whatever it was happened to Papa and she kind of quit thinking real good. Papa's something nobody talks about much at our place.

When we came 'round Hummer's Hill, a whole flock of Snappers waddled across the road and started hissing and grinding their jaws real fierce. Grandpa whacked a couple good and they scattered off quick. Snappers can't do much more'n scare you, but they do a pretty fair job of that. So while Grandpa was shooin' them off, I dropped back to where Tyrone was pulling the wagon.

Grandpa named him Tyrone after some kind of Earthie hero—only he couldn't have been one of your real big heroes if he was anything like Tyrone. According to Grandpa, he looks a lot like a big skinny anteater with the mange. Grandpa's always saying things look like something I haven't ever seen before.

"Tyrone," I said, "you goin' to have fun at the Fair?"

"Guess so," said Tyrone.

"You got some coppers, don't you?" I knew he did, 'cause Grandpa gave him some.

"Don't know," said Tyrone.

"Sure you do." I patted the little pouch around his neck. "Right in there, Tyrone. Five big shiny new coppers. Just like last year."

"Last year?" Tyrone blinked and looked dumber than ever. That's the trouble with Noords. They work real good and do what you tell 'em, but forget what it was in about a minute.

I could *really* smell the Fair, now. Not just the other way. There was bushdog cracklin' over a fire and Ting-root pie and dusty sweet-cakes yellow as the sky. "Do you smell it, Grandpa? Do you smell it *now*?"

"Toony, I sure do," said Grandpa. He closed his eyes and sniffed real good.

"What do you smell, Grandpa? Tell me!"

"I smell mustard and cotton candy, Toony. And popcorn and cinnamon apples and lemonade so cold it makes your head hurt."

"Oh, Grandpa, you don't, either," I scolded. "You're just makin' things up again."

"Guess maybe I am," said Grandpa.

Like always, I acted like a kid, trying to see sixteen things at once. As if they'd maybe close the whole Fair down if fat Toony didn't see it *right then*. There were flags and ribbons and bright strips of cloth everywhere you looked. There were reds and blues and greens and yellows and colors I hadn't even seen before. There were stands selling all kinds of pretties. And games where you knocked over pots, or caught a tin fish on a hook. And there were cookpits full of more sizzlin' bushdog than you could eat in a year, and toadberry tarts and stripe candy and hot fly-bread right out of the oven.

"Better watch out," said Lizbeth Jean real sweetlike. "You'll get fat, Toony."

"You can't *git* fat if you're fat already," I told her.

"*You* can," giggled Lizbeth Jean, and Grandpa said, "Now, now, we come to the Fair to have fun, girls." He stuck me on one side and Lizbeth Jean on the other, and left Tyrone to look after Mother. Which was a good idea, 'cause I've been known to bust Lizbeth Jean just for the fun of it.

There were people from all over, 'cause nobody misses the Fair. There were trappers from far as Southtown, and farmers like us from High, and even folks from the Crystal Hills. *They* don't hardly talk to each other, but they all came to the Fair.

I like just 'bout everything there is to see, but I guess I like the Patchmen best of all. That's because they got something new every year, and not the same old thing. And you never know what it's going to be, 'cause like Grandpa says, the Patchmen don't either. It's kinda whatever they happen on to, and fix up good. If there's a bunch of wars going on somewhere, the fleet dumps lots of old ships and stuff on Far. If there isn't much fighting, why, you don't get a lot of new things to see that year. So anyway, it's a good way to tell how the war's going.

"Grandpa, can we? Can we *please?*"

The sign was painted in big orange letters and said:

TALK TO YUR DEAR
DEPARTED LUVED ONES
2 COPPERS

On the wagon was a rusty old box colored speckledy gray. There wasn't anything on it but a worn-out knob and a little glass window.

"I don't know," said Grandpa, scowling real hard at the sign. "It's *two* coppers, Toony."

"Please," I begged, hanging on his hand, "do it, Grandpa!"

"Does the danged thing work?" Grandpa asked the Patchman. "Reckon it does, if you're chargin' two coppers for it."

"Sure does," said the Patchman. "Come right off a Bugship, out past Dingo." He grinned real sly at Grandpa. "Hear they give them hardbacks a whole bunch of new ancestors. Took out near a sector."

"Can't hardly burn too many," said Grandpa.

"Amen to that," said the Patchman, and looked right straight at me. I guess I was kind of staring, 'cause he was real interesting to look at. He had one good arm, and one bright silver, and a shiny glass head with bright ruby eyes. Course everyone knows the Patchmen were real Spacers 'fore they got banged up bad, which is how they get first pick of all the junk comes down. Grandpa says they don't much care 'bout going back home anymore, so they just hang around Far, or someplace else.

"Isn't nothing to it," the Patchman told Grandpa, "just hold that knob real tight and talk to anyone you want."

"Anyone?" asked Grandpa.

"Well, anyone that ain't still *breathin'* real good," winked the Patchman.

You could tell what Grandpa was thinking. He was thinking awful hard about Grandma, and whether he sure enough wanted to do this. I wasn't real surprised when the little round window blinked and went bright, and there was a man grinning out 'stead of Grandma. He was young, with old-timey hair and funny-looking clothes.

"Well, I'll be damned," said Grandpa. "Jess — is that really you?"

"It's me all right," said the man. "You're looking right good, Doc."

"And you're looking a sight better'n *last* time I seen you, that's for sure."

The man laughed. "Not much sense staying eighty-nine. Not if you don't have to."

"No, guess not." Grandpa frowned at the little window and scratched his beard. "What's it like up there, Jess? I mean, they keep you busy and all?"

"Busy enough," said Jess. "There's lots to do, same as anywhere."

"I know damn well you aren't playing no *harp*."

"Never was much good at playin' things. Except maybe a little poker."

Grandpa made a face. "You wasn't *real* good at that, either. You know, I've thought about it some, being up there with all that time on your hands and not having something to do. It never did seem right to me, just switching from doin' to not d—"

Grandpa's face went white as flour. The man just kind of flicked out of sight, and there was this real pretty girl where he'd been.

"Hello, Doc. It's been a long time . . ."

Grandpa swallowed hard. "Mary, I—didn't want to do this."

"I know you didn't, Doc. And I know how hard it's got to be. I just had to see you, though."

"Well, I'm glad now you did. Real glad."

"You're looking fine, Doc."

"Oh, sure I am."

"No, really. Just as handsome as ever."

"I'm looking *old* is what I'm doing." He stopped a minute, and studied Grandma real hard. "I guess there's a lot of the old crowd up there," he said finally. "Folks we used to know and all."

"Sure is," said Grandma, "lots of 'em, Doc. Ellie's here, and Cora—you remember Cora?"

"Wasn't thinking 'bout them, Mary. Guess Will's there, and J.R., and course *Jess* is probably always hangin' around. I mean—"

"I *know* what you mean," smiled Grandma. "That isn't the way it is up here, Doc. It's not the same."

"Don't care where it is!" snapped Grandpa.

"Doc, don't do this, please."

"Well, damn it all anyway. I just—"

"Doc . . ."

"I can't change, Mary, just 'cause you're there and I'm here. I—Mary? *Mary!*"

You could see Grandma saying something, but you couldn't tell what it was, and in a minute the little window went all dark again.

"Goddamn it," roared Grandpa. "It ain't right—carryin' on like that up *there!*"

"Guess they can do 'bout whatever they want," said the Patchman.

"Well, it ain't right, I'll tell you that right now. I—hellfire, what do *you* want, Tyrone?"

Tyrone was standing right behind him, his big sad eyes staring at the little round window.

"I don't think that's too good a idea," said the Patchman, trading a look with Grandpa.

"I have two coppers," said Tyrone.

"Fine," said Grandpa, "let's you and me and Toony see if we can find some stick candy somewhere, Tyrone."

"Have two coppers," said Tyrone.

"I know you do, Tyrone."

"I have—"

"Well, just spend 'em, then," said Grandpa. "Damned if you ain't stubborn. Even for a Noord!"

Tyrone carefully laid the worn and shiny coins in the Patchman's hand and wrapped his three stubby fingers around the knob. He stood real still and looked hard as he could into the window. In a minute, it got kind of dim and gray and cold looking, like the saddest winter day there ever was. Tyrone kept on trying, but there was nothing there to see but curly-gray fog, fading way way off into nowhere.

The Patchman looked at Grandpa, and Grandpa just shrugged and sort of turned Tyrone around real easy. "Guess it ain't working right, Tyrone. Come on, let's go get that candy."

"That's it for sure," said the Patchman. "Been having a lot of trouble with it lately. And I ain't going to keep your coppers, either. No, sir, you didn't get a fair look, you don't have to pay."

"See there," said Grandpa, "you got both your coppers back. How 'bout that now?"

"I guess," said Tyrone. He let me and Grandpa lead him away, but he kept looking back at the little round window just as long as he could.

Mother and Lizbeth Jean like to stand around and watch Trading, but it seems kind of dumb to me. Everybody's got 'bout the same as everybody else, but that doesn't seem to bother folks. They'll squat on the ground all day and swap blankets, pots, candles, ropes, dull knives, and sourweed soup—the same stuff they make back home themselves. And if you squat around long enough, you can even get the same blanket back you made yourself last winter. It don't make a lot of sense, but what do I know?

The only real Trading goes on with the Patchmen, and they sure aren't interested in blankets and soup. What they want is girls and *Saba*-wings. That's about the only things worth lifting off Far. Too many girls get born here anyway, and *Saba*-moths go through wheat faster'n rain. Lizbeth Jean's thirteen and just right for selling, but Grandpa isn't ever going to do that. No matter how poor we get. And of course I don't have anything to worry 'bout. Patchmen aren't just real excited 'bout fat girls with hair like a armpit.

At noon, the sun got real hot and the sky turned close to silver. Like always, Grandpa made us go rest under the wagon till it got cooler, and, like always, me and Lizbeth Jean just whispered and giggled and punched each other the whole time. Mother kind of dozed, her face all slack and empty-looking. Grandpa curled up and started snoring, and Tyrone sat out in the sun boiling himself. Noords won't come into the shade for anything. Grandpa says it scares 'em to see the light go away. *I* think they're just too dumb to know better.

When we finally got up, and everybody was ready to go again, Grandpa said since it'd been a fairly good year and the *Saba*-moths hadn't eaten more than half the crop, maybe we could all get some real Fair-bought food for supper, 'stead of the flatcakes we'd packed in the wagon. Lizbeth Jean and me did a lot of squealing and dancing around till Grandpa said maybe we wouldn't eat *any*thing if everybody didn't shut up and behave.

Now, if anybody likes to eat, it's me, old bubble-gut Toony. Grandpa says I can eat anything that don't eat me, and then go hunting for more. This time, though, there was more food to be had than even I could handle. After 'bout a half hour of stuffing, I didn't even want to *smell* bushdog cooking. Not ever.

"You're going to bust someday," said Lizbeth Jean. "Gonna just swell up and go *bang!* Toony."

"An' you're goin' to get a big fat lip, Lizbeth Jean."

"Grandpa!" shrieked Lizbeth Jean, "she's gonna hit me!"

"Now, now, girls," said Grandpa, "this is Fair day. You know your mother don't like to see fighting."

Course Mother wasn't even paying any attention to all this. She was just staring out at nothing, like always.

Tyrone bought a knife that'd break in about a minute, and Lizbeth Jean bought a shell comb and a ring, like she does every year. I got hungry again — like *I* do every year — and bought a Ting-root pie with gooey stuff on top. Then I went back out to where the Patchmen were. There was one old beat-up machine off a Spidership, and I got what I wanted from that and had the man wrap it up real nice in a little colored cloth.

Right about then, we had some excitement. The air got hot and still, and the sun turned the sky all rusty-green. All of a sudden, every Noord at the Fair stopped dead in their tracks, big feet flat against the ground, long noses tremblin' in the air. You don't have to be on Far very long to know what *that* means. I hit it out quick and found Grandpa and Mother and Lizbeth Jean, and we all sat real quiet on the ground, not thinking 'bout anything, like everybody else. All you could see was folks sitting, and waiting, and not looking anywhere close to the sky. What you're supposed to do is think about not even *bein'* there—kind of a little old piece of nothing. Noords do it real good, of course, seein' they been at it 'bout a million years. It comes kinda natural if you don't do a whole lot of thinking anyway.

After a while, the Noords got all unspooked, and everyone got up and stretched and started thinking again. Off to the south you could see 'em— two big Portugees floatin' high and slow, flat-looking bodies all pearly blue in the sun. They weren't real hungry, or looking for anything special, they were just drifting along, trailing their stingers like long rags of rain 'gainst the ground.

"They're kinda early," said a man next to Grandpa. "Means we didn't get much rain up north this year."

"Which means there'll be a sight more here than we need," said Grandpa. "Always something, ain't it?"

"One thing or another," said the man.

Mother couldn't take a lot of sun, and squattin' down waiting for the Portugees near did her in. So Tyrone took her and Lizbeth Jean back to the wagon, and me and Grandpa walked out past the cookpits again where the Patchmen stayed. He didn't say what we was going for, but I had a real good idea. Grandpa's got a spot near home where you can find good greenstones if you know how to look. He keeps what he finds all year in a little leather sack, then brings them to the Fair. It isn't something you're *supposed* to do, but Grandpa knows a Patchman who knows a Spacer who can get things off of Far.

So I stayed outside the tent while Grandpa did his business, and pretended I was too little to know nothing, which is what grown-ups like. When he was through, we walked on back out the Patchmen's camp, and right there was when the thing in the cage started yelling at us. It shook its bars and made such a awful noise, me and Grandpa stopped to take a look.

"Pleez," it said, "you come heeer. Lizzen to me!" The thing sounded all the world like a sack full of gravel, and Grandpa told me not to get up close. I wasn't about to, 'cause it stuck a warty old hand out the bars right at me.

"Iz big miztake," it kept croakin', "Pleez, you help me!"

"Lordee," I said, "what in the world is it, Grandpa?"

Grandpa didn't answer. He just scratched his chin and

A DAY AT THE FAIR

grinned, like something real amusing come to mind. It *was* a funny-looking sight. Sort of like a fat old frog with foldy skin and pale yellow eyes. It wasn't wearing nothing but rags, and not much of that.

"Talks a blue streak, don't he?"

Grandpa and I both turned around, and there was a Patchman standing just behind us. Or rolling, really, 'cause he wasn't much more'n a head and shoulders set right on top of a big black box.

"Does, at that," said Grandpa. "Where'd you come by this little fellar?"

The Patchman made a face. "Got took is what I did. Traded him from a Spacer for a bottle of good whiskey. Back down at Rise-up. Figured folks'd pay a copper to see a Bug in a cage." He shook his head and spit on the ground. "That was damn good whiskey, too."

"I—am—not—BUG!" screamed the creature in the cage. He shook his bars so hard I hid behind Grandpa. "I am Vize Adm'ral Ch'rr of Procor Fleet! You lizzen to me—you help!"

The Patchman grinned and winked at Grandpa. "Never seen one yet wasn't Grand High Muckety-muck of somethin.'"

"Reckon so," said Grandpa.

The Patchman's box whirred inside, and he rolled up close till he was looking Grandpa right in the eye. "Listen, friend, you want to buy him, I'll make you a good price."

"What for?" said Grandpa. "What in hell'd *I* do with him?"

"You're a farmer, aren't you?"

"So?"

"Do a good day's work for you."

Grandpa looked at the creature and laughed out loud. "Son, if that there's a field hand, I'm Queen of the May."

"He's a real smart fella," the Patchman insisted, "when he ain't raving on like that. He can count, and read and write good."

"Don't take a lot of smart to run a hoe," said Grandpa.

"He plays chess, too."

Grandpa's brows shot up like a bushdog's tail. "He does what now?"

"Meanest endgame you ever saw," said the Patchman, trying hard not to look too pleased with himself.

Grandpa peered in at the creature. "That right? You any good?"

"Pleez—" The thing looked up real miserable at Grandpa. "I am not Bug. I am friend. I am Vize Adm'ral Ch'rr of—"

"I didn't ask for your goddamn war record. Do you play or don't you?"

The creature didn't say anything. It just kinda sank to the bottom of its cage and started making little whiny sounds. Grandpa looked disgusted.

"He'll come around," said the Patchman, "you get him home and settled in. He isn't much used to company."

Grandpa looked at the man real hard. "I don't think this fellar knows a endgame from a pussycat. 'Sides, he's got warts."

"I'll take just what I paid for him," said the Patchman. "A good bottle of whiskey. Throw in the cage for nothing. Isn't anything fairer than that."

"Reckon not. If you need somethin' powerful ugly that don't smell good."

"It doesn't have to be *real* good whiskey."

"Right nice of you. Seeing as how there isn't no such thing this side of—*Great God and hairy little pigs!*"

Grandpa stared right over my head and his jaw dropped about a foot. Before I could blink, he was out of there, hobbling past the wagon, shoutin' and waving his stick. Then *I* saw what it was and my heart went right down in my stomach. A Patchman was leading a string of girls into camp on a long piece of rope. There wasn't any of them over twelve or fourteen, and the very last one was Lizbeth Jean.

Grandpa didn't even look at her. He marched right up to the Patchman and poked his stick in the man's chest. "Boy, you got something there don't belong to you."

The Patchman stopped and looked real hard at Grandpa. Then he just swept the stick aside like nothing was there and walked on by. Grandpa let him go. When the end of the line came by, he whipped out his little pocket knife and cut Lizbeth Jean off the string. Lizbeth Jean started bawling and hung on his leg like a leech.

The Patchman jerked 'round and stared, like he could hardly believe what he was seeing. He studied Grandpa up and down, then shook his head and grinned. "Old man, you're startin' to bother me some."

"Figure to," said Grandpa.

"Just put that pretty back where you got her, and get on your way."

"She ain't for sale," said Grandpa.

The Patchman laughed. "The *sellin'* part's over and done." He patted his pocket twice. "Got the paper right here, all signed and proper."

Grandpa's face got terrible dark. "You got nothin' at all," he said softly, " 'cept a poor woman's mark don't have any idea what she's about."

The Patchman brought himself up real straight. He was a mean, stringy-lookin' man, split right down the middle—flesh and bone on one side, silver on the other. You could tell by his eyes he wasn't about to give up Lizbeth Jean. 'Specially now, since three or four other Patchmen had drifted up to watch.

"Be best if you just get on your way," he told Grandpa. "I'm sure takin' that pretty."

"You're sure welcome to try," said Grandpa.

The Patchman grinned. His hand kind of blurred 'round his belt and came up with a short little blade. He flipped it over twice, letting its bright catch the sun.

"Mink, just hold on there a minute," said one of the Patchmen.

"Just mind your business," said Mink, not moving his eyes off Grandpa. The first Patchman said something to the man beside him, and the man looked at Grandpa, then at Mink.

"Pardo's right," said the man. "Just let it go, Mink. Leave him be."

Mink gave him a black look, spit on the ground, and started for Grandpa. Grandpa didn't move. He pushed Lizbeth Jean away and just stood where he was. Mink walked right up to him and drove his blade hard at Grandpa's belly.

Only he didn't. Or I *guess* he didn't. Right there's where it starts gettin' real hard to explain. All I know is Mink got sort of blurry a second and then he was just looking down at his knife, and laughing, and not even thinking about Grandpa. He laughed so hard the tears came to his eyes, and then he started slashin' and cuttin' as hard as he could at his own belly, ripping and tearing away hard, and watching himself come apart. Everything inside came rolling out wet and shiny and spilling to the ground, and Mink kept laughing and slicing away like he hadn't ever seen anything funny as that.

Then, all of a sudden it wasn't even happenin' at all, and Mink was just standing there looking at his belly and screaming. There wasn't a scratch on him, but Mink wouldn't stop. A couple of men took him up and carried him off to the tents somewhere, but he was still going strong. Like maybe now he'd got started he didn't know how to stop anymore.

Nobody said anything for a long time. Then one of the Patchmen walked over to Grandpa real slow. "I'm sorry about that," he said, "just real sorry."

"It's over," said Grandpa.

"Pardo said it was you, said he recognized you right off. An' I said hell, Pardo, you know it ain't *him*, what'd *he* be doing way out here on Far?"

"Guess you still ain't sure, are you?" said Grandpa.

The Patchman looked at Grandpa, then got kind of white and funny lookin' around the mouth. "No, sir," he said, "I'm — surely not."

"Fine," said Grandpa, "that's just fine. Come on Toony, Lizbeth Jean. We best be getting on back now. . . ."

By the time we got moving, there was a light breeze from the west and the moons were full up in the sky. The razortrees sparkled and made tinkly sounds in the wind, and I could hear a bunch of Whoopers start yappin' away. Tyrone hauled the wagon up ahead, with Mother and Lizbeth Jean already asleep inside. Me and Grandpa came up behind, where old Wart was pulling his cage and talkin' to himself. Grandpa said he was keepin' a good eye on him for a while till he stopped wanting to be an admiral and settled down to some decent chess playing. I didn't figure he'd ever do much of anything, but what does a fat little kid know?

"I got you a present," I said after a while. "You want to open it now or wait'll you get home?"

"Why, right now," said Grandpa. "Once you know 'bout a present, you almost have to open it." He took the little package and unwrapped it and held up what was inside.

"You gotta open the cap and smell," I told him. "You tell this machine what kind of smell you want and it makes it right off. The Patchman said it come from a Spidership."

Grandpa took off the cap and smelled.

"It's *supposed* to be popcorn, like you're always talkin' about. Only I said throw in a little lemonade and cotton candy, too. Is it all right?"

Grandpa gave me a big grin. "Just as right as it can be, Toony. That's a real good present."

"I got Mother one, too. It's some kinda flower you can't get on Far. Maybe it'll help her remember stuff. You know, like you do."

"Maybe it will," said Grandpa. "You just never can tell."

* * *

The Snappers started grinding and hissing out in the bush again, and me and Grandpa walked along and listened. I got to thinking, and wondering about things, which I do sometimes. Like what happened to Papa, and why Grandpa had to play like bein' a farmer when he wasn't. All that stuff I'm not supposed to ask about. There isn't any end to that kind of thinking. So I started thinking 'bout bushdog sizzling and sweet-cakes and Ting-root pie and how the Fair would be next year. I figured I was growing up some, 'cause I decided right then and there it didn't do much good worrying about being fat and havin' hair like a armpit. When it comes down to it, you're either a Toony or a Lizbeth Jean, and isn't anything you do going to change it. . . .

Sallie C.

WILL WOKE EVERY MORNING COVERED WITH DUST. The unfinished chair, the dresser with peeling paint, were white with powdery alkali. His quarters seemed the small back room of some museum, Will and the dresser and the chair, an exhibit not ready for public view. Indian John had built the room, nailing it to the hotel wall with the style and grace of a man who'd never built a thing in all his life and never intended to do it again. When he was finished, he tossed the wood he hadn't used inside and nailed the room firmly shut and threw his hammer into the desert. The room stayed empty except for spiders until Will and his brother moved in.

In August, a man had ridden in from Portales heading vaguely for Santa Fe and having little notion where he was. His wife lay in the flat bed of their wagon, fever-eyed and brittle as desert wood, one leg swollen and stinking with infection. They had camped somewhere, and a centipede nine and three-quarter inches long had found its way beneath her blanket. The leg was rotting and would kill her. The woman was too sick to know it. The man said his wife would be all right. They planned to open a chocolate works in Santa Fe and possibly deal in iced confections on the side. The railroad was freighting in their goods from

St. Louis; everything would be waiting when they arrived. The man kept the centipede in a jar. His wife lay in the bed across the room. He kept the jar in the window against the light and watched the centipede curl around the inner walls of glass. Its legs moved like a hundred new fishhooks varnished black.

The man had a problem with connections. He couldn't see the link between the woman on the bed and the thing that rattled amber-colored armor in the jar. His wife and the centipede were two separate events.

The woman grew worse, her body so frail that it scarcely raised the sheets. When she died, Indian John took the centipede out and killed it. What he did, really, and Will saw him do it, was stake the thing down with a stick, Apache-style. Pat Garrett told the man to get his sorry ass out of the Sallie C. that afternoon and no later. The man couldn't see why Garrett was mad. He wanted to know what the Indian had done with his jar. He said his wife would be fine after a while. He had a problem with connections. He couldn't see the link between burial and death. Indian John stood in the heat and watched ants take the centipede apart. They sawed it up neatly and carried it off like African bearers.

Will thought about this and carefully shook his trousers and his shoes. He splashed his face with water and found his shirt and walked out into the morning. He liked the moment suspended, purple-gray and still between the night and the start of day. There was a freshness in the air, a time before the earth changed hands and the sun began to beat the desert flat.

Behind the hotel was a small corral, the pen attached to the weathered wooden structure that served as workshed, stable, and barn. The ghost shapes of horses stirred about. The morning was thick and blue, hanging heavy in the air. Saltbush grew around the corral, and leathery beavertail cactus. Will remembered he was supposed to chop the cactus out and burn it.

Indian John walked out on the back steps and tossed dishwater and peelings into the yard. He took no notice of Will. The chickens darted about, bobbing like prehistoric lizards. Will opened the screen and went in. The hotel was built of wood but the kitchen was adobe, the rough walls black with smoke and grease. The room was hot and smelled of bacon and strong coffee. Will poured himself a cup and put bread on the stove to make toast.

"John, you seen my brother this morning?" Will asked. He didn't look up from his plate. "He get anything to eat?"

"Mr. Pat say your brother make a racket before noon he goin' to kill him straight out. Like that." John drew a finger across his throat to show Will how.

"He hasn't been doing that, John."

"Good. He gah'dam better not."

"If he *isn't,* John, then why talk about it?"

"Gah'dam racket better stop," John said, the menace clear in his voice. "Better stop or you brother he in helluva big trouble."

Will kept his fury to himself. There was no use arguing with John, and a certain amount of risk. He stood and took his coffee and his toast out of the kitchen to the large open room next door. He imagined John's eyes at his back. Setting his breakfast on the bar, he drew the shades and found his broom. There were four poker tables and a bar. The bar was a massive structure carved with leaves and tangled vines and clusters of grapes, a good-sized vineyard intact in the dark mahogany wood. Garrett had bought the bar up in Denver and had it hauled by rail as far as he could. Ox teams brought it the rest of the way across the desert, where Garrett removed the front of the hotel to get it in.

There was a mirror behind the bar, bottles and glasses that Will dusted daily. Above the bottles there was a picture of a woman. The heavy gilt frame was too large for the picture. The woman had delicate features, deep-set eyes, and a strong willful mouth. Will imagined she had a clear and pleasant voice.

By the time he finished sweeping, there were pale fingers of light across the floor. Will heard steps on the back stairs and then the boy's voice talking to John, and then John speaking himself. John didn't sound like John when he spoke to the boy.

Will looked at the windows and saw they needed washing. It was a next-to-useless job. The sand ate the glass and there was no way to make them look right. The sight suddenly plunged him into despair. A man thirty-six with good schooling. A man who sweeps out and cleans windows. He wondered where he'd let his life go. He had scarcely even noticed. It had simply unraveled, coming apart faster than he could fix it.

The boy ran down the steps into the yard. He walked as if he owned the world and knew it. Will couldn't remember if he'd felt like that himself.

The front stairs creaked, and Will saw Garrett coming down. This morning he wore an English worsted suit and checkered vest. Boots shined and a fresh linen collar, cheeks shaved pink as baby skin. The full head of thick white hair was slicked back, and his mustache was waxed in jaunty curls. Will looked away, certain

Garrett could read his every thought. It made him furious, seeing this ridiculous old fart spruced up like an Eastern dandy. Before the woman arrived, he had staggered around in moth-eaten dirty longhandles, seldom bothering to close the flap. At night he rode horses blind drunk. Everyone but John stayed out of his way. Now Will was supposed to think he had two or three railroads and a bank.

Garrett walked behind the bar and poured a healthy morning drink. "Looks real nice," he told Will. "I do like to see the place shine."

Will had rearranged the dust and nothing more. "That Indian's threatening my brother," he announced. "Said he'd cut his throat sure."

"I strongly doubt he'll do it. If he does, he won't tell you in advance."

"What he said was it was you. I assure you I didn't believe him for a minute. I am not taken in by savage cunning."

"That's good to know."

"Mr. Garrett, my brother isn't making any noise. Not till after dinner like you said."

"I know he's not, Will."

"So you'll say something to John and make him stop?"

"If you've a mind to weary me, friend, you've got a start. Now how's that wagon coming along?"

"Got to have a whole new axle like I said. But I can get it done pretty fast."

Garrett looked alarmed. "What you do is take your time and do it *right*. Fast is the mark of the careless worker, as I see it. A shoddy job is no job at all. Now run out and see that boy's not near the horses. I doubt he's ever seen a creature bigger than a fair-sized dog."

Garrett watched him go. The man was a puzzle, and he had no use for puzzles of any kind. Puzzles always had a piece missing, and with Will, Garrett figured the piece was spirit. Someone had reached in and yanked it right out of Will's head and left him hollow. No wonder the damn Injun gave him fits. A redskin was two-thirds cat and he'd worry a cripple to death.

Garrett considered another drink. Will had diminished the soothing effects of the first, leaving him one behind instead of even. He thought about the woman upstairs. In his mind she wore unlikely garments from Paris, France. John began to sing out in the kitchen. *Hiyas* and such strung together in a flat and tuneless fashion. Like drunken bees in a tree. Indian songs began in the middle and worked out. There was no true beginning and no end. One good solution was the 10-gauge Parker he kept under the bar. Every morning Garrett promised himself he'd do it. Walk in and expand Apache culture several yards.

"I'll drink to that," he said, and he did.

The boy was perched atop the corral swinging his legs. John had given him sugar for the horses.

"Mr. Garrett says you take a care," Will told him. "Don't get in there with them now."

"I will be most careful," the boy said.

He had good manners and looked right at you when he talked. Will decided this was a mark of foreign schooling. He walked past the horses to the barn. The morning heat was cooking a heady mix, a thick fermented soup of hay and manure, these odors mingled with the sharp scent of cleanly sanded wood, fuel oil, and waxy glue.

Will stopped a few feet from the open door. The thing seemed bigger than he remembered. He felt ill at ease in its presence. He liked things with front and back ends and solid sides to hold them together. Here there was a disturbing expanse of middle.

"Listen, you coming out of there soon?" Will said, making no effort to hide his irritation. "I'm darn sure not coming in."

"Don't. Stay right there." His brother was lost in geometric confusion.

"Orville, I don't like talking to someone I can't even see."

"Then don't."

"You sleep out here or what? I didn't hear you come to bed."

"Didn't. Had things to do."

"Don't guess you *ate* anything, either."

"I eat when I've a mind to, Will, all right?"

"You say it, you don't do it."

"One of those chickens'll wander in I'll eat that. Grab me a wing and a couple of legs."

Will saw no reason for whimsy. It didn't seem the time. "It isn't even eight yet, case you didn't notice," he said shortly. "I promised Mr. Garrett you wouldn't mess with that thing till noon. John raised Ned with me at breakfast. Me now, Orville, not you."

Orville emerged smiling from a torturous maze of muslin stretched tightly over spars of spruce and ash, from wires that played banjo as he passed, suddenly appearing as if this were a fine trick he'd just perfected.

"I am not to make noise before noon," he told Will. "Nobody said I couldn't work. Noise is forbidden, but toil is not."

"You're splitting hairs and you know it."

Orville brushed himself off and looked at his brother. "Listen a minute, Will, and don't have a stroke or anything, all right? I'm going to try her out tomorrow."

"Oh, my Lord!" Will looked thunderstruck.

"I'd like for you to watch."

"Me? What for?"

"I'd like you to be there, Will. Do I have to have a reason?" Orville had never asked him a question he could answer. Will supposed there were thousands, maybe millions of perplexities between them, a phantom cloud that followed them about.

"I don't know," he said, and began to rub his hands and bob about. "I can't say, maybe I will, I'll have to see." He turned, suddenly confused about direction, and began to run in an awkward kind of lope away from the barn.

Helene kept to herself. Except for her usual walk after supper, she had not emerged from the room since her arrival. Herr Garrett sent meals. The savage left them in the hall and pounded loudly at her door. Helene held her breath until he was gone. If he caught her, he would defile her in some way she couldn't imagine. She ate very little and inspected each bite for foreign objects, traces of numbing drugs.

Garrett also sent the Indian up with presents. Fruits and wines. Nosegays of wilted desert flowers. She found these offerings presumptuous. The fruit was tempting; she didn't dare. What rude implication might he draw from a missing apple, a slice of melon accepted?

"God in Heaven, help me!" she cried aloud, lifting her head to speed this plea in the right direction. What madness had possessed her, brought her to this harsh and terrible land? The trip had been a nightmare from the start. A long ocean voyage and then a train full of ruffians and louts. In a place called Amarillo they said the tracks were out ahead. Three days' delay and maybe more. Madame was headed for Albuquerque? What luck, the stranger told her. Being of the European persuasion, she might not be aware that Amarillo and Albuquerque were widely known as the twin cities of the West. He would sell her a wagon cheap, and she would reach her destination before dark. Albuquerque was merely twenty-one miles down the road. Go out of town and turn left.

Her skin was flushed, ready to ignite. Every breath was an effort. Her cousin would think she was dead, that something dreadful had happened. She applied wet cloths. Wore only a thin chemise. The garment seemed shamefully immodest and brought her little relief. Sometimes she drifted off to sleep. Only to wake from tiresome dreams. Late in the day she heard a rude and startling sound. Mechanical things disturbed her. It clattered, stuttered and died and started again.

Before the sun was fully set, she was dressed and prepared for her walk. Hair pale as cream was pinned securely under a broad-brimmed hat. The parasol matched her dress. In the hall she had a fright. The savage came up the stairs with covered trays. Helene stood her ground. Fear could prove fatal in such encounters; weakness only heightened a man's lust.

The savage seemed puzzled to see her. His eyes were black as stones. "This your supper," he said.

"No, no, danken Sie" she said hurriedly, "I do not want it."

"You don't eat, you get sick."

Was this some kind of threat? If he attacked, the point of the parasol might serve her as a weapon.

"I am going to descend those stairs," she announced. "Do you understand me? I am *going* down those stairs!"

The Indian didn't move. Helene rushed quickly past him and fled. Outside she felt relatively secure. Still, her heart continued to pound. The sky was tattered cloth, a garish orange garment sweeping over the edge of the earth. Color seemed suspended in the air. Her skin, the clapboard wall behind her, were painted in clownish tones. Even as she watched, the color changed. Indigo touched the faint shadow of distant mountains.

So much space and nothing in it! Her cousin's letter had spoken of vistas. This was the word Ilse used. Broad, sweeping vistas, a country of raw and unfinished beauty. Helene failed to see it. At home, everything was comfortably close. The vistas were nicely confined.

"Well now, good evening, Miz Rommel," Garrett said cheerfully, coming up beside her to match her pace, "taking a little stroll, are you?"

Helene didn't stop. "It appears that is exactly what I am doing, Herr Garrett." The man's feigned surprise seemed foolish. After four days of popping up precisely on the hour, Helene was scarcely amazed to see him again.

"It's truly a sight to see," said Garrett, peering into the west. "Do you get sunsets like this back home? I'll warrant you do not."

"To the best of my knowledge, the sun sets every night. I have never failed to see this happen."

"Well, I guess that's true."

"I am certain that it is."

"I have never been to Germany. Or France or England, either. The Rhine, now that's a German river."

"Yes."

"I suppose you find my knowledge of foreign lands greatly lacking."

"I have given it little thought."

"I meant to travel widely. Somehow life interceded."

"I'm sure it did."

"Life and circumstance. *Herr*, now that means mister."

"Yes, it does."

"And mrs., what's that?"

"*Frau*."

"Frau Rommel. In Mexican that would be *Señora*. *Señor* and *Señora*. I can say without modesty I am not unacquainted with the Spanish tongue."

"How interesting, I'm sure."

"Now if you were unmarried, you'd be a *señorita*."

"Which I am not," Helene said, with a fervor Garrett could scarcely overlook.

"Well, no offense of course," said Garrett, backtracking as quickly as he could. "I mean, if you were, that's how you'd say it. You see, they put that *ita* on the end of lots of things. *Señorita*'s sort of 'little lady.' Now a little dog or little — Miz Rommel, you suppose you could see your way clear to have supper with me this evening, maybe nine o'clock? I would be greatly honored if you would."

Helene stopped abruptly. She could scarcely believe what she'd heard. "I am a married woman, Herr Garrett. I thought we had established this through various forms of address."

"Well now, we did but —"

"Then you can see I must decline."

"Not greatly I don't, no."

"Surely you do."

"To be honest I do not."

"Ah, well! All the more reason for me to refuse your invitation! To be quite honest, Herr Garrett, I am appalled at your suggestion. Yes, *appalled* is the word I must use. I am not only a married woman but a mother. I have come to this wretched land for one reason, and that reason is my son. As even you can surely see, Erwin is a boy of most delicate and sickly nature. His physician felt a hot and arid climate would do him good. I am no longer certain this is so."

"Miz Rommel," Garrett began, "I understand exactly what you're saying. All I meant was—"

"No, I doubt that you understand at all," Helene continued, her anger unabated, "I am sure you can't imagine a mother's feelings for her son. I can tell you right now that I see my duty clearly, Herr Garrett, and it does *not* include either the time or the inclination for—for illicit suppers and the like!"

"Illicit suppers?" Garrett looked totally disconcerted. "Jesus Christ, lady . . ."

"*Language,* Herr Garrett!"

Garrett ran a hand through his hair. "If I've offended you any, I'll say I'm sorry. Far as that boy of yours is concerned, you don't mind me saying, he looks healthy enough to me. If he's sickly, he doesn't show it. John says he takes to the desert like a fox."

"I would hardly call that an endorsement," Helene said coolly.

"John knows the country, I'll hand him that."

"He frightens me a great deal."

"I don't doubt he does. That's what Indians are for."

"I'm sorry. I do not understand that statement at all."

"Ma'am, the Indian race by nature is inured to savage ways. Murder, brutalizing, and the like. When he is no longer allowed these diversions, he must express his native fury in some other fashion. Scaring whites keeps him happy. Many find it greatly satisfying. Except of course for the Sioux, who appear to hold grudges longer than most."

"Yes, I see," said Helene, who didn't at all. The day was suddenly gone; she had not been aware of this at all. The arid earth drank light instead of water. Garrett's presence made her nervous. He seemed some construction that might topple and fall apart.

She stopped and looked up and caught his eye. "My wagon. I assume you will have it ready quite soon."

The question caught Garrett off guard. This was clearly her intention.

"Why, it's coming along nicely, I would say."

"I don't think that's an answer."

"The axle, Miz Rommel. The axle is most vital. The heart, so to speak, of the conveyance."

He was fully transparent. He confirmed her deepest fears. She could see his dark designs.

"Fix it," she said, and the anger he had spawned rose up to strike him. "Fix it, Herr Garrett, or I shall take my son and *walk* to Albuquerque."

"Dear lady, please . . ."

"I will *walk*, Herr Garrett!"

She turned and left him standing, striding swiftly away. He muttered words behind her. She pretended not to hear. She knew what he would do. He would soothe his hurt with spirits, numb his foul desires. Did he think she didn't know? God preserve women! Men are great fools, and we are helpless but for the strength You give us to foil them!

There was little light in the west. The distant mountains were ragged and indistinct, a page torn hastily away. Garrett had warned her of the dangers of the desert. Rattlesnakes slithering about. He took great pleasure in such stories. She had heard the horrid tale of the centipede. From Garrett, from Will, and once again, from Erwin.

Turning back, she faced the Sallie C. again. How strange and peculiar it was. The sight never failed to disturb her. One lone structure and nothing more. A single intrusion on desolation. A hotel where none was needed, where no one ever came. Where was the woman buried, she wondered? Had anyone thought to mark the grave?

Drawing closer, she saw a light in the kitchen, saw the savage moving about. Another light in the barn, the tapping of a hammer coming from there. She recalled the clatter she'd heard that afternoon. Now what was that about? Erwin would surely know, though he had mentioned nothing at all. The boy kept so within himself. Sometimes this concerned her, even hurt her deeply. They were close, but there was a part of this child she didn't know.

Helene couldn't guess what made her suddenly look up, bring her eyes to that point on the second story. There, a darkened window, and in the window the face of a man. Her first reaction was disgust. Imagine! Garrett spying on her in the dark! Still, the face made no effort to draw away, and she knew in an instant this wasn't Garrett at all but someone else.

Helene drew in a breath, startled and suddenly afraid. She

quickly sought the safety of the porch, the protecting walls of the hotel. Who was he, then, another guest? But wouldn't she have heard if this were so?

She smelled the odors of the kitchen, heard the Indian speak, then Erwin's boyish laughter. Why, of course! She paused, her hand still on the door. The savage had carried *two* covered trays when she met him in the hall. At the time, she had been too fearful of his presence to even notice. The other tray, then, was for the man who sat in the window. He, too, preferred his meals in his room. Something else to ask her son. What an annoying child he could be! He would tell her whatever she wanted to know. But she would have to ask him first.

It was Pat Garrett's habit to play poker every evening. The game began shortly after supper and lasted until Garrett had soundly beaten his opponents, or succumbed to the effects of rye whiskey. Before the game began, Garrett furnished each chair with a stack of chips and a generous tumbler of spirits. Some players' stacks were higher than others. A player with few chips either got a streak of luck or quickly folded, leaving the game to better men. Bending to the harsh circle of light, Garrett would deal five hands on the field of green, then move about to each chair in turn, settle in and study a hand, ask for cards or stand, sip from a player's glass and move on, bet, sip, and move again. After the first bottle of rye the game got lively, the betting quite spirited, the players bold and sometimes loud in their opinions. Will, lying awake in the shed out back, and on this night, young Erwin at the bottom of the stairs, could hear such harsh remarks as "Bet or go piss, McSween," "You're plain bluffing, Bell, you never saw kings and aces in your life . . ."

More than once, Will had been tempted to sneak up and peer in a window to assure himself Garrett was alone. He thought about it but didn't. If Garrett was playing with ghosts, Will didn't want to know it.

Sometime close to three in the morning, Helene awoke with a start. There was a terrible racket below, as if someone were tossing chairs and tables across the room, which, she decided, was likely the case. Moments later, something bumped loudly against the wall outside her window. Someone muttered under his breath. Someone was trying to climb a ladder.

Helene woke Erwin, got him from his bed and brought him to her, holding the boy close and gripping her parasol like a saber.

"God save us from the defiler," she prayed aloud. "Forgive me all my sins. Erwin, if anything happens to me, you must get to cousin Ilse in Albuquerque. Can you ride a horse, do you think? Your father put you on a horse. I remember clearly he did. At Otto Kriebel's farm in Heidenheim?"

"*Nein, Mutti,*" he assured her, "it is all right, nothing is going to happen."

"Hush," she scolded, "you don't know that at all. You are only a boy. You know nothing of the world. You scarcely imagine the things that can happen."

At that moment, a most frightening shout came from just below the window. The cry receded, as if it were rapidly moving away. The ladder struck the ground, and half a second later something heavier than that. The night was silent again.

"Perhaps someone is injured," Erwin suggested.

"Go to sleep," Helene told him. "Say your prayers and don't forget to ask God to bless Papa. We are far away from home."

There was no question of sleeping. To the usual morning noise of men stomping heavily about, of chickens clucking and horses blowing air, was now added the hollow ring of timber, of hammering and wheels that needed grease. Helene dressed quickly, recalling her promise to Erwin the night before. Before she could sweep her hair atop her head he was back, eyes alight with wonder, those deep, inquisitive eyes that seemed to see much more than a boy should see.

"*Komm' schnell, Mutti!*" he urged her, scarcely giving her time to pause before the mirror. Holding tightly to her hand, he led her quickly down the stairs and out into the brightness of the morning. The Indian leaned against the wall, drinking a can of peaches from the tin, practicing looking Mescalero mean. Garrett slumped in a rocker, his leg propped testily on a stool.

Helene could not resist a greeting. "Are you hurt, Herr Garrett? I do hope you have not had an accident of some sort."

"I am in excellent health, thank you," Garrett said shortly.

"Well. I am most pleased to hear it." The man seemed to have aged during the night. His flesh was soft as dough. Helene wondered if he would rise, swell like an ungainly pastry in the heat.

"There, *Mutti,* see?" said Erwin. "Look, they are coming. It is most exciting, yes!"

"Why yes, yes, I'm sure it is, Erwin," Helene said vaguely. In truth, she had no idea what she was seeing. The strange sight appeared around the corner of the hotel. It seemed to be an agricultural device. Helene framed a question for Erwin, but he was gone. "Have a care," she called out, but knew he didn't hear.

Two men guided the wagon toward the flats. One of the two was Will. She guessed the other was his brother. Will looked stricken, a man pressed into service, who clearly hoped no one would notice he was there.

As Helene watched, the first flash of morning touched the horizon, a fiercely bright explosion that scarred the earth with light and shadow. A silver lance touched the strange device; the thing seemed imbued with sudden magic. Light pierced the flat planes of muslin and spruce, and Helene imagined transparent flesh and hollow bones. A dragonfly, a golden fish in a dream.

"Oh. Oh, *my*," she said aloud, deeply touched by the moment.

"Looks to me like a medicine show hit by a twister," said Garrett.

"I think it has a certain grace," said Helene. "The rather delicate beauty one associates with things Oriental."

"Chink laundry," Garrett countered. "Got in the way of a train."

"They say strong spirits greatly dull the imagination," Helene said coolly and took herself to the far end of the porch.

Out on the flats, Will and his brother carefully lifted the device off the wagon onto the ground. Broad wooden runners that might have come from a horse-drawn sleigh were attached to the contraption's undercarriage. Helene knew about sleighs. The runners seemed strangely out of place. Snow was clearly out of the question.

Suddenly, the engine in the device began to snarl. The latticed wooden structure, the wire and planes of fabric began to shake. In the rear, two enormous fans started churning plumes of sand into the air. Orville donned a long cotton duster and drew goggles over his eyes. He climbed aboard the device, perched on a bicycle seat, and looked carefully left and right.

"Erwin, *nein*," Helene cried out, "get back from that thing!"

Erwin, though, was too engrossed to hear. He held a rope attached to the lower muslin plane. Will held one on the other side. The engine reached a shrill and deafening pitch. Orville raised a hand. Erwin and Will released their hold.

The contraption jerked to a start, a dog released from its chain. Helene made a small sound of surprise. Somehow, the possibility of motion hadn't occurred. The device moved faster and faster. Orville leaned hard into the wind. His hands clutched mystical controls. Muslin flapped and billowed. Suddenly, with no warning at all, the thing came abruptly off the ground.

"Holy Christ Colorado," said Garrett.

Helene was thunderstruck. The device, held aloft by forces unseen and unimagined, soared for ten seconds or more then wobbled, straightened, and gently kissed the earth. The engine fluttered and stopped. Will and Erwin ran frantically over the flats, waving their arms. Orville climbed to the ground. Will and Erwin shook his hand and clapped him firmly on the back. Then all three made their way to the hotel.

Erwin was elated. He might explode from excitement any moment. Even Will seemed pleased. Orville was curiously restrained. His goggles were pushed atop his head. His eyes were ringed with dust.

"*Mutti*, it was something to see, was it not?" Erwin cried.

"It certainly was," said Helene.

"I've got to admit," said Garrett, "I never saw a man ride a wagon off the ground."

"Now I can fix that," Orville said thoughtfully. "I know exactly what happened. This was only the first trial, you understand."

Garrett seemed confused. "You planning on doing that again?"

"Why, yes sir. Yes, I am."

Garrett pulled himself erect. "Not till after noon you're not, Orville. That racket assaults the nerves. I doubt if it's good for the digestion." He turned and went inside.

"It was most entertaining," Helene said, thinking that she ought to be polite.

"The elevator needs more weight," said Orville, as if Helene would surely agree. "That should keep the front firmly down. And I shall tilt the sail planes forward. Too much vertical lift the way they are."

"Yes, of course," said Helene.

"Well, we had best get her back to the barn," Orville said. "Lots of work to do. And thank you for your help, young man."

Erwin flushed with pride. "Sir, I was honored to assist."

Will and Orville walked back into the sun.

"*Mutti*, it is a marvel, is it not?" said Erwin.

"Yes, it is," Helene agreed. "Now you stay away from that thing, do you hear? I want you to promise me that."

Erwin looked stricken. "But Herr Orville has promised that I shall have a ride!"

"And *I* promise that you shall do no such thing," Helene said firmly. "Just get that out of your head."

Erwin turned and fled, holding back the tears that burned his eyes. Helene released a sigh, wondering how she would manage to handle this. Everyone was gone. She seemed to be all alone on the porch.

The sounds of Orville's labor continued throughout the day. When Helene returned from her regular evening walk, a lantern still glowed within the barn. Orville disturbed her more than a little. The man had a fire in his eyes. Such a look in a man frightened her. Her husband's eyes were steady and reassuring. When she saw the two together, Orville and her son, a vague disquieting shadow crossed her heart. Erwin had such a light as well.

"Evening, Miz Rommel," said Garrett. The glow of his cigar came from the porch.

"I did not see you standing there," said Helene. Her tone was clearly distant.

"I suppose you're put out with me some."

"With reason, I should think."

"I guess there is."

"You only guess?"

"All right. I would say you have some cause."

"Yes, I would say that indeed."

"Look, Miz Rommel—"

"Is this an apology, then?"

"I was getting to that."

"Then I shall accept it, Herr Garrett."

Garrett shifted uncomfortably. "That wagon will be ready in the morning. Now Albuquerque's a hundred and twenty miles through real bad country in the heat. There can be no question of such a trip. On the other hand, it is only fifty miles down to Roswell and the train. I shall have Will ride along and see that you get there safely."

"I am grateful, Herr Garrett."

"You don't have to be at all."

"Perhaps you could pack a nice lunch."

"I don't see why I couldn't."

"And rig some kind of shade for the wagon."

"I could do that, yes."

"How nice. A very thoughtful gesture."

"Miz Rommel—"

"Yes, Herr Garrett?"

Garrett was on the brink of revelation. He had steeled himself for the moment. He would bare the fires of passion that burned within. She would be frightened and appalled, but she would know. He saw, then, as the words began to form, that her skin matched the pearly opalescence of the moon, that her hair was saffron-gold, spun fine as down from a baby duck. In an instant, his firm resolve was shattered. He muttered parting words and turned and fled.

A most peculiar man, thought Helene. A drunkard and a lecher without a doubt, yet God was surely within this wayward soul, as He is within us all.

She had meant to go directly to her room. Yet she found her steps taking her to the barn and knew the reason. Erwin was surely there. The matter must be settled. She loved the boy intently. Anger struggled with the pain she felt in her heart. They had never quarreled before as they had that morning. She had sternly forbidden him to have anything to do with Orville's device. Yet, he had openly disobeyed. Helene had no desire to quell his spirit. Still, she could not brook open rebellion in her child.

The moon was bright with chalky splendor. The broad backs of the horses moved like waves on a restless sea. A man came toward her through the dark. From his quick, awkward gait she knew at once that it was Will.

"Good evening," she said, "can you tell me if my son is back there, please?"

"Yes, ma'am, yes he is," said Will. "He's surely there, Miz Rommel."

Why did the man act in such a manner? He was ever bobbing about like a cork. As if there might be danger in standing still.

"He is *not* supposed to be there," Helene sighed. "I am afraid he has disobeyed."

"That wagon will be ready in the morning," said Will.

"Yes. So Herr Garrett has explained." She felt suddenly weary, eager to put this place behind her. "Do you know Erwin well? Have you talked to him at all?"

"No ma'am. Not a lot. He mostly talks to Orville."

"He feels some kinship with your brother."

"Yes, he surely does."

"He is a free spirit, your brother. I see that in him clearly."

"I guess he's that, all right."

"A man pursuing a dream?"

"He has never been different than he is. The way you see him now. When we were boys, he'd say Will, there is a thing I have to do. And I'd say what would that be, Orville, and he'd say man sails boldly before the wind across the seas. I would set him free to sail the land. And I'd say, Orville, why would you want to do that? Lord, I guess I've asked that question a million times."

"And what would Orville say?"

"Same thing every time. Why not, Will?"

"Yes. Yes, of course," Helene said softly. Oh, Erwin, have I lost you to your dreams so soon!

"Miz Rommel . . ."

"Yes, Will?"

Will bobbed about again. "Maybe I have no business speaking out. If I don't, you just tell me and I'll stop. That boy wants to ride in Orville's machine. Wants it so bad he can taste it. I hope you'll relent and let him do it. He's a boy bound and determined is what he is."

"I think I know that, Will."

"I am a man of practical bent, Miz Rommel. I will never be anything more. I used to see this as a virtue in myself. In some men maybe it is. In me it is a curse, the great failing of my life. Mr. Garrett thinks Orville is a fool. That I am a man who's lost his spirit. Perhaps he is right about us both. But he does not know the truth of the matter at all. It is not my brother's folly that brought us here but mine alone. *I* failed. *I* brought us down. We had a small shop where we repaired common household items. Coffee mills, lard presses, ice shavers, and the like. Not much, but it kept us going. I felt there was something more. I reached for a distant star and invested quite heavily in the windmill acccssory business. I think Orville sensed that I was wrong. Out of kindness, he did nothing to dissuade me. When we left Ohio, we had nothing but our wagon. A few days' food and the clothing on our backs. And Orville's wood and muslin and his motors. Our creditors demanded these as well. I have never stood up for myself. Not once in all my life. But I stook my ground on this. Your Erwin is a good boy, Miz Rommel. Let him be what he will be."

"Yes. Yes," said Helene. "I understand what you are saying. And I am grateful to you, Will."

Helene was taken aback by this long and unexpected declaration. She hadn't dreamed the man owned so many words, or that he had the passion within him to set them free. Now, as he tried to speak again, he seemed to see what he had done. He had tossed away countless nouns and verbs, spent whole phrases and contractions he couldn't retrieve. Clutching his hat, he bolted past her and disappeared. Helene listened to the horses stir about. Orville laughed and then her son. It seemed one voice instead of two. She made her way quickly to her room.

*   *   *

Erwin's mother had asked him if he knew about the man, and Erwin did. He knew John took him all his meals. He knew the man never left his room. He was much too angry at his mother to tell her that and so he lied. The lie hurt. It stuck in his throat and stayed, no matter how hard he tried to swallow. Late the night before when he came in from working in the barn, she was sitting waiting quietly in the dark. They burst into tears and cried together. Erwin told her he was sorry. She said that it was over now and done. He didn't feel like growing up and yet he did.

It took all the courage he could muster. Just to stand in front of the door and nothing more. What if John came up the stairs? He wasn't afraid of John and yet he was.

The door came open with ease. Erwin's heart beat wildly against his chest. The room was musty, heavy with unpleasant odors. Stale air and sour sweat. Food uneaten and chamber pots neglected. Mostly the smell was time. The room was layered with years. Erwin saw yesterdays stuffed in every corner.

A window centered the wall. The morning burned a harsh square of brightness, yet the light failed to penetrate the room. It was stopped, contained, it could go no further than this. The sound of Orville's machine worried the quiet, probed like a locust through the day.

"You stand there, boy, you'll turn to stone. Or is it salt, I can't recall. Salt or stone one. Get over here close so I can see."

Erwin jumped at the voice. He nearly turned and ran.

"It's salt. Salt for certain. Lot's wife. Sodom and Cincinnati. Lo the wicked shall perish and perish they do. I have seen a great many of them do it."

Erwin walked cautiously to the window. The man sat in shadow in a broken wicker chair. The chair had once been painted festive yellow. Down the arms there were eagles or maybe chickens in faded red. Cactus the pale shade of leafy mold. For a moment it seemed to Erwin that the man was wicker, too, that the chair had fashioned a person out of itself, thrust brittle strands for arms and legs, burst dry backing from Chihuahua, Mexico, for springy ribs. The whole of this draped with tattered clothes of no description. Hair white silk to the shoulders and beyond. The head newspaper dry as dust, crumpled in a ball and tied with string about the brow, a page very likely blown six hundred miles from Fort Worth across the flats. Eyes and nose and shadow mouth vaguely nibbled into shape by friendly mice.

Or so it all seemed on this attic afternoon.

"Well, what's your name now?" the man asked, in a voice like rocks in a skillet.

"Johannes Erwin Eugen Rommel, sir," said Erwin, scarcely managing to find his voice at all.

"By God. That's more name than a boy needs to have, I'll tell you sure. What do they call you for short?"

"Erwin, sir."

"Erwin sir and two more. Might be handy to have a spare at that. Knew a man called Zero Jefferson White. Couldn't remember who he was. What does your father do?"

"He is a schoolmaster, sir."

The paper mouth crinkled in a sly and knowing way. "I am aware of that, you see. John has told me all. I am kept informed, and don't forget it."

"Are you a hundred, sir?" The words came out before he could stop them.

The mouse-nibble eyes searched about. "I might be, I couldn't say. What year you think it is?"

"Nineteen-hundred-and-three, sir."

"It is? Are you sure?" The man seemed greatly surprised. "Then I am likely forty-four. I have lived a fretful life and half of that in this chair less than a man. It's a wonder I look no worse. How old are you?"

"Eleven, sir. I shall be twelve in November. When I am eighteen I shall become a *Fahnenjunker*. I will be a fine officer cadet, and I shall excel in fencing and riding."

"I doubt a soldier's life would have suited me at all. Parades. Lining up and the like. That kind of nonsense and wearing blue shirts. Never trust a man in a blue shirt. You do, I can promise you'll live to regret it."

The man seemed intrigued by the sight beyond his window, by the sleek muslin craft cutting graceful figure-eights across the sand. The engine clattered, the fans roared, and Orville sped his dream across the desert, raising great plumes of dust in his wake. The dust rose high in the still hot air and hung above the earth like yellow clouds.

"Charlie Bowdrie and old Dave Rudabaugh would go pick the best horses they could find and start out from Pete Maxwell's place and ride the mounts full out. Ride them full out without stopping, you understand, until one or the other dropped dead, the horse still running being the winner. The other horse too would generally die, as you might expect. A senseless thing to do. Dangerous to the man and plain fatal to the horse."

"I am sorry that you are ill, sir."

"What? Who said that I was?" The paper eyes came alive. "Definitions, boy. I am done, mortally hurt. That is not the same as ill. Ill, as I recall, is simply sick. Taken with disease. An affliction or discomfort of the body. I am mortally hurt, is what I am. Cut down, stricken, assaulted by violent hand. Felled with a bullet in the spine. God in Oklahoma, that's a wonder," the man said, following Orville's path. "A marvel of nature it is. I wish Charlie Bowdrie could see it. I would give some thought to the army. I can think of nearly thirty-two things I'd rather do. 'Course that's entirely up to you. I went to Colorado one time, me and Tom O'Folliard driving horses. Came back quick as I could. The cold there not to my liking at all."

"You got to go now," said John, and Erwin wasn't sure just how long he'd been standing there in the room.

"That canopy will shade you from the sun," said Garrett. "I don't expect the heat will be bad. You'll reach Roswell before dark, and Will'll see you settled before he leaves."

"Thank you," said Helene, "we are grateful for your help."

Will sat straight as a rod beside Erwin and his mother. He was proud of this new, if only temporary, post as wagon driver, and was determined to see it through. Orville wore his duster and his goggles. Earlier, after he had taken Erwin racing over the flats for nearly a full half-hour, he had given him a finely rendered pen-and-ink sketch of his muslin craft. John gave him two brass buttons, which he said had belonged to a U.S. Army major prior to a misunderstanding with Apaches in the Sierra Diablo country, which is south of the Guadalupe Mountains in Texas.

Garrett extended his hand. "Take care of your mother, boy. I have confidence that you will make yourself proud."

"Yes, sir," said Erwin.

"Well, then." Garrett extended his hand again, and Helene laid white-gloved fingers in his palm for just an instant. He studied the fair lines of her face, the silken hair swept under her bonnet. Strangely enough, he found he no longer regretted her departure.

To be honest, he was glad to see her go. Keeping real people and phantoms apart was increasingly hard to do. Delusions he'd never seen were lately creeping into his life. An old lady crying in the kitchen. A stranger at the table betting queens. The woman only served to cause confusion, being real enough herself while his fancy made her something she never was.

"I'm giving you the shotgun, Will," said Garrett, "I don't see trouble, but you use it if there is."

"Yes sir, I surely will."

"You know where the trigger is, I guess."

"I surely do."

"And which way to point it, no doubt."

"Quite clearly sir, yes, I do."

"Then make sure you—"

"Oh. Oh, my! said Helene, and brought a hand quickly to her lips.

Garrett turned to see her concern. The sight struck him in the heart. "Christ Jesus California!" he said at once, and stepped back as if felled by a blow. John stood in the door with the wicker chair, his great arms around it like a keg, the chair's pale apparition resting within. Garrett was unsure if this image was whiskey-real or otherwise and greatly feared it was the latter.

"John," he managed to say, "what in *hell* is he doing out here!"

"Mr. Billy say he ride," John announced.

"Ride what, for God's sake?"

"Ride that," John nodded. "He say he ride in Orville's machine."

"You tell him he's lost his senses."

"Mr. Billy say to tell you he going to do it."

"Well, you tell Mr. Billy that he's not," Garrett said furiously. "This is the most damn fool thing I ever heard."

"Tell Mr. Garrett I can kill myself any way I want," Billy said. He looked right at Garrett with a wide and papery grin. "Tell him I do not need advice from a fellow can't shoot a man proper close up."

"So that's it, is it," said Garrett. "You going to come downstairs every twenty-odd years now and pull *that* business out of the fire. By God, it's just like you, too. I said I was sorry once, I don't see the sense in doing it twice."

"Miz Rommel," said Billy, "I do not think your boy ought to look to the army. That is a life for a man with no ambition or gumption at all, and it is clear your boy is a comer. Bound for better things. May I say I have greatly enjoyed watching you take your evening walk. I said to Sallie Chisum once, you've likely seen her picture inside if Mr. Garrett hasn't thrown it out or burned it, which wouldn't surprise me any at all, I said Sallie, a woman's walk betrays her breeding high or low. She might be a duchess or the wife of a railroad baron or maybe even a lady of the night, a woman dedicated to the commerce of lust and fleshly delight, but the walk, now, the walk of a woman will out, the length and duration of her stride will tell you if she comes from good stock in a moment's glance, now am I right or am I not?"

"I would—I would really—I would really hardly—" Helene looked helplessly at Garrett.

"Will, Miz Rommel is sitting around in the heat," Garrett said firmly. "Would you kindly get this wagon headed south sometime before Tuesday?"

Will bobbed about with indecision, then flicked the reins and started the team moving with a jerk. Erwin waved. Garrett and John and Orville waved back.

Billy waved, too, though in no particular direction. "If you are headed for Roswell," he advised, "there was a fair hotel there at one time. Of course it may have changed hands, I can't say. Mr. John Tunstall and I stopped there once, and I recall that the rates were more than fair. A good steak is fifty cents, don't spend any more than that. The cook is named Ortega. His wife cooks a good *cabrito* if you can find a goat around that's not sick. Don't eat a goat that looks bad or you'll regret it. They are too bitter, though I've known those who prefer it that way to the other. Mr. John Chisum took four spoons of sugar. I could not fathom why. He kept an owl in a cage behind his house. That and other creatures some considerably less than tame . . ."

When the wagon reached the rise sightly east of the Sallie C., Erwin looked back and heard the engine running strong and saw the white planes of muslin catch the sun, saw the runners racing swiftly over the sand. Orville's duster flew, his goggles flashed, his hands gripped the magic controls. John gripped the chair at Orville's back, and though Erwin from afar couldn't see Billy at all, spiderweb hair like a bright and silken scarf trailed past the wicker arms to whip the wind.

From the Novel:
The Hereafter Gang
1: High Fashion

DOUG'S FATHER DIDN'T LIKE HIS WIFE'S CLOTHES. HE didn't know beans about the subject, but he knew the stuff he liked. He got fashion ideas from the funnies. Every Sunday morning he'd get off by himself and figure that new trends were coming up. "Boy, that Dragon Lady sure looks smart," he might say. He'd study some skimpy little number Wilma Deering slipped on to run to the Piggly Wiggly on Mars. "Don't tell me Buck Rogers isn't puttin' it to ol' Wilma now and then," he'd mutter half to himself. "He's loony if he don't." He thought Dale Arden had the best legs in the business. That Flash Gordon was getting some of that. So did Doug, but he came to this conclusion on his own. It didn't bother Doug's father that you couldn't stuff a Mary Worth body in a Brenda Starr dress. He'd circle the panels he liked and leave them lying by the mop or on the stove where his wife couldn't miss taking a look. Doug's mother didn't take to this at all. She let it go awhile, then started dropping sartorial hints of her own. Mandrake the Magician in a silk maroon sock. Dick Tracy on a godawful tie she couldn't stand. Doug's father felt betrayed. He sulked around the house. "You don't listen to a soul but that goddamn sister of yours," he'd say. "That woman wears clothes come out of a tree. Just look at that thing you're wearin' now. Why, they'd chase you out of Wichita Falls. You'd look right good in this outfit Blondie's got on."

Doug's mother listened. When he finished, she walked up and stabbed a finger through his heart. "Now you listen to me," she said. "Don't you' give me any funny papers again. Not ever. A man buys his shorts at the hardware store hasn't got room to talk. A pig can read your *Esquire* magazine all day long, and he isn't going to be Walter Pidgeon when he's done. You're no better'n that pig, so I doubt you'll make it, either. So you just leave me the hell alone. I dress to fit the company I'm in, and I reckon that says a lot."

After that Doug's father kept the funnies to himself. Doug discovered you could trace Dale Arden and make it look like she wasn't wearing anything at all. . . .

Cush

THE CARS STARTED COMING IN THE EARLY HOT LOCUST afternoon, turning off the highway and onto the powder-dry road, cars from towns with names like Six Mile and Santuck and Wedowee and Hawk, small-print names like Uchee and Landerville and Sprott, cars from big cities like Birmingham and Mobile and even out of state, all winding down the narrow choked-up road, leaving plumes of red dust for the other cars behind, down through the midsummer August afternoon into deep green shade under sweet gum and sycamore and pine.

The cars hesitated when they came to the bridge. The rust-iron bolt-studded sides looked strong enough to hold the pyramids, but the surface of the bridge caused some alarm. The flat wooden timbers were weathered gray as stone, sagged and bent and bowed and warped every way but straight. Every time a car got across, the bridge gave a clatter-hollow death-rattle roll like God had made a center-lane strike. Reason said that the Buick up ahead had made it fine. Caution said this was a time to reflect on mortal life. One major funeral a day was quite enough. The best way to view these events was standing up.

Aunt Alma Cree didn't give two hoots about the bridge. She stopped in the middle of the span, killed the engine, and rolled the window down. There was nobody coming up behind. If they did, why, they could wait. If they didn't want to wait, they could honk and stomp around, which wouldn't bother Alma Cree a bit. Alma had stood on the steps of Central High in Little Rock in '56, looking up at grim white soldiers tall as trees. Nine years later, she'd joined the march from Selma to Montgomery with Martin Luther King. Nothing much had disturbed her ever since. Not losing a husband who was only thirty-two. Not forty-three years teaching kids who were more concerned with street biology than reading *Moby Dick*.

She sure wasn't worried about a bridge. Least of all the one beneath her now. She knew this bridge like she knew her private parts. She knew that it was built around 1922 by a white man from Jackson who used to own the land. He didn't like to farm, but he liked to get away from his wife. Alma's grandfather bought the place cheap in '36, and the family had lived there ever since. The timber on the bridge had washed away seven times, but the iron had always held. The creek had claimed a John Deere tractor, a Chevy, and a '39 La Salle. Alma knew all about the bridge.

She remembered how she and her sister Lucy used to sneak off from the house, climb up the railing, and lean out far enough to spit. They'd spit and then wait, wait for the red-fin minnows and silver baby perch to come to lunch. They never seemed to guess it wasn't something good to eat. Alma and Lucy would laugh until their sides nearly split because spit fooled the fish every time. Didn't nobody have less sense, Mama said, than two stringy-legged nigger gals who couldn't hardly dry a dish. But Alma and Lucy didn't care. They might be dumb, but they didn't think spit was a fat green hopper or a fly.

Alma sat and smelled the rich hot scent of creek decay. She listened to the lazy day chirring in the trees, the only sound in the silent afternoon. The bottom lay heat-dazed and drugged, tangled in heavy brush and vine. The water down below was still and deep, the surface was congealed and poison green. If you spit in the water now, it wouldn't sink. The minnows and the perch had disappeared. Farther up a ways, someone told Alma a year or two before, there was still good water, still cottonmouth heaven up there, and you could see a hundred turtles at a time, sleeping like green clots of moss on a log.

But not down here, Alma thought. Everything here is mostly dead. She remembered picking pinks and puttyroot beside the creek, lady fern and toadshade in the woods. Now all that was gone, and the field by the house was choked with catbrier and nettle, and honey locust sharp with bristle thorns. The homeplace itself had passed the urge to creak and sigh. Every plank and nail had settled in and sagged as far as it could go. The house had been built in a grove of tall pecans, thick-boled giants that had shaded fifty years of Sunday picnic afternoons. The house had outlived every tree, and now they were gone, too. A few chinaberries grew around the back porch, but you can't hang a swing on a ratty little tree.

"One day, that house is going to fall," Alma said, in the quiet of the hot afternoon. One day it's going to see that the creek and the land are bone dry and Mr. Death has nearly picked the place clean. Driving up from the creek on the red-dust road, she could feel the ghosts everywhere about. Grandpas and uncles and cousins twice removed, and a whole multitude of great aunts. Papa and Mama long gone, and sister Lucy gone, too. No one in the big hollow house except Lucy's girl Pru. Pru and the baby and Uncle John Fry, dead at a hundred and three. Dead and laid out in the parlor in a box.

Lord God, Alma thought, the whole family's come to this. A dead old man and crazy Pru, who's tried to swallow lye twice. John Ezekiel Fry and Pru, and a one-eyed patchwork child, conceived in mortal sin.

"And don't forget yourself," she said aloud. "*You* aren't any great prize, Alma Cree."

They couldn't all get in the parlor, but as many came in as they could, the rest trailing out in the hall and through the door and down the porch, crowding in a knot in the heat outside. The window to the parlor was raised up high so everyone could hear the preacher's message fairly clear.

Immediate family to the front, is what Preacher Will said, so Alma had to sit in a straight-back chair by her crazy niece Pru. Pru to her left, a cousin named Edgar to her right, a man she had never laid eyes on in her life.

Where did they all come from? she thought, looking at the unfamiliar faces all about. Forty, maybe fifty people, driving in from everywhere, and not any three she could recall. Had she known them in the summer as a child, had they come to Thanksgiving sometime? They were here, so they must be kin to Uncle Fry.

It was hot as an oven outside the house and in. Before the service got fully underway, a stout lady fainted in the hall. And, as a great ocean liner draws everything near it down into the unforgiving sea, Mrs. Andrea Simms of Mobile pulled several people with her out of sight. Outside, an asp dropped from a chinaberry tree down the collar of an insurance man from Tullahoma, Tennessee. Cries went out for baking soda, but Pru had little more than lye and peanut butter in the house, so the family had to flee.

Preacher Will extolled the virtues of John Ezekiel Fry, noting that he had lived a long life, which anyone there could plainly see. Will himself was eighty-three, and he was certain Uncle Fry had never been inside his church at any time. Still, you had to say *some*thing, so Will filled in with Bible verse to make the service last. He knew the entire Old Testament and the New, everything but Titus and part of Malachi, enough to talk on through the summer and the fall, and somewhere into June.

Alma felt inertia settling in. Her face was flushed with heat, and all her lower parts were paralyzed. Pru was swaying back and forth, humming a Michael Jackson tune. Cousin Edgar was dead or fast asleep. Not any of us going to last long, Alma thought, and Will isn't even into Psalms.

The Lord was listening in, or some northern saint who was mindful of the heat. At that very moment, the service came abruptly to a halt. A terrible cry swept through the house, ripped through every empty hall and dusty room, through every mouse hole and weather crack, through every wall and floor. No one who heard the cry forgot. The sound was so lonely, so full of hurt and woe, so full of pain and sorrow and regret, a cry and a wail for all the grief and the misery the world had ever known, all the suffering and sin, all gathered in a single long lament.

Crazy Pru was up and on her feet, the moment the sound began, Crazy Pru with her eyes full of fright, with a mother's primal terror in her heart.

"Oh Lord God," she cried, "oh sweet Jesus, somethin's happened to my child! Somethin's wrong with little Cush!"

Pru tore through the crowd, fought to reach the hall, Aunt Alma right behind. The people gave way, parting as they came, then trailed right up the stairs, leaving Uncle John Ezekiel Fry all alone with a row of empty chairs, alone except for Leonard T. Pyne.

When Pru saw her child, she went berserk. She shrieked and

pulled her hair, whirled in a jerky little dance, moaned and screamed and gagged, and collapsed in an overstuffed chair. Aunt Alma looked into the crib and thought her heart would surely stop. The child was bleeding from its single awful eye, bleeding from its mouth and from its nose, bleeding from its fingers and its toes, bleeding from its ears and from every tiny pore.

Alma didn't stop to think. She lifted up the child, this ugly little kicking screaming pinto-colored child with its possum arms and legs and its baked potato head, lifted up the child and shouted, "Get the *hell* out of my way, I'm coming through!"

Alma ran out of the room and down the hall, the child slick and wet and pulsing like a fancy shower spray. In the bathroom, she laid Cush quickly in the tub and turned the faucet on full. She splashed the child and slapped it, held it right beneath the rushing tap. The red washed away, but Alma didn't care about that. She prayed that the shock would trigger something vital inside and make the bleeding go away.

The child howled until Alma thought her ears would surely burst. It fought to get free from the water streaming down upon its head, it twisted like an eel in her hands, but she knew that she couldn't let it get away.

And then the bleeding stopped. Just like that. Cush stopped crying and the color in the tub went from red to pink to clear, and Alma lifted up the child, and someone handed her a towel.

"There now," Alma said, "you're going to be all right, you're going to be just fine."

She knew this was a lie. You couldn't look at this poor little thing with its one eye open, and one forever shut, and say everything'll be just fine. There wasn't anything fine about Cush. There wasn't now and there wouldn't ever be.

At the very same moment the child stopped bleeding upstairs, Uncle John Ezekiel Fry, dead at a hundred and three, farted in his coffin, shook, and gave a satisfying sigh. In the time it takes a fly to bat its wings, Fry remembered every single instant of his life, every word and past event, every second since May 24 in 1888, things that had touched him, and things that he didn't understand, things that he had paid no attention to at all. He remembered the Oklahoma Run and the Panic of '93. He remembered getting knifed when he was barely twenty-two. He remembered Max Planck. The Sherman Silver Purchase Act. Twenty-one-thousand, four-hundred-sixty-two catfish he'd eaten in his life. A truckload of Delaware Punch. Sixteen tank cars of whiskey and gin. Seven tons of pork. John Maynard Keynes. Teddy up San Juan Hill. Iwo Jima and Ypres. Tiger tanks and Spads. A golden-skinned whore named Caroline. Wilson got four hundred and thirty-five electoral votes, and Taft got only eight. The St. Louis Fair in 1904. Corn bread and beans. A girl in a red silk dress in Tupelo. Shooting a man in Mobile and stealing his silver watch. A lady in Atlanta under a lemon moon, wet from the river, diamond droplets on her skin, and coal-black moss between her thighs.

All this came to Uncle John Ezekiel Fry as he gripped the wooden sides of his box and sat up and blinked his eyes, sat and blinked his eyes and said, *"Whiskey-tit-February-cunt . . . Lindy sweet as blackberry pie . . ."*

There was no one in the room except Leonard T. Pyne. Walking hurt a lot, so he hadn't chased the crowd upstairs. He stared at John Fry, saw his hands on the box, saw a suit that looked empty inside, saw a face like an apple that's been rotting in the bin for some time. Saw tar-ball eyes that looked in instead of out, looked at things Leonard hoped to God he'd never see.

Leonard didn't faint and didn't scream. His hair didn't stand on end. He didn't do anything you'd think he ought to do because he didn't for a minute believe a thing he saw. Dead men don't sit up and talk, he knew that. And if they don't, you wouldn't see them do it, so why make a fuss about that?

Leonard T. Pyne got up and walked out. He forgot he had knees near the size of basketballs. He forgot he couldn't walk without a crutch. He walked out and got into his car and drove away. He forgot he'd brought his wife Lucille. He drove back up the dirt road, across the bridge, and headed straight for New Orleans. He'd lived all his life south of Knoxville, Tennessee. He'd never gone to New Orleans, and couldn't think of any reason why he should.

When the folks came down from upstairs, Uncle John Ezekiel Fry was in the kitchen, pulling open cabinets and drawers, looking for a drink. Some people fell down and prayed. Some passed out, but that could have been the heat. People who'd come from out of state said it's just like Fry to pull a stunt like this, he never gave a shit about anyone else. The next time he died, they weren't about to make the trip.

Crazy Pru, when she gathered up her wits, when the baby

looked fine, or as fine as a child like that could ever be, said God worked in wondrous ways, anyone could plainly see. What if she hadn't been broke, and they'd gone and had Uncle Fry embalmed instead of laid out in a box? He'd have been dead sure, and wouldn't have a chance of waking up and coming back.

The town undertaker, Marvin Doone, could feel Preacher Will's accusing eyes, and he couldn't think of anything to say. Will had felt sorry for the family, and slipped Doone the cash to do the body up right. Which Marvin Doone had *done*, sucking out all of Uncle Fry's insides, pumping fluids in and sewing everything up, dressing the remains in a black Sears suit, also courtesy of Will. There wasn't any question in Marvin Doone's mind that Fry had absolutely no vital parts, and how could he explain that to Will?

Preacher Will never spoke to Doone again.

Doone went home and drank half a quart of gin.

Uncle John Ezekiel Fry said, "*Nipple-pussy-Mississippi-rye,*" or words to that effect, walked eight miles back to his own farm, where he ate a whole onion and fried himself some fish.

"Pru, you ought to sell this place and get you and the child into town," Alma said. "There isn't anything left here for you, there's not a reason in the world for you to stay."

"Place is all paid for," said Pru. "Place belongs to me."

They were sitting on the porch, watching the evening slide away, watching the dark crowd in along the creek, watching an owl dart low among the trees. Pru rocked the baby in her arms, and the baby looked content. It played with its little possum hands, it watched Aunt Alma with its black and sleepy eye.

"Paid for's one thing," Alma said. "Keeping up is something else. There's taxes on land, and somebody's got to pay for that. The place won't grow anything, the soil's dead. Near as I can tell, stinging nettle's not a cash crop."

Pru smiled and tickled the baby's chin, though Alma couldn't see that it had a chin at all.

"Me and Cush, we be just fine," Pru said. "We goin' to make it just fine."

Alma looked straight out in the dark. "Prudence, it's not my place to say it, but I will. Your mother was my sister and I guess I got the right. That is *not* a proper name for a child. I'm sorry, but it simply is not."

"Cush, that's my baby's name," Pru said.

"It's not right," Alma said.

Pru rocked back and forth, bare feet brushing light against the porch. "Noah woke," Pru said, "and he know his son Ham seen him naked in his tent. An' Noah say, 'I'm cursin' all your children, Ham, that's what I'm goin' to do.' And lo, that's what he did. An' one of Ham's sons was called Cush."

"I don't care if he was or not," Alma said. "You want a Bible name, there's lots of names to choose, it doesn't have to be Cush."

Pru gave Alma a disconcerting look. The look said maybe-I'm-present-but-I-might-have-stepped-out.

"Lots of names, all right," Pru said, "but not too many got a *curse*. I figure Cush here, he oughta have a name with a curse."

Alma wasn't certain how she ought to answer that.

Alma found retirement a bore, just like she'd figured that she would. Her name was on the list for substitutes, but the calls that came were few and far between. She worked part-time for the Montgomery NAACP, taking calls and typing and doing what she could. She grubbed in the garden sometimes, and painted the outside of the house. She had thought for some time about a lavender house. The neighbors didn't take to this at all, but Alma didn't care. I might be into hot pink next year, she told Mrs. Sissy Hayes across the street. What do you think about *that?*

She hadn't been feeling too well since fall the year before. Getting tired too soon, and even taking afternoon naps. Something that she'd never done before. Painting the house wore her out, more than she cared to admit. I'm hardly even past sixty-five, she told herself. I'm a little worse for wear, but I'm not about to stop.

What she thought she ought to do was drop by Dr. Frank's and have a talk. Not a real appointment, just a talk. Stop by and talk about iron, maybe get a shot of B.

Dr. Frank gave her seventeen tests and said you'd better straighten out, Alma Cree. You're diabetic and you've got a bad heart. You're maybe into gout. I'm not sure your kidneys are the way they ought to be.

Alma drove home and made herself some tea. Then she sat down at the table and cried. She hadn't cried since Lucy passed away, and couldn't say when before that.

"Oh Jesus," Alma said aloud, the kitchen sun blurring through her tears. "I don't want to get old, and I sure don't want to die. But old's my first choice, I think you ought to know that."

Her body seemed to sense Alma knew she'd been betrayed. There were no more occasional aches and pains, no more little hints. The hurt came out in force with clear purpose and intent.

The pills and shots seemed to help, but not enough. Alma didn't like her new self. She'd never been sick, and she didn't like being sick now. She had to quit the part-time job. Working in the garden hurt her knees. Standing up hurt her legs and sitting down hurt everything else. What I ought to do, Alma said, is take to drink. It seems to work for everyone else.

All this occurred after Uncle Fry's abortive skirt with death and her trip down to the farm. In spite of her own new problems, Alma tried to keep in touch with Pru. She wrote now and then, but Pru never wrote back. Alma sent a little money when she could. Pru never said thanks, which didn't surprise Alma a bit. Pru's mother Lucy, rest her soul, had always been tight with a dollar, even when she wasn't dirt poor. Maybe cheap runs in Pru's blood, Alma thought. God knows everything *else* peculiar does. Lucy flat cheap, and her husband a mean-eyed drunk. No one knew who had fathered Pru's child, least of all Pru. Whoever he was, he couldn't account for Cush. Only God could take the blame for a child like Cush. Heredity was one thing, but that poor thing was something else. There weren't enough bad genes in Alabama to gang up and come out with a Cush.

Alma felt she had to see Pru. She was feeling some better, and Dr. Frank said the trip would do her good. She had meant to come before, but didn't feel up to the drive. In her letters to Pru, she had mentioned that she wasn't feeling well, and let it go at that. Not that Pru likely cared—Alma wouldn't know her niece was still alive if it wasn't for Preacher Will. Will wrote every six months, the same two lines that said Pru and the child were just fine. Alma doubted that. How could they be just fine? How were they eating, how were they getting by? It had been nearly—what?—Lord, close to three years. That would make Cush about four. Who would have guessed the child would live as long as that?

As ever, Alma felt a tug from the past as she drove off the highway and onto the red dirt road. She was pleased and surprised to see the land looking fine, much better than it had the time before. The water at the creek was much higher, and running nearly clear. Wildflowers pushed up through the weeds and vines. As she watched the dark water, as she tried to peer down into the deep, a thin shaft of light made its way through the thick green branches up above, dropping silver coins in the shallows by the bank. Alma saw a sudden dart of color, quick crimson sparks against the citron-yellow light.

"Will you just look at that!" she said, and nearly laughed aloud. "Redfin minnows coming back. I'll bet you all still fool enough to eat spit!"

If her back wasn't giving her a fit, if she hadn't stiffened up from the drive, Alma would have hopped out and given spit a try. Instead, she drove through the trees and back out into the sun, up the last hill through the field and to the house.

For a moment, Alma thought that she'd gotten mixed up somehow and turned off on the wrong road. The catbrier and nettles were gone. The field was full of tall green corn. Closer to the house, the corn gave way to neat rows of cabbages, okra and tomatoes, squash and lima beans. The house was freshly painted white. All the windows had glossy black trim and new screens. A brick walk led up to the porch, and perched on the new gravel drive was a blue Ford pickup with oversize tires.

Alma felt a sudden sense of hopelessness and fear. Pru's gone, she thought. She's gone, and someone else is living here. She's gone, and there isn't any telling where that crazy girl went.

Alma parked behind the pickup truck. There wasn't any use in going in. Maybe someone would come out. She rolled the window down. A hot summer breeze dissolved the colder air at once. Alma thought about honking. Not a big honk, not something impolite, just a quick little tap. She waited just a moment, just a small moment more. Then something in the field caught her eye, and she turned and heard the rattle of the corn, looked and saw the green stalks part and saw the scarecrow jerk-step-jiggle down the rows, saw the denim overalls faded white hanging limp on the snap-dry arms, saw the brittle-stick legs, saw the mouse-nibble gray felt hat, stratified with prehistoric sweat, saw the face like a brown paper sack creased and folded thin as dust, saw the grease-spot eyes and the paper-rip mouth, saw this dizzy apparition held together now and then with bits of rag and cotton string.

"Why, Uncle John Ezekiel Fry," Alma said, "it's nice to find you looking so spry. Think the corn'll do good this year?"

"*Crowbar-Chattahoochee-suck,*" said Uncle Fry. "*Cling peach-sourdough-crotch* . . ."

"Lord God," Alma said. She watched Uncle Fry walk back into the corn. Either Uncle John Fry or a gnat got in her eye, either John Ezekiel Fry or a phantom cloud of lint. If *he's* still here, Alma thought, then Pru's around, too, though something's going on that isn't right.

At that very moment, Alma heard the screen door slam and saw Pru running barefoot down the steps—Pru, or someone who looked a whole lot like Pru, if Pru filled out and wasn't skinny as a rail, if she looked like Whitney what's-her-name. If she did her hair nice and bought a pretty pink dress and didn't look real goofy in the eyes. If all that occurred, and it seemed as if it had, then this was maybe Lucy's only daughter Prudence Jean.

"Aunt Alma, sakes alive," Pru said. "My, if this ain't a nice surprise!"

Before Aunt Alma could drag her aches and pains upright, Pru was at the car, laughing and grinning and hugging her to death.

"Say, you look fine," said Pru. "You look just as fine as you can be."

"I'm not fine at all, I've been sick," Alma said.

"Well, you sure look good to me," Pru said.

"It wouldn't hurt you much to write."

"Me and the alphabet never got along too good," said Pru. "But I sure think about you all the time."

Alma had her doubts about that. Pru led her up the brick walk across the porch and in the house. Once more, Alma felt alarmed, felt slightly out of synch, felt as if she'd found the wrong place, felt as if she might be out of state. A big unit hummed in the window and the air was icy cold. The wood floor was covered with a blue-flowered rug. There were pictures on the walls. A new lamp, a new couch, and new chairs.

"Pru," Alma said, "you want to tell me what's going on around here? I mean, everything sure looks nice, it looks fine. . . ."

"I bet you're hot," Pru said. "You just sit and I'll get some lemonade."

I'm not hot now, Alma thought. Isn't anybody hot, you got the air turned down to thirty-two. She could hear Pru humming down the hall. Probably got a brand-new designer kitchen, too. A fridge and a stove colored everything but white.

Lord Jesus, the place painted up, a new truck and new screens and a house full of Sears! No wonder Preacher Will never said a whole lot.

Alma didn't want to think where the money came from, Pru looking slick as a fashion magazine, all her best parts pooching in or swelling out. What's a person going to think? A girl doesn't know her alphabet past *D*, she isn't working down at Merrill Lynch. What she's *working* is a Mobile dandy with a mouth full of coke-white teeth and a Cadillac to match.

It's not right, Alma thought. Looks like it pays pretty good, but it's not the thing a girl ought to do. That's what I'll say, I'll say, Pru,

I know you've had a real bad time with Cush and all, but it's not the thing to do.

Pru brought the lemonade back, sat down and smiled like the ladies do in *Vogue* when they're selling good perfume.

"Aunt Alma," she said, "I bet you want to hear 'bout all this stuff I got around. I got an idea you maybe would."

Alma cleared her throat. "Well, if you feel like you *want* to tell me, Pru, that's fine."

"I sorta had good fortune come my way," Pru said. "I was workin' in the corn one day when my hoe hit somethin' hard. I dug it up and found a rusty tin can. Inside the can was a little leather sack. And inside *that*, praise God, was nine twenty-dollar gold coins lookin' fresh as they could be. I took 'em to the bank and Mr. Deek say, nine times twenty, Miz Pru, that's a hundred and eighty dollars, but I'll give you two hundred on the spot. An' I say I don't guess you will, Mr. Deek, I said I ain't near as touched as I maybe used to be. I said I seen a program 'bout coins on the public TV."

"So what I *did*, I took a bus down to Mobile an' found an ol' man cookin' fish. I say, can you read and write? He says he can, pretty good, and I say, buy me a book about coins and read me what it say. He does, and he reads up a spell and says, Lord Jesus, girl, these here coins is worth a lot. I says, tell me how much? He says, bein' mint condition like they is, 'round forty-two-thousand-ninety-three, seems to me. Well, it took some doing, but I ended up gettin' forty-six. I give the man helped me a twenty-dollar bill, and that left me forty-five, nine-hundred-eighty to the good. Now isn't that something? God sure been fine to me."

"Yes, He — well, He certainly has, Pru. I guess you've got to say that. . . ."

The truth is, Alma didn't know what to say. She was stunned by the news. All that money from an old tin can? Money lying out in that field for more than a hundred years? Papa and Mama living rag-dirt poor, and nobody ever found a nickel till Pru. Of course, Pru could use the money, that's a fact. But it wouldn't have hurt a thing if one or two of those coins had showed up about 1942.

Pru served Alma a real nice supper, and insisted she stay the night. Alma didn't argue a lot. The trip down had flat worn her out. Pru said she'd fixed up her grandma's room, and Alma didn't have to use the air.

All through the long hot brassy afternoon, while the sun tried to dig through the new weatherstripping and the freshly painted walls, Pru rattled on about the farm and Uncle Fry and how well the garden grew and this and that, talked about everything there was to talk about except Cush. Alma said maybe once or twice, how's Cush doing, and Pru said real quick Cush is doing fine. After that, Alma didn't ask. She tried to pay attention, and marvel at the Kenmore fridge and the noisy Cuisinart, but her mind was never far from the child. Pru seemed to know, seemed to feel the question there between them, felt it hanging in the air. And when she did, she hurried on to some brand-new appliance colored fire-engine red or plastic green. And that was as far as Alma got about Cush.

Then, when the day was winding down, when the heat let up and Alma sat on the porch with a glass of iced tea, Pru came up behind her and touched Alma gently on the arm.

"I know you got to see him," Pru said. "I know that's what you gotta do."

Alma sat very still for a while, then she stood and looked at Pru. "The child's my kin," Alma said. "Just because he isn't whole doesn't mean I don't love him all the same."

Pru didn't say a thing. She took Alma's hand and led her down the front steps. The chinaberry trees had grown tall. Their limbs brushed the screened-in porch by the kitchen out back. The ground all around was worn flat, like it always used to be. Worn where the cistern had stood years before, worn on the path that led out behind the house. Alma could see the twisted ghosts of peach trees inside her head. She could see the smokehouse and the outhouse after that, the storm cellar off to the right, and Papa's chicken coop. And when she turned the far corner of the house, there was Cush, sitting in a new red wagon by the steps.

Alma felt herself sway, felt her legs give way, felt her heart might come to a stop. The creature in the wagon looked nothing like a child, nothing like anything that ought to be alive. The baked potato head seemed larger than before, the warped little body parched and seared, dried and shriveled to a wisp. The patchwork pattern of his skin was thick with suppurating sores, pimples and blisters, blots and stains and spots, pustules and blotches, welts and bug bites, rashes and swellings and eruptions of every sort. Alma saw the possumlike hands were bent and twisted like a root, saw there wasn't any hair on Cush's head, saw Cush had somehow lost a leg, saw the child wore every conceivable deformity and flaw, every possible perversion of the flesh.

And then Pru sat down on the ground and said, "Cush, this here's your great-aunt Alma Cree. You was too young to recall, but you seen her once before. You want to try an' say hello, you want to try an' do that?"

Cush looked up at Alma with his black and milky eye, looked at Alma through his misery and pain, looked right at Alma Cree and smiled. The smile was something marvelous and terrible to see. One side of Cush's mouth stayed the same while the other side cut a crooked path past his cheek and past his nose, cut a deep and awful fissure up his face. When you hiccup while you try to sign your name, when the line wanders up and off the page, this is how the smile looked to Alma Cree. Cush's lips parted and secreted something white, then Cush scratched and croaked and made a sound.

"Haaalm'ah-ah . . . Haaalm'ah-ah," Cush said, and then the smile went away.

"Alma," Pru said with pure delight, "that's *right*. See, Aunt Alma? Cush went and said your name!"

"That's real good, Cush," Alma said, "it sure is." She felt the sky whirl crazily about, felt the earth grind its teeth and come apart. She hoped to God she'd make it to the house.

"Pru, you can't take care of that child," Alma said. "You just can't do it by yourself. I know you've done all you could, but poor little Cush needs some help."

"I *got* help, Alma," said Pru, looking at her empty coffee cup. "Since I come into money, Cush has seen every kind of doctor there is. They give me all kinds of lotions, and ever' kind of pill they got. Ain't nothin' works at all, nothin' anyone can do."

"Pru," Alma said, "what happened to his leg?"

"Didn't anything happen," Pru said. "Jus' one day 'bout a year ago spring it dropped off. Cush give a little squeal an' I 'bout passed out, and that was all of that."

Tears welled in Pru's eyes. "Aunt Alma, I lay 'wake nights and I wonder just what's going on in God's head. I say, Pru, what's He thinking up there? What you figure He means to do? The farm's all shiny like Jesus reached down and touched the land. It hasn't ever been as fine before. The Lord's took the crazy from my head and got me looking real good, and give me everything there is. So how come He missed helpin' Cush, Aunt Alma? You want to tell me that? How come little Cush is somethin' Jesus flat forgot?"

"I don't know the Lord's ways," Alma said. "I wouldn't know

how to answer that." Alma looked down at her hands. She couldn't look at Pru. "What I think I ought to say, what you ought to think about, is you've done about everything you can. There isn't much else you can do. You're young and you've got a life ahead, and there's places where Cush'd maybe be better off than he is . . ."

"No!"

The word came out as strong and solid as the hard red iron that held the bridge. "Cush is my child," Pru said. "I don't know why he's like he is, but he's mine. Alma, he isn't going anywhere but here."

Alma saw the will, saw the fierce determination in Pru, and knew at once there was nothing she could say, nothing that anyone could do.

"All right," she said, and tried her best to smile at Pru, "I guess that's the way it's got to be. . . ."

Cush liked the winter and the fall. In the summer and the spring, everything that creeped and flew and crawled did their best to seek him out. Fire ants and black ants and ants of every sort. Earwigs and stinkbugs and rusty centipedes. Sulphur butterflies made bouquets about his head to suck the sores around his eyes. Horseflies and deerflies bit his cheeks. Mosquitoes snarled about like Fokker airplanes, and black gnats clotted up his nose. Bees and yellow jackets stung his thighs. If a certain bug couldn't find Cush, Cush would somehow seek it out. With his single bent foot, he'd push his wagon down the road. A scorpion would appear and whip its tail around fast and sting his toe.

His mother tried to keep him in the house. But Cush didn't like it inside. He liked to sit out and watch the trees. He liked to watch the hawks knifing high up in the sky. There were so many wonders to see. Every blade of grass, every new flower that pushed its way up through the soil, was a marvel to Cush's eye. He especially loved the creek. By the time he was five, he stayed there every day he could. He loved to watch the turtles poke their heads up and blink and look around. He loved to see the minnows dart about. There were more things that bit, more things around the creek that had a sting, but Cush was used to that.

Besides, staying indoors didn't help. Fresh paint and new doors and super-snug-tight screens couldn't keep the biters out. They knew Cush was there and they found a way in. Anywhere Cush might be, they wriggled in and found him out.

Cush didn't think about pain. Cush had hurt from the very

first moment of his life. He didn't know there was anything else. It had never crossed his mind what *not* to hurt was like. A deaf child wonders what it might be like to hear, but he never gets it right.

Cush knew there was something different other persons felt, something that he sensed was maybe missing in his life. He didn't look like other people did, he knew that. Other people did things, and all he did was sit. Sit and look and think. Sit and get gnawed and stung and bit.

Once, in the late evening light, when Cush sat with his mother on the porch, the fan brought out from inside to try and keep the bugs at bay, Cush tried to sound a thought. That's how he looked at talk—sounding out a thought. He didn't try to sound a lot. Nothing seemed to come out right.

Still, on this night, he tried and tried hard. It was something that he knew he had to do. He worked his mouth up as best as he could and let it out.

After Pru ruled out strangulation or a stroke, she knew Cush was winding up to talk. "Hon, I'm not real sure what you're saying," Pru said, "you want to run through that again?"

Cush did. He tried again twice. Legs from old bugs, bits of vital parts, and something like liver-ripple tofu spewed out.

"*Whuuuma faar?*" Cush said. "*Mudd-whuum-spudoo?*"

Pru listened, and finally understood. When she did, she felt her heart would break in two. She nearly grabbed up Cush and held him tight. She hadn't tried that in three years, but she nearly did it then. "What am I *for?*" Cush had said. "Mother, what am I supposed to *do?*"

Oh Lord, thought Pru, how am I supposed to answer that? Sweet Jesus, put the right words inside my head. Pru waited, and nothing showed up that seemed divine.

"Why, isn't anything you *supposed* to do, Cush," Pru said. "God made the trees and the flowers and the sky, an' everything else there is to see. He made your Aunt Alma and he made you an' me. We're all God's children, Cush. I reckon that's about all we're supposed to be."

Cush thought about that. He thought for a very long time. He looked at his mother's words backward and forward, sideways and inside out. He still didn't know what he was for. He still didn't know what to do. Something, he was sure, but he couldn't think *what*. He was almost certain being one of God's flowers wasn't it.

* * *

The trip wore Alma to a nub. She took to her bed for three days, and slept through most of two. When she finally got up, she felt fine. Hungry, and weak in the knees, but just fine. All that driving, and seeing Cush and Pru, Alma thought, that's enough to do anybody in.

She thought about Pru and the farm. How nice Pru looked and how she didn't seem crazy anymore, and how the land and the creek were all coming back again. Everything was doing fine but Cush. Even Uncle Fry. It was like Pru said. All that good flowing in, and Cush not getting his share. It didn't seem right. It sure didn't seem fair.

Alma looked at the garden and decided it was far beyond repair. She dusted the house and threw the laundry in a sack. She went to the grocery store and back. Late in the afternoon, she got a notebook out and started writing things down. Not for any reason, just something she thought she ought to do. She wrote about the funeral and Uncle John Fry. She wrote about Pru and she wrote about Cush. She wrote about how the land had changed and how the creek was full of fish. Nothing that she wrote told her anything she didn't know before, but it seemed to help to get some things down.

Two weeks back from her trip, Alma got a call. Dotty Mae Kline, who'd taught school with Alma for thirty-two years, had retired the year after Alma did. She lived in Santa Barbara now, and said, Alma, why don't you come and stay awhile?

The idea took her by surprise. Alma thought of maybe fourteen reasons why she couldn't take a trip, then tossed them all aside. "Why not?" she said, and called to see when the next plane could fly her out.

Alma meant to stay a week and ended up staying four. She liked Santa Barbara a lot. It was great to be around Dotty Mae. They saw and did everything they could, and even came close to getting tipsy on California wine. Alma felt better than she'd ever felt before. Dotty Mae said that was the good Pacific air. But Alma knew air couldn't do a whole lot for diabetes, or a heart that now and then made a scary little flop.

When she got back home, Alma found a letter in her mailbox from Pru. The postmark was two weeks old. Alma left her bags in the hall and opened Pru's letter at once. She saw the scrawly hand running up and down the page, and knew this was likely the only letter Pru had ever written in her life.

"Dir Ant Alma," it said.

"I bet yur supriz to here from me. The farm is luking fine. A agerkultr man is bout houndin me to deth. He says he don no how corn can git nin feet hi and cabig grow big as washtubs on a place like this. He says there isn no nutrunts in the soil I said I cant help that. Cush dropt a arm last week. Somethin like moss is startid growing on his hed. Otherwiz he doin fine. Uncl Fry is fine too.

Luv Pru

P.S. Friday last I wun 2 milun dollars from Ed McMahon. Alma heres a twenny dollar bill I got more than I can spend."

"Lord God," Alma said, "all that money to a dumb nigger girl!"

She crushed the letter in her fist. She was overcome with anger, furious at Pru. Things didn't *happen* like that, it wasn't right. All Pru had ever done was get herself knocked up. She hadn't done a full day's work in all her life!

Guilt rushed in to have its say, anger fighting shame, having it out inside her head. Alma was shaken. She couldn't imagine she'd said such a thing, but there it was. She'd tucked it away and out of sight, but it came right up awful quick, which meant it wasn't hiding out too deep.

The anger was there, and it wouldn't go away. Anger at Pru, who was everything she'd spent her life trying not to be. Mama and Papa and Lucy, too. Never bringing college friends home because *their* folks were black doctors and CPAs, and she didn't want anyone to know that her family was dirt-poor Alabama overall and calico black, Deep South darkies who said "Yassuh" all the time, and fit the white picture of a nigger to a tee.

She remembered every coffee-chocolate-soot-gray-sable-black face that had passed through her class. Every face for forty-three years. Her soul had ached for every one, knowing the kind of world that she had to send them to. Praying that they'd end up where she was, instead of where she'd been, and all the time saying in her heart, "I'm glad I'm me and I'm not one of *them*."

Alma sat on her couch in the growing afternoon. She looked at her luggage in the hall. She thought about smart-as-a-whip bright and funny Dotty Mae. She thought about Little Rock and Selma, and she thought about Pru.

"I'm still who I am," Alma said. "I might've let something else creep in, but I know that isn't *me.*" She sat and watched the day disappear, and she prayed that this was true.

In the morning, when she was rested from the trip, when the good days spent in California seemed to mingle with the pleasure and relief of coming back, when she could look at Pru's letter without old emotions crowding in, Alma got her notebook out and found a brand-new page, and wondered what she ought to say.

Alma didn't care for things she couldn't understand. She liked to deal in facts. She liked things that had a nice beginning and an end. Dotty Mae Kline had taught Philosophy and Modern English Lit. Alma Cree had been content with Geometry and French.

She looked at Pru's letter. She looked at what she'd written down before. Everything good seemed to fasten on Pru. Everything bad came to Cush. The farm was on drugs, on a mad horticultural high. Uncle Fry was apparently alive, and she didn't want to think about that. Alma tried to look for reason. She tried to find a pattern of events. She tried to make order out of things that shouldn't be. In the end, she simply set down the facts—though it went against her nature to call them that. She closed up her notebook and put it on the shelf. Completely out of sight. But not even close to out of mind.

Alma kept her quarterly appointment with Dr. Frank. Dr. Frank said, how are we doing, Alma? and Alma said we're doing just fine. Dr. Frank's nurse called back in a week. Dr. Frank wants to make a new appointment and redo some tests. What for? Alma said, and the nurse didn't care to answer that.

Alma hung up. She looked at the phone. She knew how she *felt,* she felt absolutely great. And she wasn't in California now, she was breathing plain Alabama air.

Alma knew what was wrong with the tests, she didn't have to think twice. Everything was fine inside, she didn't need a test to tell her that, and she'd never been more frightened in her life.

Pru woke up laughing and half scared to death. She sat up and looked around the room, making sure everything was fine, making sure everything was sitting where it should. Pru didn't like to dream. She had real good dreams now, everything coral rose and underwater green, nice colors floating all about, and a honey-sweet sax off somewhere to the right. Real good dreams, not the kind she'd had before. Not the kind with furry snakes and blue hogs with bad breath. Good's a lot better'n bad, thought Pru, but I could do without any dreams at all.

Pru's idea of what you ought to do at night was go to sleep and wake up. Dreams took you off somewhere that wasn't real, and Pru had come to cherish *real* a lot. Once you've been crazy, you don't much want to go back. It's sort of like making out with bears, once seems just about enough.

Pru drank a cup of coffee and started making oatmeal for Cush. Cush wouldn't likely touch it, but she felt she ought to try. The sun was an open steel furnace outside, and she turned all the units down to COLD. When the oatmeal was ready, she covered it with foil, found her car keys, and stepped out on the porch.

A light brown Honda was sitting in the drive. A white man was standing on the steps. Pru looked him up and down. He had blow-dry hair and a blue electric suit. He had rainwater eyes and white elevator shoes.

"What you want 'round here," Pru said. "What you doin' on my place?"

"I want to see the child," the man said.

"You ain't seein' any child," Pru said, "now git."

"God bless you," said the man.

"Same to you."

"I'll leave a few pamphlets if you like."

"What I'd *like* is you off my land now, an' you better do it quick."

The man turned and left.

"My boy isn't any freak," Pru shouted at his back. "I better not see your face again!"

She watched until the car disappeared. "Lord God," she said, and shook her head. They'd started showing up about June. She'd put a gate up, but they kept coming in. Black men in beards. White men in suits. Bald-headed men in yellow sheets. Foreign-looking men with white towels around their heads. Pru shooed them all out, but they wouldn't go away. I want to see the child, is what they said. The way they looked her in the eye flat gave Pru the creeps.

Pru stalked out to the truck. She looked for Uncle Fry. "You all goin' to leave my Cush alone," she said, mostly to herself. "I have to get me a 12-gauge and sit out on the road, you goin' to let my child be."

Uncle John Ezekiel Fry appeared, standing in the corn.

"Uncle Fry," Pru said, "you seen little Cush anywhere?"

"Goat shit," Uncle Fry said. *"Rat's ass-Atlanta, strawberry-pee . . ."*

"Thanks," said Pru, "you're sure a lot of help."

Pru knew where to find Cush. She left the pickup on the bridge, got her oatmeal, and started down the bank. You could leave that child in the house or on the porch. You could leave him on the steps out back. Whatever you did, Cush found his way to the bridge. The bridge was where he wanted most to be.

Pru squatted down and tried to see up in the dark, up past the last gray timbers of the bridge, up where the shadows met the web of ancient iron.

"You in there, Cush?" Pru said. "You tell me if you in there, child."

"*Mmmm-mupper-mudd*," said Cush.

"That's good," said Pru. She couldn't see Cush, but she knew that he was there. Up in the cavern of the bank, up where the pale and twisted roots hid out from the hot and muggy day.

"I'm leavin' your oatmeal, hon," Pru said. "I'd like you to eat it if you can."

Cush wouldn't, she knew, he never did. The bowls were always where she left them, full of happy ants and flies.

Pru drove up to where the highway met the road to make sure the gate was shut. The man in the Honda was gone. No one else was snooping 'round, which didn't mean they wouldn't be back. I might ought to hire someone, Pru thought. I might send up Uncle Fry. Uncle Fry just standing there would likely keep 'em out.

Driving back across the creek to the house, Pru could see the farm sprawled out in lush array. She could feel the green power there, wild and unrestrained. The air was thick with the ripe and heady smell of summer growth. Every leaf and every blade, every seed and every pod, seemed to quiver in the damp and steamy earth. Every fat green shoot pressed and tugged to reach the light, every blossom, every bud, fought to rip itself apart, fought to reach chromatic bliss.

Pru felt light-headed, slightly out of synch, like the time in Georgia when she'd found some good pot. The land seemed bathed in hazy mist. The corn and the house and the chinaberry trees were sharply etched in silver light. Everything was lemon, lavender, and pink, everything was fuzzy and obscure.

"Huh-unh," Pru said, "*no* way, I ain't havin' none of *that*."

She slammed on the brakes and ran quickly to the house. She moved through every single room and pulled all the curtains tight.

She took a cold shower and changed her clothes twice. Then she went to the kitchen and made herself a drink.

Pru knew exactly where all the funny colors came from. They were leftover colors from her dream, and she didn't care for that. She didn't need pastel, she needed bright. She didn't need fuzzy, she needed flat solid and absolutely right. Primary colors are the key. Real is where it's at. Special effects don't improve your mental health.

Pru had watched a TV show that said you ought to learn to understand your dreams. Lord help us, she thought, who'd want to go and do *that?*

Pru fixed herself another drink. "I don't want to see funny colors," she said. "I don't want to know about a dream. I don't want to know 'bout *any*thing, God, I don't already know *now*. . . ."

It surprised Cush to find out who he was. Sometimes, knowing made him glad. Sometimes, it frightened him a lot. One thing it did, though, was answer the questions he'd always had burning in his head. He knew what he was for. He knew for certain now what he had to do.

Cush didn't know *how* he knew, he just did. Mother didn't tell him and he didn't think it up by himself. Maybe he overheard the minnows in the creek. Minnows whisper secrets after dark. Maybe he heard it from the trees. Trees rumble on all the time. If you listen, you can learn a whole lot. If you listen real close, if you can stand to wait them out. A tree starts a word about April twenty-six, and drags it out till June.

Now I know, Cush thought. I know what it is I have to do. He felt he ought to be satisfied with that, he felt it ought to be enough. But Cush was only five. He hadn't had time to learn the end of one question is only the beginning of the next. He knew what he was for. He knew what it was he had to do. Now maybe someone would come and tell him *why* . . .

Cush heard the car stop on the bridge. The doors opened up and the people got out. Cush could see daylight through the planks. All the people wore white. The man and the woman and the boy, everybody spruced up, clean and shining white.

"Y'all stay here," the man said. "I'll drive up to the house."

"I'll read a verse and say a prayer," the woman said.

"Amen," said the little boy.

The man drove off. The woman sat down on a log. The little

boy leaned on the railing and spat into the creek.

"Don't wander off," the woman said, "don't wander off real far."

The woman sat and read. The boy watched minnows in the creek. He heard a bird squawk somewhere in the trees. He saw a toad hop off behind a bush. Mother said toads were Satan's pets, but the boy thought toads were pretty neat. He walked off the bridge into the woods. He followed the toad down to the creek.

Stay away, Cush cried out in his head. *Stay away, little boy, don't be coming down here!*

The little boy couldn't hear Cush. The woman was heavy into John 13, and didn't know the little boy was gone. The boy saw the toad a foot away. Cush heard the cottonmouth sleeping in the brush. He heard it wake up and find the toad, heard it sense breakfast on the way.

Cush sat up with a start. Nerve ends nibbled by gnats began to quiver with alarm. Blood began to flow through contaminated pipes. He knew what was coming, what had to happen next.

Don't do it, snake, Cush shouted in his head. *Don't you bite that little boy!*

Snake didn't seem to hear, snake didn't seem to care.

Can't you see that boy's dressed up clean and white? Can't you see that's someone you shouldn't oughta bite?

Cush tried hard to push the words out of his head, tried hard to toss them out, tried to hurl them at the snake. Snake didn't answer. Snake was trying hard to figure where toad ended and little boy began.

Cush could scarcely breathe. He felt the ragged oscillation of his heart. *You want to bite something, bite me,* he thought as hard as he could. *Leave that little boy alone and bite me!*

Snake hesitated, snake came to a halt. It listened and it waited, it forgot about toad and little boy. It turned its viper will to something down below the bridge.

Something white as dead feet slid down a pale vine, something black and wet moved inside a tree. Green snakes, mean snakes, snakes with yellow stripes, king snakes, ring snakes, snakes of every sort began to ripple whip and slither through the bush, began to find their way to Cush. They coiled around his leg and bit his thigh. They wound around his neck and kissed his eye. Rat snakes, fat snakes, canebrake rattlers, and rusty copperheads. Coral snakes, hog snakes, snakes from out of state. Snakes with cool and plastic eyes smelling dry and stale and sweet. White-bellied cottonmouths old as Uncle Fry, some big as sewer pipes, some near as fat as tractor tires.

Snakes hissed and snapped and curled about until Cush was out of sight. Snakes cut and slashed and tried to find a place to bite. And when the fun was all done, when the snakes had managed all the harm they could, they crawled away to find a nap.

Cush lay swollen and distended like a giant Thanksgiving Day balloon, like a lacerated blimp, like a great enormous bloat. Eight brands of venom chilled his blood and couldn't even make a dent. Seventeen diseases, peculiar to the snake, battled the corruption that coursed through Cush every day, tried and gave it up and did their best to get away.

"Mom, guess what," the boy said on the bridge, "I found me a big green toad."

"Sweet Jesus," mother said, "don't touch your private parts until you wash. You do, your thing'll fall right off!"

Mother turned to Psalms 91:3. A few minutes later, the car came back down the road. The man picked his family up fast. He'd faced Pru once and didn't care to try again.

Cush thought he heard the car drive away. He thought about the clean little boy. He thought about the nice white clothes. He wondered if his brand-new bites would bring the beetles and the gnats and the horseflies out in force.

It was nearly ten at night when Alma got the call from Preacher Will. Alma's heart nearly stopped. Oh Lord, she thought, it's Cush. Nothing short of death would get Will to use the phone. It's Pru, Will said, and you ought to come at once. What's wrong with Pru? Alma said, and Will rambled on about bad hygiene and mental fits.

Alma hung up. She was on the road at dawn, and at the gate at ten. There were cars parked up and down the highway, RVs and campers and several dozen tents. People stood about in the red dirt road. They sat and ate lunch beneath the trees. Uncle Fry stood guard, and he wouldn't let them in.

"Uncle Fry," Alma said, "what exactly's going on? What are these people doing here, and what on earth is wrong with Pru?"

"*Oyster pie*," said Uncle Fry. "*Comanche-cock-Tallahassee-stew* . . ."

"Well, you're looking real fine," Alma said.

Uncle Fry unlocked the gate and let her in. Alma drove down the narrow dusty road toward the bridge. It hadn't been a year since she'd been to see Pru, but she was struck by the way the place had changed. It had flat been a wonder before, springing up new from a worn-out tangle of decay, to a rich and fertile farm. She had marveled at the transformation then, but the land was even more resplendent now, more radiant and alive. The very air seemed to shine. Every leaf shimmered, every blade of grass was brilliant green. There were flowers that had certainly never grown here before. Birds that had never come near the place flashed among the trees.

Alma wondered how she'd write it down. That the worst farm in Alabama state was getting prettier every day? That scarcely said a thing. She wished she'd never started taking notes. All she had accomplished was to make herself more apprehensive, more uneasy than before. Putting things down made them seem like they were real. When you saw it on paper, it seemed as if the farm and little Cush and Uncle Fry, and Prudence Jean the millionaire, were just everyday events. And that simply wasn't so. Nothing was going on that made a lick of sense. Nothing that a reasonable person who was over sixty-five liked to think about at all.

"All right, I'm here," Alma said. "I want to know what's happening with Pru. I want to know what's going on. I want to know *why* those people are camping at the gate."

Preacher Will and Dr. Ben Shank were in the kitchen eating Velveeta cheese and ginger snaps. Oatmeal cookies and deviled ham. There were Fritos and Cheetos, Milky Ways and Mounds, dips and chips of every sort. Every soft drink known to man. Junk food stock was very likely trading high.

"Folks say they want to see the child," said Preacher Will, popping up a Nehi Orange. "More of 'em coming ever' day."

Alma stared at Will. "They want to see Cush? What for?"

"There's blueberry pie on the stove," said Will.

"You make sure those people stay out," Alma said. "Lord God, no wonder poor Pru's in a snit! What's wrong with her, Ben, besides that?"

"Hard to say," said Dr. Shank, digging in a can of cold pears. "Pixilation of the brain. Disorders of the head. Severe aberrations of the mind. The girl's unsettled somewhat. Neurons slightly out of whack."

Alma had never much cared for Ben Shank. What could you say about a man who'd spent his whole adult life working on the tonsil transplant?

"Fine," Alma said, "you want to kind of sum it up? What's the matter with her, Ben?"

"Pru's daffy as a duck."

"I wouldn't leave Satan out of this," said Will.

"Maybe *you* wouldn't, *I* would," Alma said. "Where's Pru now?"

"Up in her room. Been there for three whole days, and she won't come out."

"That girl needs care," said Dr. Shank. "You ought to keep that in mind. I know a real good place."

"The arch fiend's always on the prowl," said Will, "don't you think he's not."

"What I think I better do is see Pru," Alma said.

Alma made her way through the parlor to the hall. Through cartons from Kmart, Target, and Sears. Through tapes and cassettes, through a stack of CDs, past a tacky new lamp. Coming into money hadn't changed Pru's taste a whole lot.

Pru's room was nearly dark. The windows were covered up with blankets and sheets. The sparse bit of light that seeped in gave the room an odd undersea effect.

"Pru," Alma said, "you might want to talk me in. I don't care to fall and break a leg."

"I'm not crazy anymore," Pru said. "An' I don't care what that fool preacher says, I haven't got a demon in my foot."

"I know that," Alma said. She groped about and found a chair. "What you think's the matter with you, Pru? Why you sitting up here in the dark?"

Pru sat cross-legged in the middle of her bed. Alma couldn't see her face or read her eyes.

"If I'm sittin' in the dark, I can't *see*," Pru said. "I don't want to see a thing, Alma, seeing's what messes up my head."

"Pru, what is it you don't want to see," Alma said, almost afraid to ask. "You want to tell me that?"

"I ain't going to a loony house, Alma, that's a fact."

"Now, nobody's going to do that."

"I sit right here, I'll be fine. Long as I keep out the light."

"You don't like the light?"

"I flat can't take it no more," Pru said. "I can't stand anything *pink*. Everything's lavender or a wimpy shade of green. Everything's got a fuzzy glow. I'm sick to death of tangerine. I feel like I fell into a sack of them afterdinner mints. Lord, I'd give a dollar for a little piece of brown. I'd double that for something red."

Pru leaned forward on the bed. Alma reached out and found her hands. Her eyes were big and round and her hands were like ice.

"I'm scared, Aunt Alma," Pru said. "Corn don't come in baby blue. I never seen a apricot lettuce in my life. I *know* what's going on, I know that. Them Easter egg colors is leakin' through out of my dreams. They're comin' right in and I can't hold 'em back!"

Alma felt a chill, as if someone had pressed a cold Sprite against her back. She held on to Pru real tight.

"I haven't seen any blue corn," Alma said, "but I know what you're telling me, Pru. I want you to think on that, you understand? Hon, it isn't just *you*, it's not just something in your head. I could feel it driving in, like everything's humming in the ground. Like every growing thing on the place is just swelling up to bust."

Alma gripped Pru's shoulder and looked right in her eyes. "You've got about the prettiest farm there is, but you and I know it isn't how it *ought* to be. It doesn't look right, Pru, and it isn't any wonder that you're having color problems in your head. Shoot, this place'd send van Gogh around the bend."

"Oh God, Aunt Alma, I'm scared," said Pru. "I'm scared as I can be!"

Tears trailed down Pru's cheeks, and Alma took her in her arms.

"It's going to be fine," Alma said. "Don't you worry, it'll be just fine."

"You ain't goin' to leave me here, are you?"

"Child, I am staying right here," Alma said. "I'm not going anywhere at all."

Alma held her tight. She could feel Pru's tears, she could feel her body shake. I'm sure glad you're hugging real good, Alma thought, so you won't know that I'm scared, too.

Alma shooed Will and Dr. Shank out the door and started cleaning up the house. The kitchen took an hour and a half. She worked through geologic zones, through empty pizza cartons and turkey pot pies. Through Ritz Cracker boxes and frozen french fries. It might be that malnutrition was affecting Pru's head, Alma thought. A brain won't run in third gear on potato chips and Mounds.

She had the house in shape by late afternoon. Pru seemed

better, but she wouldn't leave her room. Alma was alarmed to learn that Cush stayed at the creek all the time, that he wouldn't come back to the house at all.

"It isn't right," Alma said. "A little boy shouldn't live beneath a bridge."

"Might be he shouldn't," Pru said, "but I reckon that he *is*."

Alma fixed Pru supper, and took a plate up to the gate for Uncle Fry. If Uncle Fry had moved an inch since she'd left him there at ten, she couldn't tell. The cars were still there. People stood outside the gate and looked in. They didn't talk or move about. Some of the men had awful wigs. Some of the men were bald. Some of the men wore bib overalls. More than a few wore funny robes. They all gave Alma the creeps. What did they want with *Cush*? What did they think they'd *see*? As far as that goes, how did they even know that Cush was *there*?

"I don't want to think about that," Alma said as she drove back toward the creek. "I've got enough on my mind with just Pru."

Alma left the car on the road and took some oatmeal down to Cush. She walked through tall sweet grass down a path beside the bridge, down through a canopy of iridescent green. The moment she saw the creek, she stopped still. The sight overwhelmed her, it took her breath away. Thick stands of fern lined the stream on either side. Wild red roses climbed the trunk of every tree. Fish darted quicksilver-bright through water clear as air. Farther toward the bend, red flag and coralroot set the banks afire.

There was more, though, a great deal more than the eye could truly see. Standing on the bank in dusky shade, standing by the creek in citron light, Alma felt totally at peace, suspended in the quiet, inconceivably serene. The rest of the farm seemed far away, stirring in the steamy afternoon, caught up in purpose and intent, caught in a fever, in a frenzy of intoxicated growth.

The creek was apart from all that. It was finished and complete, in a pure and tranquil state. Alma felt certain nothing more could happen here that could possibly enhance this magic place. She felt she was seven, she felt she was ten, she felt her sister Lucy by her side. And as she stood there caught up in the spell, lost in the enchantment of the day, her eyes seemed to draw her to the bridge, to the shadows under old and rusted iron.

Alma held her breath. Something seemed to flicker there, vague and undefined, something like a dazzle or a haze. A pale shaft dancing for an instant through the quiet. Dust motes captured in an errant beam of light. It was there and it was gone and it wasn't gone at all.

"Hello, Aunt Alma," Cush said.

Alma stood perfectly still. She felt incredibly calm, she felt frightened and alarmed, she felt totally at ease.

"Are you there, Aunt Alma, are you there?"

"I'm right here, Cush," Alma said. "I'm glad to see you're talking some better than you could." His voice was a croak, like gravel in a can. "I've brought you some oatmeal, hon. You need to eat something hot and good."

"Tell mother that I'm doing just fine," Cush said. "You tell her that for me."

"Now, you ought to tell her that yourself," Alma said, "that's what you ought to do. Cush, you shouldn't be staying down here. You shouldn't be out beneath a bridge."

"I'm where I ought to be," Cush said.

"Now, why you say that?"

"This is where I got to stay, this is where I got to be."

"You already told me that. What I'd like to know is *why*."

"This is where I am, Aunt Alma. Right here's where I got to be."

He may be different, Alma thought, but he's just as aggravating as any other child I've ever known.

"Now, Cush—" Alma said, and that's as far as Alma got. Words that might have been were never said. Alma was struck by a great rush of loneliness and joy, shaken to her soul by a wave of jubilation and regret, nearly swept away by chaos and accord.

As quickly as it came, the moment passed and let her go. Let her go but held her with the faint deep whisper of the earth. Held her with a hint of the sweet oscillation of the stars. She tried to remember the universal dance. Tried her best to hum the lost chord. There were things she had forgotten, there were things she almost knew. She hung on the restive edge of secrets nearly told, a breath away from mysteries revealed. She wondered if she'd died or if she'd just come to life. She wondered why they both looked just the same.

And when she found herself again, when her heart began to stir, she looked into the shadow of the bridge. She looked, and there was Cush. Cush, or a spiderweb caught against the sun; Cush, or a phantom spark of light.

"Cush, I know you're there," Alma said. "Cush, you *talk* to me, you hear?"

Alma stood and listened to the creek. She listened to a crow call far off in the trees. She listened and she waited in the hot electric summer afternoon. . . .

Pru wasn't any better and she wasn't any worse. Pastel shades were still clouding up her head. Mint seemed the color of the day. She said she felt she had a rash, and took three or four baths before dark. She soaked herself in European soap and rubbed Chinese lotions on her skin. Every hour and a half, she completely changed her clothes.

Alma couldn't take all the bathing and the changing and the scurrying about. It made her dizzy just to watch. She prowled through the kitchen, searching for anything that wasn't in a can or in a sack. Lord God, Alma thought, there's a garden outside that would bring Luther Burbank to tears, and Pru's got a corner on Spam.

She went outside and picked several ears of corn. She yanked up carrots big as Little League bats. She made a hot supper and a salad on the side, and took it up to Pru. Pru picked around awhile and wrinkled up her nose.

"What kinda stuff is this?"

"Those are vegetables, Pru. You probably never saw one before. We grow 'em all the time on Mars."

"I ain't real hungry right now."

"Pretend you've got Froot Loops and a Coke," Alma said. "I'll leave your plate here."

Alma went back downstairs and ate alone. She took a lot of time cleaning up. She did things she didn't have to do. She didn't want to think. She didn't want to think about Cush or what had happened at the bridge.

Nothing did any good at all. Cush was in her head and he wouldn't go away. "I don't even know what *happened* out there," Alma said. "I don't know if anything *did*."

Whatever it was, it had left her full of hope and disbelief, full of doubt and good cheer, full of bliss and awful dread. She felt she was nearly in tune, on the edge of perfect pitch. She felt she nearly had the beat. That's what he did, Alma thought. He gave me a peek somewhere and brought me back. Brought me back and never told me where I'd been.

Alma left the house and walked out onto the porch. The air was hot and still. Night was on the way, and the land and the sky were strangely green. It looked like Oz, right before the wizard came clean.

Oh Lord, Alma thought, looking out into the quickly fading light, I guess I knew. I knew and I didn't want to see. I wrote it all down and I thought that'd make it go away. The farm and the money and Uncle John Fry, nothing the way it ought to be. And all of that coming out of Cush. Coming from a child with awful skin and a baked potato head.

"Who *are* you, Cush?" Alma called into the night. "Tell me who you are, tell me what you got to do!"

The cornfield shimmered with luminescent light. The air seemed electric, urgent and alive, she could feel it as it danced along her skin, she could feel the night press upon the land, she could feel the deep cadence of the earth.

"It's going to happen," Alma said, and felt a chill. "It's going to happen and it's going to happen here. *Who are you, Cush?*" she said again. *"Tell me what it is you've got to do. . . ."*

Alma tried to rest. She knew she wouldn't get away with that. Not in Pru's house, and not tonight. She dozed now and then. She made tea twice. The wind picked up and began to shake the house. It blew from the north, then shifted to the south. Tried the east and tried the west, and petered out.

A little after one, she fell asleep. At two, she woke up with a start. Pru was screaming like a cat. Alma wrapped her robe around herself and made her way back up the stairs.

"Don't turn on the light!" Pru shouted when Alma opened up the door.

"Pru, I'm getting tired of trying to find you in the dark," Alma said. She felt her way around the walls. A glow from downstairs showed her Pru. She was huddled on the floor in the corner by the bed. She was shaking like a malted-milk machine, and her eyes were fever bright.

"Pru, what's the *matter* with you, child?" Alma sat down and held her tight.

"Oh God," Pru said, "my whole insides are full of fleas. It might be fire ants or bees, it's hard to tell. They're down in my fingers and my toes. They're crawling in my knees."

Alma felt Pru's head. "I'd say you're right close to a hundred and three. I'll find you an aspirin somewhere. I'll make a cup of tea."

"I've got some Raid beneath the sink, you might bring me

some of that. Oh Jesus, Aunt Alma, I'm scared. I think something's wrong with Cush. I think he needs his mama bad. I think I better go and see."

"I don't think Cush needs a thing," Alma said. "I think Cush is doing fine. Pru, you better come downstairs and sleep with me. We'll keep off all the lights."

"Don't matter," said Pru. "Dark helps some, but it don't keep the pinks from sneakin' in. I can take them limes, I can tolerate the peach, but I can't put up with pink."

"I'll get a pill," Alma said. "You try and get some sleep."

Alma helped Pru back into bed and went out and closed the door. Lord God, she thought, I don't know what to do. You can't hardly reason with a person's got decorator colors in her head.

Alma's watch said a quarter after three. She didn't even try to go to bed. She sat in the kitchen and drank a cup of tea. She tried not to think about Cush. She tried not to think about Pru. Everything would work itself out. Everything would be just fine. She could hear Pru pacing about. Walking this way and that, humming a Ray Charles tune. Likely works good in the dark, Alma thought.

At exactly four o'clock, the lights began to flicker on and off. The wind came up again, this time blowing straight down. Alma knew high-school science by heart, and she'd never heard of *that*. Cups and dishes rattled on the shelves. The teapot slid across the sink. Cabinets and drawers popped open all at once. Peanut butter did a flip, and food from overseas hopped about.

Alma held on to the Kenmore stove. She knew that Sears made their stuff to last. In a moment, the rumbles and the shakes came abruptly to a halt. The wind disappeared, and Alma's ears began to pop. Something spattered on the window, something drummed upon the roof, and the rain began to fall. Alma ran into the parlor and peeked out through the blinds. Pink lightning sizzled through the corn. Every bush and every tree, every single blade of grass, was bathed in pale coronal light. Light danced up the steps and up the porch and in the house. It danced on the ceiling, on the walls, and on the floor. It crawled along the tables and the lamps.

Lord, Alma thought, this isn't going to set well with Pru. She listened, but she didn't hear a sound from upstairs. Pru wasn't singing anymore, but she wasn't up stomping or crying out.

The rain stopped as quickly as it came. Alma stepped out onto the porch. The very air was charged, rich and cool and clean. It made Alma dizzy just to breathe. The sky overhead was full of stars. The first hint of morning started glowing in the east, darts of color sharp as northern lights. And as the day began to grow, as the shadows disappeared, Alma saw them everywhere about, people standing in the road, people standing in the corn, people standing everywhere, and everyone looking past the field and through the woods, everyone looking toward the bridge.

Alma looked past the corn, past the people and the trees. Something pure and crystal bright struck her eyes, something splendid as a star, something radiant and white. Alma caught her breath. She looked at the light and she laughed and cried with joy. She felt she ought to sing. She felt goofy in the head, she felt lighter than a gnat. She felt as if someone had shot her up with bliss.

"It's going to happen," Alma said, "it's going to happen and it's going to happen here!"

Alma couldn't stay put. She couldn't just stand there with glory all about. She sprang off the porch and started running down the road. She hadn't run like that since she was ten. She ran down the road past the people, toward the bridge. The people sang and danced, the people swayed and clapped their hands. Alma passed Uncle John Ezekiel Fry. Uncle Fry grinned from ear to ear, and the light sparked off his tears.

"He's coming!" people shouted. "He's coming and he's just about here!"

"I can see him," someone said. "I can see him in the light!"

Alma was sure she heard bells, a deep sonorous toll that touched her soul and swept her clean. A noise like a thunderclap sounded overhead. Alma looked up, and the air was full of birds. Storks and cranes and gulls, hawks and terns and doves, eagles and herons, every kind of bird there was.

Alma laughed at the sky, Alma laughed at the bells, Alma laughed at the music in her head. It was Basin Street jazz, it was Mozart and Bach, it was old-time Gregorian Rock.

Alma couldn't see the road and she couldn't see the bridge. She felt enveloped and absorbed. She felt like she was swimming in the light. It dazzled and it glittered and it sang. It hummed through her body like carbonated bees. It looked like the center of a star. It looked like a hundred billion fireflies in a jar.

"I *knew* you were something special, Cush," Alma cried. "I knew that, Cush, but I got to say I never guessed *who!*"

The light seemed to flare. It drowned her in rapture, an overdose of bliss. It was much too rich, too fine, and too intense. It drove her back with joy, it drove her back with love. It lifted her and swept her off her feet. It swept her up the road and past the field and past the yard, and left her on the porch where she'd begun.

"Better not get too close," someone said. "Better not get too near the light."

"That's my grand-nephew," Alma said, "you likely didn't know that. I guess I can do about anything I please."

Cush knew who he was. He knew what he was for. He knew what it was he had to do. And now, for the first time in his short and dreary life, in a life full of misery and pain, in a life filled with every dire affliction you could name, Cush knew the reason *why*. When he knew, when it came to him at last, Cush was overwhelmed with the wonder of the thing he had to do. It was awesome, it was fine, it was a marvel and a half, and Cush laughed aloud for the first time in his life.

And in that very instant, in the echo of his laugh, the spark that had smouldered in his soul, that had slept there in the dark, burst free in a rush of brilliant light. The light was the power, and Cush was the light, and Cush reached out and drew everything in. Everything wrong, everything that wasn't right. He drew in envy and avarice and doubt. He called in every plague and every blight. He called in every tumor, every misty cataract. He called in AIDS and bad breath. Ingrown toenails, anger, and regret. The heartbreak of psoriasis, the pain of tooth decay. Migraines and chilblains, heartburn and cramps. Arthritic joints and hemorrhoids. Spasms and paralytic strokes. Hatred and sorrow and excess fat. Colic and prickly heat and gout.

Cush drew them all in, every sickness, every trouble, every curse, and every pain. Cush called them down and drew them into healing light, where they vanished just as if they'd never been.

"*I got it all sopped up, I did what I came to do,*" Cush cried. "*I got everything looking real fine!*"

Cush was the power, and Cush was the light. He was here and he was there, he was mostly everywhere. He could see Cincinnati, he could see Bangladesh. He could see Aunt Alma, see her rushing up the stairs. He could see his mother's room filled with swirls of pastel light. He could see her as she cried out with joy and surprise, see the wonder in her face, see the beauty in her smile as something blossomed inside her, blossomed for a blink and then appeared with silver eyes.

"*Got it all ready for you, little sister,*" Cush called out from the light. "*Got it looking real fine, just as pretty as can be. I've done about all there is to do!*"

All the people standing in the road and in the field saw the light begin to quiver hum and shake, saw it rise up from the bridge, saw it rush into the early morning light.

"*Hallelujah,*" said Uncle John Fry, standing in the tall green corn. "*hallelujah-Chattanooga-bliss. . . .*"

Class of '61

Daniel spent the afternoon hacking weeds and second growth off the runway. Sweating felt reasonably good. Maybe he'd start helping in the garden. Not every day, but now and then. In the sparse shade of mesquite, he watched ants dismember a beetle. He felt they were overrated. Sheer number gave the appearance of organization. A thousand of anything looked efficient. He drank from a Mason jar, and ate the sandwiches Doreen had fixed. The plane appeared at six out of a hard metallic sky, engines high-pitched and out of synch. It circled and drifted in slightly askew, buoyed on distorting waves of heat. The plane was something odd and unexpected, a museum-quality relic the color of slag. It gave him a childish surge of pleasure to see the boxy shape of corrugated iron and know its name. Junkers Ju-52 trimotor. Milk Duds, seven years old, Movietone News.

The wheels touched down and puffed rubber, engines stopping almost at once. A ladder appeared, and John and Hannah climbed down—Hannah, without hesitation; John, as if the ladder might keep on extending down until the earth swallowed him up. The Junkers revved up and rattled off, lumbering like a goose. Hannah looked good. The years had scarcely touched her. She wore a loose Moroccan robe, slate gray and mixed with the color of some yellow desert fruit. In the backdraft of the engines, the robe defined her figure. Susan Hayward on safari. John looked detached. Lean and awkward in a rumpled black suit. He held a panama hat in both hands, working the brim like beads. His white hair was receding, cut short by someone in a hurry. Hannah took the lead, quick assertive steps through the weeds. Hoppers got out of the way. She grasped the small duffel like a weapon, telegraphing her mood, stopping short of Daniel.

"You asshole," she said, "what *is* this?"

"Hello, Hannah. It's been a long time."

"What the fuck am I doing here, Daniel? I want to know that right now."

"You might not want to show anger," Daniel said. "They're not that close, but they don't like it."

"Oh Jesus." Hannah looked dismayed.

"You've no right to bring us here," John said. Daniel waited, but that was it. John still wasn't good at getting mad.

"Let's get going," Daniel said. "I want to be in before dark." He turned and walked toward the pickup across the field.

"I am flat *not* leaving here," Hannah said.

Daniel got in the truck. Hannah's string of curses were lost in a sudden wave of sound. The plane teetered around and gathered speed. The pilot waved at no one in particular. A dark man in a turban. A crazed Azerbaijan, more than happy to be gone.

He drove from the airport through empty streets, now and then stealing a glance at Hannah. Still the classic nose, the Nefertiti neck or maybe Lubbock—now strung with copper and silver hammered in the North African fashion. There were white strands in her hair, but not many. Hannah and John didn't speak. Daniel flushed a herd of white-tailed deer. The deer raced behind a Safeway and disappeared. He drove John and Hannah past the college, thinking they'd like to see it. John showed marginal interest. Hannah looked straight ahead. He wound through residential streets into the hilly part of town. Light was beginning to fade. He turned off at the curving gravel drive and stopped almost at once under the trees.

"We walk from here," he said. "I don't take the truck any closer." He was startled by Hannah's look. She seemed on the edge of bolting. "It's okay," he said.

"You just shut up. You just goddamn don't talk to me."

He turned her around, touching her for the first time. "Don't do that, Hannah. You're mad at me, that's fine. Just don't show it *here*."

Hannah didn't answer. She looked angry but subdued. He couldn't guess what John was thinking. The cross on John's chest caught the feeble light. He led them up the road, past hot summer smells, live oak and dust. Cicadas droned in the trees. He sensed a certain thickness in the air. The lake was dark through heavy branches. There were lanterns in the downstairs windows of the house. The house was white, columned, and imposing. Country club out of Tara, close to what Daniel's father had imagined. The paint was peeling badly, gentility gone to pot.

"It's still there," John said, with some wonder. Hannah gave him a look, as if he might be simple-minded. Still, Daniel saw she felt it, too, coming back after all these years, and was trying not to show it.

Katie met them at the door, looking kittenish and sly. Doreen came partway out of the kitchen, holding back, tall and elusive. Daniel made introductions. Hannah let him know that she knew exactly what was going on here.

"Katie'll take lamps up to your rooms," Daniel said. "You can clean up if you like, and we'll have supper."

Hannah stood her ground. "What I want now is a drink. Then I want to talk. Right now. In that order."

John nodded vague agreement.

"All right," Daniel said, "that's fine. I just thought you'd like to rest, get something to eat."

"Don't look wounded," Hannah said. "You don't do it nearly as well as you used to." She smiled sweetly at Katie. "I'll bet you're a comfort to Uncle Dan."

"I'll bet I am," Katie said.

"Christ. I hope you've got Scotch."

John took the chair by the empty fireplace. Hannah found a bottle and plopped on the sofa. Far right side. Daniel stood by the mantel. Everyone knows their places, he thought. Nothing and everything has changed.

"I know you don't want to be here," he said. "I'm sorry. They want something, They just do it. We've got to go along with that. If something goes wrong, that's not good."

"Not good for you," Hannah said.

"Maybe not good for anyone, Hannah." Daniel downed his drink. "What we've got is this *apparition*. Something like that, I don't know. They've seen it down there, and They don't like it. They want me to get rid of it."

Hannah looked startled. "They've got a *ghost?* You're talking about a spook?"

"Maybe. Whatever it is, They want it out of their burrows."

"I wish you'd left me alone," Hannah said. She looked at John. "You going to just sit there, or what? Well, of course you are. You always did."

"What do you want me to do?" John said.

"You see?" She turned on Daniel. "I know what goes on in your head. You get some crazy idea, and that's it. Well, I don't do that anymore, so you're wasting your time. You can't just call up spirits any time you happen to feel like it. Anyway, I think I was a fake."

"We can talk about it tomorrow," Daniel said.

"This room looks just like it did," John said. His smile seemed out of place. He stood and fingered the spines of books.

"I hope I'm dreaming all this," Hannah said.

"John looks the same. You look good, Hannah. You haven't changed a lot."

"Oh, that's *real* nice," Hannah said.

"I didn't mean any offense."

"You never did. That's what makes you such a son of a bitch, Daniel. Christ. I haven't had good whiskey in years." She looked unsteady. John was simply wandering around.

"You've had a long trip," Daniel said. "Be a good idea to get some rest."

"Uh-huh." Hannah looked sly and slightly fierce. "Don't want to keep your chippies waiting."

"All right, now."

"All right, now," Hannah mocked.

John came over and helped her to her feet. Hannah didn't resist.

"I don't have to tell you to stay inside," Daniel said.

"You're interfering with our lives," John said. It seemed another conversation entirely. "I feel you're assuming a lot."

"I'm sorry."

"I'm going to pray for you, I think."

"It couldn't hurt."

"You talk to Jesus," Hannah said, "you tell Him I don't need this shit. You tell Him that."

He thought about Hannah and John. He counted years in his

head. It seemed to be twenty-seven. It didn't seem that long . . . and it did. Hannah and John and Daniel, musketeers, flaunting their friendship, reminding each other daily how close they were. And then Daniel and Hannah taking the friendship a big step further, John shyly backing off and accepting. They invented threesome tennis, roared through the hill country in Daniel's MG, or rushed down to Houston for a party. Daniel played at architecture; Hannah made a brief stab at English. John took every philosophy course he could find. Wore his Nietzsche shirt every day. This was before he startled the other two by announcing, out of the blue, that he'd found a higher calling than German thinkers. All that long and steamy summer, before a senior year that never came. Lovemaking that John always pretended not to hear, just as he pretended not to see Hannah sleek as an otter in the lake, and Daniel knowing he did, and wondering what God could possibly have that Hannah didn't. And Hannah's famous séances, every Saturday night. John scoffing, during his philosophical phase, disapproving later for reasons at the other end of the spectrum.

And then it was over, although it seemed as if they'd hardly started on their lives. Something came from somewhere, quietly and with no fuss at all. No starships or death-rays, no sense of the dramatic. They simply *came*. Nothing changed. Everything was exactly as it had been. Except for the people. Most of the people were simply *gone*. There one minute, and not the next. And nearly thirty years later, neither Daniel nor anyone else knew where all the people had gone, or what *They* were. He knew that They'd apparently come to stay. He knew that there weren't many of Them. That not many was enough. He knew that the ones that lived close by his house, under the earth, had a spook, and wanted it gone.

Daniel watched the curtains billow and heard the clock downstairs, heard frogs at the lake and felt Doreen's sweet breath on his shoulder. The young slept soundly. Nothing seemed to wake them. He pulled on his shorts and opened the wide French doors, stepped out on the balcony that circled the upper floors, and saw that John was already there. The night was half gone, and he was still fully dressed.

"You shouldn't be out here," Daniel said.
"Couldn't sleep. Did you think I could?"
"I'd feel a lot better if you just cussed me out good, John."
"Would that help?"

"I hope this isn't a sermon."

"I can't get over this. It all looks the same."

"It's not," Daniel said.

Clouds whipped over the moon. The grounds, the dark lawn that swept up from the house to the terraced hill, wavered and seemed fluid. His father had built a colonnaded temple atop the hill during a brief Ionic fit. A copy of something-or-other in Greece, Daniel couldn't remember what. It seemed chalky and tenuous among the trees.

"That was my favorite place," John said. "It looks best at night. Sort of Maxfield Parrish. Very unchristian, I suppose." He didn't look at Daniel. "Where are They? I mean, do you know?"

"No," Daniel said. He didn't want to talk about this. "The burrows are all over. Deep, I guess."

"They don't stay down there all the time."

Daniel didn't answer.

"I don't think I can handle this," John said. His voice seemed oddly detached.

"Don't think about Them."

"We've got a hundred and seven people in Cardiff. It's a nice little place. Maybe a hundred more up at Glasgow. There's a burrow at York, but They don't seem to bother anyone. Hannah says there are eighty-two people in Morocco. A few more in Kenya. Nobody's in Europe, I know that."

"I don't think it does any good to count," Daniel said.

"Those girls you have here. . . ."

"There's a settlement in Fort Worth. Pretty big one. They come from there. Why don't you get some sleep, John? There's a bottle of good brandy downstairs."

"Those young people being here is a sin, Daniel."

"They don't mind sinning that much," Daniel said. "You think about that brandy."

"I wonder what They *did* with everyone?" John said. "I wonder where everybody is?" He looked at Daniel, but didn't appear to see him. He seemed to wander accidentally back to his room.

Daniel heard Doreen sigh in her sleep. The temple seemed misty, indistinct. A slight hot breeze, and last year's leaves rattling across marble steps. Trees formed ragged shadow, the night seemed tangible and immense. Daniel went back to bed. If anything was out there, he didn't want to know it.

Hannah looked fresh, ready to go ten rounds with Daniel. John looked wasted, as if Hannah's hangover had somehow found the wrong room. Doreen stayed in the kitchen. Katie served breakfast and Hannah looked her over. Katie met her eyes, confirming mischief. No way Hannah could put her down, and Hannah began to see this and left her alone. She went through venison steak and hotcakes and tea. John picked at his food, and Daniel said nothing about it.

"I'm not saying I can or I can't," Hannah said, picking up the conversation from the night before. "It'll have to be at night. I guess in the library, the way we used to do it." She winked at John. "I'll flush it out, you toss wine and cookies on its tail."

"I guess you think that's funny," John said. He crossed himself, a halfhearted gesture. He spoke to Daniel but looked at Hannah. "I don't want any part of this. You've got your medium. You don't need a priest."

"I don't know exactly what I need," Daniel said.

"The Church doesn't recognize spiritualism," John said. "You ought to know that."

What church? Daniel wondered. John might be the only priest in the world. John would be aware of that, too, but it wasn't a point Daniel cared to make.

"I'm glad you're willing to try," Daniel said. "I appreciate it, Hannah."

"Fuck appreciation," Hannah said. "I want to get *out* of this place."

John stayed in his room, maybe storing up grace. Daniel showed Doreen how he wanted the fence done to keep deer out of the lettuce. He looked for Hannah, and found her past the house near the lake. She had trimmed down jeans to make shorts. Moroccan sun had browned her; twenty-seven years didn't seem that long ago. She heard him coming but didn't face him. The tennis courts were flat desolation, veined with tufts of grass hard as rope. Trumpet vines covered the high backdrop fence, a sagging plane of green.

"I wasn't ever much good," Daniel said. "It was mostly your game. You and John."

Hannah almost smiled, but thought better of it. "I didn't think I could get out of the house. I've never been this close to where They stay. I'm scared out of my socks, you want to know. I guess you've seen Them; I don't know if I want to ask that or not."

"Daytime's all right," he told her. "Stay down here and around the house. Don't go up the hill."

She looked at him, a question put quickly aside. He counted

years in her face, the planes of her cheeks. If drink had done damage, he couldn't see it. She wasn't nineteen anymore, but her eyes were clear as crystal.

"You got everything ready for tonight? Anything you need, ask the girls."

"It's a *séance*, Daniel, not a Broadway play." She looked at the house, shuddered at something she couldn't see. "Jesus. How do you stay in this place?"

"I've never lived anywhere else."

"That's not a reason."

He walked past her to the lake. Willows hung in the water, a sunfish flashed in the shallows. "We used to have a lot of fun here."

"Oh God, don't start on that!" The acid in her laughter surprised him. "I don't need any shit about fun college days and the big game. I've had a pretty lousy life."

"I'm sorry."

"Thanks."

"I wish you'd stayed here, Hannah. I wish you hadn't gone."

Hannah looked pained. "As I recall, Daniel, one girl wasn't enough. You had to try whoever was left. For Christ's sake, you're still doing it."

"Why do you take everything the wrong way?"

"Oh, right." She gave him a curious look. "You want to tell me something, Daniel? How did you get us back here? You just have Them send us a ticket? Did you see that goddamn plane?"

The idea was frightening and absurd. "I don't *talk* to them, Hannah."

"Just leave little notes under a rock, right?"

"It's not like that at all. They—let you know things sometimes."

"Not me, they don't," Hannah said.

Daniel looked somewhere else. Hannah was still there. "I've been here a long time. Maybe it's different when They live this close to people. Once They wanted old books. I *knew* that. I don't know how. I knew they had a ghost. I knew you and John were coming. Maybe They got you out of my head; hell, I don't know." He faced her. "Look. Before that, I didn't even know if you and John were still alive."

"Well, we are. My luck's running rotten as ever. What happens when this is over? What happens to *me?*" The life seemed to go out of her eyes. He thought that he'd feel better without her anger. Instead, he was somehow uneasy, disconcerted, as if he'd seen her more than naked.

"They don't care, Hannah," he said. "They just want this done."

"Is that so?"

"They don't care," he said, aware that he was saying this again.

"Go molest someone," Hannah said. "Leave me the hell alone."

"The lady doesn't like you very much," Katie said.

"I expect she's got a reason," Daniel said.

"You two used to get it on, huh?"

"He doesn't want to talk about that," Doreen said. "That's private."

"Well, I am *so* sorry, everyone." Katie cleaned mud off a bottle of wine. She cooled wine deep in the lake and pulled the bottles out on a string.

"It doesn't matter," Daniel said.

"The priest isn't feeling real good," Doreen said. "I took him up soup, but he didn't eat it."

"Religious people don't eat a whole lot."

"Why not?"

"They just don't."

"He's not bad looking," Katie said. "For a guy your age, I mean."

"He'll be delighted," Daniel said. "I know I am."

Katie laughed. Doreen looked disapproving. Doreen was a ferret in bed, a prude during most of her waking hours. Katie was just the other way. Daniel couldn't figure either one. "Water the wine good," he told Katie. "I don't want our witch getting whacked."

"We don't have to be *in* there, do we?" Doreen asked. It was easy to see how she'd vote.

"No," Daniel said, "of course you don't. Go to bed and stay there, is my advice."

They seemed relieved. As if they were afraid he might have asked them to do something they didn't want to do. Maybe he didn't really know them at all.

"This is ridiculous," Hannah said. "I feel like a complete fool."

"It'll come back to you," Daniel said. "You used to be great."

"I used to put on a great show, is what I did."

"That's not true. Some spooky things happened."

"You saw what you wanted to see. You lifted up the table with your legs."

"Not always," Daniel said.

"I am not staying in here for this," John announced.

"I think you need to, John. You're part of it." Doreen was right. John had lost his color.

"Wait," Hannah said, "I'm getting something now." She pressed her fingers to her head and closed her eyes. "Yes, I *see* it. Katie's missed her period. You are greatly distressed."

"Damn it, Hannah!" John was clearly furious. Hannah looked surprised and slightly askew. Daniel decided that the liquor wasn't secure. She'd likely filched a bottle during the day.

"Is it all right if I ask a simple question," John said, "or is that out of order in all this?"

"Ask," Daniel said.

"How long has this—haunting thing been going on? Do we know that?"

"Why the sudden interest?" Hannah said.

"I'm asking as a person, not as a priest. This isn't a priest question, Hannah."

"I can't give you a good answer," Daniel said.

"Why not?"

"I don't know. I know maybe three things about Them, John. They don't like machines. They like it quiet. They don't mind us if we're not—aggressive. I don't think They pay much attention to us at all. I can't answer your question, because I don't think They see *time* passing the way we do. Don't ask me for ten examples, Hannah, which is what you're about to do. I can't explain that. I've been here for a long while, and I've got ideas about things. I'm saying that I don't know if this spook's been around six weeks or six years. I don't think they *measure* time like that."

"Oh, that's a big help," Hannah said.

"Anyway, what difference does it make?" Daniel asked.

"Not any, I guess." John shrugged and crossed his legs. "Just wondered if it was their ghost or ours."

"Jesus." Hannah looked alarmed.

"It's a pointless question," Daniel said, irritated at John.

"Not to me, it isn't," Hannah said. "I'm not calling up a dead one of *theirs*."

"You're a fake. What do you care?"

"What if I'm not?" Hannah said. "Someone get me a goddamn drink."

Daniel felt frightened and foolish. It was an odd and unstable emotional mix. The darkness was complete, the moon playing tricks. Maybe a dog would howl. He tried to remember what Lon Chaney looked like, and couldn't. John sprawled in his chair, protesting all this with bad posture. A candle sputtered in a dish. They held hands. Hannah's hand was wet, or maybe his. John's was dry as stone.

"Okay," Hannah said suddenly, "so is anybody here, or what?"

John laughed, apparently unable to help it.

"Get serious," Daniel said.

"You want to be medium, go ahead."

Hannah leaned back and took a breath. Getting serious, Daniel supposed, or giving it a try. Her hand tightened in his, and Daniel watched the candle set them apart, isolate them with some sort of magic. The old high ceilings, the dark polished shelves, were outside this sphere of light, the three of them within. Hannah's lids fluttered, possibly part of the act. She muttered to herself, the sound reaching Daniel like summer bees. He caught John's eye. John was looking right at Hannah, head tilted to one side and slightly perplexed. The expression dogs get when they try to understand what people say.

Daniel was thinking that this was pleasant in a way, that the three of them were here. They weren't who they'd been, but who was? And, nudging this thought like one layer of water slightly cooler than the next, what he was going to do when this gypsy act folded and he still had a ghost or whatever it was down below, disturbing Things he didn't want disturbed in any way. The thought never went further than that because Hannah suddenly went rigid and hurt his hand. Something terrible and cold had found them. Something clearly puzzled by them as well, ethereally confused. There was a cry Daniel imagined as that of a mouse in the clutches of an owl, but apparently coming from Hannah, who was pressed flat against her chair, shaking like electric shock treatment forty-nine.

"Oh Jesus, oh Jesus. . . ." Hannah seemed stuck on this and made no effort to move. Daniel thought to look at John, and found a sack of kittens. Drowned maybe three or four days. John soaked in sweat, hair and clothes stuck to his skin. Daniel carried him without effort to the couch. Katie and Doreen appeared in the door, frightened and disheveled, scared out of an adolescent ménage he'd seemingly missed.

"Get some water," Daniel said, "hurry."

The girls vanished. Daniel checked Hannah and saw nothing new. And then he *felt* it, a clearly perceptible grind, massive and unconfined, somewhere below the house. He knew at once that the spook had been down there as well, that it was still haunting the burrows. That Something wasn't very happy about it at all. He hoped his heart would stop. Katie and Doreen returned with water. John opened his eyes, but didn't speak. Daniel left him to the girls, and found Scotch behind Blackwood and Poe.

"You okay?" he asked Hannah.

"Oh, I'm just fine," Hannah said. "Do I look fine to you?" She drank out of the bottle, glancing over at John. "I wish I had something to shoot you with."

"I didn't know this would happen."

"You're getting me out of this place in the morning. Early. You're going to do that, Daniel."

"We stirred up our spook, Hannah. I don't know if it's gone."

Hannah looked appalled. "You think I'm going to do that *again?*"

"We'll have to think of something else."

"Like what?"

"I don't know. Get some sleep."

"You better not have any guns around here. You better not, or I'll find them."

Doreen and Katie seemed to enjoy playing nurse. They fussed over John and got him to sit in a chair on the porch. John drank tea, and when the girls would leave him alone, he watched the morning sun pattern the temple on the hill. Daniel studied him from the yard, and decided that he wasn't looking at anything at all. He was filtering out images maybe two or three feet in front of his eyes.

"The lady's bombed out real good," Katie reported. "I looked in a couple of times."

"Let her be," Daniel said. He watched Katie assume an unlikely angle in the cane-bottom chair in the kitchen, brown limbs tangled in the legs. Doreen stopped moving sometimes, but Katie didn't.

"Me and Doreen were scared," Katie said.

"I guess you were," Daniel said.

"You going to fix this?"

"I hope maybe I can. You want to stay or go? You do whatever you want."

"I think maybe stay. Doreen says we're better off."

"What do you say?"

"Nothing. I don't care. I don't want to be scared too much, is all."

"I'm sorry that happened," Daniel said.

"I guess so," John said.

Daniel didn't like the way he looked. He hadn't seemed bad in the morning. Now his skin had the texture of stuff on a pond. As if he'd had some disease a long time and wasn't getting any better.

"My house in Cardiff is quite small," John said. "I could get one bigger if I liked. There are hundreds of houses around. A smaller place seemed better for a priest. I guess that's a sin of false something. If I think about having a finer house, the sin's the same."

"I think you ought to do what you want," Daniel said.

"You mean get a better house? What kind do you recommend?"

"I don't know anything about that, John."

"I think maybe Georgian. There's a certain dignity to that. Of course dignity's close to pride. It seems to me it is."

"You know anything about exorcism, John?"

"Do I what?"

"Exorcism, you know. The Church has something on it. I don't know just what, that's your department. You feel a little better, we could talk."

John seemed to partially emerge. "Go fuck yourself, Daniel. Go fuck yourself in a ditch. I'll live anywhere I like. Architectural style is up to me. Go in peace, if you want."

"That was a shitty thing to do," Hannah said. "Katie told me. You ought to just leave him alone."

Girl talk with Katie. This was something new. "John's doing theological battle," Daniel said. "He experienced something he didn't think he believed."

"That's good. Psychology coming from you."

"I've got to get this ghost business cleared up," Daniel said. "If John can help, I've got to ask. That spook didn't come from any table tipping, Hannah."

"He's not going to help in the state he's in," Hannah said. "Anyway, how do you know that? You said it last night. That you didn't think it was gone. How do you *know?*"

"I don't. That's what I think." He couldn't tell her that there was great dissatisfaction below the ground. She wouldn't want to hear about that. "What else did Katie tell you?"

"Don't worry. We discussed Moroccan cooking."

"Katie's never cooked anything in her life."

"Maybe she's getting domestic. Maybe she's building a nest." Hannah laughed at Daniel's alarm. "Should have thought of that, friend. You can't run a Girl Scout troup without maybe baking a cookie."

Katie seemed perplexed at Daniel's concern. He realized that Hannah was still adroit at hooking him cleanly through the gills. He didn't need that at the moment. There was a problem that needed solving. *Right now.* He couldn't tell them what would happen if it wasn't. He didn't have the slightest idea, and didn't want to try to guess.

It was clear now that John couldn't help. The séance had left him addled. Escaping the girls' care, he had left the front porch and wandered off. Doreen called Daniel. Daniel found John at the tennis courts, chopping with a hoe at thirty years of weedy neglect. He worked at a fever pitch. Divine infusion had given him strength. He worked in pajamas and a straw hat.

"God wants me back in tennis," he said cheerfully. "My backhand was a problem. I think I've got it licked."

"Good," Daniel said. "You want to come in for supper?"

"We'll have to resurface the whole thing."

"I'll see to it." He led John back to the house. John voiced concern with misuse of the Doric arch. Katie got him to bed.

Doreen burned supper, and that seemed to set the tone for the evening. Katie asked pointless questions about birds. Only Hannah seemed unaffected. She didn't drink, which told Daniel something. He caught expectant looks around the table. As if he might announce a lottery winner.

"I went up to Tangier," Hannah said. "Last winter. There are twenty-two people up there. Mostly men. They all live in this one house. The whole city's vacant, but they live in this one crappy house. I made them Swedish meatballs and creole shrimp. It seemed to have some aphrodisiacal effect."

Doreen wanted to know what that was.

"I'll be in the library," Daniel said, uncertain he could handle any more of this. It seemed the thing to do. He felt he was a barometer for the group. That if they didn't have him there, the pressure would ease. That didn't make a lot of sense. He couldn't tell them what to do. He didn't know himself. The books he'd found were popular tales of ghosts in British castles. They didn't seem to apply. In no case were the hauntees more frightening than the haunters.

Hannah came in. "I thought I'd get a drink," she said.

"I'd feel a lot better if you did," Daniel told her.

"You look like Vincent Price in here. The girls wanted to know who Mickey Mouse was. That led in several odd directions. They don't know anything, do they? I forget how much is gone."

"I guess so." Hannah moved with remembered grace. When she'd stepped off the plane, he'd seen a past Hannah projected. There was no longer the illusion that she was young, which likely meant he wasn't, either.

"They giggled about Kotex," Hannah said. "Doreen said she thought she'd seen a Coke once. Daniel, I am fairly scared right now. I feel *something* . . . I don't know what."

"I'm sorry, Hannah."

"I don't know how you could do this to me. If you say you're sorry again, I'll break this bottle over your head."

"I think maybe I'll check on John."

"You do that," Hannah said. "He's talking about a doubles match with Jesus. He thinks Katie's a nun. I hope you're happy with this circus."

He couldn't imagine sleep. Doreen tried to get something going, mostly out of the jitters. Daniel didn't respond. He lay awake and listened to her breathe. When he was little, he was frightened every night. In this house. He'd thought every night about gorillas. Gorillas were very big in the forties. They terrorized natives in the movies, and followed you home to bed. You had to fight sleep and watch the window. And now he was watching it again. He'd learned to live with what was there because They were more abstract than something real. Like being frightened of God. You vaguely followed the rules and hoped for the best. Now it didn't seem like that at all.

He thought about Hannah. Lazy afternoons in the bed he was sleeping in now. Hannah scarcely older than Doreen. The smells sharp and clean, the heady odor of love and Pall Malls, the residue of baby oil and iodine that turned Hannah gold as a magazine ad. The memory maybe sweeter than it was, but how could you know for sure? He wandered off into that and imagined he was asleep, dreaming he was awake. That she came to him and everything was fine. That she held him and said, "Christ, Daniel—please!"

Katie just past her, and that was food for thought. Had they come in together or what? And then a look in Hannah's eyes that brought him up and fully awake.

"What is it?" he said. "What's wrong?"

Hannah didn't answer. Katie whispered Doreen awake and drew her away. Hannah's hand was cold in his. She led him to the high French doors, stopped behind him. It was clear she wasn't going any farther, and this didn't help Daniel at all. He knew he'd have to look. Nothing would get him out of that. He felt a great sense of relief when nothing was there, that Hannah had let her fears get out of hand. He couldn't blame her for that. They all had reason enough to jump at shadows. And then, as if he hadn't seen clearly before, as if he hadn't really allowed himself to look, this delusion was stripped away, shifting to a heart-stopping understanding of *mass*, of a presence between the temple and the house. Daniel smelled wet earth, deep burrows and years, felt a ponderous weight of displeasure that left him shaken. All this real and illusory at once, there in an instant or half the night, and he was uneasily certain that a season or half a breath meant nothing to what was there. . . .

"Daniel, come look at John," Katie said. "Daniel, *please!*"

Daniel turned from the window, the quality of her voice telling him more than he wanted to know. Katie tried not to cry. Doreen held her close. When Daniel looked out at the night, he saw the temple on the hill, familiar trees, the dark stretch of lawn and nothing more. He sensed that what was out there had seen what It wanted to see. He didn't want to go and look at John.

Between the tennis courts and the lake seemed as good a place as any. John had liked the temple, but Daniel wasn't about to bury him there. On the way back to the house, the girls started to cry. Daniel told them it was all right. They said they'd miss him, they didn't want to go. But only half of that was true. He couldn't ask them to stay, and wouldn't. They'd never be easy here now, and they knew it.

"You'll be fine," he said. "It's what I want you to do." They took too long saying good-bye. Daniel shooed them off. "Don't sell them to the Arabs," he told Hannah.

"That's you, all right," Hannah said. "Jokes at a time like this."

"Leave the pickup at the runway. I'll get it sometime."

"That goddamn plane better come."

"Hold the good thought," Daniel said. He looked after the girls. Tried to snap leggy pictures in his head.

"I think you're a son of a bitch, Daniel," Hannah said. "I think you knew something awful like this would happen."

"I didn't know anything at all," Daniel said wearily.

"I hope it gets around to haunting *you*. I sure as hell would, if it were me."

"I can use the company," Daniel said. "Just so it leaves the burrows alone."

It was easier to tell her that. Easier than trying to tell her that the spook was gone. A hell of a lot easier than telling her that it was *John* who'd done the haunting. Just not in the usual order you might expect. Dying usually came first, and *then* the ghost, but that didn't bother Them down below. He'd guessed long ago that whatever lived in the burrows had kinky clocks. It was half-past purple down there, a quarter till yesterday.

No use going over that, he decided. It wasn't what Hannah wanted to hear. Getting mad was what she wanted. Mad was easier than double reverse daylight zonker time, the plausibility of predeparted spooks. Daniel didn't much want to think about it, either. John's ghost scaring John into dying. Watching movies backward from the middle hurt his head.

She didn't say good-bye. She picked up her duffel and walked away, and Daniel went inside. The house seemed big and empty. He walked from room to room, the way cats assure themselves that no one else is around. No one was. He wondered about simply walking away. Going somewhere else, or catching up with Hannah and the girls. He'd thought about it before. Maybe They wouldn't know. Maybe They'd notice last September. He decided not to think about it again. He found a bottle of wine Katie had left him, and pulled his chair to the kitchen door. He dipped cold corn bread in the wine. When the sun was down an hour, two does and a buck came up and stuck their heads between the fence and ate his lettuce. Daniel drank and watched.

Trading Post

With the glasses, lying on the flat gravel roof across the street, he could follow ant dramatics on the worn brick facing of the center. The place looked thoroughly abandoned. Dry summer grass followed cracks along the broad parking lot, sprouting in small explosions. Wild azalea had taken hold in rusted cars. He slipped the binoculars into his pack and out of the heat. The south Texas sun bleached the sky of any color, and there was no shade at all on the roof. He thought about beer in sweaty bottles. He'd tried making beer but it was flat, both in chemistry and emotion. Fruit jars lacked the ambience of TV taverns.

What the Snakes had done was set up their operation in an old shopping mall on the far edge of Beaumont, close to the Port Arthur road. There was a Kmart and a Safeway and a discount appliance store, and a dozen smaller shops all connected by an inside mall. Josh was sure they weren't using the whole place. The real operation would be hidden in some inaccessible corner, past a wall that had crumbled on its own or gotten help. You could walk through rubble all day and satisfy yourself there was nothing to see. Proper measures would be taken.

A noise from the street brought him about, and he bellied across the roof and parted a tangle of dead vines. A one-wheeler took the corner fast, raising white dust and heading south. The motor was strangely flat in the humid air. The Snake sat high on his perch, awkward as Orville Wright. The sun glanced off copper scales. His whip tail snapped in the breeze. A moment later, the convoy followed. Nine boxy shapes painted the familiar vomit yellow. They made no sound and rode meters above the road.

There was nothing else to see. He backed off and dropped through a hole in the roof. The store was dark and cool. He laid on his pack and slept amid the ghosts of plumbing supplies. He dreamed that a dog came in and saw him. When it was dark, he slipped out and walked back to the Neches River. The black gelding was hobbled in a thick grove of willows near the water. The mount jerked away when he approached; he held its nose and spoke to it quietly. A few miles north he turned west and followed Black Creek into the Thicket. A big magnolia grew near the creek, as broad as three men. He stepped down and allowed himself a smoke.

That was how they worked it, then; the convoy turning right past the mall had shown him the answer. The Snakes had a small repair base out past the Eastex Freeway. He had no idea what they repaired. The fact that it was there had gotten him thinking about how his buddy Howard Johnson ran his scam. Traffic came off the base and past the mall. All Howard had to do was bring his goods out the mall's back door, circle around and edge in a convoy going south. The Snakes had a setup over east of Sabine Pass, a fair-sized town and a landing pad for the big space freighters that took everything in and out of the Gulf Coast. Howard would grease some palms and his stuff would go out clean with everything else. Someone would pick up the goods at the other end. Fucking larceny among the lizards. So much for advanced civilizations.

He mounted up again and took a long pull from the bottle he kept in his pack. The moon was nearly full. He could see flat water, a dense stand of thick-boled cypress. The mosquitoes found him out, and he kicked the gelding into a trot.

He was up and out back splashing his face with cold water out of the bucket before the sun came over the trees, regretting the fact that he'd ridden in late and finished off the whiskey on the way. One of the men was chopping wood, and the sound rang sharply over the clearing. The smell of breakfast led him into the cabin.

"Dry off before you sit," Ellie told him. She didn't turn from the stove. He wiped his dark beard on a cloth and filled his plate with fried fish and biscuits and sorghum. The hands had already eaten. He'd seen their plates stacked on a stump.

"You had to go and see," Ellie said. "That's what this is all about."

"Don't start on me now."

Ellie faced him, a big wooden spoon in her hand. She was a long-limbed girl with a country-strong jaw and yellow hair. "What good did it do? Will you just tell me that?"

"I know old Howard's a crook."

"Big surprise."

"Ellie. I wanted to see how he does it."

Ellie turned back to the stove.

"He's got a slick operation, which is how he better do it. They ever catch him at it, they'll make him into eighty-dollar shoes and a belt."

"And what'll they do to you?"

"Commerce is a risk."

"The way you do it it is."

He got up and pushed back his chair and walked up behind her and touched her waist. She stiffened slightly under his hands.

"You didn't bathe this morning. You smell like whiskey and horses."

"You smell pretty good. Like flour and a woman in heat."

"That last part's wishing." She squirmed out of his grasp. Josh saw her flush and knew evening would find her content. He drank down his coffee and walked out into the yard. The land below the cabin sloped down to a narrow inlet, the water there still and dark as slate. The wind had picked up right at dawn and the fog had burned off early. Moss-bearded tall oak trees lined the edge of the water. The world came to an end twenty yards into the swamp, choked off in dense vegetation. When the sun broke through, the feeble light was pale as butter.

Sol and Jim and the two new hands were waiting in the shade of the live oak that spread its branches over the cabin and the barn, the smokehouse and the hands' quarters back past the corral. The red flag was down; Ellie had taken breakfast out to the men and disarmed the traps. Still, they waited past the last white line. They seldom came closer unless they were asked.

Josh didn't much care for the new hands, but Sol said they

were all right. They came from up past Votaw, and Sol was vaguely related to them both. Which said nothing at all, as everyone in the Thicket was somebody's cousin. The two would bear watching. They both had the tallow-colored skin and spare frames of backcountry men who were never more than a day this side of hungry. They knew who Josh was and what he had, and they wouldn't stop thinking about that.

Sol and Jim stood as Josh appeared. The new men followed their lead, one deliberately slower than the other.

"We got a lot to do," Josh said without greeting. "I want those horses fit and clean. Jim, you see the trading stock gets some extra feed." He turned to the new hands. "You all get started on those stumps past the barn. I want that patch flat as a table."

One of the men looked down at his feet. The other faced Josh for an instant and scratched at his chin. He didn't want to chop out stumps. It was backbreaking work in the heat of summer.

Sol stayed on when the others left. "Anything special you want me to do today, Josh?"

It was part of their morning rite. Josh would give him paper and a pinch of tobacco in acknowledgment of his status as top hand. Sol would roll a smoke and carefully put it away. Josh had never seen him light up. Sol took his pleasure in private, or did a little trading of his own.

"That storm last week took some cedar shakes off the barn," Josh said. "You can see it from right here. In the unlikely event it ever rains again, we'll have a ton of sour feed to fork out."

Sol looked down at his hands. It was something he should have noticed and he knew it. "I'll get right to that, Josh. I sure will."

"I found a bee tree yesterday evening coming back. Two miles down past that stand of palmetto. You might take a look at that."

"Right after I get to that roof," said Sol. "You have any luck out in the bush? See anything at all?" He pretended the question had suddenly struck him, but it wasn't a thing he did well at all.

"A little sign, maybe," Josh told him. "There's wild porkers out there. One day I'll get 'em."

"You take me out, I'll find them. I got a good nose for game."

"I might do that," said Josh. Sol knew it was a lie. He hadn't gone out three days looking for pigs that didn't exist.

Josh stood and Sol sprang up like his shadow. He showed Josh an open cheerful grin. A dog eager to fetch. "All right, get to it," Josh told him. Sol trotted off and Josh rolled a smoke. You couldn't help like Sol, and it was better to have a snoop on the property who was easy, than one who wasn't. It had to be Sol that told everything he knew to Martin Bregger. Jim was too dumb. Nobody could act that ignorant unless he was.

Josh sighed and walked back to the house. The sun was up strong, the air already too thick to breathe. On one side he had Martin Bregger, who ran everything clear up to the Red River and over east to Louisiana. Martin was too smart to try and kill the golden goose, but he wouldn't mind at all if the goose was his own man instead of Josh. And on the other end he had the Snakes, Howard Johnson and whoever else was in it. He wasn't sure which he trusted the least. If either one got foolish, he was standing in the middle. He tossed down the smoke and stubbed it out. Maybe he was getting too old for this business. Except the only other business was going hungry, and he was sure as hell too old for that.

It seemed like a night for a treat; no good reason except Beaumont had left him feeling edgy. That, and Ellie's disapproval. When he finished up his rounds and locked up, he ran the patch of red cloth above the roof. The flag told the hands and whoever might decide to wander in that he'd armed the traps again and it wouldn't be smart to poke around. No one had since the boys from Liberty County had decided to come in and try for the horses. Martin Bregger said it wouldn't happen again and had come down himself to look at the bodies. Josh knew Bregger had likely sent them himself to see what the traps could do.

He went to the cellar and got the Herradura Añejo tequila, ninety-two proof and still in the bottle, that and two good joints, and then climbed to the bedroom upstairs. Ellie was moving about, fluffing pillows. She slept in the raw year 'round, as he did himself, there being little need for bedclothes in the Thicket. The lamp was out, but there was a candle. He liked the way the light kissed her skin. She turned and saw the bottle and the joints and gave him a curious smile.

"What's the occasion, something special?"

"Make one up if you want."

She got a single glass from beside the bed and watched him pour, then waited while he lit up the joints, closing her eyes and drawing smoke into her lungs.

"God, it isn't going to take much of that."

"It's all right, is it?"

"Better than all right."

Josh tasted the tequila on his tongue. Quick picture of a fountain, red tiled roof and bright color.

"I'm sorry my leaving upset you."

"I don't ever like you going. Specially if it's got to do with a town. That wasn't something you really had to do."

"Maybe not."

"I don't like staying here, Josh. Making a little circle around the house."

"Isn't any other way I know to do it."

"I still don't have to like it." She flipped ash on the floor, using her whole arm in the motion. He gave her the glass again and she held it in both hands, bringing it to her mouth like a child. Her eyes came up, and she caught him checking her out.

"You didn't need to get out the goodies. I can be had."

"Isn't what it was for."

"Well, then. Let's pretend it was." She touched his chest and smiled. "I'll fight you off a little."

"Not if you finish that toke."

"Then I guess I finish the toke. I can get you whenever I want."

"That's true."

"While you were gone, Sol acted real funny."

"Funny how?"

"Walking around the yard all the time, stopping to get a rock out of his shoe. That kind of thing."

Josh grinned. "He's trying to map out the traps. I've caught him at it before."

"You think it's funny?"

"Ellie, you know how to find the traps? Step on 'em. That's not a practical solution." There were two trap perimeters around the cabin. When he was gone, Ellie armed the outside perimeter day and night, and shut off the inside perimeter during the day. It left her a little room to walk around, and was better than being shut up in the house.

"You're not going again soon, are you?" she asked.

"No, you know I'm not."

"Good. Just don't." She pinched out the candle and came in close against his shoulder. The loving was good and they surprised each other with their needs. When Ellie was asleep, he looked up at the ceiling and thought about Sol. He was getting a little cocky. He never did anything he wasn't told to do, so Martin was egging him on. Pushing him into something or maybe nothing at all. The whole idea was to keep Josh from getting any sleep, and sometimes it worked better than others.

He spent his days mostly in the cellar, getting his goods in order for Howard Johnson's next visit, the squares on his homemade calendar diminishing much faster than he liked. The cellar was as large as the cabin space above, lined with concrete blocks Josh had hauled in from Batson by team and wagon three summers before. It was caulked, painted, and generally proof against the wet ground pressing on every side, and had the virtue of being twenty degrees cooler in the summer. Ellie was from northern Minnesota and had no tolerance for hot and humid weather. More than once he'd been tempted to bring her down, when her skin flushed red and she could hardly get a breath. He hated to see her suffer, but it was a rule he couldn't break. He'd made it clear to Martin that no one but himself had ever been in the cellar or knew how to get in or what was there. It was the only way he had of protecting Ellie. After the boys from Liberty County had taken the short course in fragmentation mines and other surprises, Josh had broken his rule about no one in the cabin. He had brought Martin in and shown him the heavy steel door to the cellar, which was really the front half of a safe, and let him read the sign he'd painted just above the combination:

> **WARNING!**
> NO ONE CAN OPEN THIS BUT ME. EVEN IF YOU HAD THE COMBINATION THE DOOR IS RIGGED TO BLOW THE WHOLE FUCKING CABIN UNLESS THE DOOR IS FIRST DISARMED IN SEVERAL PLACES.
> SINCERELY YOURS,
> JOSHUA T. RAINES

Martin had seemed impressed. He had stopped looking crazed for several moments. Of course the flaw in all this was if Martin somehow got past the traps outside and got to Ellie, he could make Josh open up the door. If things ever went that far, it was over anyway and wouldn't matter. The best guarantee against trouble was that Martin was a businessman first and a loony-tune second. That, and the fact that he was scared to death of the Snakes. Josh knew this for certain. It was easier just to let him keep dealing with Howard Johnson than try to cut him out and learn what he traded to the Snakes. Sol's little capers simply reflected Martin's feeling that Josh ought to worry a little more. It was a sound corporate tactic. One that told him Martin was probably only marginally unhinged.

The flyer dipped low over the swamp, scaring up bright-colored birds from the trees. The craft was a dull mustard yellow, shaped like half a melon, its power source vaguely asthmatic, a man sucking air through his teeth. It settled on runners in the clearing where Josh had whitewashed a circle. A blister set asymmetrically forward was tinted against the sun. It slid back to reveal the four Snakes. Pilot. Two armed guards. Howard Johnson stepped out and came quickly toward Josh, walking in the springy deliberate manner that made Snakes appear to move in slow-motion—even when they ran as fast as deer, which Josh had watched them do from a distance.

Josh differed from Martin in that he feared them for what they were, and not for the way they looked. Reasonably they were no more alien than upright chameleons. Seven-foot lizards that talked. Rust-sienna skin, salmon underbelly. Whip tail and apparently no use for any clothing. Howard Johnson wore a weapon, slung from a decorative webbing about his throat. To Josh, it looked like a lubricating tool, but would likely prove effective.

The Snake came to a stop. Forty-weight eyes found Josh. "Have a nice day," said Howard.

"Right, Coke is it," said Josh. "Hang on, I'll get the stuff." He left the Snake standing in the yard and went in and got his goods, packed on a dolly and covered with a tarp. Ellie didn't come out of the kitchen. Howard Johnson made her nervous. Josh wheeled the dolly across the yard and into the barn, waited until Howard was inside and shut the door. Sol and Jim and the new hands were off in the woods. They had left before sunup with no urging. In the hot, heavy air of the barn, Howard smelled musty and slightly sweet. Dead leaves and pollen. Josh pulled back the tarp and set his wares on a weathered plank table. Light from the slanted window was slightly muted.

"Some real good items this time," he told Howard. "You're lucky. First-rate stuff isn't all that easy to find. Rats get to the canvas. They take to that pigment like candy." As he talked he fooled with the paintings, turning one a little to the light, brushing at the frame of another.

"I like the people dancing," said Howard.

"Well, sure," said Josh, "that's a Degas."

"Degas is good, I think."

"Degas is good." He knew Howard really didn't care about names. While he talked about dancers, his eyes were flicking over the other paintings. It irritated the hell out of Josh that the Snake had a fine critical eye. Bluebonnets and moon-eyed children wouldn't cut it. Howard knew better. Josh had only tried it on him once.

"Just five, Josh?" Howard shook his head sadly in human imitation. "This is all?"

Not unexpected, but a direction Josh had hoped they might avoid. "We're talking masterpieces, Howard. These are first-rate goods."

"I know that, Josh."

"Then what are we saying here?"

"Last time there were nine."

"It can't be the same every time," Josh said patiently. "You know that. It depends on what I find."

"Five is not enough, Josh." His voice was slightly nasal, the words faintly musical and extended, as if he might have learned English from a Chinese waiter.

Josh studied the paintings while he thought about what to do next. He couldn't tell Howard he had only found two the last trip, that the others were from his hold-back stash. Besides the Degas, he had the Miró and the Klee and the Andrew Wyeth, and a Lennart Anderson that looked as good as Gauguin. Back in the cellar he had the Freilicher landscape and the Cézanne and what he thought was maybe a Titian. And that was it. He wanted to tell Howard Johnson that it hadn't been his idea to flatten Houston. That devastation hindered the earnest collector. He was fast running out of museums, concentrating now on well-to-do residential rubble. This last avenue hit or miss, wealth not always reflecting taste.

He showed Howard the other stuff he had, the Kazak carpet and the three good Teotihuacán heads and a Minoan beaker jug, a salesman winding up his pitch and saving a little kicker for the last. Howard had a weakness for good glass, and he brought out the Baccarat crystal and held it up to the light, flipping the rim so Howard could hear it ring. A tulip-shaped glass, clear as air and whisper-thin.

"Oh, yes, very nice," said Howard. He took the piece carefully from Josh. Their hands didn't touch. He held the crystal by its base, fingers long and spatulate at the tips. Needles of light flecked his skin, for a moment a disco lizard.

"I would like more of these. In other shapes as well."

"So would I," Josh said carefully. Howard had an ear for human inflection. "I found this item in a shop that handled fine crystal and china. Spoke, Wedgwood, Steuben, everything the best. Two floors of it. I never saw so much broken glass in my life. This was the only piece intact."

"You should find other shops such as that."

"That's a real good idea. As a matter of fact, I'm working on another site now. There might be something, I can't promise."

The other site was pure fiction, and maybe Howard knew it. If there was a Mason jar left in Houston, Josh couldn't find it. In the cellar he had a single, exquisite Lalique, a crystal piece with a frosted satin finish that would knock the Snake on his tail. Howard would expect something big next time, and he'd have to bring it out.

The Snakes came in from the flyer and loaded everything up, packing the items carefully under Howard's watchful eye. Josh handed Howard the envelope with his samples for next time, then loaded up the goods Howard had brought him and wheeled the dolly into the house.

Howard was waiting in the yard.

"Bring Ellie outside," he told Josh.

"Ellie? What for?"

It shook Josh badly, and Howard caught his concern. "I'm not going to hurt her, Josh. I am going to take her up in the flyer. I will bring her back safely. She can look at the countryside and see the Gulf from great heights."

"Howard, I don't think Ellie'd like to do that."

"Bring her out, Josh."

He was overcome by a terrible fear, a helpless rage. There was nothing he could do, and there was no use asking the Snake what he wanted. He turned and went inside. Ellie looked up from the kitchen table and read his face. She stood quickly, and Josh held her shoulders and sat her down and told her.

"Oh Jesus . . ." She looked like a bird caught in a trap.

"You'll be all right," he said. "If he was going to do something, he'd just do it. That's his way. I can't stop him, Ellie."

She pulled away and stood and walked out of the cabin, past Howard without looking. Howard nodded to Josh and followed Ellie. Josh watched the flyer lift from the clearing and bank out of sight above the trees. He went inside and found the Remington 12-gauge, which he wasn't supposed to have, and leaned it by the door. Howard was trying to tell him something. He didn't much care what it was. If he didn't bring Ellie back safe, he'd try to kill him. Pointless. But the only gesture he could imagine.

It was a full two hours before he heard the flyer again. It

settled in afternoon shadow, and Howard got out and then Ellie. Josh ran to meet her. Her face looked pale and unfinished. She'd thrown up and stained the front of her dress.

"Ellie . . ."

"Just leave me the fuck alone, all right?" She pushed him off and walked shakily to the cabin.

"She became ill," said Howard.

"Yeah, I can see that. You want to tell me what this is all about?"

"Let's walk," said Howard. He left the front of the house and started past the barn to the corral. The horses shied and trotted away at his approach, bunching up at the far side of the pen, afraid of the unfamiliar smell. There were six pack animals and nine riding horses. Howard drew his weapon and began firing methodically into the pens. Josh stared in dismay, certain this was something he only imagined. A big sorrel mare went down heavily and thrashed in the dust. The other animals went crazy with fear. They shrieked and kicked out at each other and ran blindly into the fence. Howard killed five of the riding horses. He left the pack animals alone, a point not wasted on Josh. Finally, he put the weapon away. Josh couldn't take his eyes from the corral.

"It was not a good idea to approach my place of business," said Howard. "I am greatly concerned about this, Josh."

Josh made no attempt to deny it, or ask Howard how he'd found him out. That's what it was all about, then. Ellie and the horses. Things could be taken from him. Returned or not returned.

"All right, you made your point," said Josh. "Here's one you maybe didn't consider. People see you and me having trouble, that isn't good for business. It gives them ideas."

"You'd better take care of that."

"You got any suggestions?"

Howard nodded toward the corral. "Fresh meat is scarce. Give some to Martin Bregger." He had never mentioned Bregger before. He was letting Josh know something else.

"I will be back in one month," Howard announced. "One instead of four. Have more goods ready."

"Now Christ, that doesn't make sense!" Josh was tired of holding back his anger. "I can't make a run that fast and you know it. What are you trying to do?"

"If the canvases are difficult to find, you may substitute crystal for some of the paintings. One good piece will equal three paintings."

"It doesn't work like that. The glass is just as scarce."
"Try harder, Josh."
"All right, I don't know. I'll do what I can."
"I know you will. Good-bye, Josh."

He waited until the flyer disappeared and then turned and stomped back into the cabin and armed the traps, not even bothering to raise the flag. Maybe Sol would come back and blow his ass off. Ellie was upstairs. She had changed clothes and washed herself off. The bedroom smelled sour.

"You all right?" He knew it was a useless thing to say.

"I got sick and threw up and passed out. I've never been so scared in my life. I'm fine, Josh."

"I'm sorry, Ellie."

"He shoot all the horses?"

"Just the ones I don't need for business."

"Beaumont. Your goddamn adventure."

"How do you know that?"

"He told me."

"If you want, I can get you something to eat. Some soup or I'll fry up those potatoes."

"No, thanks. You want you can bring me the rest of the Herradura."

"I wish this hadn't of happened."

"So do I." She looked at him for the first time, and he saw less anger there than despair. "I'll be okay. Just leave me alone for a while."

Sol and Jim and the new hands came in before dark. The new men took one look at the corral and ran off into the woods. Josh got Sol and Jim butchering before the flies could do more damage. Sol knew better than to ask any questions. Martin would know something had happened here before morning.

Josh took his goods off the dolly and into the cellar, lit a lamp and locked himself in. The way the operation worked, Josh would give Howard a few grams of what he wanted and Howard would work it up. The goods came back in square plastic containers. Some standard Snake measure that came out to roughly four and a half gallons. The Snakes were clearly hotshot chemists; anything Josh had in mind they could make it. Howard never seemed concerned with the sample packets. All he told Josh was the process was risky and expensive; Josh had to take his word for that.

The Snakes leveled the cities with sonic disaster, some weapon that shattered buildings and fine crystal. The best casualty figures

Josh had heard were 80 percent. Maybe more, and the same for other countries. The Snakes went away and let pestilence take its course. Disease and famine took another hefty percent. Survivors looted shopping centers and homes and grocery stores. Cattle and pigs quickly vanished. Cats and dogs. Nine years later, the Snakes came again, quashing feeble resistance and settling in to stay. They left people alone and went about doing whatever they did. Howard Johnson caught Josh looting a 7-Eleven ruin and made him a deal. Supply determined trade. Most items were spoiled or lost forever. Canned goods, Hershey bars, and Sprite. Josh concentrated his efforts on items that had lasted. Salt. Sugar. Tea. Coffee. Tobacco. Isolated pockets of whiskey and wine. Seeds that would still come up. Occasional caches of gasoline. Marijuana, and selected recreational and medicinal drugs. Some of the food items had gone stale, but nobody cared. Josh gave samples to Howard Johnson, and Howard brought the goods back in bulk. There was never very much. Maybe seven hundred pounds each trip.

So Josh traded art to Howard Johnson, which Howard smuggled out to distant worlds. Howard made formerly staple items, which Josh traded off to Martin Bregger. Martin stayed in power through control of rare goods. He gave Josh vegetables and fruit, flour and clothing and nails, axe handles and protection from Martin himself. Howard Johnson got paid in some measure; Josh had never even thought about that. All he needed to know was that Howard would never let him out of the business. If he couldn't get out, he had to make certain he stayed in. An indispensable link in the chain of commerce and trade. Why was Howard suddenly making that difficult to do? It could be the Beaumont thing or something else. Maybe lizards thought like Martin Bregger. Keep Josh from getting any sleep. It had a perverse sense of logic, the ring of truth.

Martin appeared in the yard with the morning fog. Four men, a wagon, and a team were in the clearing. One man held Martin's reins while he stood under the trees and waited for Josh. Josh had the goods ready and waiting, stacked on wooden pallets a few yards past his inside perimeter of traps. The goods had been transferred from the Snakes' plastic containers to canvas sacks, Josh having skimmed off portions for personal use.

Josh appeared in the door and Martin nodded. "Morning, friend. It's going to be a scorcher."

"Martin . . ."

Bregger was tall and stringy, a man with possum eyes. His height seemed wrong, as if something might have stretched him out of shape. One leg was shorter than the other, causing him to stand like a tree grown up in the wind. This didn't bother Martin; other men found themselves leaning off balance to catch his eye.

"Josh, my boys blow up if they get those goods?"

"Not now they won't, Martin."

Martin smiled in appreciation. He nodded and his crew brought over the wagon and loaded up. As soon as the pallets were empty, they filled them with the goods they'd brought along. Sweet corn and tomatoes, sacks of onions, strips of metal strapping and bolts of cloth. The men worked quickly. They didn't like walking in Josh's yard. Once they were clear, Josh ducked inside and armed the perimeter again, making a big show of raising the flag. Martin was still standing in his spot.

"Understand you had some trouble," he said to Josh.

"Nothing I can't handle."

"That's good to know."

"I got you some fresh meat. Be a good idea to start it smoking or eat it fast."

"Sure kind of you. Hate to see you shoot prime horses just for me." Josh waited for Bregger to get to it. "Your trouble with the Snakes goin' to interfere with business?"

"I can handle the Snakes just fine."

A wide possum grin. "I know you can, Josh."

He decided there was no use putting it off. "I'll need a couple of escorts, Martin. Sunup four days from now. I'm going back to Houston."

Martin smiled. "Did put the screws to you, didn't he?"

"The business that doesn't grow stands still."

"Uh-huh." Martin picked at a tooth. "I'll have the boys here. Pleasant trip to you." He turned back to the wagon, listing to the right. A man handed over the reins and he mounted up. Sol and Jim brought meat out of the barn and slung it off their shoulders into the wagon. Blood had soaked the sacking and left stains along their arms. Sol pretended he didn't know Martin or the others.

Ellie seemed better. There was still a distance between them. Maybe that would change with time. She walked through her days like a woman coming back from a sickness, brushing against life out of habit. Josh would find her standing in the kitchen in a pool of morning light, clutching a spoon or teacup to her breast. He sensed she was drawing some strength from the familiar.

She was reconciled to the trip; that, or too much within herself to show concern. "I'll be all right," she told him. "Don't worry about me."

"I do worry, Ellie."

"Worry about yourself. And come back safe." She rested her hands on his shoulders. The action seemed an effort. When she kissed him, her lips were dry as paper.

Sol and Jim had the packhorses ready. Josh had decided on three. He'd likely find goods to warrant one, but no use advertising that. Martin Bregger's two men were waiting under the big stand of cypress by the road. The older of the two reached up and flicked at moss with his knife. Josh had worked with the pair before. Sol brought over the black gelding and told Josh he'd hold down the fort. Sol's open, boyish grin irritated Josh more than usual.

By early midmorning they had passed the marshy lake with its forest of skeletal trees. Yellow iris dotted the shore. The way south twisted through willows and sharp-leaved holly. Farther, the willows gave way to a steep hammock of pine and welcome shade. A sound like applause startled Josh, and he turned to see hundreds of white herons overhead. Birds reassured him. Wildlife was apparently holding its own, the hunger less intense across the land. Creatures mating and reproducing, faster than people could eat them. He kept a running tally of survivors. Gray squirrels. Swamp rabbits. No more deer or wild turkey, but now and then a possum or a coon. Coons were as sly as people. He told himself the Thicket was no place to take a poll. Wildlife had always gathered here, and what he saw didn't reflect true conditions.

He didn't talk to Martin's riders. There was nothing he had to say. They were there to protect him, make sure he and the horses got to Houston and back safe. Raiders were always about; protecting Josh was essential to Martin's business. The men carried pistols but never showed them. It wasn't smart to let another see you owned something of such great value.

Josh picked up the pace and led them through a tricky piece of swamp. Gnats followed the men and the horses. The trip was settling down in his head. Going back this soon wouldn't hurt. He was running out of goods; Howard had simply nudged him into action, a little sooner than he liked. The Beaumont business or something else entirely—it didn't matter. Motives here were futile. A lizard mind was razor-blade jelly.

Just after noon he called a halt and stepped out of the saddle. He ate biscuits and honey and sat down under a tree and listened to the lazy sound of cicadas. The riders ate and kept to themselves. Branches crowded in overhead; the air itself was lemony-yellow. Cinnamon fern grew thickly under the trees. Josh saw a canebrake rattler slip through the grass. There were still plenty of snakes—the other kind. Snapping turtles and frogs, and 'gators back in the worst parts of the swamp. He wondered how Snakes viewed the reptile population. Probably the same way people thought of apes.

A hundred years before, black bear had roamed the Thicket. Bears couldn't run as fast as hogs. They tracked the razorbacks and caught them when they bedded down for the night. Bit the back of the neck and started eating. Wild hogs feared nothing in the world except bears. Josh remembered the taste of bacon. Pleasures now extinct seemed all the sweeter.

He was coming to his feet when the unmistakable sound reached his ears. He looked at Martin's riders. They led the animals quickly back in the trees, held the reins, and squatted on their heels. Josh crawled up through the brush. He'd come due south through the Thicket, intending to skirt 90 and cross over past the Liberty County line. The Snakes kept 90 open for their convenience. Now there was traffic on the road. Four landcars and three flyers overhead. The striped cursive symbol was one everyone knew. Lizard law and order. They'd have to hole up or go back. Travel was out of the question.

The direction of the traffic worried Josh. East, into Beaumont or past it, and past it wasn't likely. He could tell himself it had nothing to do with Howard Johnson, but making himself believe it was something else. Avoidance seemed a temperate solution. Reptile fuzz was the worst kind of trouble you could find.

He walked back and squatted by the riders. "I'll catch up with you later," he told them. "Don't expect me till noon maybe tomorrow. Take the horses back up Jackson Creek and wait for me there."

The older of the two looked at Josh. "We're supposed to stay with you."

"You're supposed to stay with me if I go to Houston. We can't go to Houston right now."

The man wore a straw hat frayed at the edges. "Where is it you're going?"

"That's not your business. You don't want to go."

The man thought about that, putting together the Snakes'

appearance and Josh's sudden change of plans. Coming up with indeterminate answers. Each possibility worse than the last.

"We'll be at the creek," he said finally.

"Don't get attached to those horses," Josh told him. "They don't belong to you."

The shopping center was no longer deserted. A flyer sat untended near the rows of rusted cars. The three squat sedans reminded Josh of boll weevils. Three at the Safeway, one farther down at the Kmart entrance. Winking yellow lights illumined Snakes on official errands. There was no more room for question. Howard Johnson was busted. Which meant, essentially, that Josh was busted, too. They'd want to know connections and Howard would tell them. There was no way to guess whether they had him—Josh had to assume they didn't, that he still had time to get Ellie out of the cabin and into the Thicket. He backed away from the broken fence. The gelding was in an alley, two blocks away and to his right. He stood and started back across the street. Light stabbed out of the dark, nearly catching him in the open. He leaped for the cover of tall weeds. The one-wheelers drew tight circles on the road, came to a stop in a line. Josh guessed four, maybe five. They made Snake-talk and purred their engines. They weren't looking for him, but they clearly didn't intend to go away. Someone had told them to keep everyone clear of the center.

Josh considered. There was no way to get across the street. Ahead, a warehouse wall blocked the way. He would have to follow the ditch to the back of the mall. Go all the way around and hope for no Snakes on the other side. It would take a good hour. He needed to be heading for the Thicket.

A building had collapsed, leaving a mountain of broken brick. Debris lapped the rear of the center. Boxlike carriers nosed the concrete dock where Kmart shoppers had loaded their goods. The carriers floated just above the ground. Bright cones of light lit up the dock, the reeflike strands of rubble. Josh viewed the scene without pleasure. He could easily break his neck if he climbed the rubble. The area near the docks was bright as day. Josh watched the procedure. Workers wheeled dollies out of the mall, loaded them into carriers, turned and went back for more. More what? Josh wondered. The Snake cops were hauling off a hell of a lot of goods. What else was Howard into besides art?

One way out. If he kept to the shadow below the dock, worked his way under the carriers past the rubble to the other end of the center. He watched the routine once more. There were maybe four minutes when all the Snakes were gone. Loading up inside or going back with empty dollies. Check it out again. He saw he was losing his nerve, waiting for intercession. He took a deep breath and bolted from cover.

The Snakes loaded a dolly directly above. The carrier dipped slightly under the weight. When they left, he made for the next carrier in line. A barrier of rubble intervened. For a moment, he was level with the floor of the dock itself. He hesitated, checked quickly for Snakes. Poked his head inside the carrier for a look. The space was packed with long rectangular containers. Pressure sealed in plastic, accordion ridges along the sides. They reminded Josh of crackers. Individual packs for locked-in flavor. The packs were different sizes. Two feet square on up. It was a bad idea, but he knew he was going to do it. Pulling himself up, he slipped inside and moved to the far back wall. With his knife, he cut through the translucent plastic. Stretching the ridges apart, he got a glimpse of a very nice Utrillo. He'd traded it to Howard in March. Behind the Utrillo was another. Not really another, the same one. And after that another, the same painting. Josh tried another, slightly larger container. Grant Wood. All identical down to a wavy scratch on the frame.

He didn't picture for a moment a roomful of busy Snake forgers. The little bastards had a duplicating device. Something that could stamp out paintings like cookies. Josh ran a gallery operation; Howard had dimestore distribution. The egg-shapeed containers to his left would be pre-Columbian jars. Aztec culture by the gross. So much for hardworking chemists, miserly portions of pot. Howard could turn it out by the ton.

He heard them coming and knew he couldn't make it to the front. Crouching behind Utrillo, he waited until they wheeled the new load inside. They had to jockey things around to make room. For a moment, the containers hid him from view. He moved up as the load moved back. The dolly was flush against the carrier, stacked high with containers. No way to drop back to the ground. He went to his knees and crawled through the stacks, waited, then darted into the mall.

The mall was a mess. Storefronts gutted and crowded with rubble. Dark except for lights set up farther down. He ducked inside a store. Hickory Farms, the shelves stripped for more than twenty years. He guessed the big lights were where Howard had stored his goods. The lizard cops were looking it over. Part of the roof had collapsed. A cavern hung with rusted steel vines. It allowed Josh to move through stores without going back to the mall. Discount Shoes, Doubleday. A shop for skiers and divers. Loaded dollies passed in the mall. The stench hit him at Penney's. Something was recently dead; it would be deader tomorrow in the heat.

He could hear Snake voices and see the lights in the mall. He was right next door or close to it, much too bright and he moved to the back of the store. Clothing, he decided, from the jungle of empty racks. Light cast a narrow dusty beam on the floor. It came from a fist-sized puncture in the wall. The hole sprouted old electric wiring. The smell here was bad. He held his breath and went to his knees, turning his head to see in the hole. He backed off fast, throwing up in one violent constriction after another. His body was helpless to stop. Cries of alarm reached his ears, and he knew the Snakes had heard him. He tried to crawl away. The Snake poked him with something hard. Josh turned and saw a muzzle that resembled a garden hose. Two more Snakes arrived quickly. Josh wiped his face with his shirt. The Snakes gave way to another; he wore ornamental webbing around his throat. He turned a flash on Josh, then bent to study him closer. Standing, he gave quick instructions to the others and walked away.

The Snakes pulled him roughly to his feet, took his knife and his belongings and hustled him out of the store into the mall. Outside, they opened the rear door of a landcar, tossed him in, and shut him up in the dark.

Josh tried not to think, a process that only served to sharpen mental pictures. The store was full of Ellies. Hundreds of dead Ellies under a white-hot light. The Snakes were dragging them by the legs and tossing them in mustard-colored dumpsters. The Ellies wore blue cotton dresses and jogging shoes . . .

"*Jesus!*" The image was too sharp, too bright. His stomach lurched again. There was nothing left to give. He took off his shirt and tossed it away. His hands were shaking and wouldn't stop. The landcar started up smoothly. He felt it turn left, leave the lot and go north. The Ellies wouldn't go away. Dead Ellies in the store. One back at the cabin, but *which one?* He saw her in light. Sunlight finding her in the kitchen. A candle by the bed. If he looked at her now, touched her again, would she be the same? *Ellie, Ellie* . . . His throat tightened just short of closing. He shut his eyes and tried to push the image aside. He wasn't sure he wanted the answer. Maybe that wasn't a problem. The way things were going, it probably wasn't a question he'd ever get to ask.

The ride seemed to last half an hour. When the landcar stopped, the Snakes came back and let him out. Dark pines shadowed the rutted dirt road. Josh smelled stagnant water. A flash shined in his eyes, and the Snakes motioned him forward. One brought up the rear. He watched the other spring along in an awkward, peculiarly graceful manner. Finally, he stopped and motioned Josh to a halt. A square boxy light sat on the ground. It illuminated two more Snakes. They were digging a shallow grave.

Josh felt a quick little motion under his heart. Breaking glass. He'd guessed where they were going, but a guess is a speculation. A hole is to the point.

When the grave was complete, the guards and the digger left. Josh heard steps, turned and saw the official-looking Snake from the mall.

"You are the one named Josh," he said abruptly. "You worked with Howard Johnson. You gathered artifacts and traded them for goods. Howard Johnson produced the goods."

"Yes. I did." Josh saw no reason to deny it.

"The female. She came from your place? She left at some time with Howard Johnson?"

"Yes."

"And Howard Johnson brought her back."

"Yes."

"You'd like to know if she is real, or if Howard left a copy."

"The thought occurred."

" 'Real' is a personal observation."

"Is that supposed to be an answer?"

"An answer is not a solution. That was a very foolish decision on Howard's part. Smuggling is one thing. Duplicating a being is something else. This is why I put him out of business."

"A humanitarian gesture."

"A contradiction in terms."

"Look. What was Howard going to *do* with them?"

"Do with what?"

"With the Ellies."

"Trust me. You don't want to know." The Snake drew his weapon. "This is your burial spot. No one will see you again."

Josh felt himself unravel. The Snake pointed the weapon in the hole and fired twice.

Josh looked at him.

"Take a shovel and fill it up."

Josh did. The Snake held the light. Josh was wet all over when he finished. The Snake tossed him his knife and his belongings.

"Baskin-Robbins. Is that a name?"

"I guess it is."

"Then you will call me Baskin-Robbins. Don't go back and get your horse. Walk home. Tomorrow afternoon, I will officially discover your cabin and destroy it from a flyer. Don't take anything with you. Sol will guide you and the female to a place where someone will meet you and pick you up."

"*Sol* will?"

"Sol worked for the Bregger person. But mostly he worked for Howard Johnson. Now he works for me. Basically, we start all over from scratch. I have to burn those goods we took from the mall. I still have Howard's originals. I think. Doesn't matter. You can't work in Houston anymore. I want you out of the district. We'll set you up somewhere else. Maybe San Francisco. Denver."

"You're going to keep the operation like it is?"

"Yes, of course. Why not?"

Josh sat down on his grave and made a smoke. "All right," he said, "let's talk business. There are some things you got to know about art . . ."

Winter on the Belle Fourche

H‍E HAD COME DOWN IN THE COLD FROM THE BIG HORN Mountains and crossed the Powder River moving east toward the Belle Fourche, all this time without finding any sign and leaving little of his own. There were wolf tracks next to the river and he saw where they had gone across the ice, which told him they were desperate and hungry, that they would turn on each other before long. An hour before dark, he pulled the mount up sharp and let his senses search the land, knowing clearly something had been there before. Finally, he eased to the ground and took the Hawken rifle with him, stood still in the naked grove of trees, stopped and listened to the quiet in the death-cold air, heard the frozen river crack, heard the wind bite the world. He looked south and saw the Black Hills veiled in every fold, followed them with his eyes until the land disappeared in the same soot color as the sky. He stood a long time and sniffed the air and the water moving slow beneath the ice. He let it all come together then and simmer in his head, and when it worked itself out, he walked down in the draw and started scooping off the snow.

A few inches down he found the ashes from the fire. They had camped right here the night before, made a small supper fire and another in the morning. He ran the ashes through his fingers then brought them to his nose. They were real smart Injuns. They hadn't broken dead sticks off the trees but had walked downstream to get their wood. Cupping more snow aside, he bent to smell the earth. Six, he decided. If he dug a little more he'd find they all had mounts, but he didn't need to bother doing that. They wouldn't be on foot out here.

This close to the Powder and the Belle Fourche, they could be any kind of red nigger and not any of them friends. He knew, though, this bunch wasn't Sioux or Cheyenne, but Absaroka. He'd smelled them right off. Crow warriors certain, and likely from Big Robert's camp.

He straightened and looked east, absently touching the bowie at his belt, the scalp ring next to that. That's where they'd gone, east and a little north, the way he was headed, too. They weren't after him, didn't know that he was there. And that was something to chew on for a while.

The snow came heavy in the night, slacking off around the dawn. He was up before light and keeping to the river. Soon he'd have to figure what to do. It was two hundred miles to Fort Pierre on the Missouri, a lot more than that if he kept to every bend in the river. Del Gue would be waiting at the fort; he didn't need to be chasing after Crow, there were plenty out sniffing after him. Still, it wouldn't take much time to see what kind of mischief they were up to over here. The Absaroka were a little far east from where they rightly ought to be. He didn't think they'd want to keep on riding and maybe tangle with the Sioux, who would go without breakfast any day to skin a Crow.

At noon he found the answer. The snow had lightened up enough for tracks and he saw where the Crow had taken off, digging up dirt in the snow and hightailing it across the frozen river, heading back northwest into Absaroka country. Now he went slowly, keeping his eyes open for whatever had spooked the Crow. Sioux, most likely, though the Cheyenne could be around, too. Hard winter and empty bellies made everybody brave, and a man might go where he hadn't ought to be.

He smelled the death before it saw it. The cold tried to hide it, but it came through clear and he was off his horse fast, leading it down to cover in the draw. The dead were in the trees just ahead, and though he knew there was no one there alive he circled wide to make sure, then walked into the clearing, the Hawken crooked loose against his chest.

Three men, mostly covered by the snow. He brushed them off enough to see they were soldiers, a white lieutenant and two buffalo troopers. Each had been shot and soundly scalped, then cut up some in the playful manner of the Sioux. The soldier's clothes and boots were gone; the Sioux had taken everything but long-handle underwear and socks.

A quick look around showed the Sioux hadn't taken them by surprise. They'd stood their ground and gotten off a few shots, and that was of some interest in itself. North, he found high ground and lighter snow and saw where the Sioux had walked Army-shod mounts northwest among their own. Ten or twelve riders. They'd gone back to the river with their trophies; the Crow had seen them then and turned for home. About this time the day before, the massacre a little before that.

He stopped and tried to work the thing out. What had the three troopers been doing up here? And why only three? It was maybe a hundred and fifty miles to Fort Laramie, a powerful lot to go in heavy snow and the cold maybe thirty-five below. Troopers didn't have a lot of smarts, but anyone'd know more than that.

He mounted up and crossed the river, circled and crossed again. Two miles down he found the trail. Something about the tracks caught his eye, and he eased out of the saddle and squatted down. Now there was puzzle for sure. One of the horses had ridden double—*before* those boys had been hit by the Sioux. But there were only three bodies in the snow. Which meant the red coons had likely taken one alive, carried him back home for Injun fun. Nothing you could do for that chile, except hope he got to die, which wasn't real likely for a while. Del Gue had been taken by the Sioux the year before, and barely got out with his topknot intact. A trooper would get an extra measure sure, a skinning and worse than that.

He had the whole story now. There was no use following tracks back to the clearing, but he did. He'd kept his scalp for twelve years in the wilds, and part of that from being thorough, taking two stitches in a moccasin when one might do as well, winding up a story like this to see how it came about.

He came upon the cabin without knowing it at all, reined the horse in and just sat there a minute and let the sign all around him sink in. The cabin was built low against the side of a ravine, nearly covered by a drift and he'd damn near ridden up on the roof. He cursed himself for that. It was the kind of aggravation he didn't like, coming on something like this after he'd gotten the whole story put away. He could see it clear now, like he'd been right there when it happened. The troopers had ridden past this place into the trees, sensed trouble up ahead, and the man riding double had ridden back, stopped at the cabin, then turned and joined his comrades again. Which meant he'd left someone behind. There were no more tracks in the snow, so whoever that'd be was still there, unless they'd sprouted wings and flown to Independence like a bird.

Snow was nearly three feet high against the door, and he carefully dug it clear. Jamming the stock of his Hawken in the snow, he pulled the Colt Walker and the bowie from his belt and stepped back.

"You inside there," he called out. "I'm white an' I don't mean ye any harm, so don't go a-shootin' whatever it is you got."

There was nothing but silence from inside. Edging up close, he bent his head to listen. There was someone in there, all right. He couldn't hear them but he knew.

"Mister," he said, "this chile's no Injun, you oughter have the sense to know that." He waited, cussed again, then raised his foot and kicked solidly at the door. It was old and split and snapped like a bone. Before it hit the floor he was in, moving fast and low, sideways like a bear, coming in with the Colt and the knife and sweeping every corner of the room. Kindling and dead leaves. The musty smell of mice. A fireplace nearly caved-in. Half a chair and a broken whiskey crock. An Army blanket in the corner, and something under that. He walked over and pulled the blanket aside with his foot.

"Great Jehoshaphat," he said aloud, and went quickly to the still and fragile form, touched the cold throat and felt for signs of life he was sure he wouldn't find.

* * *

She woke to the memory of cold, the ghost of this sensation close to death, a specter that consumed her, left her hollow, left her numb with the certainty there was no heat great enough to drive the terrible emptiness away. She woke and saw the fire and tried to draw its warmth to her with her eyes. The walls and the ceiling danced with shadow. The shadows made odd and fearsome shapes. She tried to pull her eyes away but could find neither the strength nor the will for such an effort. The shadows made awful deathly sounds, sounds she could scarcely imagine. And then with a start that clutched her heart she remembered the sounds were real; she had heard them all too clearly through the walls from the trees across the snow.

"Oh Lord Jesus, they are dying," she cried aloud, "they are murdered every one!"

Darkness rose from the floor and blocked the fire. It seemed to flow and expand to fill the room, take form as a broad-shouldered demon cloaked in fur; it grew arms and a dark and grizzled beard, a wicked eye.

She screamed and tried to push herself away.

"Ain't any need for that," the demon said. "Don't mean ye any harm."

She stared in alarm. His words brought her no relief at all. "Who—who are you?" she managed to say. "What do you want with me?"

"My name's John Johnston," the figure said. "Folks has mostly took out the *t*, but that ain't no fault of mine. Just lie right still. You oughter take in some soup if ye can."

He didn't wait for an answer, but moved across the room. Her heart pounded rapidly against her breast. She watched him carefully, followed his every move. He would likely attack her quite soon. This business of the soup was just a ruse. Well, he would not catch her totally unaware. She searched for some weapon of defense, pulled herself up on one arm, the effort draining all her strength. She was under some heavy animal skin. It held her to the floor like lead. She saw a broken chair, just beyond her reach. With the help of Lord Jesus it would serve her quite well. David had very little more and brought another fearsome giant to his knees.

As she reached for the chair, stretched her arm as far as it would go, the heavy skin slipped past her shoulders to her waist. She felt the sudden cold, stopped, and caught sight of herself. For an instant, she was too paralyzed to move. Frozen with terror and disbelief. She was unclothed, bare beneath the cover! Her head began to swim. She fought against the dizziness and shame. *Oh Lord, don't let me faint,* she prayed. *Let me die, but don't let me faint in the presence of the beast!*

Using every ounce of will she could find, she lay back and pulled the cover to her chin. With one hand, she searched herself for signs of violation, careful not to touch any place where carnal sin resides. Surely he had done it in her sleep. Whatever it was they did. Would you know, could you tell? Defilement came with marriage, and she had no experience in that.

The man returned from the fire. She mustered all her courage. "Stay away from me," she warned. "Don't take another step."

He seemed puzzled. "You don't want no soup?"

"You—you had no right," she said. "You have invaded my privacy. You have looked upon me. You have sinned in God's eyes and broken several commandments. I demand the return of my clothing."

He squatted down and set the soup on the floor. "Ma'am, I didn't do no sinnin' I recall. You was near froze stiff in them clothes."

"Oh, of course. That is just what you would say to excuse your lust. I would expect no less than that."

"Yes, ma'am."

"I cannot find it in my heart to forgive you. That is my failing. I will pray that our Blessed Savior will give me the strength to see you as His child."

"You feel a need fer this soup," Johnston said, "it's on the fire." With that he rose and left her, moved across the room and curled up in a buffalo robe.

He woke at once and grabbed his heavy coat and picked up the Hawken rifle, all this in a single motion out of sleep. The woman hadn't moved. He had propped the broken door back up as best he could, and now he moved it carefully aside and slipped out into the night. The world seemed frozen, silent and hard as iron, yet brittle enough to shatter into powder at a touch. He couldn't put his finger on the sound that had broken through his sleep. The horse was all right, safely out of the wind by the cabin's far wall. The ground was undisturbed. He circled around and watched, stopped to sniff the air. Nothing was there now, but something had left its ghost behind.

Inside he warmed his hands by the fire. The woman was still asleep. It wasn't fair to say that she hadn't roused him some, that the touch of her flesh as he rubbed life back into her limbs hadn't started up some fires. Not like an Injun girl now, but some. He'd seen maybe two white women stark naked in his life. They seemed to lack definition. Like a broad field of snow without a track or a rock to give it tone. An Injun girl went from one shade to another, depending where you looked. John Hatcher had kept two fat Cheyenne squaws all the time. He kept them in his cabin in the Little Snake Valley and offered Johnston the use of one or both. He had politely declined, preferring to find his own. Hatcher's squaws giggled all the time. An Injun woman tended to act white after a spell and start to giggle and talk back. His wife hadn't done that at all. She'd been pure Injun to the end, but there weren't very many like that.

When she woke once again she felt sick, drained and brittle as a stick. The man was well across the room, squatting silently by the wall.

"I would like that soup now if you please," she said as firmly as she could. She would show him no weakness at all. A man preyed upon that.

He rose and went to the fire, filled a tin cup and set it by her side.

"Take a care," he said, "it's right hot." He returned to the fire and came back and dropped a bundle on the floor. "Your clothes is all dry," he said.

She didn't answer or meet his eyes. She knew any reference to her garments would encourage wicked thoughts in his head. The soup tasted vaguely of corn, meat a little past its prime. It was filling and soothed the hurt away.

"Thank you," she said, "that was quite good."

"There's more if you want."

"I would like you to leave the cabin for a while. I should think half an hour will do fine."

Johnston didn't blink. "What fer?"

"That is no concern of yours."

"You want to get dressed, why you got that buffler robe. Ain't no reason you can't do it under there."

"Why, I certainly will not!" The suggestion brought color to her cheeks.

"Up to you," he said.

"I shall *not* move until you comply."

"Suit yerself."

Oh Lord, she prayed, *deliver me from this brute. Banish transgression from his mind.* Reaching out beneath the robe, she found her clothing and burrowed as far beneath the cover as she could, certain all the while he could see, or surely imagine, every private move she made.

"Certain rules will apply," she said. "I suppose we are confined here for the moment, though I trust the Lord will release us from adversity in good time."

She sat very close to the fire. The warmth never seemed enough. The cold came in and sought her out. The man continued to squat against the wall. It didn't seem possible that he could sit in this manner for long hours at a time. Only the blue eyes flecked with gray assured her he had not turned to stone. He was younger than she'd imagined, perhaps only a few years older than herself. His shocking red hair and thick unkempt beard masked his face; hard and weathered features helped little in determining his age.

"You will respect my privacy," she said, "and I shall certainly respect yours. There will be specific places in this room where you are not to venture. Now. I wish to say in all fairness that I believe you very likely saved my life. I am not ungrateful for that."

"Yes'm," Johnston said.

"My name is Mistress Dickinson. Mistress Emily Elizabeth Dickinson to be complete, though I caution you very strongly, Mr. Johnston, that while circumstances have thrown us together, you will *not* take the liberty of using my Christian name."

"Already knew who you was," Johnston said.

Emily was startled, struck with sudden fear. "Why, that is not possible. How could you know that?"

"Saw yer name when I went through yer belongin's," Johnston said.

"How dare you, sir!"

"Didn't mean to pry. Thought you was goin' to pass on 'fore the morning. Figured I ought git yer buryin' name."

"Oh." Emily was taken aback. Her hand came up to touch her heart. "I . . . see. Yes. Well, then . . ."

Johnston seemed to squint his eyes in thought. For the first time, she detected some expression in his face.

"Ma'am, there's somethin' I got to say," Johnston said. "Them soldiers you was with. I reckon you know they're all three of 'em dead."

"I . . . guessed as much." Emily trembled at the thought. "I have prayed for their souls. Our Lord will treat them kindly."

"Some better'n them Sioux did, I reckon."

"Do not take light of the Lord, Mr. Johnston. He does not take light of you."

Johnston studied her closely again. "Jes' what was you an' them fellers doin' up here, you don't mind me askin'."

Emily paused. She had kept this horror repressed; now, she found herself eager to bring it out. Even telling it to Johnston might help it go away.

"Captain William A. Ramsey of Vermont was kind enough to ask me to accompany him and his troopers on a ride," Emily said. "There were twelve men in all when we started. The day was quite nice, not overly cold at all. We left Fort Laramie with the intention of riding along the North Platte River a few miles. A storm arose quite quickly. I believe there was some confusion about direction. When the storm passed by, we found ourselves under attack, much to everyone's alarm. Several men were killed outright. It was . . . quite terrifying."

"Cheyenne, most likely," Johnston said, as if the rest was quite clear. "They kept drivin' you away from the fort. Gittin' between you an' any help."

"Yes. That is what occurred."

"Pocahontas an' John Smith!" Johnston shook his head. "Yer lucky to be alive whether you know that or not."

"The men were very brave," Emily said. "We lost the Indians the third day out, I believe. By then there were only three men left and myself. Whether the others were cruelly slain or simply lost in the cold, I cannot say. We could not turn back. I think we rode for six days. There was almost nothing to eat. One of the colored troopers killed a hare, but that was all."

"You got rid of the Cheyenne an' run smack into the Sioux," Johnston finished.

"Yes. That is correct."

Johnston ran a hand through his beard. "You don't mind me sayin', this end of the country ain't a fit sort of place fer a woman like yerself."

Emily met his eyes. "I don't see that is any concern of yours."

Johnston didn't answer. She found the silence uncomfortable between them. Perhaps he didn't really mean to pry.

"Mr. Johnston," she said, "I have lived all my life in Amherst, Massachusetts. I am twenty-five years old and my whole life to now has passed in virtually one place. I have been as far as Washington and Philadelphia. I had no idea what the rest of God's world was like. I decided to go and see for myself."

"Well, I reckon that's what ye did."

"And yes. I confess that you are right. It was a foolish thing to do. I had no idea it would be like this. In my innocence, the Oregon Trail seemed a chance to view wildlife and other natural sights. Soon after departing Independence, I sensed that I was wrong. Now I am paying for my sins."

"I'd guess yer folks ain't got a idea where you are," Johnston said, thinking rightly this was so.

"No, they do not. I am certain they believe I am dead. I only pray they think I perished somewhere in the New England states."

"You ain't perished yet," Johnston said.

"I fear that is only a question of time," Emily sighed.

This time he was waiting, fully awake and outside, hunched silently in a dark grove of trees. It was well after midnight, maybe one or two. There was no wind at all and the clouds moved swiftly across the land. He thought about the woman. Damned if she wasn't just like he figured, white in near every way there was, stubborn and full of her own will. It irked him to think she was stuck right to him and no blamed way to shake her loose. There wasn't any place to take her except back to Fort Laramie or on to Fort Pierre, and either way with one horse. He thought about White Eye Anderson and Del Gue and Chris Lapp, and old John Hatcher himself, seeing him drag in with this woman on a string. Why, they'd ride him for the rest of his life.

The shadow moved, and when it did Johnston spotted it at once. He waited. In a moment, a second shadow appeared, directly behind the first. He knew he'd been right the night before. How many, he wondered. All six or just two? What most likely happened was the Crow ran back toward the Powder, then got their courage up when the Sioux were out of mind. One was maybe smarter than the rest and found his trail. Which meant there was one red coon somewhere with a nose near as good as his own. Now that was a chile he'd like to meet. Johnston sniffed the world once more and started wide around the trees.

Now there was only one shadow. The other had disappeared while he circled past the grove. He didn't like that, but there was not much for it. He sat and waited. Part of the dark and the wind-blown striations of the snow. Part of the patch of gray light that swept the earth. He knew what the Crow was doing now. He was waiting to get brave. Waiting to get his juices ready for a fight.

When it happened, the Indian moved so quickly even Johnston was surprised. The Crow stood and made for the cabin door, a blur against the white and frozen ground. Johnston rose up out of nowhere at all, one single motion taking him where he had to be. He lifted the Crow clearly off the ground, the bowie cutting cold as ice. It was over fast and done and he knew in that instant, knew before the Crow went limp and fell away, where the other one had gone. Saw him from the corner of his eye as he came off the roof straight for him, and knew the man had buried himself clean beneath the snow, burrowed like a mole and simply waited out his time. Johnston took the burden on his shoulder, bent his legs and shook the Indian to the ground. The Crow came up fighting, brought his hatchet up fast and felt Johnston's big foot glance off his chest. He staggered back, looked fearfully at Johnston as if he knew a solid blow would have stopped his heart at once, as if he saw in that moment the widows in the Absaroka camp whose men had met this terrible sight before. Turning on his heels, he ran fast across the snow, plowing through drifts for the safety of the trees. Johnston tugged the Walker Colt from his belt, took his aim and fired. The Crow yelled but didn't stop.

Johnston cussed aloud; the red coon was bloodied but still alive. He didn't miss much, and this sure was a poor time to do it. He'd counted on horses. Now the Crow would take them off. He maybe should have gotten the horses first. The Crow would go and lick his wound and come back and that was pure aggravation.

He dragged the dead body well back behind the cabin. He sat beside the corpse, cut the heavy robes away. He saw a picture in his head. He saw his woman. He saw his unborn child within her womb. The child sprang to life. It played among the aspens on the Little Snake River and came to him when he called. The picture went away. He drew the knife cleanly and swiftly across the Indian's flesh below the ribs and thrust his hand inside the warmth.

With no windows at all, with the cold outside and no difference she could see between dismal day and night, the hours seemed confused. She was often too weak to stay awake. When she slept, the rest seemed to do her little good.

She felt relieved to wake and find him gone. Relief and some alarm. His size, his presence, overwhelmed her. Yet these very qualities, the nature of the man, were all that stood between her and some greater menace still. He cannot help being what he is, she told herself. God surely made him this way for some reason, for some purpose, though she could scarcely imagine what that purpose might be.

The soup tasted good. That morning he had made some kind of bread out of corn, and there was still a little left. The fire was getting low and she added a little wood. The wood caught and snapped, for an instant lighting every dark corner of the room. He had set his belongings along the wall. A buffalo robe and a saddle. Leather satchels and a pack. His things seemed a part of the man. Fur and hide greased and worn, heavy with the raw and sour smells of the wild.

She had never ventured quite this close to his things. It seemed like a miniature camp, everything set the way he liked. Her eyes fell upon a thick leather packet. She looked away and then quickly looked back. The corner of a paper peeked out, and there was writing on the edge. How very strange, she thought. Literacy was wholly unexpected. She knew this wasn't fair, and chastised herself at once.

Certainly, she did not intend to pry. She would never touch Mr. Johnston's things. Still, what one could plainly see was surely no intrusion. I should not be here at all, she decided. I must turn away at once. Should dizziness occur, I might very well collapse, and this is not the place for that. Indeed, as she turned, this very thing happened. Her foot brushed against the leather packet, and slipped the paper free.

"Now look what I have done," she said, and bent to retrieve the paper at once. In spite of her good intention, the words leaped up to meet her eyes:

> It makes no difference abroad,
> The seasons fit the same,
> The mornings blossom into noons,
> And split their pods of flame.

And then, from the packet, another scrap of paper after that:

> The sky is low, the clouds are mean,
> A traveling flake of snow
> Across a barn or through a rut
> Debates if it will go.

"Oh. Oh, dear," Emily said aloud. "That last one's quite nice. Or at least I *think* it is." She read the lines again, frowning over this and that, and decided it was slightly overdone.

Still, she wondered, what was verse doing here? Where had this unlettered man of the wilds come across a poem? Perhaps he found it, she reasoned. Came across it in a cabin such as this where some poor traveler had met his fate.

The sound of the shot nearly paralyzed her with fear. "Oh blessed Jesus!" she cried. The papers fluttered from her hand. She fled to a corner of the cabin, crouched there and stared at the door.

An Indian would enter quite soon. Possibly more than one. They would not slay her, though they would take her to their camp. She would tell them about Christ. They would renounce their savage ways. They would certainly not touch her in any way.

It seemed forever before the door opened again and Johnston appeared. "Oh, thank the Lord you're all right," Emily sighed. "That shot. I thought—I thought you had surely been killed!"

"Took a shot at a deer," Johnston said. "Wasn't nothin' more'n that." He shook his coat. His beard seemed thick with ice.

"God be praised," Emily said.

Johnston set his Hawken aside. Stomped his feet and ran his hand through a bushy nest of hair. He looked down then and saw the papers on the floor and picked them up. He looked right at Emily and didn't say a thing.

Emily's heart began to pound. "I . . . I'm very sorry," she said. "I certainly had no right."

"Don't matter none," Johnston said. He stood with his backside to the fire.

"Yes, now yes it does," Emily said firmly. "It is I who have transgressed. I am clearly in the wrong. I do not deny my sin."

"I ain't never hear'd so much about sin," Johnston said.

Emily felt her face color. "Well, there certainly is sin abroad, Mr. Johnston. Satan has his eye upon us all."

"I reckon," Johnston said. He scratched and sat down. Leaned against the wall in his customary manner.

Emily wondered if she dare break the silence. He didn't seem angry at all, but how on earth would one know? And they could not simply sit there and look at one another.

"Mr. Johnston, I do not excuse my actions," she said, "but perhaps you'll understand when I say I have an interest in poetry myself. As a fact, one small effort has seen the light of publication. Three years ago. February 20, 1852, to be exact. In the *Springfield Daily Republican*." She smiled and touched her hair. "I recall the date clearly, of course, There are dates in one's life one remembers very well. One's birthday, certainly—" Emily blushed, aware she was chattering away. "Well, yes, at any rate . . ."

Johnston said nothing at all.

"You must be quite chilled," Emily said. "There is still a little soup."

"I ain't real hungry," Johnston said.

This time would have to be different; the Crow was wary now and hurt, and an Injun like that was the same as any other creature in the wild in such condition, the same as he'd be himself, Johnston knew, as deadly as a stirred-up snake. The Crow would be in place early this night, out there in spite of the cold, because the first man out could watch and see what the other man would do. It was a deadly advantage, and Johnston was determined to let the Absaroka have it.

The Indian was cautious and he was good. Johnston could scarcely hear him, scarcely smell his fear. He seemed to take forever, moving when the wind rose some, stopping when it died.

Tarnation, Johnston thought, *come on and git it done, chile, 'fore I freeze these bones to the ground.*

At last the Crow struck, coming in swiftly without a sound. The hatchet fell once, slicing the heavy furs, withdrew and hacked again, and Johnston, even in the dark, saw emotion of every sort cross the Absaroka's face, saw surprise and alarm and then final understanding that the furs crouched there against the tree didn't have a man inside, that it was simply too late to remedy that.

Johnston shook the snow aside. "That war your trick, son, not mine," he said aloud. "Ye got no one to blame but yourself . . ."

She hated the boredom most of all. It overpowered fear and apprehension. Now she sorely missed being scared. Now there was nothing at all to do. Was it day outside or was it night? Sometimes Johnston would tell her. For the most part, he sat like a stone or wandered out in the night. Worse than sitting in the cabin were the times when she had to go out to attend to bodily needs. It was horrid, a humiliation she could scarcely bear. She had to *ask*. He would not let her venture out alone. He would stand by the door with his weapon while she struggled as far as she dared through the snow. And the cold! That fierce, and unimaginable cold. Winter, she saw now, gave New England a fleeting glance. This terrible empty land was where it was born.

She heard him at the door and then he stepped inside, letting in the cold. "Found us a couple of horses," Johnston said, and dropped his heavy coat on the floor.

"You did?" Emily was surprised. "Why, isn't that odd."

"Ain't nothin' odd to it," Johnston said.

"Yes, well . . ." He seemed very pleased with himself. It dawned on her then that horses had meaning in her life. "Heavens," she said, "that means we can leave this place, does it not?"

"First thing in the mornin'," Johnston said. He didn't even glance her way. He simply wrapped up in his robes and turned his face against the wall.

Emily felt the heat rise to her cheeks, and this brought further irritation. Anger at Johnston, but mostly at herself. What did *she* care what he did? They certainly had nothing to talk about. No topic that would interest her in the least. Still, the man's rudeness had no bounds at all. He had no concept of social intercourse.

"You are just going to—sleep?" she said. "Right now?"

"I was plannin' on it," Johnston said.

"Well, you could at least impart information. There are things one needs to know."

" 'Bout what?"

"About the trip." Emily waited. Johnston didn't answer. "What I mean, is how long will it take? I have no idea of the distance to Fort Laramie. As you know, I left under unusual circumstances."

"Ain't goin' to Fort Laramie. Goin' to Fort Pierre."

Emily sat up. "Mr. Johnston, I demand to be returned to Fort *Laramie*. I have no intention of going anywhere else."

"Fort Pierre's whar I'm headed," Johnston said.

"Whatever for?"

"Meetin' someone."

"Well, who?"

"Like you're fonda sayin', Miz Dickinson, that ain't no concern of yours."

Emily tried to contain herself. To show Christian restraint. A sudden thought occurred. A woman, that was it. He was going to see a woman. Possibly a wife. The thought defied imagination. What sort of woman would this backwoods ruffian attract?

"Are you married, Mr. Johnston?" Emily asked. "I don't believe you've ever said. But of course you're quite correct. That is no concern of mine."

Johnston kept his silence. He had likely gone to sleep and hadn't heard a word she said. The man had no consideration.

"My wife's dead," Johnston said. The tone of his words brought a chill. "Her an' the chile, too. Crows killed 'em both."

Emily felt ashamed. "I'm . . . terribly sorry, Mr. Johnston. Really."

"Reckon I am, too."

"You are angry with me, I know."

"Ma'am, I ain't angry at all."

"Yes, now, you are. I do not fault you for it, Mr. Johnston. I have intruded upon your life. I am guilty of certain violations. And you are still upset about the poems."

"No I ain't."

"Yes you are. That is quite clear to me. I want you to know that I have since shown respect for your possessions. I was tempted, yes. We are all weak vessels, and there is nothing at all to do in this place. Still, I did not succumb. Lord Jesus gave me strength."

"Git some sleep," Johnston said, and pulled the buffalo robe about his head.

He awoke in fury and disbelief, clutched the Hawken and came to his feet, saw the dull press of dawn around the door, heard the faint sound of horses outside, hardly there at all, as if they'd come up with him out of sleep.

Great God A'Mighty, they'd played him for a fool, him sleeping like a chile and sure he'd got the only two. Maybe it wasn't Crow, he decided. Maybe it was Sioux coming back. And what in tarnation did it matter which brand of red coon it might be—they flat had him cold like a rabbit in a log.

The woman came awake, a question on her face. "Jes' get back in yer corner and keep quiet," Johnston said harshly. He turned to face the door, made sure the Walker Colt was in his belt. How many, he wondered? The horses were silent now.

"Come an' git your medicine," he said softly, "I'm a-waitin' right here."

"Inside the cabin," a man shouted. "This is Lieutenant Joshua Dean. We are here in force, and I must ask you to come out at once, unarmed."

Johnston laughed aloud. He decided he was plain going slack. A man who couldn't tell shod horses in his sleep was a man who maybe ought to pack it in.

* * *

"I am grateful for what you have done," Emily said. "I owe you my thanks, Mr. Johnston."

"Nothin' to thank me for," Johnston said. The troopers had stopped fiddling about and seemed ready to depart. He wondered why a soldier took an hour to turn around. The lieutenant had eyed the Indian ponies but didn't ask where their riders might be. If he recognized Johnston or knew his name, he didn't say.

"We have had our differences, I suppose," Emily said.

"I reckon so."

"God has a reason for what he does, Mr. Johnston. I am sure this adventure serves a purpose in His plan."

Johnston couldn't figure just what it might be. "You have a safe trip, Miz Dickinson," he said.

"I will do just that," Emily said. "I expect Massachusetts will seem dear to me now. I doubt I'll stray again."

She walked away through the snow, and the lieutenant helped her mount. Johnston watched till they were well out of sight, then went inside to get his things.

As he rode through the flat white world with the slate-dark sky overhead, he thought about the Bitter Root Mountains and the Musselshell River. He thought about the Platte and the Knife and the Bearpaw Range, every peak and river he'd ever crossed clear as glass in his head. He thought about Swan, eight years dead in the spring, and it didn't seem that long at all, and in a way a lot more. Dead all this time, and he still saw her face every day.

Before dark, he found a spot near the Belle Fourche and staked the horses out safe. One Crow pony had a blaze between its eyes. He favored an Injun horse with good marks. He wondered if Del Gue was still waiting at Fort Pierre. They'd have to get moving out soon to get some hides. He thought again how he'd waited too long to get in the trapping trade, the beaver near gone when he'd come to the mountains and hooked up with old Hatcher. Just bear and mink now and whatever a man could find.

Scooping out a hole in the snow, he snapped a few sticks and stacked them ready for the fire, then walked back and got his leather satchel and dipped his hand inside. Johnston stopped, puzzled at an unfamiliar touch. He squatted on the ground and started pulling things out. There was nothing but an old Army blanket. His paper was all gone.

"Well, cuss me fer a Kiowa," he said aloud. That damn woman had filched the whole lot. He was plain irritated. It wasn't like he couldn't spark a fire, but a man fell into easy habits. A little paper saved time, especially if your wood was all wet. Came in handy, too, if you had to do your business and there wasn't no good leaves about.

She'd gotten every piece there was. He hadn't ever counted, but there were likely near a thousand bits and scraps, rhymes he'd thought up and set down, then saved for the fire. This was by God pure aggravation. He grumbled to himself and found his flint. A man sure couldn't figure what was stewing in a white woman's head. An Injun wasn't like that at all.

Stairs

MARY LOUISE MADE WHEAT-CRACKLE MUSH AND THE last of the cabbage rose tea. "I think what I will do is I will book," she decided. "I will book about the boy with amethyst eyes." The thought made her blush. A naughty flew in her ear and buzzed about. She hurried through supper quick as a wink. Rinsed out the bowl and the long copper spoon and the milk-blue cracked china cup. Moved about the room and fussed and straightened this and that. Made everything neat as it could be.

"That's that," she said at last, and sat down in the straight-back chair and took the big brown book from the table. The binding was chip-brittle, dry and cracked. Mary Louise turned pages limp as soup. A word came off on her finger. She held it up and looked. The word said ƎJIMƧ. Mary Louise made a face and licked it off. Words became pictures in her head. She saw the young man with amethyst eyes. The crisp black hair and cheery grin. She saw the olive coat and the soot-black trousers and the fine high boots brown as wood. She saw how the clothes fit tight across his chest and muscled arms. Her heart beat faster and a warm touched her lightly on the cheek. She turned the page as quickly as she could. Words slipped off and disappeared. *Thigh* and *quicksilver*, and *mute anticipation.*

Mary Louise booked. The lamp with the red paper shade made a cozy circle of light. The light stayed where it belonged. Never reached dusty corners, wallpaper waterstained and marbled with coffee clouds and the ghosts of tiny flowers. Left undisturbed places sad and torn and worn, a lace dress buried in the wall.

Tap-tap-tap, came a sound or maybe didn't come at all.

Tap-tap-tap, it maybe didn't come again.

Mary Louise stopped booking and watched the dark around the room. The colors time-soft like ash and russet and plum. Colors that smelled of dustballs, whits and spiderbreath, places dry and hollow. She listened to the drone and the rumble on the stairs, listened to the hum of the people passing by.

"Who's there," Mary Louise said softly. "Is that you I hear, Mrs. Wood?"

"Hello, Mary Louise," said Mrs. Wood. "And how are we doing this lovely day?" Voice dry as paper, chipped as a china cup.

"Why, I'm just fine, Mrs. Wood."

"And how old are we today, Mary Louise?"

"Nineteen," said Mary Louise, knowing that Mrs. Wood could never remember. "You're feeling well, I hope?"

"As well as I can be," said Mrs. Wood.

"Are you sewing, Mrs. Wood?"

"No I'm not, Mary Louise."

"Are you sweeping, Mrs. Wood?"

"No I'm not, Mary Louise."

"What are you doing, Mrs. Wood?"

"I'm doing a book, Mary Louise."

"Why, so am I!" said Mary Louise.

"My book's a book about mice," said Mrs. Wood. "Every possible kind of mice that you can name. Feelmice, realmice, mice that live in a jar."

"I don't suppose I know about a myce," said Mary Louise.

"I can guess what your book's about," said Mrs. Wood. "I can guess it's a book about a boy."

"It is not," said Mary Louise, feeling another warm behind her ears. "It's nothing of the sort!"

"I know young ladies like you," said Mrs. Wood. "I know what they like to do."

"I had a cup of tea," Mary Louise said quickly. "I fixed a fine cup of tea a while ago."

"That's nice," said Mrs. Wood. "Do you know what I'm doing right now? I'm looking at the water. I've been looking at the water all day."

"I see," said Mary Louise, who didn't see at all. She tried to picture Mrs. Wood. Mrs. Wood sat in a chair. Mrs. Wood booked myce and looked at water. Now why would she want to do that?

"How old are you now, Mary Louise?"

"Still nineteen, Mrs. Wood."

"Do you like to dress up, Mary Louise?"

"I only have two dresses, Mrs. Wood."

"Are you pretty, Mary Louise?"

"I wouldn't know, Mrs. Wood."

"Do you play with your little whoozie, Mary Louise?"

"Mrs. *Wood!*" Mary Louise was so startled, the book fell from her lap and struck the floor. "If that's the way you're going to be," she said crossly, "I'm not going to talk to you at all!"

But Mrs. Wood was gone. There was nothing there at all but the rumble of the people on the stairs.

Mary Louise didn't like to go out, but there was nothing in the pantry but a biscuit hard as stone. She found a few monies in the drawer. Her big brass key and a broken comb. Monies in her pocket, she unlocked the door and slid the wooden bolt aside. The stairs were people thick. People and the smells that people do. A woman with a nose like a knife tried to peek into her room. She said, *"paste lethal, globally remiss."*

Mary Louise shut the door and locked it tight, thrust the brass key in her pocket. People bumped and pushed and squeezed. Jabbed and poked. Stuck her in the ribs and kicked her shins. She was caught in the crowd and swept along. She passed her orange number on the wall. 320,193. The rumbles and the hums picked her up and sucked her in. Mary Louise struggled and shoved, dug and grabbed. Turned and found the lane going down. The stairs twisted pinch-tight and narrow, twisted dizzily round and round. She breathed in feet smells, armpit and teeth smells, cheese smells, sweat smells, he smells and she smells. Squeezed down the stairs in a flatulescent fog. The walls and the ceilings and the stairs were dark wood caked and clotted with people stuff, and the people wrote and scribbled as they passed. Made fingernail names, drew acts they'd like to commit. Mary Louise never read what people wrote.

A woman with a face gray as lead touched her hair. A man found her ear, whispered, *"carp bridal, imminent intent."* Wormed clever fingers down her neck and pinched her pointy. Mary Louise bit her lip and clutched her key. That was a trick they liked to use. Do something awful, make you let go of your key for just a wink. Steal it and get your things while you were gone. Wait and pull you in when you returned.

A yellow bulb made bleary light on every floor. The bulbs were thick with people-soot and spiders. The spiders came to eat and warm their eyes. Mumble-mumble shove. People wearing dun and slate and gray. People wearing patch-torn black and burnt sienna.

320,193
320,189
320,185
One floor one door one more.

Mary Louise shoved and pushed. Popped out of people like a cork. A beggar with putty eyes sat on the floor. A man with a yellow tongue stepped on his hand. The beggar said, *"miscarry, continental mire."*

Grocer Bill ran a store in his room. Mary Louise held her breath and made her way along the wall. There were thirty-seven people inside. The table was lined with brown paper sacks. Grease sacks, used sacks, patched with other sacks. There was a curtain on a string.

"Well, I haven't seen you for a while, Mary Louise," said Grocer Bill. He wore a green paper hat shaped like a box. Grocer Bill always gave her funny looks, gave her sly funny looks when he knew Mrs. Bill wasn't around. Mary Louise clutched her key and squeezed her monies in her pocket.

"I need a few things," said Mary Louise. "What do you have that's good today?"

"I have some very fine lardstring noodles," winked Grocer Bill. "Very fine indeed."

Mary Louise made a face. Sniffed into brown paper sacks. Fat noodles, skinny noodles, noodles white as the skin between her toes.

"I guess I'll take wheat-crackle if you have it," said Mary Louise. "And fatcake and sourmeal pie. There's no dirtsugar, I don't suppose?"

"Oh, all out of that, I'm afraid."

"Any cabbage rose tea?" she said, really afraid to ask.

"Now that's hard to get, Mary Louise," said Grocer Bill. "Real hard to get is what it is." His shiny black eyes darted about, searching for Mrs. Bill. One hand snaked under the counter and came up with a small twist of paper. Pressed it in her palm and squeezed her fingers under his. "That's just for you," said Grocer Bill. "Don't tell anyone where you got it."

"Thank you," Mary Louise said politely, "I surely won't."

"Anything else you need today?"

"I don't guess," said Mary Louise.

"That'll be, let's see." Grocer Bill flicked his tongue about his teeth. "About seven monies, Mary Louise."

"Goodness, that much?"

"Hard times, Mary Louise."

Mary Louise dug monies from her pocket. There were six pearl buttons and a black steel washer. A thumbtack without any point, and a marble as blind as an eye. A military button with important swirly lines.

"Let's see what we have," said Grocer Bill. Poked at her palm, sneaked a tickle. Snatched up the button and went right for the cloudy eye. Mary Louise snapped her fist shut tight.

"That's a real good monies that first one," she said firmly. "That *ought* to be enough. It's probably a nine is what it is."

"Well now, I wouldn't say a nine," grinned Grocer Bill, the grin telling her he'd gotten the best of the bargain. She wished she hadn't shown him the button at all.

Grocer Bill put her goods in a sack. Mrs. Bill poked her head through the curtain, saw Mary Louise and made a face. Mary Louise smiled. Turned to go. Stopped, and looked curiously down the table. A boy was leaning against the wall. Not buying a thing, just leaning against the wall. He was tall and knobby-kneed with a thatch of yellow hair. The hair seemed to perch upon his head, as if it didn't intend to stay. He carried a wooden box on a string. The string hung over his shoulder to his side. And his clothes— He had a *most* peculiar clothes. Mary Louise had never seen such a clothes in all her life. It was a patchwork of bright and raggedy squares. Reds and blues and greens. Yellows and silvers and golds. Colors she couldn't name and didn't want to if she could. How awful, she thought. How terribly ugly and bright. What a frightening thing to wear!

The boy looked up. Looked right at her as if he'd guessed what she was thinking all along. There were tiny blue lights in his eyes. The lights sparked and danced. He smiled at Mary Louise. The smile seemed to slice his face in two. Mary Louise felt a warm in her tummy. A fidget behind her knees. She grabbed her sack and ducked into the crowd.

The first floors were slow, slower than ever. At three-two-oh, one-eight-eight, everything came to a stop. Nothing moved ahead. Crowds backed up behind. People mumbled and shoved. Officer Bob came bounding up the stairs, banging his stick against the wall.

"Flatten up, everyone, flatten up," he called out. "Train coming through right now!"

"Oh no," groaned Mary Louise, and everyone else groaned, too.

Before long the train came plodding up from below. Both lanes crowded against the wall, but there was still scarcely room for the train to pass. First came a skinny little man in coal-black, gray paper stripes across his chest. He beat on a can with a wooden stick.

Clack, clack — clack-clack-clack!

Then came the train, each man moving at a slow and steady pace.

"Huh, huh — huh-huh-huh!
"Huh, huh — huh-huh-huh!"

Big heavy boxes were strapped to their backs. Their backs were broad and strong. They were built just like the boxes, chests and shoulders square and hard. Legs thick as poles, ankles the same as thighs. Mary Louise could smell the sharp and tingly sweat, the heat as hot as a stove.

"Huh, huh — huh-huh-huh!
"Huh, huh — huh-huh-huh!"

A little girl began to count. "Seventy-nine . . . seventy-ten . . . seventy-leven . . ."

"Hush," said the little girl's mother.

Numbers were scribbled on the boxes. Numbers as thick as the scribbles on the walls. Numbers over numbers and over numbers still. Mary Louise read them as the train rumbled past her up the stairs.

344,119
  351,444
    377,920

"Goodness!" Mary Louise said aloud, doing quick sums in her head. Doing numbers minus her floor from the boxes passing by. What a long way to go — what a terribly *long* way to go. Of course they got to rest, she decided. Surely they got to rest. She'd never seen a train stopped, only trains going up and going down.

One of the trains raised his head and looked right at Mary Louise. His eyes were noodle-white, his mouth a crooked nail. He said, *"indigo confection, common oversight."*

"Hello," said Mary Louise to be nice.

Officer Bob gave the signal. The crowd raised a cheer and surged ahead. Traffic began to move in both lanes.

"Why hello, Mary Louise," said Officer Bob. "How have you been I'd like to know?"

"Why I've been fine," said Mary Louise, feeling a warm on the tip of her chin. Officer Bob was tall and strong, nearly the size of some of the train. He wore a blue paper hat and kindly eyes.

"It's awfully crowded today," said Mary Louise. "I thought I'd never get to the store."

Officer Bob shook his head. Leaned in close to Mary Louise. "Stair wars," he said, so low that only Mary Louise could hear. "Real bad trouble down below."

"Oh my!" said Mary Louise.

"Now that's all down in the two-eighties, not here," Officer Bob added quickly. "But a thing like that'll back up a long ways. You have a care now, Mary Louise." He tipped his blue hat, and Mary Louise climbed the rest of the way home.

Back in the safety of her own 320,193, Mary Louise locked the door and slipped the big wooden bar in its place. Tossed off her dress and didn't bother to put it away. Set the kettle on the stove and washed and scrubbed beneath the faucet till the smell of the stairs was nearly gone. Slipped on her other dress and poured a fresh cup of cabbage rose tea.

"I *guess* I'll have to drink a cup in the morning and one at night," she sighed aloud. "If I want to make it last any at all." And after that what would she do? She was nearly out of monies and couldn't think where to find any more.

"Oh well," she said, catching the last spicy drop on the tip of her tongue, "there's no use worrying about *that*." Turning back the covers, she slipped quickly into bed and in a moment she was fast asleep on her pillow.

She dreamed of drinking tea with Mrs. Wood. Mary Louise booked myce and Mrs. Wood looked at water. The water wasn't clear like water ought to be, it was the color of amethyst eyes. Mary Louise enjoyed the dream until she saw the boy's terrible clothes. Raggedy-patch clothes in awful colors that hurt her eyes. "That's *not* who you're supposed to be," said Mary Louise. The boy grinned. Lardstring noodles fell out of his mouth.

Mary Louise ate and slept and drank cabbage rose tea. She wouldn't talk to Mrs. Wood. She wouldn't sit by the table and the lamp. She took her chair to the wall between the pantry and the bed. Sometimes, if she closed her eyes and listened, she could hear the singers there. They sang like bells if bells could sing. Close and far away. She could never hear the words, but she could tell when the singers were happy or sad. Sometimes she wondered where they were. Sometimes she wondered if they were anywhere at all. They were certainly much nicer than Mrs. Wood.

Someone knocked at the door. Mary Louise gave a start. She opened the little hole but didn't peek right away. That's what they liked to do. Wait until you looked, then squirt something awful inside. Or poke out your eye with a stick. This time it was only Postman Jack, and Mary Louise slid the big bolt aside and opened the door.

"Hello, Mary Louise," smiled Postman Jack, "and how are you? Like to buy a mail today?"

"Oh, I would," said Mary Louise, "but I don't have monies to spend now."

"Real sorry to hear that," said Postman Jack. He wore a brown paper hat. Gold paper buttons pinned to his coat. A shabby gray bag drooped from his shoulder to his knees. "I've got one here I can let you have cheap," he told Mary Louise. "Hardly any monies at all."

"I'm afraid that's still too much for me," sighed Mary Louise.

"This is a very special mail," said Postman Jack. "Very special mail indeed."

"Special how?" said Mary Louise.

"You'll see," said Postman Jack, "you'll see." And with that he dipped a hand into his bag and drew a mail out with a flourish. "There now," he said, with a sparkle in his eye, "what do you think of that?"

Mary Louise wanted to be polite, but she really didn't think much at all. The mail was thin as air, a pale and sallow green. It looked as if it might simply whoof and disappear.

"It doesn't look very special to me," said Mary Louise. "It looks like a mail nobody wants."

"Well now, there's two halves to every mail," winked Postman Jack, "and you haven't seen the other." He flipped the mail over and held it right before her eyes.

"Oh," said Mary Louise, bringing a finger to her lips, "oh my!"

"See," said Postman Jack, "didn't I say it was special? What do you say now, Mary Louise?"

Mary Louise knew she shouldn't, but she really wanted the mail. Before she could change her mind, she dug a hand in her pocket and came up with the marble like an eye.

"This is all I can afford," she said sadly, "and I can't really *afford* to spend that."

"I'll take it," said Postman Jack, snapping up the monies quick as air. "I'll take it, since it's you."

"Oh, thank you," said Mary Louise, pleased and surprised at her good fortune. "Thank you, Postman Jack!"

"My pleasure," said Postman Jack. He tipped his brown hat and he was gone.

Mary Louise swore she'd just put the mail aside, save it for when there was nothing else to do. Since that was right now or most any time at all, she ran to the kettle and made tea, cut a piece of fatcake, and sat in the chair beneath the lamp. For a long time she looked at the pale green paper, at the paper so sheer she was certain a spider had made it. A spider as old as Mrs. Wood. Whoever had written the mail had drawn a very nice stamp to go along. It wound in sepia lines like a wispy tangle of wire that didn't end and didn't begin. Finally, she turned the mail over and looked at the tiny faded script. Caught her breath in wonder once again.

668,110

Goodness, thought Mary Louise, how could you even imagine a place so terribly far away? What was it like? How did it look? What did the people do? Mary Louise couldn't wait another moment. She carefully opened the mail. Dreamed of far adventure, strange customs and rites. The words on the paper were so delicate and tiny she could scarcely make them out, words drawn with a mite-whisker pen. She held her breath, afraid she'd blow them away. Brought the mail up close to her eyes. What the mail said was this:

Tailor John said he would make me a clothes for three monies. He is a liar and he knows it. If my legs hadn't give out bad I would go up there and tell him.

"Is that *all?*" Mary Louise cried. She stomped her feet on the floor. "Well, I'm certainly going to tell Postman Jack what I think about that!"

"What are you doing, Mary Louise?" said Mrs. Wood.

"I'm booking a mail, Mrs. Wood," said Mary Louise, then remembered she wasn't speaking to Mrs. Wood.

"My son writes me every week," said Mrs. Wood. "Even when he's out to sea."

"Out to see what?" Mary Louise said crossly.

"You are a sassy, impudent girl," said Mrs. Wood. "I doubt you have education or bearing. I expect you go naked under your clothes."

"Just go *away*, Mrs. Wood," said Mary Louise.

Mary Louise booked about the boy with amethyst eyes. She slept and got up and ate sourmeal pie and drank the last of the cabbage rose tea. She fussed about the room and washed her cup and washed her spoon and listened to the traffic on the stairs. Rumble-rumble hum. Sometimes it came through the door and over the floor and went tingling up her legs. Sometimes it buzzed about in her head. Why couldn't everyone stop going up or going down? Why couldn't everyone stay where they belonged?

The knock gave her a start. "Who's there," she called out, "what do you want?"

"You're never going to know if you don't look out and see," said the voice. "You'll have to look and see, Mary Louise."

It was a very *nice* voice, thought Mary Louise. But that didn't fool her for a minute. "I can do very well without looking," she said firmly. "Now please go away and leave me alone."

The voice became a laugh. A laugh sharp as glass that cut cleanly through the heavy wooden door and rattled dishes on the shelf.

"My goodness," said Mary Louise. She opened the hole a crack. Saw a patch of yellow hair. Saw a mouth so wide it could make a laugh any size it wanted. Eyes like crackly blue hot electric lights. The eyes made a warm at the hollow of her neck. Mary Louise caught her breath and backed half a step away.

"I know who you are," she said at last. "You're the boy with the funny clothes from Grocer Bill's."

"Right you are," said the boy. "Open up and let me in, Mary Louise."

"I'll do nothing of the sort," said Mary Louise. "I don't even know you at all."

"But I know you," said the boy. "I've brought you a fine present, and my name is Artist Dan."

"What kind of a present?" Mary Louise asked cautiously.

"A present like this," said Artist Dan, and waved a fat paper sack where she could see. "Cabbage rose tea, Mary Louise, and lots of it. The finest you'll ever taste, I promise you that."

"Oh my." The sack grew larger as she looked. Of course it could be full of stones and dead spiders for all she knew, and likely was.

"You can't come in," she said boldly. "I don't know who you are, and besides your awful clothes are hurting my eyes. No one wears a clothes like *that*."

"Not here they don't," said Artist Dan. "And there are places I've been where they don't wear pitch and soot and dead-grub yellow. Lead and drab and shadow-black and slug-dung madder. Colors dull as belly button fuzz in the dark of night."

"Well, if people dress like you somewhere," said Mary Louise, "I hope it's far away."

"Far is near and near is far," said Artist Dan.

"That's the silliest thing I've ever heard."

"Maybe so, maybe not."

"I have a mail from six-six-eight, one-one-oh," said Mary Louise.

"Far is where you aren't," said Artist Dan.

"See, you keep doing it," Mary Louise said sharply. "What do you art, anyway? I'll bet you art on the stairs is what you do."

"I paint," said Artist Dan.

"Paint what?" said Mary Louise.

"Paint people," said Artist Dan. "People is what I paint. I'll paint you if you like, Mary Louise."

"Well I wouldn't," Mary Louise said shortly. "I wouldn't like it at all."

"I have colors in my box you've never seen," said Artist Dan. "Bottle-green and apricot and cream. Violet and lilac and seven shades of blue. Saffron and vermilion, tangerine and pearl . . ."

"Go away," cried Mary Louise, "go away and leave me alone!" She snapped the hole shut, turned and leaned against the door, and heard her heart beat loudly in her ears. Pressed her head against the wood and imagined she heard him breathe. That's as foolish as it can be, she thought at once. All you can hear are the people on the stairs.

She waited long and listened, didn't breathe. What if he didn't go away? What if he stood there with all his awful colors? With his dreadful vermilions and his blues and bottle-greens? After a while she was certain he wasn't there. What she really needed now was a nice cup of cabbage rose tea. The kettle was nearly hot before she remembered the tea was gone. She tore Grocer Bill's little twisty brown paper in a hundred tiny pieces, dropped them in the drawer with the key and the broken comb. She wanted to cry, but couldn't remember how. All she wanted was some tea. What was the matter with that? And it *wasn't* tea he'd dangled before the door. It was just another trick is what it was.

Mary Louise slept and ate wheat-crackle mush. Cleaned up her room and sat in her chair and booked the boy with amethyst eyes. Slammed the book shut and saw words fly this way and that. The olive coat was gone and the soot-black trousers and the fine high boots as brown as wood. The colors in her head were amber and gold and ultramarine. Cobalt and cadmium and chrome. The crisp black hair was lemon-yellow and hurt her eyes.

"Mary Louise," said Mrs. Wood, "Mary Louise?"

Mary Louise took her chair across the room. The singers were silent and wouldn't sing. She threw herself on the bed and pulled the covers over her head. She dreamed he painted indigo waves beneath her eyes, brushed silver across her lips. Circled her waist with emerald indecision, dappled crimson on her thighs. Drew a raw and florid rainbow to her toes. When she woke, her heart was louder than the hum and the mumble on the stairs. When she stood, her legs were weak and there were spiders in her head.

"Are you there, Mrs. Wood?" called Mary Louise. If Mrs. Wood was there, she didn't say. The singers were back again, but she could scarcely hear their song. She carried her chair to the far end of the room. The corners that smelled old, where the light from the lamp would never go. She never ever came here because there was nothing here to do. No one talked or sang or said hello. There was nothing but the dust-smell, wallpaper waterstained, colors faded and gone.

And here, thought Mary Louise, is exactly where I want to be, not anywhere at all. I don't want to smell awful people on the stairs. I don't want to see bad colors or yellow hair, or blue electric eyes. I don't want dreams that leave warms in funny places. I don't even want a cup of tea. What I want is for everyone to simply leave me alone.

"Plover leech regatta," someone said, *"gainfully intact."*

"Please go away," said Mary Louise . . .

From the Novel: *The Hereafter Gang*
2: Mummies

Doug turned past the cemetery just on the edge of town. Yesterday reached out and gathered him in. His grandparents were buried right here in weedy plots under rusted marble stone. Greats and great-greats and uncles and aunts. Men in black suits and black high-top shoes, black socks thin as a woman's hose. White shirts buttoned at the top without a tie. Watch chains draped across a vest, chains attached to ivory pocket knives and watches the size and weight of river stones. Pearl gray Stetsons set straight above the eyes, the brim out flat and the crown stained with sweat. A pink rosebud in the lapel. A Prince Albert tin in one pocket, a Morgan silver dollar in the other. Their faces farm red, never tan. There's no such thing as a tan in Phara, Texas. The women wear flower-print dresses, corsets underneath hard as iron. Their hair is braided tight and bound in buns on either side. Hatpins lethal as a dagger hold a black straw firmly in place atop the head. The hat is set straight like a man's. No jaunty angles in Phara, Texas. The black straw hat is for the week. White hat, white shoes, and white gloves for Sunday service at the First Methodist Church. Powder and lilac water, a bright circle of rouge for the cheeks. Pearls and a brooch handed down, brought west from Tennessee or Alabama, and Virginia before that. Back further still, from Ireland and Wales.

At night, the shades drawn, the woman puts the flowered dress aside and quickly slips into a white cambric gown. Her back to the empty dressing room, she reaches under the gown and strips the armor of the day, corset and corset cover, drawers and underskirt. She sits before a mirror and a kerosene lamp and draws the many pins from her hair. The hair falls down to her waist. She brushes each side a hundred times. She thinks about the day. Her son has married a hussy from Kansas City. She works in a shop and smokes Old Gold cigarettes on the sly. The woman turns down the lamp and peeks into the other room. Her husband is safely asleep. She slips into bed, careful not to wake him. He smells of corn shucks and tobacco, dust and axle grease. She lays awake a long time. She hears a train far away, and wonders where it's going. She's been to Galveston, Texas. Weatherford and Dallas. The St. Louis World's Fair. She can't think of anywhere else.

Doug remembers them all, these people long dead who seemed old when he was young, people in their fifties when he was eight, people who were part of his summer days, his Easters and Christmas Eves. He remembers the great-uncles and great-aunts, pioneer mummies so old they struck terror in his heart. A visit to these survivors was an annual flagellation, a somber rite of the clan. The family would gather for this outing, arriving in great number, people Doug had never seen before, slate-eyed kinfolk in strange exotic garb, cousins with eyes a quarter-inch apart, haircuts straight out of 1386, all motored in from some rural quarter of Mars for the occasion, people who couldn't possibly be related in any way, boys his own age who spoke of livestock romance, girls who farted when they walked. Everyone packed into black Chevrolets and black Fords, then a drive to some clapboard house on the edge of desolation, some house in a field where the land had gone to seed, set amid hackberry trees with warty leaves, the porch and the roof bowed with age, the wood bare of paint for fifty years, flat gray and dry the color of mice, the yard choked with weeds and nettle, snapdragons and roses gone wild, a maze hiding rusty tractor parts and old tires, a trace of brick paths neatly laid in younger days. As the cars pulled up, scrawny pullets squawked and scattered; a pack of crazed dogs would erupt from under the house, dogs that had mange as a strong genetic trait handed down with family pride. And then the mothers, one by one, would parade their young quietly through the faded yellow halls, across the warped pine floors, beneath the dark high ceilings, and into the tomb itself. And there would be a man or maybe a woman, who could say, a paper leather husk, fragile as dried flowers under glass, a creature from *Weird Tales,* part human and part rocker, wood and flesh grown together. Say hello to Uncle Jess/Aunt Irma, mother would say, and Doug would mumble and shrink away, knowing if he looked too long, if he let those black bullet eyes draw him in, that the thing in the rocker would take possession right there, would pop into his head and take his youth, leave him stranded in that dry and hollow shell. And when the visit was all done, this prefunereal caravan would stop along the way for ice cream, something to cut the taste of death, and mother would say now Doug, Uncle Jess/Aunt Irma's real old, and won't be here very long, that's likely the last chance you'll ever have, you remember how he/she looks. And next year they'd do it once again, and the year after that, for maybe five more years or maybe ten, one last visit fading easily into the next, this indestructible zombie still sitting right there, inhabited or not Doug couldn't say, but there it was, rocking through another somber visit, determined to escape, to steal young eyes and live again. . . .

Under Old New York

$\int$TAY IN LINE AND KEEP YOUR GOODS HID, THAT'S TWO things to do. That's what the kid said. No, he hadn't been up there himself, but he knew a guy who had. He told her all this and she gave him half a roll. They sat and talked in a rusted-out car. He said he came from Tennessee. He said there wasn't any work down there and he didn't think he'd ever go back. He ate the roll without chewing it at all. Hannah couldn't spare the food. But she couldn't stand to eat while the boy sat and watched with hungry eyes. The boy had a pinched-up Southern kind of look. He was skinny as a rail. He said his name was Cadillac. He liked it when she smiled at the name. This was clearly what he wanted her to do. His skin smelled bad, like soured-up milk, like something was wasted inside.

The rain came hard in the night, but the car was okay. Cadillac slept in the front. Hannah in the back. She listened to the rain. She stayed awake a long time. The boy was maybe fourteen, fifteen tops, but that was old enough. She slept with her food between her legs. She slept with an ice pick in her hand. The rain let up toward morning, but the sky was still low and hard as iron. When she woke, the boy was gone.

This was after Newark when she found out she'd come the wrong way. The old filling station map said tunnels ran into New York. The man in the store had to laugh. He said they didn't anymore. He said the niggers had stopped them all up. He said the only way over was the bridge. He said he was about to close up and she could stay on for supper if she liked. He had a place above the store. Times were hard, he knew that, and he liked to help people when he could. The big coat fit her like a tent; she knew this didn't fool the man at all. He could see right through, he could see her in his head. The store was hot and smelled of mold. Hannah said no thanks, she had to go. Her brother, who had done a lot of boxing in North Platte, Nebraska, was waiting down the street. Her brother knew right where she was, and he didn't like to wait. She bought an apple and some rolls and sliced meat. The meat had gone bad. She spent the next day doubled up sick in a culvert by the road.

That night she found the rusted-out car and Cadillac. In the morning, she ate her apple and a roll and started off again. There were plenty of people on the road. Most everyone was headed up north, but some were walking back the other way. Hannah kept to herself. She didn't talk to anyone. Cadillac had told her that, too. There are all kinds of folks out there, is what he said. You get in the line, you make friends with someone, they're going to find out what you got. What kind of food and how much. If you've got any money in your sack. You get all cozy then you get across the bridge, this friend tells a nigger what you said, something you didn't mean to say. What if I didn't say anything at all? Hannah said. Don't matter if you didn't or you did. They'll make something up and say that. There's only so many jobs over there, and folks will do anything they can to get work. This is what the guy told *him*, and he'd been across the bridge and back. He met a girl in line, and she messed him up good. Ate all his food and then stole the job that should've been his. That's just the way it is.

Hannah figured Cadillac was right or close enough. Three weeks on the road, and she'd learned a whole lot by herself. They nearly had her in Decatur, Illinois. Migrants camped out in a field. She woke in time and got away. Not a one of them was over nine or ten, kids running in a pack. Pittsburgh was good. A lot of the plants were going full. Knock on any back door, and they'd most of them fix a plate of food. It wasn't bad everywhere. Some towns were doing okay. If people had work, they'd treat you fine. They knew how it was to do without.

Around noon, the rain started up again; not the hard and steady rain that had drummed her to sleep the night before, but a rain you couldn't see, like a cloud come to earth, a dirt-cold rain that you knew could settle in, just hang there heavy for a week, until it soaked right through to the bone. Hannah drew her collar up high and pulled the woolen cap down about her ears. The rain formed a chill oily mist on her face. She licked her upper lip and tasted salt. Road dirt from West Virginia. Handout food from Indiana, wood smoke from Illinois. You stay in the shower till you're weak in the knees, till the walls begin to sweat. A million little drops sting hot against your skin. The room's full of steam, and the bathroom cabinet's full of all the white towels in the world.

Lord God, Hannah thought, when could she remember doing that? She knew exactly where and when, and thrust the picture out of her head, tossed it as far as it would go.

Merchants from Newark had set up stands along the highway out of town, lean-tos and tents, makeshift counters and stands. The owners were delighted with the rain. It brought people in off the road. They huddled inside from the cold. The stalls were mostly family affairs. A husband and his wife. The man sold goods while the woman watched the customers like a hawk. Road people didn't have a lot to spend, but they all knew how to steal.

Cadillac had said buy before you get too far. Don't buy nothing on the bridge, it'll cost you an arm and a leg. Hannah looked at the pitiful display. The vegetables were wilted, the fruit was overripe. The sight made her feel helpless, helpless and angry and hungry all the same. She knew this was stuff the people couldn't sell in town. There were peaches, no bigger than limes, pulpy with the smell of sweet decay. Apples that had laid on the ground. Back home, her father had raised a few hogs, just to eat and not to sell. Hannah had taken out a bucket of scraps from the kitchen every day; every scrap in that bucket was fresher than the crap they had here.

She picked out some apples that didn't seem entirely brown. Two long loaves of hard bread. You could chew on bread and get it soft. The carrots went limp in her hand, but she bought some anyway. A bunch of green onions. one orange. She stayed away from meat. It added up to forty-eight cents, three times what everything was worth. Hannah counted out the coins she had left. Seventeen cents. Two pennies, a nickel, and a dime. Not a lot, but she would have to make do. Cadillac said you could make two dollars a day in New York, three if you had any skills.

For some time, Hannah had sensed a presence nearby. She felt vaguely ill at ease, felt the touch of curious eyes. She didn't turn around. She put the things she'd bought in a string sack she kept beneath her coat. She closed her change tightly in her fist and edged her way toward the front of the stall. An old woman blocked her path. Hannah backed off. The aisle was too narrow and there was nowhere to go.

"Excuse me," Hannah said, and tried to squeeze herself by.

The old woman looked right at her, determined not to move, looked right at her with predatory eyes, black eyes circled by halos of loose discolored flesh, looked right at her like an owl looks at a shrew.

Hannah was annoyed, startled by the dark and foreign face, by the tiny blue lips, by the nose that was sharp enough to cut.

"Listen, I have to get by," Hannah said, "you have to move."

"My husban' is dead," the woman said. "This is no matter to me, I tell you that. I can get along. I don' fock with no one, okay?"

Hannah took a deep breath, squeezed and shoved and forced her way free. She hurried through the stall into the rain. The old woman followed on her heels. Hannah looked the other way.

"Hey, I don' like to be push, okay? Is easy to push an ol' lady. What do you care?"

"Well, you just refused to let me by," Hannah said.

"My husban' is dead. He is driving this trock he falls dead."

"I'm very sorry for your loss."

"What's it to you? You got your youth, you got your looks. We live in one house thirty years. He says, I don' want to drive a trock no more. He says, I don' want to work for focking Japs. I say, what do you care? They pay, so what do you care?"

Hannah thrust her hands deep into the pockets of her coat. Everyone walked hunched up against the rain. Everyone's head disappeared. The woman was short; she scarcely came up to Hannah's chest. She took three steps to Hannah's one.

"I wish I had a egg," the woman said. "Luis, he wouldn't eat a egg. Any way you fix it, he don't touch a egg. Those apples you got, they no good. They gonna spoil plenty fast."

"I guess they'll have to do," Hannah said.

"I'm Mrs. Ortega. You don't say your name."

"Hannah," Hannah said, and wished she'd said Mary or Phyllis Ann.

"I know a Hannah once. I think she's a Jew. I guess a Jew's okay."

"That's nice," Hannah said. She wasn't listening at all.

The people on the road seemed a mix. Men and women, young and old, black and white. Spanish, like Mrs. Ortega. A few Orientals now and then. Mrs. Ortega told Hannah, wanted Hannah to know, that she was Puerto Rican, that she wasn't any Mex. That her cousin by marriage owned a store in New York. Didn't just run it but owned it by himself. The cousin would meet her when she got across the bridge. That was the thing; if you knew someone who was already there, someone who would give you a job, then they wouldn't send you back. Everyone else—and Mrs. Ortega included Hannah in the lot—everyone else had to trust to their luck, had to take what they could get.

Hannah didn't care to hear this at all. It was something she had tried hard not to think about. That there were just as many people coming back along the road as going north. People who had been across the bridge. People who couldn't get a job. What kind of people did they want? Hannah wondered. Who got hired, and who got turned away? After a while, everyone seemed to look alike. They looked just like the people going north.

She guessed it was early afternoon. With the rain you couldn't tell. The world ended just beyond the road. There were buildings and houses and telephone poles on either side, all ghostly shapes behind a veil.

"A man, he give you trouble all your life," said Mrs. Ortega. "This is what a man he's gonna do. He give you trouble all your life then trouble when he's dead."

"I wouldn't know about that," Hannah said.

Horns began to blare down the road, and Hannah turned to see circles of yellow light through the rain. Everyone moved to the side. A long line of trucks lumbered by, headed north. The trucks were full of scrap iron and heavy metal drums and left the smell of oil and rust. Hannah watched them pass. Mrs. Ortega kept her eyes straight ahead, as if the trucks weren't even there.

A few minutes after that, a car came up from the south, bright lights cutting through the mist. It was long and low and black, and its tires hissed on the road. The car was moving fast. It whined past Hannah in a blur. The taillights winked and disappeared.

"Focking Japs," said Mrs. Ortega.

"Well, I don't know why you say that." Hannah knew she

couldn't see inside. The windows were as black as the car.

Mrs. Ortega looked at Hannah like she didn't know anything at all. "They got a big car, it's a Jap. Take my word it's a Jap."

"I guess so," Hannah said. She let it go at that. There was no sense arguing with Mrs. Ortega. Mrs. Ortega had her own set opinion on everything there was, and didn't much care to hear yours.

And this time, Hannah had to admit, she was likely close to right. There weren't many cars on the road. You had to be rich to run a car, and there weren't a lot of poor Japanese. Not any Hannah had ever seen.

She thought about the car. About the slick black paint, about the fine black tires, about the chrome that was shiny silver bright, silver bright even in the rain. She wondered how it looked inside. It was warm and it was dry. A woman sat in back. She didn't have to wear a coat. She listened to the car radio. She had a long white dress and gold shoes. She had a ring. The ring had a big green stone. If she lost the ring, a nice-looking man would say fine, I'll get you another at the store. We'll go out to dinner somewhere, then we'll go and get a ring. They go out to dinner, and the woman has corn and fresh tomatoes and some cake. The man has a steak. Then they both order ice cream.

Hannah felt beneath her coat and found the string sack she kept inside. She pulled out two green onions, and tore off a hard piece of bread.

Mrs. Ortega shook her head. "You eat while you walk is no good. Eat when you stop. You go and eat ever'thing now, you run out."

"I won't run out," Hannah said. "And I'll eat whenever I please."

"Hah!" said Mrs. Ortega. "You don' know nothing. You don' know nothing at all."

When Hannah saw the end of the line, she nearly cried. It simply wasn't right. It wasn't how she saw it in her head. In her head there was the line and the bridge and then New York City after that. Everything together, everything there where she could see. Instead, the line stretched off down the highway and vanished in a dismal shroud of rain. Everybody disappeared, just the way they had before.

"Where is it?" she said aloud. "I can't see the bridge."

"Up about a mile," someone said. "A mile or maybe two."

"A *mile?*" Hannah turned and saw the man. He was tall, he was old, or maybe young. Rain dripped off his felt hat. "Why, we've already walked about ten!"

"Ten's about it," the man said.

"Don' talk to him," said Mrs. Ortega, who had already edged past Hannah to get ahead.

"I'll talk to anyone I want," Hannah said.

The man grinned. "Your mother don't care for me at all."

"She is *not* my mother," Hannah said.

"Well then, I'd guess you're all alone. I'd say you're by yourself. Hey, you're a pretty little thing. That coat don't show it, but I bet you look fine. I'm Dutch, and I didn't get your name."

Hannah felt the color rise to her face. "Listen, I don't much care for your manners or your talk."

"So? What did I tell you?" said Mrs. Ortega. She didn't bother to turn around.

"I didn't mean no offense," said Dutch. His eyes were rimmed with red. His face was too long, and he clearly hadn't shaved in several days.

"You don't even know someone, you shouldn't ought to talk like that," Hannah said. "Even if you know this person, that is not the thing to say."

Dutch looked properly subdued. "I just figured we could talk. There's nothing else to do."

"I don't guess you and I have a thing to talk about."

"You think you'll get a job in New York?"

"I'm sure I don't know. I'll do the best I can."

"Shoot, that's all anyone can do." Dutch grinned again. "I got me a skill. I can fix things good. Anything that's broke. Something comes apart, I can put her back right." Dutch showed Hannah a wink, not the wrong kind of wink, but a wink in confidence. "See, that's the thing, you get over 'cross the bridge. You got to have a skill. That's what they want to hear. And even if you don't, if you can't do anything at all, that sure ain't what you want to say. You won't know what they're lookin' for, but you got to say a skill. That's the only chance you got."

"That seems a little risky to me," Hannah said. "I think I'd be scared to say I could do something if I can't."

Dutch looked at Hannah. "You know what scary is, girl? Scary's comin' back across the bridge with no work. You thought you had a quarter, but you don't. Isn't nothin' any scarier than that."

"No. I guess not." He didn't have to tell her that he'd done all this before. Hannah didn't have to ask. She didn't know exactly what to say. She knew she had encouraged him to talk. She wished she hadn't but she had. Now she wasn't certain how to stop.

The rain began to pound the road, much harder than before. Not straight down like a rain ought to do, but slanting in furtive and sly, cunning and cold, from here and then from there, whipping in so fast that you couldn't fight it off, couldn't duck inside your coat, couldn't hide beneath your hat. The rain swept down Hannah's collar, bit her face and stung her legs, but she was grateful for the chance to turn away, grateful not to have to talk, grateful not to have to think about coming back across without a quarter to her name.

The sound came back down the line, first in a whisper like the wind from far away, then swelling to a rush, one voice drowning out the next.

"*The bridge! The bridge! The bridge is right ahead!*"

Everyone stretched for a look. The rain had slacked off, settled to a chill and steady drizzle once again. Day was winding down, and the saturated sky was a dull oppressive gray. At first Hannah couldn't see a thing. Everything was near, everything was far away. Then she saw the lights, caught her breath, saw the pale white stars strung in long and lacy patterns through the rain, saw the stars loop down in a roller coaster arc, climb again and disappear. Once she saw the lights, Hannah could pick out the towers of the bridge, two immense shadows looming high and out of sight, lost in the mist, in the fast approaching night.

"It's so big," Hannah said. "I never imagined it would look like that."

"George Washington Bridge," said Dutch. He grinned like people do when they've been somewhere before. "There she is, right there, there she is, straight ahead."

"We can see," said Mrs. Ortega. "Nobody here is blind."

"Just pointing out the sights," said Dutch.

"Watch him," said Mrs. Ortega. "I don' like his looks."

"You don't much like nothin'," said Dutch.

As the line grew closer to the bridge, Hannah saw they had come upon a tangle of roads on either side, roads that passed below and overhead, roads that swept in from every side. Trucks rumbled by underneath the people road, going east toward the bridge and coming back, trucks of every shape and size and even black and shiny cars. The highways whispered and hummed. Headlights pierced the vaporous night.

Now there was a new line of people, a new line that came in from the west, a new line moving toward the bridge. The new line kept to the left side of the road, Hannah's to the right. Not a word passed between the two lines. There was nothing anyone had to say. It was clear to everyone in either line: Those people aren't the same as the people over here. They might look the same, but they aren't the same at all. They're over there and we are here. They are not in our line. People who had never said hello to whoever was behind them or ahead had something to talk about now. You might be talking to the woman or the man who would steal your job away. But at least they weren't in the other line.

Now the dark towers were directly overhead. The lines moved onto the bridge. At once, Hannah was aware of a new and greater cold, a cold that didn't come from the rain. It swept in from the north. It sang through the great webs of cable and steel. It cut through her coat like vicious darts of ice.

"Real bitch, ain't it? That's the Hudson," said Dutch. "You can't see it, but it's there."

"Mr. Guidebook," said Mrs. Ortega. "Mr. Know-It-All."

"Hey. Excuse me for livin'," said Dutch.

Hannah wondered why they didn't try to keep the bridge clean. There was garbage everywhere. Tin cans and broken glass. Scraps of food ground into the road. Cardboard boxes. Broken wooden crates. Candy wrappers, newspapers, papers of every sort, pressed wet against the rust-colored metal of the bridge.

And the smell. The smell was worst of all. A smell too strong for the wind to blow away. It came from the little tin stalls they'd set up along the sides of the road. Hannah thought about the stalls with growing dread. She had to go. She had to go real bad. She couldn't stand the thought of going *there*. But there was no place else to go.

"Listen, I'll be right back," she told Mrs. Ortega, softly so Dutch couldn't hear. Mrs. Ortega was huddled in her coat. She didn't say anything at all.

Hannah walked quickly along the line. She didn't look at anyone, she kept to the side of the bridge. She saw the flash of headlights from the trucks on the level down below. She saw a red light on the river to the south, but it quickly disappeared.

A man was selling food in a shack he'd made from cardboard and wood. He wore a hunting cap pulled down about his ears. His face was bright red from the cold. He had a flashlight hung inside the shack. Hannah could read the prices tacked up against a wall. An apple was a quarter. A sandwich was seventy-five cents. Lord God, on the road you could eat on that for a week. Still, people were lining up to buy.

Hannah tried to hold her breath inside the stall. She got out as quickly as she could. There wasn't any paper, and she tore off a piece of her filling station map and used that. Walking back along the line, she heard her name. She turned and looked and there was Cadillac. Up the line maybe twenty yards ahead. Hannah was delighted to see someone she knew. She smiled and started up to say hello. She stopped and looked at Cadillac again. He was standing between two men. One man was heavy, the other was thin. Both of the men had coats as good as new. Cadillac had a coat, too, a red plaid coat that nearly swallowed him whole, and a red cap to match. He grinned at Hannah with a big piece of chicken in his hand. Hannah hadn't tasted chicken in a month or maybe two. One of the men saw Hannah. He saw her wave at Cadillac. He looked right at her and didn't smile. He raised his hand and touched Cadillac's face, touched his face and touched his hair.

Hannah felt as if the cold had reached in and found her heart. She looked at the man. She couldn't look at Cadillac. She turned away and ran back down the line. People glanced up to watch her pass.

"Wha's the matter with you?" said Mrs. Ortega. She looked Hannah up and down. "Huh? You fall ina toilet or what?"

"I am just *fine,* thank you," Hannah said. Good. Now everyone knew where she'd been.

"Okay. You don' look fine to me. You look like you eat something you ought to t'row up." Mrs. Ortega stomped her feet against the cold. "You back jus' in time. Mr. Big Shot here is telling lies. Like I don' know a lie. Like I don' live with a liar forty year."

"I didn't tell you no lie," Dutch said. "You ain't got the sense to know the truth."

"I know what I know. I don' got to hear a lie."

"Hey, ol' lady. You don't have to do nothin' but complain."

"Mrs. *Ortega*—" It suddenly occurred to Hannah that something wasn't right somewhere. That something had changed while she was gone. That the line wasn't moving anymore. That everyone had stopped. "Do you think something's wrong?" Hannah said. "Why aren't we going anywhere?"

Mrs. Ortega rolled her eyes in patience and despair. "See? You don' know nothing at all."

Dutch laughed as if Hannah had told a joke that he already knew. "The line don't go at night. Not when it's dark. It don't go nowhere in the dark."

"Well why not?"

"It just don't. They hire all day and they close her down at night. Even the niggers and the spics, they gotta sleep."

"You watch your mouth," said Mrs. Ortega.

Hannah stared at Dutch. "You mean we have to stay out here? Out here on the bridge?"

"You got it, babe."

"But there's no place to *sleep*."

"This is the line. It ain't a hotel."

"Well, I guess I know that. I guess I've been on the road as long as you."

Hannah knew at once it was the wrong thing to say. Dutch didn't answer. He looked at her a while then hunched down in his coat and turned away. He looked beyond the bridge, past the river and the rain, as if there might be something there to see.

Hannah tried to sleep, tried to huddle up against the cold. She found a piece of cardboard and folded it up across her head. It didn't do a lot of good. It kept out the rain, but it kept the smells in. The smells were there and they wouldn't go away. She thought about the garbage, the food and the trash and the paper and the glass, pressed in forever on the surface of the bridge. Like the cliff by the creek on the farm, layers of time stacked together like a cake. Her father had known all the names, what the different rocks were called. He told her the names of all the rocks and all the years. But the names were too long, and Hannah couldn't remember them at all.

She wondered if some of the smell was her. She wondered if she smelled as bad as everyone else in the line. Sometimes she'd found a river or a stream. A place far enough from the road. She had tried to get clean, tried to wash as best she could, but she was scared to take everything off. Afraid that someone might come along.

Some people slept. Some people stayed awake and talked. You weren't supposed to make a fire on the bridge, but a lot of people did. Sometimes a policeman came by and made them put the fires out. He drove a little three-wheeled car and wore a heavy leather coat. When he was gone, the people lit the fires again.

"My husban', he don't like to work for Jap," said Mrs. Ortega. "He don' like the way they look."

"I talked to a Jap feller once," said Dutch, "me and him had a drink. He gets to drinkin' real hard he says, hey, I don't like the way you look."

"I think you tell a lie. I don' think he give you any drink."

"Listen, this guy was okay. I'm cutting up scrap for this place and the Jap says, Dutch, it's gettin' hot. Stop and have a drink."

"A Jap is not gonna say that. He don' say this to you."

"Sure he did. He don't like the way I look, that's fine. Hey, you're going to work for whoever's got the pay. Don't make no difference to me, niggers, Japs, an' spics. Some guy gives me a dollar a day, I say fine. Where you want me to dig? What you like me to fix? It's all the same to me."

"You don' talk like that, Mr. Smart Aleck, you get across the bridge."

"You think I'm nuts?" Dutch laughed. "Damn right I don't. I say, good morning, Nee-grow, how you doin' Poortoe-rican, sir? Say, I'm glad you burned down the fuckin' town so ol' Dutch can get some work. I sure appreciate that."

"See, now tha's a lie," said Mrs. Ortega. "You gotta tell a lie. Nobody burn it down. Nobody doin' that."

"Right. I guess it burned down all by itself. I guess the city gets up one mornin' says look, I got nothing else to do. I guess I'll burn myself down. I guess that's what I'd like to do."

"I wish you would kindly shut up," Hannah said. "Some people don't want to talk all night. Some people like to sleep."

"So sleep," said Dutch.

"Don' listen," said Mrs. Ortega. "You don' want to listen, put somet'ing in you ear. Tha's what I think you oughta do."

Hannah turned away. She pretended not to hear. She pretended that the day was just ahead and the sun was warm and bright.

"What I'm going to do," Dutch said, "I'm going to get a good job, maybe fixin' machinery and stuff. They can always use a guy can fix things up. I get this job, I'm going to eat myself sick, I'm going to sleep in a bed."

"You goin' to dream about a bed," said Mrs. Ortega. "Tha's what you goin' to do."

"This ain't no dream, ol' lady. I'm gettin' me a job. Right now it's a real good time to be going 'cross the bridge."

"Right. Tha's why ever'body coming back."

"Everybody's coming *back*," Dutch said, " 'cause they haven't got a skill. See, I got a skill. What I'm thinking is, I'll maybe get on at Times Square. There's all kinds of shit going on there. That's what I'd like to do."

"Hah!" said Mrs. Ortega, "now you a liar again. They don't got a Times Square anymore. Anybody know that. My cousin, he got his own store in New York."

"Big deal," said Dutch. "Listen, they got a Times Square, okay? What they done is a bunch of rich niggers and spics, they're fixin' it up again nice. Bright lights, the whole bit. You got the bread, you can eat and see a show. A nigger, he knows how to make a buck, you gotta hand them that. Fuckin' Jap tourists'll eat it up."

"This is another big lie," said Mrs. Ortega.

"I seen it in a paper," said Dutch. "It's in the paper, it ain't a lie."

"I think you make up the paper, too," said Mrs. Ortega. "I think the paper is a lie. This is what a bum he's goin' to do."

She heard the trucks and the cars as they rumbled by below. She heard the wind, she heard the rain. She heard a man singing on a boat. She heard the people talk. She slept and woke up and heard a fight. The policeman came again, riding in his three-wheeled car. He told the people not to fight. He told them not to light a fire.

Once Hannah woke to find the rain had gone away. Dutch was sleeping close against her back. His knees were tucked up against her legs. His big arm was heavy on her waist. Hannah sat up with a start. She waved her ice pick in his face.

"Look, you better not do that again," Hannah said.

"Fine. Okay," Dutch said. "Freeze your ass off. What do I care?"

Dawn was bleak and ashen gray. Mist hugged the river and the cold steel heights of the bridge, and left a little open space between. Hannah itched all over. She ached everywhere. She felt her eyes were full of sand. People stood up and stirred about. People lined up for the stalls. Hannah swore she wouldn't do that again. She smelled the morning fires, smelled someone cooking food. She chewed on an onion and some bread to make the hunger go away.

Dutch looked awful. His skin was white as paste. He took a paper sack from his coat, took a long swallow, and made a face. He saw Hannah watching, grinned and wiped his mouth, and put the sack away.

Hannah reached under her coat, got half a loaf of bread, and handed it to Dutch. Dutch looked surprised. He mumbled something like "thanks," as if the word was real hard to get out. He dug past the crust for the softer bread inside.

"Don' give this bum nothing to eat," said Mrs. Ortega.

"I will if I want to," Hannah said.

"Hah! You don' get a job you don' eat. What you say then?"

The line began to move. Hannah tried to find New York, but she couldn't see the end of the bridge. At least the rain had gone away.

"Listen, last night," said Dutch. "I'm sorry 'bout that. I didn't mean nothin' wrong."

"Yes, you did," Hannah said. "Why do you say you didn't if you did?"

"You want a drink, I got a little left. It'll warm you up good inside."

"No, thank you," Hannah said.

The line stopped. Someone shouted up ahead. A woman began to scream. Someone took her off and made her stop. A crowd started to gather near the right side of the bridge.

"What's wrong," Hannah said. "Can you see what's going on?"

"What am I, a giant?" said Mrs. Ortega.

Several people ran back along the bridge. People in the line behind Dutch asked what was going on. Dutch said he didn't know. After a while, two policemen appeared in their three-wheeled cars. They told everyone to stand back. They told the line to move along. The line moved slow. Everyone had to see. Whatever it was, Hannah didn't want to look. But when she passed the place she had to look, too. There was blood on the bridge. The policemen bent over something white. The blood was dark in the somber morning light. One of the men stood and moved away.

"Oh, *God!*" Hannah said. She stumbled and brought a hand up to her face.

"Hey, so somebody's dead, it's not you," said Mrs. Ortega.

"Jesus," said Dutch. He gripped Hannah's arm.

"I'm just fine," Hannah said. She threw up her onions and her bread.

They'd cut him up bad, cut him bad everywhere. She wondered what they'd done with his clothes, with his red plaid coat and his hat. They cut him everywhere, but they didn't cut his face. His face was just fine. Were the men still on the bridge, did they go back to the end of the line? His face looked nice. Everything else was real bad, but his face was just fine.

It seemed to take forever for the lines to leave the bridge. They wound down ramps and over this and under that, wound past buildings pressed one against the next, packed so tight it was hard to tell which belonged to what. Down through a grim and narrow street to a dark red building where the lines disappeared.

"Hiring hall," said Dutch before Hannah had to ask. He nodded vaguely to the left. "You don't get work, they send you out another door. You don't get to talk to nobody goin' back across the bridge."

"Why not?" Hannah said.

Dutch grinned and picked his teeth. "Shoot, they let you do that, everybody out here's all of a sudden got carpenter skills. They're plumbers or they're good at fixing trucks. Whatever the hell they're hirin' inside."

"Maybe they looking for a dronk," said Mrs. Ortega. "Maybe you get a job quick."

"Maybe you'll have a fuckin' stroke," said Dutch.

As the line drew closer to the door, Hannah was struck by a sudden sense of loss, a feeling like a shudder, like a tremble, like a quake, like a chill that swept back along the line, like a wave of dark despair. She tried to shake away the fear, tried to lose the sense of dread, tried to think good thoughts, but nothing good would come to mind. She was left with the chill and with the fear, with the image of the long walk back across the bridge.

"The line moves slow, that's a sign," said Dutch. "That means the hiring's good. It means they're takin' time to talk. You move too fast means they ain't finding anyone they want."

"It looks like we're moving fast to me," Hannah said.

"Yeah, maybe. I'd say kinda in between."

"Don' listen to him," said Mrs. Ortega. "Don' listen to a bum."

The scene inside did nothing to temper Hannah's fears. The room was immense, as wide as the building itself, a big room with harsh white lights and a concrete floor. People sat behind long and narrow desks. They wrote things down. They picked up papers and took them to a desk across the room. The papers were blue and pink and white.

You had to stop at a broad yellow line on the floor. The line was twenty feet from the desk up ahead. You couldn't see, you couldn't hear what people said. The lines were moving fast. Hannah's line and the other to her left. Hannah watched. When you didn't get a job, you went out through a door painted red. Hannah counted in her head. Seven-eight-nine-ten . . . nineteen-twenty-twenty-one. Hannah's heart sank. Everyone was going through the door.

"Oh, Lord," Hannah said. "They aren't hiring anyone at all!"

"Hey, you don't know, you can't never tell," said Dutch.

They hired someone at twenty-five. Another at twenty-nine. Then no one clear to forty-one. Mrs. Ortega was forty-two.

Hannah stood with her toes on the line. A black man sat behind a desk. He wore a blue shirt and blue tie. He spoke to Mrs. Ortega. Mrs. Ortega spoke to him. The man shook his head. There was a coffee cup full of yellow pencils on the desk. Mrs. Ortega picked them up, cup and all, and threw them at the man. The man stood and backed away.

"I don' need you focking job," screamed Mrs. Ortega. "I got family. I got a cousin owns a store!"

The man looked shocked and surprised. Yellow pencils rolled about the floor. Two men rushed in from the left. They picked up Mrs. Ortega and hurried her quickly across the room.

"My cousin he is coming," shouted Mrs. Ortega. Her short legs kicked at the air. "You wait. He is coming soon. My husban' is dead. He drives a Jap trock an' he is dead. My cousin owns a store."

"Oh, dear," Hannah said, "I hope she'll be okay."

"Serves her right," said Dutch.

"It does not. Don't you talk that way."

"Yeah, right."

"Next," said the man at the desk.

Hannah could scarcely move. The twenty feet seemed like a mile. The man looked her up and down. Hannah stopped before the desk. The man looked at her again. He opened his mouth to speak. Another man came up behind his chair. The man at the desk turned away. He leaned back to talk. Hannah looked at the papers on his desk. The man had them covered with his hand. Hannah looked again. There were only two words she could see. The words said ꓱ⅂ꓔꓔ ⅄∀M. ⅄∀M was half a word. The rest lay beneath the man's thumb. The man turned back, and Hannah quickly looked away.

"Experience," said the man.

"I beg your pardon?" Hannah said.

The man pointed a pencil at her chest. "What do you do, what kind of work?"

"Oh, sorry." Hannah's mind raced. She didn't want to say tile. Not right off. Tile might give her away.

"Brick," Hannah said. "I've done a lot of work in brick."

"You work in brick?" The man seemed surprised.

"Brick, stone, tile, anything like that."

"Doing what?"

"I can lay brick good. I've made a lot of walls. I can do 'bout anything with tile."

"Let me see your hands," said the man.

Hannah held out her hands. The man ran a finger down her palm. Hannah held her breath, thankful for the first time in her life that she had grown up on a farm.

The man made a mark on a blue piece of paper and handed it to Hannah. "Table Five," he said. He didn't look up. He didn't look at Hannah again.

Hannah was stunned. She couldn't believe she had a job. She had work in New York. She didn't have to go back across the bridge. She found Table Five. It was two rows down. A black girl her own age took the paper from her hand. The girl was awfully clean.

"Here's your chits," said the girl. "The yellow's for housing, the green one's for a meal. This is your button. Put it on and don't take it off. Hang on to your button and your chits. We don't give 'em out twice. Go through the door that says Nine." The girl made a mark on the paper and gave it back.

Food. Housing, Hannah thought. Things were looking better all the time. She found Door Nine. She turned and looked back. Mrs. Ortega was in a chair across the room. The chair looked big. Or Mrs. Ortega looked small. At least she was still inside the room. She wasn't out the red door.

Hannah suddenly remembered she hadn't even thought about Dutch. She felt bad about that. She looked about the room, and couldn't find him anywhere at all. She looked at the button on her coat. It said 939. It occurred to her, then, that no one had asked her for her name.

*   *   *

Hannah was shocked when the woman said take off your clothes, but she did as she was told. The woman handed her a towel and a bar of yellow soap. Leave your stuff here, the woman said, and Hannah did.

The shower was a pleasant surprise. The soap had a medicine smell, but the water was strong and steamy hot. There were seven other women in the showers nearby. Hannah didn't look at them and they didn't look at her. You could stay five minutes, a sign told you that. Hannah wanted to spend the day. She wanted to let the water wash every mile away.

In a room off the shower, a woman gave Hannah a green jumpsuit and a pair of tennis shoes. The suit wasn't new and didn't fit too well, but it was clean. It smelled just like the yellow soap. Hannah's old clothes and her button and her chits were in a sack. Her food was there, too, and her seventeen cents and her map. The ice pick was gone.

A long hall led to a big room with tables and chairs. Hannah could smell the food before she even reached the room. The smell went right to her belly, and the pain nearly brought her to her knees. She tried not to cry, but the hurt spilled over to her eyes.

The stew was hot and thick. There was fresh bread and coffee and sugar in a bowl. The sign said you could go back for more, and Hannah did. The room was half full. The women sat apart from the men. There were green jumpsuits like her own, blues and blacks and reds.

"Where you from?" said a girl at Hannah's right.

"Nebraska," Hannah said.

"South Carolina," said the girl. She had a long face. Hollow cheeks and hollow eyes. "I wish I wasn't scared. I hope it's goin' to be all right."

"I guess we'll be fine," Hannah said.

"I'm LuAnn," the girl said.

"Hannah," Hannah said.

"You ever heard of Scotia? That's in Hampton County, right close to Estill."

"I don't think I have. I've never been too far from home until now."

A loudspeaker on the wall said, "Greens to the bus. Two minutes. Give your paper to the driver outside."

"That's me," Hannah said. She wolfed down the last of her stew. "You take care, okay?"

"I'll sure try," said LuAnn.

Hannah took her bowl and her cup back to the line. The girl looked lonely and afraid. Maybe I do, too, Hannah thought. Maybe everyone here looks the same.

The street signs passed in a blur. 155th . . . 146th . . . Lord, who'd ever guess streets could go that high! Traffic was light. There were people everywhere, but Hannah saw few trucks or cars. The bus raced south like it was going to a fire. There was so much to see, too much to take in at one time, but Hannah tried. The broad street was called Amsterdam Avenue. Long rows of buildings stretched out on either side, grim red buildings with tiny shops and markets jammed between. A movie and a church. A park with no trees. Everyone Hannah saw was black. Sometimes a street looked shabby and dark. Sometimes it looked nice. A man selling food on a corner waved at Hannah, and Hannah waved back.

Leaden clouds still drifted overhead. Hannah thought about the people on the bridge. She wondered if Mrs. Ortega was still sitting in her chair. She wondered if Dutch was headed back.

"Hey, you like New York okay?"

Hannah nearly jumped when the girl swept into the seat beside her. "Yes. I mean I guess I like it fine."

The girl flashed a smile. She looked at Hannah's button. She thumbed through the stack of blue papers in her hand. Hannah was struck by the dark and startling beauty of the girl. Black hair and black eyes, cinnamon colored skin that seemed to shine. A new red jumpsuit that fit. Hannah touched her own hair, and wished she had a brush.

"So, a construction worker, no? Brick and tile." The girl looked at Hannah and laughed. "Boy, that is a big lot of bullshit, 939, you know that?"

"It certainly is not." Hannah was alarmed. "That's what I do."

"Right. Who cares? I'm Catana Pérez. So who are you?"

"I'm Hannah."

"Hannah what?"

"Hannah Gates."

"Gates. Like you swing in and out alla time, huh?"

"They used to tease me some in school."

"And where is that?"

"Nebraska. My father had a farm."

"Had. He don't got it now?"

"It went broke. He couldn't pay it off."

"An' your father, now he is *muerto*, he is dead."

"I didn't say that."

"You don' have to say. You are what, fifteen?"

"No! I'm seventeen, eighteen in May."

"*Dios.*" Catana made a face. "You watch yourself, okay? The dogs, the *perros,* they gonna bark plenty at you. You're a real pretty girl. You got nice yellow hair. I guess you got tits somewhere, I don' know. See, you gonna blush a little, huh? The *perros,* they goin' to bark. You don' listen. You don' bark back, you okay. You understand what I say?"

"I think I do."

"Ah, *sí.* That's exactly what I mean. What am I gonna do with you?"

"You don't have to do a thing," Hannah said. "I'm just fine."

Catana leaned in close. Hannah smelled a light flower perfume.

"Okay. I can see what's in your head," Catana said. "This girl, she ask a lot of questions to me. Why she want to do that? Because this is what I do. I ask people stuff all day. I see you get on the bus and get where you gotta go. That's my job, that's what I do. It's better than construction work, no?"

Hannah had to smile. "Yeah, I guess so."

"You bet."

"Listen, are you a Puerto Rican? Is it all right to ask?"

"Cuban. *Cubano.* That's even better, but don't tell the PRs, they don' know."

Hannah glanced out the window again. She was surprised how things had changed. The buildings weren't so grim anymore. Most of the shops had a fresh coat of paint. The streets were fairly clean. People ate under red and white umbrellas outside. A store that sold flowers spilled its wares out on the street. It looked as if a garden had blossomed in cement.

Catana seemed to read Hannah's thoughts. "Looks a little better, right? You're out of the Heights now, girl. You on the Upper West Side." Catana touched the tip of her nose and raised it a quarter of an inch. "Pretty good place to be. Very nice."

Hannah shook her head. "I guess I'm getting real confused. Everybody says the city burned down, but it doesn't look very burned to me. Everything looks fine. You can't tell anything at all."

Catana showed no expression at all. "Hannah Gates. Hannah Gates from off the farm. I bet you milk a focking cow."

"I just asked," Hannah said.

"Yeah. Okay." Catana traced a shape like a pickle on the seat. "It don't burn up here. The fire is down there. Everything from Downtown to Midtown. Up to Central Park. On the East Side, maybe little more. Sixty-seventh, okay? On the West Side, up to fifty-ninth. That's where you gonna go. Fifty-ninth." She looked up at Hannah. "This don' mean a thing, right? You don' know where you are. You don' know where you go. You don' know what you gonna do."

"I do tile," Hannah said, "tile and brick."

"Yeah, right." Catana rolled her eyes like Mrs. Ortega. "Miss 939 tile and brick. I don't think you ever *see* a tile before, but that's what you gonna do. You chip and shine, you fix the subway up fine. All the tourists say, hey, everything is lookin' nice. I bet Miss 939 she been by."

"The subway?" Hannah tried not to show her alarm.

"Sure, the subway, what you think? That's why you got a green suit." Catana laughed. "You work real hard, maybe you shine all the way to Times Square. Maybe you get to see the sights."

"I know all about Times Square," Hannah said. "I read about it in a paper one time."

"Hey, she can read a paper, too. We are plenty locky you come across the bridge." Catana paused. "Listen, I tell you a couple things. Stuff you need to know. You learn where you stay. How to get to work. You don' go out after dark until you know pretty good where you are. They give you a meal tonight after work. You don' gotta have a chit. After that, buy your own food at the *bodega* where it's cheap."

Catana glanced over her shoulder, then turned to face Hannah again. "What you don' do most of all is go asking someone about the fire. That's ten, eleven years back, okay? That's gone. Don' go talking 'bout that. Nobody wants to hear."

Hannah was startled. "I just *asked*. I don't see anything wrong with that."

Something changed in Catana's eyes. "You don' see nothing wrong because you got a white face. Everybody got a white face thinks they know about the fire. They got all the answers in their head."

"I don't think anything at all," Hannah said.

"Yeah, right. So I tell you this. Then you don' gotta ask. The fire don' start up here. Where it starts is down *there*. Okay? Where everybody had a face as white as you. You think about tiles. You think about making two dollars every day."

Catana touched Hannah on the shoulder and stood. "Hey, you gonna do real good. You gonna do fine."

Hannah didn't want to be mad at Catana, but she was. The girl didn't have to get up and walk away. She didn't have to leave. What did I do? Hannah thought. I asked a question is all. I asked about the fire. What's so bad about that? It isn't any secret, everybody knows about the fire. I didn't talk like Dutch. I didn't say nigger and spic. The girl tried to act pleasant after that, but she did get up and walk away.

The bus moved south. The farther south they went, the nicer things became. Traffic picked up at eighty-sixth. The bus slowed down at eighty-first. There were places to eat everywhere. The people were black and brown. A few were even white. Hannah saw a fine hotel. A place to eat Japanese food. The bus stopped again at sixty-ninth. On the corner, there were six men hanging from a pole. Six men and a girl. Hannah couldn't tell what color they had been. Everyone's face had turned black. Someone had made a sign, and hung it at the base of the pole. The sign said, MAKE BIG MONEY IN DRUGS. No one glanced at the people who were hanging from the pole. People bought flowers on the street, but no one looked up at the pole.

The bus moved on. Hannah saw places to eat and things to buy. People rushing everywhere about, people walking little dogs. Someone behind her said, hey, there's Lincoln Center, I read about that, and Hannah looked and saw pretty white buildings, a big opera house. But mostly she saw the people hanging on the corner with their faces turning black.

The bus came to a stop, and the driver said, "Columbus Circle, everybody out."

Everyone in the bus began to talk. Hannah made her way down the aisle and outside. Catana was there and she smiled and said hello. Maybe everything was all right.

Hannah marveled at the big traffic circle, a column with a statue on the top. A tall glass building, a corner of the park. There were people everywhere, trees and grass, a man selling bright balloons. A dozen sights to see, but every eye turned to the south. To the burned and ragged spires, to the towers black as night, to the dark and ruined shells of steel and glass stark against a sullen sky.

Hannah was chilled by the grim and awesome sight. The dead

city cast a charred shadow on the city still alive. It's much too close, Hannah thought. It shouldn't be as close as that. It ought to be somewhere far away. I don't want to live in a place that's all dead, I don't want to clean tiles. I don't like it here at all.

"Okay, Greens," Catana said, "line up, let's go." She laughed, as if the sound might make the shadows disappear. "Let's get under New York, let's get to work, let's make a couple dollars today."

Highbrow

Will gave his weight to the sling, thrusting his feet firmly against the broad granite face. The crews worked above and to his right. The sound of chisels was swept away at once by the wind that razored the heights. He leaned half a mile into California air. The rope gave him forty feet of slack. Higher, it clipped to the A-ring and the less flexible cable. The cable stretched up and out of sight to the winch station at Hairline, fifty yards above. He could lean in and snake-whip the rope and move about in an arc either way. When the angle gave out, he'd have to signal the callboy to pass the word to the winch. He decided to let it go. The kid was likely asleep. He pushed off and swung twenty feet and caught the webbing, got a sound grip and loosed himself from the sling. Hooked the sling to the webbing so the boy wouldn't decide to haul it up.

Eyebrow was twenty feet below. His crew crawled about the granite hedge, cutting and chipping furred striations. The scaffolding snaked crookedly over Eyelid, seventy-five feet to the bridge of Nose. The other brow was Mink's. Mink was perched in a sling, pretending to watch his crew on the other side. What he was doing was watching Will's people work. Will didn't care. He could look all day if he liked. All of Mink's craft was in his hands.

He had no feeling for the stone. You had to feel the stone in your head and in your heart.

A shadow slid over Face. Will looked up. A steam-driven flyer clattered by. Rods pumped and thrashed, driving eight bat wings in partial accord. Streamers flew from the tail. The gondola was painted gold, hung from a fine confusion of wires and struts. Japanese tourists took pictures. Quaker, standing by the winch station above, shook his fist and waved a small red flag. The craft lurched off, leaving a trail of soot. Three weeks before, Eva Duke had mooned Norwegian balloonists. Will decided this accounted for increased aerial traffic.

Taft-Hartley wasn't looking at the flyer. He was leaning on the scaffolding, frowning out to sea. "I don't much like the weather," he told Will. "I don't plan to work up here in no storm. Quaker can ground my ass if he likes. I saw Eddie House after lightning got him working on Nose. Welded him to the rock like snot."

Will dropped goggles around his neck and sniffed the air. T.H. was right. Something was forming off the coast. A smudge on the horizon, air thickening into a haze. The sun was still bright up top, but San Clemente was a blur, a sight through dirty glass. A steamer hugged the coast, sluggishly towing barges loaded with granite into port. Will looked up and studied his work. The furrowed crest of granite was a honeycomb ridge brooding twenty-four feet out from Face to shade the Eyes. Close, it appeared to be sedimentary art, the tunnels of ants exposed, uncovered and petrified. Seen from San Clemente, the road that followed the coast, from the decks of clippers at sea, tourists and sailors marveled at the sight. The brows lived; sun and shadow worked their magic, tricks of corrugation and the subtle play of light. Stone became the stern and somber visage. The left brow and the right were in theory of equal craft, but Will knew the right had the touch. That Mink knew, too, and was totally unable to guess why.

"You'll get it," said Taft-Hartley, seemingly reading Will's thoughts. "Odds are eight to five, but I figure it'll go higher than that."

Will was irritated and showed it. There was something wrong with betting on his career. The sky was growing darker by the moment. Clouds considered wearing slate. The breeze was stiff and cool and heavy with salt.

"Get the crew started up," said Will. "I don't want anyone down here when it hits."

"I don't wager any myself, you understand," said T.H. "I'm just telling you so you'll know."

"Yeah, right." Will looked up at Mink. Mink appeared to be taking notes.

Others could see the storm as well, and soon finishers and joiners, polishers and pointers, were scrambling up from Eyebrows and Nose, climbing up to Hairline to beat the threatening wind. A callboy finally dared to tell Quaker. He lurched out of the winch shack, hoisted the weather flag, and sent the steam whistle wailing over the heights. By then all but stragglers were on top. Bright crooked wires kissed the sea. Wind shivered the surface, sweeping flat water from blue to gray. San Clemente vanished as the front curled to shore in a fierce convexity of rain, slashing at coastal roads and the worktowns to the south. The first heavy drops measled granite the color of sand. Droplets formed tears, and tears coursed streams. Rain gathered to sweep down Nose across Cheeks, part and come together at the grim curve of Mouth, drawn in small rivers to the great cleft of Chin, where a rushing cascade fell to Chest. Other currents swirled from Neck and Shoulders, surged and met in a torrent past Beltline and Statesman's Cape and Trousers, gaining speed and power for some two thousand feet until a cataract drummed with a roar on the roofs of hall and cloister, gatehouse and tower, barbican and bridge, those mammoth structures carved in Greco-Brit-California splendor, nestled between colossal granite Shoes. And when this great swell of water reached the ground, it was quickly carried away in pipes and gutters, cleverly channeled and directed by engineering marvel, rushed to vast reservoirs that nourished the formal gardens and graceful fountains, which delighted Serbian tourists and retired assassin couples from as far away as Spain.

Above, Will made his way through substantial blocks of granite, the site of his future or maybe Mink's. These giant squares rested, waited to be joined and shaped and formed to crown the glory of the Work. In his heart, Will knew Quaker wouldn't fuck him up. Quaker was old and fuddled, but he was still a Master pointer. He wouldn't give the hair to Mink. Even if he didn't care for Will, he loved the Work. He'd started as a boy, a rough-shaper, worked his way to carver, then chief assistant pointer to Don Debate, and finally to Master when Debate had a seizure and fell from Mole. Fifty years on Face, and he wouldn't turn that over to Mink. Will couldn't see him doing that.

Lightning struck the tall iron beam raised above the winch station for that purpose. Will ducked. Rain blew in his eyes. The sharp crack of sound pressed his skin. He smelled burning air. The crews were huddled up before the cages. The steam engines wheezed and snaked cable. The crews waited, standing in the rain or under the narrow tin roof when there was room. Their faces were granite white, rain-streaked now like weary tigers. Hammer and rasp and chisel hung heavy from their belts.

The crews kept to themselves. Mink's crew and Will's and the polishers who worked for Court. Up here they didn't talk. Down below they'd drink beer, mix, and fornicate with ease. Will couldn't see it. He didn't feel close to the others. Just his own. The others were like strangers; he didn't know their skills and didn't trust them.

Taft-Hartley nodded, and Will crowded into the next available cage. There were three elevators for the crew. Will had the clout to take Express, but that would mean riding down with Quaker. Maybe listening to Mink suck up to the old man. Will would rather swing down on a rope.

The crews squeezed into place. Tight and smelling of rain and rock and sweat. No one talked. The elevator rattled and jerked. Because of the height of the Work, each crew elevator was really a bank of five. That meant a change every four hundred feet.

T.H. punched Will, and Will glanced out the side. The elevators hugged the back of the Work, adjacent to the step-angle ramps that wound ziggurat fashion from Base to Head, a mountain of rock and soil that let the mules haul granite to the top. Will saw a mule team in trouble. They'd been caught in the downpour at Beltline, and ten-ton blocks had slipped precariously close to the edge. The crews were running about trying to figure what to do.

"Those guys are nuts," said Taft-Hartley. "I wouldn't do that for nothing."

Will didn't answer. Annie Page gave him a wink. Will nodded politely. The elevator rumbled to a halt. The engine house protested, offered death-rattle sounds. Cables seemed appeased. Will hated the ride twice a day, every day of his life. It was far safer to be at work than leave it.

"You want a beer, you're welcome to come," said T.H. "Be glad to have you." A ritual invitation, but T.H. was determined to pursue it.

"Thanks. I got to do some stuff for Pop."

"You don't want to worry about Mink. You got it for sure, Will."

Will stopped. "Just quit doing this, all right?"

"Well, sure. Okay." T.H. looked hurt, as if he had some deformity of the jaw. "The whole crew's pulling for you, is all."

"All right."

"People care, you know."

"Fine."

"Listen. I'm not going to bring this up again. I don't think you want to talk about it much."

"You see right through me, T.H."

"Well, hell, we been working together a long time, you know?"

Taft-Hartley trotted off. There was a bigger crowd than usual by the steamhouse, the taverns and stores clustered about. Rain had brought the topsiders down at the same time the grounder shift changed. Yellow jumpsuits mixed with green. Workers spilled from tunnels that led to vaulted halls and chapels, columned rooms that channeled through the vast expanse of Base. The storm was passing on. The sun was overly bright, and steam rose from the ground. Rooftops made a thousand flashing mirrors in Milhous, and the worktowns to the south.

It was then that Will saw her. Striding with a purpose through the crowd as if people were no obstruction. She appeared to be practicing for a race. He was struck by her at once. He felt a great sense of loneliness for someone he didn't know. A tall girl with bony features and a fiercely defiant chin. He longed to know in defiance of what. And then she was suddenly gone. A cropped head of hair catching the sun.

He thought about her all the way home. Imagined knowing her name and where she lived. What he would say. What she would say to him. He enjoyed small fantasies and walked with new purpose.

It was well after three, and the low roofs, the cobbled streets of Milhous were in the shadow of the Work. The rain had left the town smelling clean. Pop was in his room, the wheelchair pulled to a table and his maps. The paper shades were drawn, the wicks turned high. Charts covered the walls depicting the density of lizards in the Orocopia Range.

"I've got new thoughts on the Western Ground Gecko," said Pop. "Serious errors have been made. We know less than we think about diversity of diet. Those fuckers will scarf any spider that crawls."

"You eat anything, or just drink?" asked Will.

"Don't start on me, boy."

"Pour me one, too, you got anything left."

Pop brought a quarter bottle of gin from under the table. Two glasses followed. Will started poking through cabinets for something marginally close to supper.

"You get down before the rain?"

"Quaker's too old to know he's wet."

"Shit. I'm three years older'n him."

"My point exactly."

Pop showed restraint. Will discovered sausage, sliced a piece, and sniffed.

"You get Quaker over here and let *me* talk to him, there won't be any wonder 'bout who gets Hairline and who don't."

"Now you know I'm not about to do that."

"Me and that old fart started topside together. Worked Upper Lip and Nose. Your ma's buried just below Nostril, bless her soul. Right next to Quaker's Sarah. I'd of been Master pointer if I hadn't gone and fell, and he knows it. Where you going now?"

"Out back and clean up."

"And then where?"

"I don't know, Pop. Out."

"I thought maybe we'd talk. You know the chuckwalla's flesh was highly prized by Indians? It can use its thick tail in defensive situations."

"I won't be much late."

"Don't give a fuck if you are. Don't go thinking I do."

He didn't feel he'd have trouble finding the girl. If she lived in Milhous, he'd know her. She wasn't a topsider, the green jumpsuit told him that. A carver, then, or a painter. Someone with a craft. Living in Agnew maybe, or Checkers.

He tried Checkers first, and couldn't believe his luck. A topsider he knew who'd got the dizzies named her at once from Will's description. Carrie Deeds. He said the name to himself. It sounded right. She looked like a Carrie Deeds.

At her door he had a brief moment of doubt. Up to now they were comfortably together in his head. She laughed readily and had a fairly agreeable nature. She appeared to smell faintly of cloves. She opened the door and gave him a vague, yet penetrating look. Measured him for some purpose he couldn't guess.

"I'm Will Taypes," he said. "I saw you this afternoon. You came out of Tunnel Nine."

"I didn't see you."

"I know. I was wondering if you'd like to go out."
"No."
"What?"
"No, I wouldn't like to go out." She laughed. It seemed pleasant and not demeaning at all. "I'm sorry. Didn't anyone ever turn you down before?"
"Well, sure."
"But not much."
"What's that got to do with us?"
"Listen, thanks for asking."
"You're not making this real easy."
"I guess you're right. Good night, Will Taypes."

Her image was still clear on the face of the door. He found her quite appealing. He was intrigued by contradiction. There was confidence in her eyes, which were attractively wide-set, yet he felt this masked a certain shy and vulnerable nature. A firm, yet faintly indolent chin. A sense of frailty about her face that concealed an inner strength. Possibly wanton restraint. She had clearly said *no*. But what did that mean in a woman so adept at hiding her feelings from the world?

In the morning he left early and tried to catch her going to work. Waited at Tunnel 9 until the whistle blew for his shift. He was less than pleased with himself. It was not his way to let a woman trouble his sleep. The truth was, Carrie Deeds had kept him awake. He had prowled about, unearthing a cache of Pop's bad gin. Spent some time looking whomper-eyed at a poster of the eight-lined whiptail lizard.

Taft-Hartley was hung over, and several others as well. Annie was entwined wlth Abel Passage, looking silly. Will snagged them all on the hook of his sullen mood. Told them he could ground them as work hazards, but he'd rather give them the chance to break their necks. All appeared subdued. Will felt better as they ascended. He was sluggish on the ground, heavy and oppressed. On topside, a man was alive. He knew why Pop had taken to drink.

Mornings, the front of the Work was in shadow. The job went quickly until noon, when the sun flared over Head and started pounding white granite in the thin upper air. The fresh cuts of stone mica-bright, the Face hot as a stove. Will worked his crew hard. They cursed behind his back, sweating beer and passion. Will stalked through every hollow, T.H. at his heels, Will chalking burrs and nodulations for further work, fashioning new striations in his mind, crawling from cleft to fissure breathing stone. A finer groove with point and hammer, better delineation with the three-point chisel and the rasp. Will could see it take form, feel the crude chisel hatching, the honeycombing stone, an unfinished sketch from where he stood but something more from far away. Half a mile straight down, five miles off to San Clemente where every tourist took a picture. Clear and sharp from there and even further, past Liddy Point and out to sea. The brows had been brooding black in nature; granite is cold and undefined. Will could only capture this dark intense emotion with depth and shadow, with the play of light that changed from one moment to the next. Yet he was certain he was right. That his brow lived and breathed. That Mink had no feeling for the Work. You could look in Mink's eye and see it plain. If he wasn't too addled or disconnected, Quaker could see it, too. If he came to some decision before they started feeding him coffee with a spoon.

As if the thought had brought him to life, Will looked up and saw Mink. He sat in his sling some thirty yards away, following the feverish activity of Will's crew. Will displayed a finger. Mink would tell Quaker, who disliked perverse behavior of any sort.

He left an hour early, turning the reins over to T.H., certain this was a sign that his mind was mushy as Quaker's. If she left Tunnel 9, he didn't see her. He couldn't go to her house again. Home seemed a bad idea. Pop was out of sorts. During periods of irritation, he tended to piss on Will's socks and extra shirts. Barring that, there was gin and lizard lore. Leaving the work tunnels he started walking, taking the long road past the five-story collonaded Base. Took his time and gave a craftsman's admiring eye to the great wall of stones, slick as glass, each fashioned so carefully to the next that, like the Work far above, there was no room for the thinnest blade between. The walk took an hour. Shadow said it was likely past six. He bought a cold drink and watched tourists. Black women from King, stately and thin as wires. A green Duesenberg hitched to six matched geldings. Arabs sat in back, feeding chocolates to small Apache boys. Will found the sight faintly disturbing.

Pop was drunk in his chair. A balsa-wood Gila was half complete. Will made supper, avoiding kitchen sounds. Drinking coffee out back and watching clouds play over the heights. Weather moved swiftly above Shoulder. He felt a surprising sense of relief, a lightness of the spirit that seemed wholly without reason. He realized he'd come to some decision about the girl. He'd decided not to look for her again. There were other women he wouldn't have to chase. He'd see her somewhere, but he would bring resolution into play. Stand up against her disturbing sense of motion. Forget soft distraction.

"I get supper or what?" Pop called from inside. "You here or out ruttin' around?"

Will spooned hash from the stove and brought coffee. Pop looked unsteady, erratic about the eyes. He poked food carefully with his fork, maybe looking for mines.

"I don't like the idea of being buried someplace I didn't work. 'Course that's what happens if you're fool enough to wind up a cripple. My mamma's in Lapel, and papa's close by in Knot-of-the-Tie. His pa's in Coat Button Four. My great-grandad fell from Herringbone Bend at eighty-six. Used to listen to his tales. He clearly recalled several electrical appliances. Your mother's people were prominent in the Crotch. That's sometime back, and she couldn't recall names. There was some kind of scandal, but I can't say what it was. One thing's certain, we go back on both sides down to Shoe."

"There's more of this hash."

"Be lucky to keep down what I got."

Will dreamed he could see through the Work. It seemed as if stone had turned to glass. He could see every person inside. Multitudes and throngs. Legions of prone bodies facing west. The sun came up in sweet fury and set the Work afire. He saw that each body was interlinked. A tracery of veins carried blood throughout the Work. The Work moved, took a ponderous step toward the sea. Will woke and guessed he'd slept maybe an hour. He was still in his clothes. The sound that roused him came again. The moon painted a window on the floor, and when he opened the door, the same waxen light struck her face.

"I couldn't sleep," she said. "I thought we might talk. You look a little surprised."

"I guess that's what I am."

"I wouldn't go out, and you felt that was some kind of rejection."

"I think that's it."

"The truth is, I'm somewhat attracted. I just don't like topsiders who figure they can knock a girl over with their charms."

"I don't recall charming you at all."

"Well. There's that."

He walked along with her through silent streets. Admired the way she moved. The quick determined stride. There was no one about. Shuttered windows, and even the taverns still. At Tunnel 9 she found a lantern. The glow lemoned her eyes. She took his hand without hesitation, a touch that seemed new and yet familiar. He didn't ask where they were going. A cool and steady draft swept through the tunnel, the smell of stone perpetually damp and clean. There were small rooms, lithic indentations on either side, places for folded canvas, scaffolding and tools, paints and other things.

She left the tunnel and led him down a short granite passage, through a wooden door. The space about him seemed hollow and immense. A high vaulted ceiling was revealed. Stone ribbing soared to dizzy heights and disappeared. Carrie Deeds drew him swiftly past fluted marble columns, carved groups, and figures. Will began to find scraps of paper, the notes of student guides.

crowned in the classical sense . . .
    symbolic of naval supremacy and plentiful reign . . .

The vaulted hall gave way to Knight's Chapel. Deep-relief sculptures of great battles and achievement. Elders, counselors, and maidens.

"Over here," Carrie whispered, a sound that fled like quick escaping birds for some time. She made the lamp brighter and held it high. "There. That's what I do. What do you think?"

A hint of challenge in her voice. A frieze done in subtle coloration. Gracious woods, the trunks of massive trees, framing stately homes and folded hills. A spaniel in the old heroic style, rampant on a lawn.

"I like it," said Will. "It's damned good work. I can almost hear that little fella bark." He meant it, and looked right at her as he spoke, knowing this was a woman who would smell idle praise in an instant, would sense any patronizing air and likely hit him with the lantern.

"I just wanted you to see," she told Will. "I wanted you to know what I do." Her words seemed to bridge something between them, words spoken and unsaid as well. She was a carver, too, and if topside was a problem, they could end whatever there was right there.

She took him past Early Years, past Piety and Truth stripped to the waist, entwined in marble and quartz. He kissed her before the high bronze gate of Funerary Hall, held her beneath brooding obsidian guards. Her breath was sweet, her body firm and yielding at once. He wanted her then, and knew she would come to him gladly. Instead, he gathered the lantern and took her quickly the way they'd come. She seemed to understand. A pulse beat patiently in her throat. She looked composed and yet intent.

Clouds had gathered to mask the moon. The steamhouse was dark, engine-dreams growling back behind. Will roused old Butz out of sleep. Butz was clearly annoyed. He had no authority to raise Express in the middle of the night. Will suggested a costly breed of gin.

"This is crazy," said Carrie Deeds. "This is crazy as it can be." She held to him tightly, her head against his shoulder, fearful of what she'd see yet curious about the ground dropping away at a rapid pace. "I got to prove myself or what? That better not be what I'm doing."

"You don't have to prove a thing. I want you up there with me."

"I asked people about you."

"What did they say?"

"That you're eight to five to get Hair."

"Me or Mink. Odds don't mean a thing to old Quaker. He'll take us on the boat one day, maybe three miles out, then he'll stand there studying on the brows, making me and Mink sweat. If he's constipated bad, he'll pick Mink. If he's thinking straight at all, he'll choose me. He knows I'm the one ought to get it."

"You ever think about if he doesn't?"

"No. Not any. Your folks carvers, too?"

"Dad is. Mom's dead. Sis is a nun at our Lady of Pat. That didn't seem the life for me."

"I wouldn't think."

"What's that supposed to mean?"

"Now don't start that. We're getting along fine."

"So you say."

The elevator trembled to a stop. He led her through a maze of granite blocks. Clouds swept the moon, and planes of stone seemed to vanish and reappear. At Hairline he stopped and held back. Newcomers never understood what they would see. Carrie, though, walked boldly ahead, the high night wind sweeping her hair and snapping at her clothes. The earth below was fluid. Chalky ribbons scratched the sea.

"Lord," she said, "I didn't even imagine."

She didn't speak as he took her hand and guided her to the webbing. Snapping a safety line about his waist, he linked a shorter rope to hers. Before, he might have asked, told her how it would be. He knew, now, she would never make the descent to impress him, or show him that she could. She would do it because this was what she wanted, what she'd decided to do. She stayed close beside him on the webbing, making the fifty yards without looking above or below, the wind whipping sharply about her. Forehead seemed the curve of another moon, a luminous world fleeing in the night.

When it was over, she turned to him and smiled. A mix of emotions. Daring and hesitation. Wonder, an honest touch of fear.

"You do this every day?"

"Like falling off a log."

"I won't say you've got a way with words."

She gripped his hand as he moved from the webbing to a smooth granite fissure, a brooding hollow near the thickest point of the brow. The wind seemed to die. She rested in his arms. When he kissed her, she brought her hand between them, found the zipper at her neck. He looked into her eyes, saw bold and wicked purpose. Her skin was uncanny, another shade of moon and granite. Her features seemed lost in gentle confusion. He drew his strength from the rock itself, from the spirit of the Work. When the sweet rage consumed him, he felt as if a great stone heart beat from below. She sighed, and seemed much smaller than before. Ragged cloud tangled in her hair. He shuddered at the wonder of what had occurred. Bracing his hands on frigid granite, he saw past her to the night. The moon rippled the earth. The sea mirrored the sky. The lights of houses and small towns winked here and there, distorted by the wind.

"Come back down here," she said. "I'm cold."

He leaned against her to give her warmth.

"I think you've turned my head, Will Taypes."

"I'm doing the best I can."

"You're doing pretty good."

In the unnatural light, he could see far to the north, to the towers of Traitors' Gate, the L.A. Wall that stretched forever, and behind it nothing but dark. The Work was all there was.

"My father's obsessed with lizards. I think you ought to know."

"I can live with that. What else?"

"I don't ask a lot."

"Good. I won't do just anything you want."

"I'm not surprised to hear it."

"I'm guessing we'll get along."

Ginny Sweethips' Flying Circus

D EL DROVE AND GINNY SAT.
"They're taking their sweet time," Ginny said, "damned if they're not."

"They're itchy," Del said. "Everyone's itchy. Everyone's looking to stay alive."

"Huh!" Ginny showed disgust. "I sure don't care for sittin' out here in the sun. My price is going up by the minute. You wait and see if it doesn't."

"Don't get greedy," Del said.

Ginny curled her toes on the dash. Her legs felt warm in the sun. The stockade was a hundred yards off. Barbed wire looped above the walls. The sign over the gate read:

First Church of the Unleaded God
& Ace High Refinery
WELCOME
KEEP OUT

The refinery needed paint. It had likely been silver, but was now dull as pewter and black rust. Ginny leaned out the window and called to Possum Dark.

"What's happening, friend? Those mothers dead in there or what?"

"Thinking," Possum said. "Fixing to make a move. Considering what to do." Possum Dark sat atop the van in a steno chair bolted to the roof. Circling the chair was a swivel-ring mount sporting fine twin-fifties black as grease. Possum had a death-view clean around. Keeping out the sun was a red Cinzano umbrella faded pink. Possum studied the stockade and watched heat distort the flats. He didn't care for the effect. He was suspicious of things less than cut and dried. Apprehensive of illusions of every kind. He scratched his nose and curled his tail around his leg. The gate opened up and men started across the scrub. He teased them in his sights. He prayed they'd do something silly and grand.

Possum counted thirty-seven men. A few carried sidearms, openly or concealed. Possum spotted them all at once. He wasn't too concerned. This seemed like an easygoing bunch, more intent on fun than fracas. Still, there was always the hope that he was wrong.

The men milled about. They wore patched denim and faded shirts. Possum made them nervous. Del countered that; his appearance set them at ease. The men looked at Del, poked each other and grinned. Del was scrawny and bald except for tufts around the ears. The dusty black coat was too big. His neck thrust out of his shirt like a newborn buzzard looking for meat. The men forgot Possum and gathered around, waiting to see what Del would do. Waiting for Del to get around to showing them what they'd come to see. The van was painted turtle-green. Gold Barnum type named the owner, and the selected vices for sale:

Ginny Sweethips' Flying Circus
SEX*TACOS*DANGEROUS DRUGS

Del puttered about with this and that. He unhitched the wagon from the van and folded out a handy little stage. It didn't take three minutes to set up, but he dragged it out to ten, then ten on top of that. The men started to whistle and clap their hands. Del looked alarmed. They liked that. He stumbled and they laughed.

"Hey, mister, you got a girl in there or not?" a man called out.

"Better be something here besides you," another said.

"Gents," Del said, raising his hands for quiet, "Ginny Sweethips herself will soon appear on this stage, and you'll be more than glad you waited. Your every wish will be fulfilled, I promise you that. I'm bringing beauty to the wastelands, gents. Lust the way you like it, passion unrestrained. Sexual crimes you never dreamed!"

"Cut the talk, mister," a man with peach-pit eyes shouted to Del. "Show us what you got."

Others joined in, stomped their feet and whistled. Del knew he had them. Anger was what he wanted. Frustration and denial. Hatred waiting for sweet release. He waved them off, but they wouldn't stop. He placed one hand on the door of the van—and brought them to silence at once.

The double doors opened. A worn red curtain was revealed, stenciled with hearts and cherubs. Del extended his hand. He seemed to search behind the curtain, one eye closed in concentration. He looked alarmed, groping for something he couldn't find. Uncertain he remembered how to do this trick at all. And then, in a sudden burst of motion, Ginny did a double forward flip, and appeared like glory on the stage.

The men broke into shouts of wild abandon. Ginny led them in a cheer. She was dressed for the occasion. Short white skirt shiny bright, white boots with tassels. White sweater with a big red G sewn on the front.

"Ginny Sweethips, gents," Del announced with a flair, "giving you her own interpretation of Barbara Jean, the Cheerleader Next Door. Innocent as snow, yet a little bit wicked and willing to learn, if Biff the Quarterback will only teach her. Now, what do you say to *that*?"

They whistled and yelled and stomped. Ginny strutted and switched, doing long-legged kicks that left them gasping with delight. Thirty-seven pairs of eyes showed their needs. Men guessed at hidden parts. Dusted off scenarios of violence and love. Then, as quickly as she'd come, Ginny was gone. Men threatened to storm the stage. Del grinned without concern. The curtain parted and Ginny was back, blond hair replaced with saucy red, costume changed in the blink of an eye. Del introduced Nurse Nora, an angel of mercy weak as soup in the hands of Patient Pete. Moments later, hair black as a raven's throat, she was Schoolteacher Sally, cold as well water, until Steve the Bad Student loosed the fury chained within.

Ginny vanished again. Applause thundered over the flats. Del urged them on, then spread his hands for quiet.

"Did I lie to you gents? Is she all you ever dreamed? Is this the love you've wanted all your life? Could you ask for sweeter limbs, for softer flesh? For whiter teeth, for brighter eyes?"

"Yeah, but is she *real*?" a man shouted, a man with a broken face sewn up like a sock. "We're religious people here. We don't fuck with no machines."

Others echoed the question with bold shouts and shaking fists.

"Now, I don't blame you, sir, at all," Del said. "I've had a few dolly droids myself. A plastic embrace at best, I'll grant you that. Not for the likes of *you*, for I can tell you're a man who knows his women. No, sir, Ginny's real as rain, and she's yours in the role of your choice. Seven minutes of bliss. It'll seem like a lifetime, gents, I promise you that. Your goods gladly returned if I'm a liar. And all for only a U.S. gallon of gas!"

Howls and groans at that, as Del expected.

"That's a *cheat* is what it is! Ain't a woman worth it!"

"Gas is better'n gold, and we work damn hard to get it!"

Del stood his ground. Looked grim and disappointed. "I'd be the last man alive to try to part you from your goods," Del said. "It's not my place to drive a fellow into the arms of sweet content, to make him rest his manly frame on golden thighs. Not if he thinks this lovely girl's not worth the fee, no sir. I don't do business that way and never have."

The men moved closer. Del could smell their discontent. He read sly thoughts above their heads. There was always this moment when it occurred to them there was a way Ginny's delights might be obtained for free.

"Give it some thought, friends," Del said. "A man's got to do what he's got to do. And while you're making up your minds, turn your eyes to the top of the van for a startling and absolutely free display of the slickest bit of marksmanship you're ever likely to see!"

Before Del's words were out of his mouth and on the way, before the men could scarcely comprehend, Ginny appeared again and tossed a dozen china saucers in the air.

Possum Dark moved in a blur. Turned 140 degrees in his bolted steno chair and whipped his guns on target, blasting saucers to dust. Thunder rolled across the flats. Crockery rained on the men below. Possum stood and offered a pink killer grin and a little bow. The men saw six-foot-nine and a quarter inches of happy marsupial fury and awesome speed, of black agate eyes and a snout full of icy varmint teeth. Doubts were swept aside. Fifty-calibre madness wasn't the answer. Fun today was clearly not for free.

"Gentlemen, start your engines," Del smiled. "I'll be right here to take your fee. Enjoy a hot taco while you wait your turn at glory. Have a look at our display of fine pharmaceutical wonders and mind-expanding drugs."

In moments, men were making their way back to the stockade. Soon after that, they returned toting battered tins of gas. Del sniffed each gallon, in case some buffoon thought water would get him by. Each man received a token and took his place. Del sold tacos and dangerous drugs, taking what he could get in trade. Candles and Mason jars, a rusty knife. Half a manual on full-field maintenance for the Chrysler Mark XX Urban Tank. The drugs were different colors but the same: twelve parts oregano, three parts rabbit shit, one part marijuana stems. All this under Possum's watchful eye.

"By God," said the first man out of the van. "She's worth it, I'll tell you that. Have her do the Nurse, you won't regret it!"

"The Schoolteacher's best," said the second man through. "I never seen the like. I don't care if she's real or she ain't."

"What's in these tacos?" a customer asked Del.

"Nobody you know, mister," Del said.

"It's been a long day," Ginny said. "I'm pooped, and that's the truth." She wrinkled up her nose. "First thing we hit a town, you hose 'er out good now, Del. Place smells like a sewer or maybe worse."

Del squinted at the sky and pulled up under the scant shade of mesquite. He stepped out and kicked the tires. Ginny got down, walked around and stretched.

"It's getting late," Del said. "You want to go on or stop here?"

"You figure those boys might decide to get a rebate on this gas?"

"Hope they do," Possum said from atop the van.

"You're a pisser," Ginny laughed, "I'll say that. Hell, let's keep going. I could use a hot bath and town food. What you figure's up the road?"

"East Bad News," Del said, "if this map's worth anything at all. Ginny, night driving's no good. You don't know what's waiting down the road."

"I know what's on the roof," Ginny said. "Let's do it. I'm itchy all over with bugs and dirt and that tub keeps shinin' in my head. You want me to drive a spell, I sure will."

"Get in," Del grumbled. "Your driving's scarier than anything I'll meet."

* * *

Morning arrived in purple shadow and metal tones, copper, silver, and gold. From a distance, East Bad News looked to Ginny like garbage strewn carelessly over the flats. Closer, it looked like larger garbage. Tin shacks and tents and haphazard buildings rehashed from whatever they were before. Cookfires burned, and the locals wandered about and yawned and scratched. Three places offered food. Other places bed and a bath. Something to look forward to, at least. She spotted the sign down at the far end of town.

MORO'S REPAIRS
Armaments*Machinery*Electronic Shit of All Kinds

"Hold it!" Ginny said. "Pull 'er in right there."

Del looked alarmed. "What for?"

"Don't get excited. There's gear needs tending in back. I just want 'em to take a look."

"Didn't mention it to me," Del said.

Ginny saw the sad and droopy eyes, the tired wisps of hair sticking flat to Del's ears. "Del, there wasn't anything to mention," she said in a kindly tone. "Nothing you can really put your finger on, I mean. okay?"

"Whatever you think," Del said, clearly out of sorts.

Ginny sighed and got out. Barbed wire surrounded the yard behind the shop. The yard was ankle-deep in tangles of rope and copper cable, rusted unidentifiable parts. A battered pickup hugged the wall. Morning heat curled the tin roof of the building. More parts spilled out of the door. Possum made a funny noise, and Ginny saw the Dog step into the light. A Shepherd, maybe six-foot-two. It showed Possum Dark yellow eyes. A man appeared behind the Dog, wiping heavy grease on his pants. Bare to the waist, hair like stuffing out of a chair. Features hard as rock, flint eyes to match. Not bad looking, thought Ginny, if you cleaned him up good.

"Well now," said the man. He glanced at the van, read the legend on the side, took in Ginny from head to toe. "What can I do for *you*, little lady?"

"I'm not real little and don't guess I'm any lady," Ginny said. "Whatever you're thinking, don't. You open for business or just talk?"

The man grinned. "My name's Moro Gain. Never turn business away if I can help it."

"I need electric stuff."

"We got it. What's the problem?"

"Huh-unh." Ginny shook her head. "First, I gotta ask. You do confidential work or tell everything you know?"

"Secret's my middle name," Moro said. "Might cost a little more, but you got it."

"How much?"

Moro closed one eye. "Now, how do I know that? You got a nuclear device in there, or a broken watch? Drive it on in and we'll take a look." He aimed a greasy finger at Possum Dark. "Leave *him* outside."

"No way."

"No arms in the shop. That's a rule."

"He isn't carrying. Just the guns you see." Ginny smiled. "You can shake him down if you like. *I* wouldn't, I don't think."

"He looks imposing, all right."

"I'd say he is."

"What the hell," Moro said "drive it in."

Dog unlocked the gate. Possum climbed down and followed with oily eyes.

"Go find us a place to stay," Ginny said to Del. "Clean, if you can find it. All the hot water in town. Christ sakes, Del, you still sulking or what?"

"Don't worry about me," Del said. "Don't concern yourself at all."

"Right." She hopped behind the wheel. Moro began kicking the door of his shop. It finally sprang free, wide enough to take the van. The supply wagon rocked along behind. Moro lifted the tarp, eyed the thirty-seven tins of unleaded with great interest.

"You get lousy mileage, or what?" he asked Ginny.

Ginny didn't answer. She stepped out of the van. Light came through broken panes of glass. The skinny windows reminded her of a church. Her eyes got used to shadow, and she saw that that's what it was. Pews sat to the side, piled high with auto parts. A 1997 Olds was jacked up before the altar.

"Nice place you got here," she said.

"It works for me," Moro told her. "Now what kind of trouble you got? Something in the wiring? You said electric stuff."

"I didn't mean the motor. Back here." She led him to the rear and opened the doors.

"God a'Mighty!" Moro said.

"Smells a little raunchy right now. Can't help that till we hose 'er down." Ginny stepped inside, looked back, and saw Moro still on the ground. "You coming up or not?"

"Just thinking."

"About what?" She'd seen him watching her move and didn't really have to ask.

"Well, *you* know . . ." Moro shuffled his feet. "How do you figure on paying? For whatever it is I got to do."

"Gas. You take a look. Tell me how many tins. I say yes or no."

"We could work something out."

"We could, huh?"

"Sure." Moro gave her a foolish grin. "Why not?"

Ginny didn't blink. "Mister, what kind of girl do you think I am?"

Moro looked puzzled and intent. "I can read good, lady, believe it or not. I figured you wasn't tacos or dangerous drugs."

"You figured wrong," Ginny said. "Sex is just software to me, and don't you forget it. I haven't got all day to watch you moonin' over my parts. I got to move or stand still. When I stand still, you look. When I move, you look more. Can't fault you for that, I'm about the prettiest thing you ever saw. Don't let it get in the way of your work."

Moro couldn't think of much to say. He took a breath and stepped into the van. There was a bed bolted flat against the floor. A red cotton spread, a worn satin pillow that said DURANGO, COLORADO and pictured chipmunks and waterfalls. An end table, a pink-shaded lamp with flamingos on the side. Red curtains on the walls. Ballet prints and a naked Minnie Mouse.

"Somethin' else," Moro said.

"Back here's the problem," Ginny said. She pulled a curtain aside at the front of the van. There was a plywood cabinet, fitted with brass screws. Ginny took a key out of her jeans and opened it up.

Moro stared a minute, then laughed aloud. "*Sensory* tapes? Well, I'll be a son of a bitch." He took a new look at Ginny, a look Ginny didn't miss. "Haven't seen a rig like this in years. Didn't know there were any still around."

"I've got three tapes," Ginny explained. "A brunette, a redhead, and a blond. Found a whole cache in Ardmore, Oklahoma. Had to look at 'bout three or four hundred to find girls that looked close enough to me. Nearly went nuts 'fore it was over. Anyway, I did it. Spliced 'em down to seven minutes each."

Moro glanced back at the bed. "How do you put 'em under?"

"Little needle comes up out the mattress. Sticks them in the ass lightnin' fast. They're out like *that*. Seven-minute dose. Headpiece is in the end table there. I get it on and off them real quick. Wires go under the floorboards back here to the rig."

"Jesus," Moro said. "They ever catch you at this, you are cooked, lady."

"That's what Possum's for," Ginny said. "Possum's pretty good at what he does. Now what's *that* look all about?"

"I wasn't sure right off if you were real."

Ginny laughed aloud. "So what do you think now?"

"I think maybe you are."

"Right," Ginny said. "It's Del who's the droid, not me. Wimp IX Series. Didn't make a whole lot. Not much demand. The customers think it's me, never think to look at him. He's a damn good barker and pretty good at tacos and drugs. A little too sensitive, you ask me. Well, nobody's perfect, so they say."

"The trouble you're having's in the rig?"

"I guess," Ginny said, "beats the hell out of me." She bit her lip and wrinkled her brow. Moro found the gestures most inviting. "Slips a little, I think. Maybe I got a short, huh?"

"Maybe." Moro fiddled with the rig, testing one of the spools with his thumb. "I'll have to get in here and see."

"It's all yours. I'll be wherever it is Del's got me staying."

"Ruby John's," Moro said. "Only place there is with a good roof. I'd like to take you out to dinner."

"Well sure you would."

"You got a real shitty attitude, friend."

"I get a whole lot of practice," Ginny said.

"And I've got a certain amount of pride," Moro told her. "I don't intend to ask you more than three or four times and that's it."

Ginny nodded. Right on the edge of approval. "You've got promise," she said. "Not a whole lot, maybe, but some."

"Does that mean dinner, or not?"

"Means not. Means if I *wanted* to have dinner with some guy, you'd maybe fit the bill."

Moro's eyes got hot. "Hell with you, lady. I don't need the company that bad."

"Fine." Ginny sniffed the air and walked out. "You have a nice day."

Moro watched her walk. Watched denims mold her legs, studied the hydraulics of her hips. Considered several unlikely acts. Considered cleaning up, searching for proper clothes. Considered finding a bottle and watching the tapes. A plastic embrace at best, or so he'd heard, but a lot less hassle in the end.

Possum Dark watched the van disappear into the shop. He felt uneasy at once. His place was on top. Keeping Ginny from harm. Sending feral prayers for murder to absent genetic gods. His eyes hadn't left Dog since he'd appeared. Primal smells, old fears and needs, assailed his senses. Dog locked the gate and turned around. Didn't come closer, just turned.

"I'm Dog Quick," he said, folding hairy arms. "I don't much care for Possums."

"I don't much care for Dogs," said Possum Dark.

Dog seemed to understand. "What did you do before the War?"

"Worked in a theme park. Our Wildlife Heritage. That kind of shit. What about you?"

"Security, what else?" Dog made a face. "Learned a little electrics. Picked up a lot more from Moro Gain. I've done worse." He nodded toward the shop. "You like to shoot people with that thing?"

"Anytime I get the chance."

"You ever play any cards?"

"Some." Possum Dark showed his teeth. "I guess I could handle myself with a Dog."

"For real goods?" Dog returned the grin.

"New deck, unbroken seal, table stakes," Possum said.

Moro showed up at Ruby John's Cot Emporium close to noon. Ginny had a semiprivate stall, covered by a blanket. She'd bathed and braided her hair and cut the legs clean off her jeans. She tugged at Moro's heart.

"It'll be tomorrow morning," Moro said. "Cost you ten gallons of gas."

"Ten gallons," Ginny said. "That's stealin', and you know it."

"Take it or leave it," Moro said. "You got a bad head in that rig. Going to come right off, you don't fix it. You wouldn't like that. Your customers wouldn't like it any at all."

Ginny appeared subdued but not much. "Four gallons. Tops."

"Eight. I got to make the parts myself."

"Five."

"Six," Moro said. "Six and I take you to dinner."

"Five and a half, and I want to be out of this sweatbox at dawn. On the road and gone when the sun starts bakin' your lovely town."

"Damn, you're fun to have around."

Ginny smiled. Sweet and disarming, an unexpected event. "I'm all right. You got to get to know me."

"Just how do I go about that?"

"You don't." The smile turned sober. "I haven't figured that one out."

It looked like rain to the north. Sunrise was dreary. Muddy, less-than-spectacular yellows and reds. Colors through a window no one had bothered to wash. Moro had the van brought out. He said he'd thrown in a lube and hosed out the back. Five and a half gallons were gone out of the wagon. Ginny had Del count while Moro watched.

"I'm honest," Moro said, "you don't have to do that."

"I know," Ginny said, glancing curiously at Dog, who was looking rather strange. He seemed out of sorts. Sulky and off his feed. Ginny followed his eyes and saw Possum atop the van. Possum showed a wet Possum grin.

"Where you headed now?" Moro asked, wanting to hold her as long as he could.

"South," Ginny said, since she was facing that direction.

"I wouldn't," Moro said. "Not real friendly folks down there."

"I'm not picky. Business is business."

"No, sir," Moro shook his head. "*Bad* business is what it is. You got the Dry Heaves south and east. Doom City after that. Straight down and you'll hit the Hackers. Might run into Fort Pru, bunch of disgruntled insurance agents out on the flats. Stay clear away from them. Isn't worth whatever you'll make."

"You've been a big help," Ginny said.

Moro gripped her door. "You ever *listen* to anyone, lady? I'm giving good advice."

"Fine," Ginny said, "I'm 'bout as grateful as I can be."

Moro watched her leave. He was consumed by her appearance. The day seemed to focus in her eyes. Nothing he said pleased her in the least. Still, her disdain was friendly enough. There was no malice at all that he could see.

There was something about the sound of Doom City she didn't like. Ginny told Del to head south and maybe west. Around noon, a yellow haze appeared on the ragged rim of the world, like someone rolling a cheap dirty rug across the flats.

"Sandstorm," Possum called from the roof. "Right out of the west. I don't like it at all. I think we better turn. Looks like trouble coming fast."

There was nothing Possum said she couldn't see. He had a habit of saying either too little or more than enough. She told him to cover his guns and get inside, that the sand would take his hide and there was nothing out there he needed to kill that wouldn't wait. Possum Dark sulked but climbed down. Hunched in back of the van, he grasped air in the shape of grips and trigger guards. Practiced rage and windage in his head.

"I'll bet I can beat that storm," Del said. "I got this feeling I can do it."

"Beat it where?" Ginny said. "We don't know where we are or what's ahead."

"That's true," Del said. "All the more reason then to get there soon as we can."

Ginny stepped out and viewed the world with disregard. "I got sand in my teeth and in my toes," she complained. "I'll bet that Moro Gain knows right where storms'll likely be. I'll bet that's what happened, all right."

"Seemed like a decent sort to me," Del said.

"That's what I mean," Ginny said. "You can't trust a man like that at all."

The storm had seemed to last a couple of days. Ginny figured maybe an hour. The sky looked bad as cabbage soup. The land looked just the way it had. She couldn't see the difference between sand recently gone or newly arrived. Del got the van going again. Ginny thought about yesterday's bath. East Bad News had its points.

Before they topped the first rise, Possum Dark began to stomp on the roof. "Vehicles to port," he called out. "Sedans and pickup trucks. Flatbeds and semis. Buses of all kinds."

"What are they doing?" Del said.

"Coming right at us, hauling timber."

"Doing *what*?" Ginny made a face. "Damn it all, Del, will you stop the car? I swear, you're a driving fool."

Del stopped. Ginny climbed up with Possum to watch. The caravan kept a straight line. Cars and trucks weren't exactly hauling timber ... but they were. Each carried a section of a wall. Split logs bound together, sharpened at the top. The lead car turned and the others followed. The lead car turned again. In a moment, there was a wooden stockade assembled on the flats, square as if you'd drawn it with a rule. A stockade and a gate. Over the gate a wooden sign:

FORT PRU
Games of Chance & Amusement
Term*Whole Life*Half Life*Death

"I don't like it," said Possum Dark.

"You don't like anything's still alive," Ginny said.

"They've got small arms and they're a nervous-looking bunch."

"They're just horny, Possum. That's the same as nervous, or close enough." Possum pretended to understand. "Looks like they're pulled up for the night," she called to Del. "Let's do some business, friend. The overhead don't ever stop."

Five of them came out to the van. They all looked alike. Stringy, darkened by the sun. Bare to the waist except for collars and striped ties. Each carried an attaché case thin as two slices of bread without butter. Two had pistols stuck in their belts. The leader carried a fine-looking sawed-off Remington 12. It hung by a camou guitar strap to his waist. Del didn't like him at all. He had perfect white teeth and a bald head. Eyes the color of jellyfish melting on the beach. He studied the sign on the van and looked at Del.

"You got a whore inside or not?"

Del looked him straight on. "I'm a little displeased at that. It's not the way to talk."

"Hey." The man gave Del a wink. "You don't have to give us the pitch. We're show business folk ourselves."

"Is that right?"

"Wheels of chance and honest cards. Odds I *know* you'll like. I'm head actuary of this bunch. Name's Fred. That animal up there has a piss-poor attitude, friend. No reason to poke that weapon down my throat. We're friendly people here."

"No reason I can see why Possum'd spray this place with lead and diarrhetics," Del said. "Less you can think of something I can't."

Fred smiled at that. The sun made a big gold ball on his head. "I guess we'll try your girl," he told Del. " 'Course we got to see her first. What do you take in trade?"

"Goods as fine as what you're getting in return."

"I've got just the thing." The head actuary winked again. The gesture was starting to irritate Del. Fred nodded, and a friend drew clean white paper from his case. "This here is heavy bond," he told Del, shuffling the edges with his thumb. "Fifty percent linen weave, and we got it by the ream. Won't find anything like it. You can mark on it good or trade it off. Seventh Mercenary Writers came through a week ago. Whole brigade of mounted horse. Near cleaned us out, but we can spare a few reams. We got pencils too. Mirado twos and threes, unsharpened, with erasers on the end. When's the last time you saw *that*? Why, this stuff's good as gold. We got staples and legal pads. Claim forms, maim forms, forms of every sort. Deals on wheels is what we got. And *you* got gas under wraps in the wagon behind your van. I can smell it plain from here. Friend, we can sure talk some business with you there. I got seventeen rusty-ass guzzlers runnin' dry."

A gnat-whisker wire sparked hot in Del's head. He could see it in the underwriter's eyes. Gasoline greed was what it was, and he knew these men were bent on more than fleshly pleasure. He knew with androidial dread that when they could, they'd make their play.

"Well now, the gas is not for trade," he said as calmly as he could. "Sex and tacos and dangerous drugs is what we sell."

"No problem," the actuary said. "Why, no problem at all. Just an idea, is all it was. You get that little gal out here and I'll bring in my crew. How's half a ream a man sound to you?"

"Just as fair as it can be," Del said, thinking that half of that would've been fine, knowing dead certain now that Fred intended to take back whatever he gave.

"That Moro fellow was right," Del said. "These insurance boys are bad news. Best thing we can do is take off and let it go."

"Pooh," said Ginny, "that's just the way men are. They come in mad as foamin' dogs and go away like cats licking cream. That's the nature of the fornicatin' trade. You wait and see. Besides, they won't get funny with Possum Dark."

"You wouldn't pray for rain if you were afire," Del muttered. "Well, I'm not unhitching the gas. I'll set you up a stage over the tarp. You can do your number there."

"Suit yourself," Ginny said, kissing a plastic cheek and scooting him out the door. "Now get on out of here and let me start getting cute."

It seemed to be going well. Cheerleader Barbara Jean awoke forgotten wet dreams, left their mouths as dry as snakes. Set them up for Sally the Teach and Nora Nurse, secret violations of the soul. Maybe Ginny was right, Del decided. Faced with girlie delights, a man's normally shitty outlook disappeared. When he was done, he didn't want to wreck a thing for an hour or maybe two. Didn't care about killing for half a day. Del could only guess at this magic and how it worked. Data was one thing, sweet encounters something else.

He caught Possum's eye and felt secure. Forty-eight men waited their turns. Possum knew the caliber of their arms, the length of every blade. His black twin-fifties blessed them all.

Fred the actuary sidled up and grinned at Del. "We sure ought to talk about gas. That's what we ought to do."

"Look," Del said, "gas isn't for trade, I told you that. Go talk to those boys at the refinery, same as us."

"Tried to. They got no use for office supplies."

"That's not my problem," Del said.

"Maybe it is."

Del didn't miss the razor tones. "You got something to say, just say it."

"Half of your gas. We pay our way with the girl and don't give you any trouble."

"You forget about *him*?"

Fred studied Possum Dark. "I can afford losses better than you. Listen, I know what you are, friend. I know you're not a man. Had a CPA droid just like you 'fore the War."

"Maybe we can talk," Del said, trying to figure what to do.

"Say now, that's what I like to hear."

Ginny's fourth customer staggered out, wild-eyed and white around the gills. "Goddamn, try the Nurse," he bawled to the others. "Never had nothin' like it in my life!"

"Next," Del said, and started stacking bond paper. "Lust is the name of the game, gents, what did I tell you now?"

"The girl plastic, too?" Fred asked.

"Real as you," Del said. "We make some kind of deal, how do I know you'll keep your word?"

"Jesus," Fred said, "what do you think I am? You got my Life Underwriter's Oath!"

The next customer exploded through the curtain, tripped and fell on his face. Picked himself up and shook his head. He looked damaged, bleeding around the eyes.

"She's a tiger," Del announced, wondering what the hell was going on. " 'Scuse me a minute," he told Fred, and slipped inside the van. "Just what are you doing in here?" he asked Ginny. "Those boys look like they been through a thrasher."

"Beats me," Ginny said, halfway between Nora and Barbara Jean. "Last old boy jerked around like a snake having a fit. Started pulling out his hair. Somethin' isn't right here, Del. It's gotta be the tapes. I figure that Moro fellow's a cheat."

"We got trouble inside and out," Del told her. "The head of this bunch wants our gas."

"Well, he sure can't have it, by God."

"Ginny, the man's got bug-spit eyes. Says he'll take his chances with Possum. We better clear out while we can."

"Huh-unh." Ginny shook her head. "That'll rile 'em for sure. Give me a minute or two. We've done a bunch of Noras and a Sally. I'll switch them all to Barbara Jean and see."

Del slipped back outside. It seemed a dubious answer at best.

"That's some woman," said Fred.

"She's something else today. Your insurance boys have got her fired."

Fred grinned at that. "Guess I better give her a try."

"I wouldn't," Del said.

"Why not?"

"Let her calm down some. Might be more than you want to handle."

He knew at once this wasn't the thing to say. Fred turned the color of ketchup pie. "Why, you plastic piece of shit! I can handle any woman born . . . *or* put together out of a kit."

"Suit yourself," Del said, feeling the day going down the drain. "No charge at all."

"Damn right there's not." Fred jerked the next man out of line. "Get ready in there, little lady. I am going to handle *all* your policy needs!"

The men cheered. Possum Dark, who understood at least three-fifths of the trouble down below, shot Del a questioning look.

"Got any of those tacos?" someone asked.

"Not likely," Del said.

Del considered turning himself off. Android suicide seemed the answer. But in less than three minutes, unnatural howls began to come from the van. The howls turned to shrieks. Life underwriters went rigid. Then Fred emerged, shattered. He looked like a man who'd kicked a bear with boils. His joints appeared to bend the wrong way. He looked whomper-eyed at Del, dazed and out-of-synch. Everything happened then in seconds thin as wire. Del saw Fred find him, saw the oil-spill eyes catch him clean. Saw the sawed-off barrels match the eyes so fast even electric feet couldn't snatch him out of the way in time. Del's arm exploded. He let it go and ran for the van. Possum couldn't help. The actuary was below and too close. The twin-fifties opened up. Underwriters fled. Possum stitched the sand and sent them flying ragged and dead.

Del reached the driver's seat as lead peppered the van. He felt slightly silly. Sitting there with one arm, one hand on the wheel.

"Move over," Ginny said, "that isn't going to work."

"I guess not."

Ginny sent them lurching through the scrub. "Never saw anything like it in my life," she said aloud. "Turned that poor fella on, he started twisting out of his socks, bones snapping like sticks. Damndest orgasm I *ever* saw."

"Something's not working just right."

"Well, I can see that, Del. Jesus, what's that!"

Ginny twisted the wheel as a large part of the desert rose straight up in the air. Smoking sand rained down on the van.

"Rockets," Del said grimly. "That's the reason they figured that crazy-fingered Possum was a snap. Watch where you're going, girl!"

Two fiery pillars exploded ahead. Del leaned out the window and looked back. Half of Fort Pru's wall was in pursuit. Possum sprayed everything in sight, but he couldn't spot where the rockets were coming from. Underwriter assault cars split up, came at them from every side.

"Trying to flank us," Del said. A rocket burst to the right. "Ginny, I'm not real sure what to do."

"How's the stub?"

"Slight electric tingle. Like a doorbell half a mile away. Ginny, they get us in a circle, we're in very deep shit."

"They hit that gas, we won't have to worry about a thing. Oh Lord, now why did I think of that?"

Possum hit a semi clean on. It came to a stop and died, fell over like a bug. Del could see that being a truck and a wall all at once had its problems, balance being one.

"Head right at them," he told Ginny, "then veer off sharp. They can't turn quick going fast."

"Del!"

Bullets rattled the van. Something heavy made a noise. The van skewed to a halt.

Ginny took her hands off the wheel and looked grim. "It appears they got the tires. Del, we're flat dead is what we are. Let's get out of this thing."

And do *what*? Del wondered. Bearings seemed to roll about in his head. He sensed a malfunction on the way.

The Fort Pru vehicles shrieked to a stop. Crazed life agents piled out and came at them over the flats, firing small arms and hurling stones. A rocket burst nearby.

Possum's guns suddenly stopped. Ginny grimaced in disgust. "Don't you tell me we're out of ammo, Possum Dark. That stuff's plenty hard to get."

Possum started to speak. Del waved his good arm to the north.
"Hey now, would you look at that!"
Suddenly there was confusion in the underwriters' ranks. A vaguely familiar pickup had appeared on the rise. The driver weaved through traffic, hurling grenades. They exploded in clusters, bright pink bouquets. He spotted the man with the rocket, lying flat atop a bus. Grenades stopped him cold. Underwriters abandoned the field and ran. Ginny saw a fairly peculiar sight. Six black Harleys had joined the truck. Chow Dogs with Uzis snaked in and out of the ranks, motors snarling and spewing horsetails of sand high in the air. They showed no mercy at all, picking off stragglers as they ran. A few underwriters made it to cover. In a moment, it was over. Fort Pru fled in sectional disarray.
"Well, if that wasn't just in the nick of time," Del said.
"I hate Chow Dogs," Possum said. "They got black tongues, and that's a fact."

"I hope you folks are all right," Moro said. "Well now, friend, looks as if you've thrown an arm."
"Nothing real serious," Del said.
"I'm grateful," Ginny said. "Guess I got to tell you that."
Moro was taken by her penetrating charm, her thankless manner. The fetching smudge of grease on her knee. He thought she was cute as a pup.
"I felt it was something I had to do. Circumstances being what they are."
"And just what circumstances are that?" Ginny asked.
"That pesky Shepherd Dog's sorta responsible for any trouble you might've had. Got a little pissed when that Possum cleaned him out. Five-card stud, I think it was. 'Course there might have been marking and crimping of cards, I couldn't say."
Ginny blew hair out of her eyes. "Mister, far as I can see, you're not making a lot of sense."
"I'm real embarrassed about this. That Dog got mad and kinda screwed up your gear."
"You let a *Dog* repair my stuff?" Ginny said.
"Perfectly good technician. Taught him mostly myself. Okay if you don't get his danger up. Those Shepherds are inbred, so I hear. What he did was set your tapes in a loop and speed 'em up. Customer'd get, say, twenty-six times his money's worth. Works out to a Mach seven fuck. Could cause bodily harm."
"Lord, I ought to shoot you in the foot," Ginny said.

"Look," Moro said, "I stand behind my work, and I got here quick as I could. Brought friends along to help, and I'm eating the cost of that."

"Damn right," Ginny said. The Chow Dogs sat their Harleys a ways off and glared at Possum. Possum Dark glared back. He secretly admired their leather gear, the Purina crests sewn on the backs.

"I'll be adding up costs," Ginny said. "I'm expecting full repairs."

"You'll get it. Of course you'll have to spend some time in Bad News. Might take a little while."

She caught his look and had to laugh. "You're a stubborn son of a bitch, I'll give you that. What'd you do with that Dog?"

"You want taco meat, I'll make you a deal."

"Yuck. I guess I'll pass."

Del began to weave about in roughly trapezoidal squares. Smoke started to curl out of his stub.

"For Christ's sake, Possum, sit on him or something," Ginny said.

"I can fix that," Moro told her.

"You've about fixed enough, seems to me."

"We're going to get along fine. You wait and see."

"You think so?" Ginny looked alarmed. "I better not get used to having you around."

"It could happen."

"It could just as easy *not*."

"I'll see about changing that tire," Moro said. "We ought to get Del out of the sun. You think about finding something nice to wear to dinner. East Bad News is kinda picky. We got a lot of pride around here . . ."

From the Novel: *The Hereafter Gang*
3: The Model Shop

DOUG DREAMS HE AND JESUS ARE IN OLD MAN WETZEL'S model airplane store. The store is across the street from the dark and somber fortress of Lincoln Elementary. The school is two stories high but looks higher. There are towers crowned with concrete breastworks and sentry walks behind. Small mice and pigeons stand guard. Even on a Saturday afternoon, a cold December day free of imports and exports of Brazil, this grim wet structure holds the threat of Monday morning. Doug and Jesus stay clear. They keep to the other side of the street. They avoid looking up at the crenellated roof, the windows with pointed arches, the Norman arrow loops that the swallows have stuffed with straw. Doug imagines Mr. Britton donning battered helmet and mail. He mans the tower walls with a crossbow he's cleverly made in shop. Miss Crewley brings tubs of boiling soup from the cafeteria line. The Vikings howl in pain, drop their weapons and flee. They wish they'd never heard of Oklahoma.

The thick-boled elms that line the street are wet and bare. Doug feels ice on the bark. The clouds are steel and full of winter. The wind, out of the north, cuts corduroy knickers like a knife. The paint on Wetzel's store is flecked and dry as powder. The inside is the same; clapboard siding weathered ancient silver-gray.

Wetzel's gas stove, big as a grand piano, fills one wall with its mass. Blue flame licks at the shaggy asbestos, blisters the wooden floor. The air is thick with heat. There is no way to breathe. Old man Wetzel stands stern and unforgiving behind the counter. This stupefying warmth is not enough. He longs for lazy Mesozoic days. His nose runs all year round. His chicken-bone frame is wrapped in sweaters, one woolen layer after another, each the color of attic dust. A black stocking cap is pulled down across his ears. He watches Doug and Jesus through gold-rimmed glasses. He is waiting for them to steal. He knows all boys are thieves. Boys practice thievery and self-abuse. These are the things they do.

"What are you going to get?" asks Jesus. "You still thinking about the Hawker?"

"Maybe," Doug says. "I dunno. What are you going to do?"

Jesus doesn't answer. His eyes are as blue as raw milk, blue as baby eyes. He looks at the model, hanging from a string overhead. A Spitfire shrieks through English skies. It dives on a doomed Focke-Wulf. Red yarn lances from the Spitfire's wings. White cotton smoke and orange tissue flames billow from the hapless Jerry's engine.

"Lo, the wicked shall perish," Jesus says. Doug sees sadness and understanding in his eyes. "They shall be consumed in flame, smitten over the channel and in the fields."

"Yeah, right," Doug says. "Listen, you get the Spitfire I'm still getting the Hawker. I'm not going to be no German."

Jesus keeps his silence. When he gets that look in his eyes, Doug knows there isn't any use trying to talk. Still, if he wants to be weird it's okay. He's the only kid Doug likes in 5A. When he first came to school, his folks made him wear these sandals and a robe. The other guys beat him up at recess for a week. After that he dressed like everyone else. Corduroy knickers with leather patches on the knees. The elastic is long gone out of the knickers, and they sag to his dirty tennis shoes. He has a checkered mackinaw and a checkered cap to match, earflaps down over his hair. And that's the only thing. His hair is as long as a girl's. Doug thinks Jesus is pushing with the hair. Your best friend turns up on the Sunday school lesson every week, it's asking a lot.

Doug already knows what he wants. He'll get the flying model Hawker and some glue. That'll leave twenty cents left over. Enough for the picture show and popcorn and Jujubes and a Coke. He knows what he wants, but he looks at every item in the store. He pretends he might get something different. He walks along slow, hands stuck down in his pockets. He looks at the long strips of balsa in the bin. Some strips are thin as spaghetti, some as thick as baseball hats. He covets every piece. He savors the rich smell. Sun comes in the window of your room. You sand down balsa and the air is rich with dust. He's looked up balsa in a book. Balsa trees grow in the tropics. He imagines how they look. You could pick up a whole tree and throw it.

He looks at the neat lines of airplane dope behind the counter, squat bottles of Chinese red and sky blue, black and green and silver and battleship gray. He looks at the fine blades for carving, bright as new nickels and scalpel sharp, keen enough to lace a hand with scars in a single afternoon. He studies all the blue and orange kits on the homemade shelves at Wetzel's back. Every Comet model ever made is right there, everything from small nickel solids to the fliers for a quarter or fifty cents.

And there, on the very top shelf, where it's been for as long as he can remember, is a plane nearly three feet long. It is covered in black and red tissue applied with a surgeon's skill. The wings are swept up like a gull's. A silver-chrome gasoline engine is mounted just behind the prop. Doug wants this plane, with its bold pirate colors, more than anything else in the world. He knows he'll never have it, but he'd like to touch it once and feel its magic. It has never crossed his mind to ask Wetzel for such a favor. There isn't a kid alive with the guts for that. Wetzel is watching him even now, guessing his thoughts. His eyes are cold as Spandaus, searching for hapless Bristols limping home. Wetzel knows. He knows Doug will buy a gasoline model about the same time he buys a new La Salle. Wetzel can see right through Doug's mackinaw and knickers. He can see through flesh and bone and into pockets, see the quarter and two dimes clutched hot in Doug's fist. He knows to the penny what Doug has to spend. He even knows about the popcorn, the Jujubes and the Coke. He knows what's his and what isn't.

Doug and Jesus duck their heads into the biting north wind, close their eyes against the cold. Doug's ears are numb. He has to stretch his mouth to talk.

"You want to build 'em over at my house this afternoon? I got the table set up."

"Can't," says Jesus, "I have to be about my father's business."

"Is tomorrow okay?"

"Tomorrow's *Sunday*, Doug."

"Oh, yeah. I forgot. Anyway, I got to clean up my room 'fore Mom throws a fit."

"That's good. Honor thy father and mother, Doug."

"Hey—we'll do it Monday after school. I got a new *Captain Marvel* you can borrow if you want."

"Monday's fine, Doug."

Doug wipes his nose on his sleeve. They hurry north, bent into the wind. The cold begins to chew at their bones. Doug feels the first rattle of sleet on his cap. The gray stone capitol of Oklahoma squats at the far end of the street. High steel derricks line the parkway, right to the building's front door. Ice slicks the derricks at their peaks, hammerheads groan and suck oil. The building and the derricks are the same dull color as the sky.

"What are you going to be when you grow up?" asks Doug. "I'm going to be a pilot, and shoot down Germans and Japs."

"Those who live by the sword—"

"Hey, I can be a pilot if I want."

"I know that, Doug."

"Yeah, well what are you going to be?"

"I guess I'm going to be what I am," Jesus sighs.

"What? A ten-year-old kid?"

"No. Something else."

"Like what?"

"I guess I'll be about my father's business."

"Sure, this after*noon*," Doug says, "you already told me." He's beginning to lose patience with his friend. Sometimes it's better just to walk with Jesus and not try to talk to him at all. "I mean later. When you grow up. What are you going to do then?"

Jesus doesn't answer. He stops and turns and looks back the way they came, past the bare trees and the school and the slate-colored sky. He seems to listen like a cat that hears sounds it doesn't share. Doug follows Jesus's eyes. He sees a small spot growing larger, the hard point of a pencil, punching through dark and brittle paper. The point grows, sprouts black horns and then a tail. Jesus doesn't move. He watches this dark and spinning star hurling toward him from a chill inverted sea.

"It is time," says Jesus, and Doug can scarcely hear his words. He stares in awe, in terrible disbelief. He knows the star and what it is.

"Jesus," Doug shouts, "it's a Fokker D-VII and it's coming right at us!"

He tugs at his friend, tries to throw him to the ground. Jesus is made of stone. The plane grows larger, fills the winter sky. Twin threads of yarn reach out and find their mark. Jesus cries out and falls. Doug looks up and sees the tattered double wings, the stubby shape. He sees no pilot, no one at all. Tissue paper shivers in the wind. The acid taste of glue is on his tongue. The plane snarls like a dog and disappears. Doug bends and takes Jesus in his arms. He is hit in the side and in his feet. There is blood in the palms of his hands. His face is set in pain and resignation. He looks at Doug and smiles.

"It's all right," he tells Doug, "it's okay."

"It's *not* okay, it's not!" Tears fill his eyes. He holds Jesus close against his chest. "I don't want you to die. You just can't!"

"I think I have to, Doug. I'm almost sure I do."

"You don't either. I'll never see you again, and I don't even like anyone else."

"I'll be back. I promise."

"Oh sure. When?"

Jesus thinks a minute. "How about Easter? I'll get up Easter morning early, and we'll do the Hawker and the Spitfire together."

Doug starts to tell him they go to church on Easter and eat out. He looks down and sees the fine blue eyes are white as marble. He's seen war movies and how they close a guy's eyes when he'd dead. It doesn't work. The eyes don't want to stay shut. He doesn't know what to do next. Easter seems a long time away. . . .

Three thousand copies of this book have been printed by The Maple-Vail Book Manufacturing Group, Binghamton, N.Y., for Golden Gryphon Press, Urbana, Ill. The typestyle is Elante, printed on 55# Sebago. The binding cloth is Roxite B Grade #51545. Typesetting by The Composing Room, Inc., Kimberly, Wis.

Also from Golden Gryphon Press

The Robot's Twilight Companion
by Tony Daniel

This collection of award winning science fiction includes a story that was a finalist for the Hugo Awards and one that was voted one of the 10 greatest science fiction stories to appear during the 1990s. In the title piece, geologist Andrew Mutton has obtained an intelligent mining robot and downloaded the memories of his deceased mentor into the robot's electronic brain. Together, man and robot undertake a project to bore through the crust and mantle to the very core of the planet Earth. Their work is complicated by conflict with a mysterious intelligence deep within the Earth and by the robot's own emergent humanity. The remaining stories comprise a variety of tales including a story about mountain climbing in the Chilean Andes in which the protagonist is haunted by a ghost, and a tale about a battle-weary veteran who returns from a high-tech future only to face his greatest and most sinister challenge right at home.

"The Robot's Twilight Companion"
by Tony Daniel
cover art by J. K Potter
ISBN 0-9655901-5-1 / (hardcover)
325 pages
First Edition

$24.95 postpaid
Golden Gryphon Press
3002 Perkins Road
Urbana, IL 61802

FICTION

Barrett, Neal.

Perpetuity blues and
other stories /
c2000. $21.95

APR 1 8 2000